JAN[illegible]

was brought up o[illegible] Later she went to wor[illegible] Thailand and after her marriage, lived in Japan, India and Hong Kong. She finally returned to the farm where she now lives with her husband and various animals, wild and domestic.

Her favourite pursuits are gardening, bird watching, and travel to far away places.

Bridge Over The Past is her first adult novel, although she has had several books published for the juvenile market.

[illegible] DE LAUNAY

[illegible] a farm in West Sussex [illegible]

[illegible]

[illegible]

[illegible]

Jane de Launay

BRIDGE OVER THE PAST

The Romance Club
R.002

Aspire Publishing

An Aspire Publication

First published in Great Britain 1998

ISBN 1 902035 10 0

Printed and bound in Great Britain by
Caledonian International Book Manufacturing Ltd, Glasgow.

Typeset in Palatino by Kestrel Data, Exeter, Devon.

Cover design by Gwyneth Jones/Corbis UK Ltd.

Aspire Publishing – a division of XcentreX Ltd.

For Michael

Chapter One

Anna went alone to meet her brother. She was thankful that her parents had been firm in remaining at home to welcome him there. She hadn't seen Jack for eighteen months, longer than they had ever been apart. He had joined the navy at the onset of war, two years ago, about the time that she, herself, had started her nursing training.

For the first time in her life Anna felt nervous about meeting her twin. Would he have changed, grown away from her, or would they still have that same easy way together? Would they know intuitively, as they had always done, what the other was about to say before the actual words were uttered? Even as children they had their own special language known only to themselves, which was a constant source of frustration to their mother. Unless she was with Jack, she never felt a complete person. Now they had less than forty-eight hours together, to last them for what could be, the duration of the war. Was that long enough to express all that needed to be said?

By the time she reached the station, Anna was torn between excitement at the prospect of seeing him, and apprehension at what the future held for them.

As the train drew into the station Jack barely waited for it to stop, before stepping onto the platform. Anna hadn't seen him in his naval lieutenant's uniform and it took her a moment to recognise him. He was a good deal taller than herself, well over six foot, otherwise they were remarkably similar, even for twins. Both had their mother's deep blue eyes and chestnut hair, but Jack's was straight and short cut while Anna wore her wavy mane loose, except on duty, when it was coiled under her cap for neatness.

He saw her immediately and strode over to her with a broad smile.

'Anna! I never expected you to be here.' Putting down his kit bag, he gathered her into his arms and hugged her.

'I didn't know myself till the last moment whether I'd get leave,' she said, when eventually he released her. 'Anyway I wanted to keep it a surprise.'

'How long have you got?' he asked her.

'Forty-eight hours. I've used up six of them already.'

'It will be just like old times, Anna.'

'Not exactly. This is a bit different.' So short a time and who knew how long this bloody war was going to last? Then, because this must be a cheerful time, she smiled up at him. 'Come on,' she said. 'I've parked Mum's car outside.'

They went out past the ticket office to where the black Wolsely waited.

She got into the passenger seat and passed him the keys.

'I thought you'd be overseas by now,' said Jack, squeezing in his long legs.

She shook her head. 'Not yet. I'm still at the army hospital in Aldershot. I've been there nine months already, gaining experience as they say. I'm hoping for a posting soon.'

'Any idea where?'

'Not yet. I just hope it will be overseas. What about you, Jack? Do you know where you'll be going?'

He shrugged. 'None of us know, do we? Possibly the Far East, but it could be anywhere.' He drove slowly, looking about him as they cleared Oxford and reached the quieter lanes. A deer ran across the road. It was beginning to get dark. 'Nothing changes here, does it?' he remarked.

'No, thank goodness. It's nice to feel whatever happens, little old England remains the same.'

'With the exception of some nasty bombing,' said Jack.

'I meant the countryside,' said Anna. 'Nothing can change that. Even if it was overrun with Germans, life would still be much the same in the country.'

'It will never come to that. It looks pretty grim in North Africa though, but if we can hold them there, it might be the turning point.'

'I wish I could be part of it,' said Anna, wistfully. 'I hate this uncertainty. I want to be where the action is.'

He glanced at her. 'Don't be too brave. I don't want anything to happen to you.'

When they drew up in front of the house, everything was in darkness. Anna waited while he got his kit bag out of the car.

'Dismal, isn't it?' she said, taking his arm as they walked to the front door together.'Not a light to be seen, or the air raid warden will be round. Remember how Dad always used to put all the lights on when he expected us home?'

'I bet the welcome inside will be just as warm though,' said Jack.

Once inside the house, it was warm and bright.

Commander and Mrs Bradford had heard the car and were in the hall waiting for them. It was a few moments before they had done with embraces and loving words, and they went through to the sitting room where a wood fire was roaring in the hearth. Commander Bradford went over to open the drinks cabinet.

'Just like old times,' he said. 'What will it be? Your mother and I have been hoarding for such an occasion, haven't we, Vera? But we never thought we'd have you both together. We must make the most of it.'

Their interest was centred on Jack. Anna had already given them all her news and now it was his turn. She watched him relax. He was sitting in the big armchair beside the fire, a drink in his hand, recounting stories about his life in the Navy in a light and amusing way.

'It's a great life,' he said. 'A good crowd of officers and men. You get to know them pretty well when you're out there for days, weeks sometimes, without coming in to port.

'But there's danger all around,' said his mother. 'Nowhere is safe when you're at sea.'

'You don't think about that,' said Jack, smiling at her. 'Of course we're aware of it, but that's what makes it exhilerating. We've got up to date equipment, under water detection and all that, so we've got a pretty good idea when the enemy is near. Then we've just got to outwit them.'

His mother was not convinced by his confident tone. 'And enemy aircraft. We're always hearing about them on the news.'

'Your mother does worry,' said Commander Bradford. 'Of course there's danger, but our navy has always been second to none, and let's hope they get the better of those U boats before too long.'

Anna felt sorry for her mother. With both of them away and her husband up in London every day at the Admiralty and in the thick of the bombing, she was left alone to worry. Her Red Cross work was not arduous enough to take her mind off the danger to her family, but her mother had always coped through difficult times and Anna was sure she would now. Already her anxious expression turned to laughter and she was joining in the conversation.

Jack was excited and optimistic about the future and Anna felt a pang of envy that her twin was already in action while she was kicking her heels at home, waiting to know when and where she would be sent.

Later on, they sat down to dinner at the long table. Their mother had laid it for a festive occasion, with the best china and family silver. The candles were lit and the first course was brought on.

'It's no good questioning either of you,' said their father, pouring wine into chrystal goblets. 'I don't suppose you know the answers yourselves, but it's pretty certain that you'll be sent overseas, I suppose, Anna?'

'I hope so. But at this rate the war will be over before I get there.'

Commander Bradford sighed. 'Makes me wish I was young again. I can't say I relish the Admiralty, but at least there's one person who's satisfied.' He smiled across at his wife.

'Even that's not safe,' she said. 'London's having a terrible time at the moment. Auntie Flo says they have raids every night.'

'We're not doing too well in the desert at the

moment,' said their father. 'We need someone who can stand up to Rommel. Japan coming in doesn't help either. We'll win through in the end, but it's going to be a long haul. What do you think, Jack?'

Jack frowned. 'Japan's a force to be reckoned with. They believe their country is invincible. But then they'll have to contend with our Navy, and I think we can put her in her place.'

The air raid sirens interrupted the conversation. Commander Bradford went over to check the curtains for any chink of light. They heard the planes passing over and fifteen minutes later the all clear sounded.

On Sunday Anna and Jack went for a long walk together. It was a crisp autumn day, and as they trudged through a carpet of fallen leaves Anna found Jack's buoyant mood infectious, but presently as the woodland gave way to heath, she grew serious.

'What will you do when it's over, Jack?'

'No idea. Probably stay in the Navy. I rarely think of the future.'

'How long do you think it's going to last?'

'I agree with Dad. There's a lot more to come. A couple of years, perhaps more.'

'Two years! Surely not. It's an eternity.'

'I can't see the Japs giving in easily,' said Jack.

'I don't expect we'll manage another leave together. Do you?'

'Probably not. Not till it's over and you might be married by then.'

'I doubt it.'

'Have you met anyone yet?' asked her brother. 'Anyone serious, I mean?'

'Plenty. All those war casualties coming home to be

nursed. It's heart breaking to see some of them. But all they want is to get back on their feet and have another go at Jerry. They've got incredible courage.'

'It makes one wonder if one could be as brave if it happened to oneself. But I wasn't talking about your professional life. I want to know about the personal bits.'

She laughed at him, knowing full well what he meant. 'What do you want to know?'

'No irresistibly attractive doctors?' he teased. 'You'd let me know, Anna, wouldn't you?'

She took his hand in hers and squeezed it. 'Of course. You'd be the first to hear. At the moment I love them all but none in particular.'

'You've always been discriminating.'

'That, in a way, is your fault. I suppose if I'm choosy, it's because of you. I've never found anyone to measure up to you.'

'Very flattering. Strangely enough, I've found the same thing. Whenever I meet a girl I'm interested in I find myself making comparisons. It's a sure way to end a relationship.'

She burst out laughing. 'You could have put that rather better. Sounds as though the thought of me is enough to put you off any girl.'

'Don't be an idiot. What I mean is sometimes I think we're too close for each other's good.

She looked at him, startled.

'That's ridiculous. Ours is a wonderful relationship. The most important thing in my life, in fact. What could possibly be wrong with it?'

'We understand each other so well that it tends to exclude everyone else.'

'I wonder if it's always the same with twins,' she said thoughtfully. 'I suppose when you do fall in love, I'm going to be quite jealous. I couldn't bear her to come between us.'

'That's what I mean. If I'm not there to advise you, choose carefully, won't you, Anna?'

'War's not the time to get married,' said Anna. 'I might think about it one day, but not for a long while yet.'

'I can't ever remember your having a serious boyfriend, not unless you count that fellow Charlie Fothergill. A twit if ever there was one.'

She giggled. 'As a matter of fact I did fancy him at the time but it didn't last long. My enthusiasm for him died a sudden death when you tipped him out of the boat.'

'I didn't. He lost his balance. I just refrained from helping him.'

They had come out onto a country road. Not far away was a church with a stone tower and opposite, a pub.

'The George and Crown,' said Jack. 'It's ages since I've been there.'

They found a seat overlooking the lawn, and Jack ordered a pint of bitter and a half pint for Anna.

'You wouldn't have anything to eat, I suppose?' Jack asked the landlord's wife.

'I'll see what I can do,' she said. 'I might be able to rustle up some egg sandwiches. How would that be?'

'That would be very kind,' said Anna. 'I hope we're not using your rations.'

'We've got pullets out the back,' said the woman. 'No one counts the cracked eggs and there're plenty of those.' She gave Jack a wink as she departed, and shortly afterwards brought them a plate of egg and lettuce sandwiches. 'You can pay for the beer,' she said, 'but the sandwiches are on us. You young people are doing more than your share in this war. I know that and we older ones appreciate it.'

Anna smiled at her. Folk were kind. The war brought people together.

As they munched, Anna felt a gloominess descending over her.

'Are you ever afraid, Jack?' she asked.

'I suppose everyone is. We wouldn't be human if we weren't. If my number comes up I shall probably be blown up or sink to the bottom of the ocean. Either way it would be over quickly. There's one thing though that I couldn't bear, but it's unlikely to happen.'

'What is it, Jack?'

'I'd hate to be taken prisoner. I don't think I could cope with that. Being kept in a confined space and at the mercy of prison guards would be intolerable. I'd have to escape before I went to pieces.'

'You would cope though,' said Anna, nodding confidently. 'After all, you're used to discipline in the Navy.'

'Of a kind. There's always a good atmosphere on board and if you're going into action you forget the danger. You never think that something might happen to you. I suppose it's because of the excitement.'

'The dreadful thing for me would be not knowing. If something did happen to you, we would eventually hear, I suppose, but perhaps not for a long time. One just has to carry on hoping that all is well.'

'And most likely it will be,' said Jack. 'My chances are probably better than yours. Nursing units go where the action is, don't they?'

She wished she could be as certain. She had no fear for herself but if anything happened to Jack . . . She looked across the lawn to where the trees were covered with the glorious reds and golds of autumn. A lot of leaves had already fallen and the wind chased them along the path. They lay in a pile against the hedge, their life over and while she watched, she had that strange feeling that came over her so often when she was with Jack. Would there ever be a time like this again, just the two of them together?

She looked at him, trying to commit to memory what he looked like just then, relaxed, happy. Yes, definitely happy. He wore a polo necked navy sweater and a pair of old grey slacks. He looked so healthy, so alive. She could never imagine him as a casualty, not like some of the men she had seen coming home to a life that must be forever restricted. She shuddered. She couldn't imagine what it would be like without him but she felt that, by facing the possibility, she could in some way prevent it.

He wore a puzzled expression as he waited for her to reply. 'What's the matter?' he asked.

She was startled to be brought back. 'Sorry. I've forgotten your question. Oh yes, of course. The field hospital is not in the front line. The ambulances go up and bring the men back.'

'What were you really thinking?'

She wanted to be honest. This time together was too precious for superficiality.

'I was thinking that we're not dependent on telegrams. We always know when something happens, don't we?'

'Come on,' he said, laughing at her. 'Don't get gloomy. I don't expect we shall ever have to put it to the test.'

Later he drove her to the station. Smart in her khaki uniform, her hair tucked neatly under her cap, she stood on the platform looking at him. Their parents had remained at the house. They disliked saying their farewells in public places.

'I'm glad you've got another few hours,' said Anna. 'They'll treasure that. You always were their favourite, you know.'

'Nonsense. That's purely your imagination. But I'll try and lift their spirits. It's all right for Dad. He's absorbed in his job. It's Mum I'm worried about.'

'She'll cope,' said Anna. 'She always had to and she will now.'

There were other service men and women waiting for the London train. Anna hoped they wouldn't bump into anyone they knew. She wanted these last few moments alone with Jack, though everything had been said that was going to be. She wasn't good at goodbyes.

The level crossing gates closed against the traffic and moments later the train came in. For a moment she clung to him, as though she would imprint everything about him upon her memory. She tilted back her head and looked into his eyes, seeking reassurance, willing him to come through safely and then, very gently, she kissed him on his lips.

'Take care of yourself, Anna,' he said. 'I couldn't do without you.'

'Nor I.' She bit back the tears. Then, picking up her small overnight bag, she stepped up into the compartment and lowered the window. He smiled up at her. She could tell that, like herself, he was excited by what lay ahead. They had to believe that they had a future, that they would come through this hellish war. For them it was a challenge, for those waiting at home, a time of foreboding.

As the train moved away from the platform, she leaned out of the window and continued waving to him until it rounded a bend and he was lost from sight. Then she pulled up the window and sat down in a corner seat. She was deeply thankful for the time they'd had together. It would sustain her through the dark days of war that lay ahead.

Chapter Two

It was another four months before Anna got her posting. She joined a nursing unit on a troop ship from Liverpool on a dull day in June. Then, hugging the west coast of Africa and under constant threat of attack from U boats, they rounded the Cape and made their way through the Indian Ocean to Suez. It was a vivid reminder to her of the danger which Jack was experiencing every day.

The last letter she had from him, via the services postal system, was a week before she left England. It was clear that he was enjoying life, thriving on the excitement. For her part she would rather face the tangible threat of guns and tanks, than the invisible stealth of U boats.

She had waited so long to get to the war zone, but now, at last, she would be in the thick of it. Everyone believed that the battle of El Alamein would be the turning point of the war. It was in the Western Desert that Montgomery and his troops would stem Rommel's advance and force him back to Tobruk and she had to be there when it happened. She felt so much nearer to Jack now that she, too, was involved in the action.

After three weeks, they docked at Suez. Anna stuffed her few personal belongings into her kit bag and went up on deck. The heat was intense and the noise of the troops disembarking and the shouts of Arab merchants persuading the troops to part with their currency, deafening. Giant cranes lifted tanks and guns and swung them onto the dock.

Anna waited with her unit while the hundreds of troops filed down the gangway and into trucks to take them to their staging posts. Then it was her turn. As she followed her nursing companions onto the dockside, she felt the thrill of landing on foreign soil.

She piled into a truck with others from her unit and they set off in convoy. The streets of Suez soon gave way to desert, sandy tracks along which the trucks rolled, teasing up dust which settled on the sweaty arms and faces of the occupants. By the time they arrived at the transit camp south of Cairo, she was aching in every limb and longed for a bath.

The camp was basic and under canvas and it was here that, having been kitted out with tropical uniform, all personnel were classified and allocated to their units. Some were sent to hospitals in Palestine, others to Casualty Clearing Stations all over the Middle East. When her name came up she learned that she was being posted to a Casualty Clearing Station somewhere west of Alexandria. Her war had begun.

She soon found herself in the thick of things. The distant noise of the guns and explosion of shells was a constant reminder of the casualties which would be brought in for surgery or treatment, often after a long, painful and difficult journey.

As the battle intensified, some of the nurses were sent forward to the Advanced Dressing Station, Anna was among them. Here she was required to help with amputations and other emergencies. She struggled to keep her emotions under control. If she went to pieces now she would be useless. She tried to resist involvement with her patients, but compassion twisted her heart as she looked into the beseeching eyes that pleaded with her to do something to ease the pain. She felt helpless to reassure them.

People like Chris for instance.

When she first saw Chris being carried in on a stretcher, he was scared out of his mind. One of his legs had been blown off by a mine and the other was in a shocking state. They had given him a shot of morphia but he was still conscious. Anna sat beside him in the ambulance, holding his hand and wishing she could soak up some of his pain.

'I'm not going to make it, am I?' he whispered.

'Yes,' she said, steadying her voice. 'You'd never believe how clever those doctors are. They'll patch you up all right.'

He was silent for a while watching her, then he said 'What's my girl going to think of me like this?'

'She'll think pretty highly of you, Chris. The girls back home who have men out here are as proud as punch.'

He smiled weakly. 'Would you write to her? Tell her about this? I don't think I can.'

'Let's talk about it when you're better,' she said gently.

'No. I want her to know the worst. It's only fair she should have some warning just in case I don't make it. I'd like her to know that I'm thinking of her. Tell her I've spoken to you, sent her my love.' His face twisted with a bout of pain. 'Her name's Joy. Suits her. She's like that. You'll find her address among my things.'

'I don't . . .' she began.

'Promise? It means a lot to me.'

'I promise, Chris.'

He died that night and Anna was distraught. She blamed herself for failing to give him enough encouragement to live. She asked his C.O. for permission to look through his things for his girl's address, and sat down to keep her promise, searching for the right words to break the news. She had never done anything like this before. How could she soften the blow? Wouldn't it be better for something like this to come through official sources? But her promise was sacred to her. She picked up her pen and began. She wrote dry-eyed, but she felt a tight knot of helplessness somewhere deep inside her. She knew enough to recognise that she was near breaking point.

Army trucks regularly crossed the desert to take service personnel into Alexandria for Rest and Recuperation and on the return trip brought back supplies to the camp. Anna sat in the back with eight other service men and women. She hadn't asked for leave. She didn't want to go. The nurses and doctors worked at full stretch, sometimes for sixteen hours a day and she could ill be spared, but the Medical Officer was firm.

'Forty-eight hours is not enough but we can't spare you for more. Take it and make the most of it, Anna.'

As the truck rumbled along the sixty miles of desert track, she listened to the others planning their leave. She took care not to commit herself. She desperately wanted to be alone, to please only herself after the restrictions of the battle field. The truck bounced over the uneven ground and every bone in her body ached, but tired though she was, she was vividly aware of her surroundings.

Alexandria assaulted all her senses, smelling to high heaven of the people who lived there, cooking their kebabs, roasting ears of corn on charcoal braziers. And the noise. People spitting, shouting, urinating, with little regard for privacy. Trams clanged and clattered, their conductors blowing something like minature hunting horns. From every cafe came the clatter of backgammon pieces or the blaring of radios.

A reservation had been made for her at a small hotel near the centre of the town. The first thing she did was to find the bathroom. Then, flinging off her clothes, she luxuriated in a soak. After a scrub and shampoo, she returned to her room and flung herself on the bed, revelling in the comfort of crisp, clean sheets, utter bliss after her constricting camp bed in the desert.

Tired though she was, she was determined not to squander her precious respite. She changed into a cotton dress and sandals and feeling a lot better, she set off for the shops. She had plenty of money, for there was nothing to spend it on in the desert, and she intended to indulge her passion for clothes and lash out on some expensive perfume. The place was full of service personnel and she found the carefree holiday atmosphere infectious. Bars and places of amusement thrived, providing a service for people who, like her, had come for a break from the battlefields.

She mingled with men and women, drifting in and out of shops on mammoth spending sprees. It would be months before she had another chance for such extravagance. A sense of excitement gripped her. Anything could happen in a place like this.

The heat was overwhelming and she was

desperately thirsty, but all the restaurants were full. She searched and at last turned into a side street where she found a small cafe. She went in and looked round for a vacant table.

'Come and join me, won't you? That's if you don't mind sharing.' She looked up to see a tall, good-looking young officer standing beside her. 'There's not really much alternative,' he added, smiling.

She thanked him and followed as he led the way through the restaurant to a small shady courtyard where a waiter was clearing a table. Sinking gratefully into a chair, she welcomed the long cold beer he ordered for her.

'Nigel Wainwright,' he said, introducing himself. 'And you?'

'Anna Bradford.'

'I must say I'm more than pleased to meet you,' he said with a grin. 'I was becoming extremely bored with my own company, and of course I'm always glad to be of service. I found this place two days ago. Unless you happen to know about this extension of the restaurant, you'd never expect anything like it.' He took a long pull at his beer and stood it in front of him. 'On leave, are you? How long do you have?'

'I've just arrived. Forty-eight hours.'

'What unit are you with?'

She told him. 'I'm working at a CCS. What about you?'

'Fiftieth Div.,' he said shortly. She knew then that he was in one of the hot spots and probably didn't want to talk about it. She understood the feeling.

They fell into easy conversation, talking about England and what they had done before the war. It brought back memories of days in the country spent with Jack, and the fun they had together.

'Who's Jack?' he asked her.

'My twin,' she said, eager to talk about him. 'He's in the navy. We were always together until, of course, war broke out.'

'So you are very close?' asked Nigel.

'Yes. I worry about him all the time.'

'He probably isn't in such a dangerous situation as you are,' said Nigel.

'Perhaps not, but then one doesn't worry about oneself, does one?'

'That's true. There's rarely time for thought. Where did you do your training, then?'

'At the Radcliffe in Oxford.' She went on to tell him about it and as they shared recollections, the past took on a reality more vivid than the present and the aura of war which seemed to be always with her, gradually faded, giving way to enjoyment in his company. She found his strong features and steely blue eyes distinctly attractive and, encouraged by his easy laughter, she related some of the amusing episodes of early days in the services. It was a long time since she had basked in the admiration of an attractive man and she revelled in it.

He insisted on paying for the meal and suggested that they should wander down to the front and along the corniche. Watching the lapping of gentle waves on the shore, it was hard to believe that not far away a bitter battle was being fought which was to change the course of the war.

'I'm going to take you to tea at the Cecil,' Nigel told her. 'You've no other plans I hope?'

'None.' She was delighted at the prospect of spending the rest of the day with him.

At tea in the company of other service men and women they danced cheek to cheek to the music of the Egyptian Palm Court Orchestra, and towards evening they went on to explore the countless places of entertainment that the town offered.

'I can't believe I only arrived this morning,' said Anna, as they sat sipping their drinks. 'I feel I've been here for weeks.'

'I can see a difference in you already,' he said.

'In what way?'

'You're much more relaxed. It's good to see you enjoying yourself, Anna. Almost happy, in fact.'

She smiled at him. 'I'm sorry. I was rather tired, but I'm fine now.'

'It's obvious that you've reached the end of your tether and in your job that's not surprising. Do you want to talk about it?'

'No. I don't even want to think about it until I have to.'

'Very well then. Let's decide where we want to go next. Would you like to eat here or shall we find a small restaurant somewhere? Do you like French cooking?'

Just the mention of food made her feel hungry. 'That sounds wonderful.'

'I know just the place.' He called for the bill and asked the waiter to call a taxi.

'How is it you know you way around this place so well?' she asked.

'I was here for a while before I joined my company. At the time I was frustrated. I just wanted to get on with the war. Now I wish I had longer.' His gaze lingered on her. 'You've made all the difference to my leave, you know.'

Only in the early hours of the morning when she was drooping with tiredness did she manage to persuade Nigel to take her back to her hotel. Walking the short distance hand in hand, they came to the small square where he stopped and drawing her into the shadows, he took her into his arms and kissed her. She was surprised to find that she enjoyed Nigel's kisses and far from pulling away, she found herself responding willingly.

'Till tomorrow, then,' he whispered when at last he released her.

Before she had finished breakfast a waiter came with a message that Nigel was waiting for her in the foyer.

'I'm going to take you for a picnic,' he said. 'Go and get your swim suit.'

'Wonderful. Just a minute.'

She went to fetch it and followed him from the coolness of the hotel to where he had parked his jeep. Although it was early, the heat wrapped itself around her like a blanket.

They set off along the coast road. A welcome breeze ruffled her hair and soon they were clear of the town and speeding along beside a limpid blue sea. As they rounded a bend they came upon an almost deserted beach with rocks and a few trees. He parked the jeep in the shade and brought out a hamper.

'Lunch,' he told her.'I've tried to do justice to the occasion.'

'How on earth did you put that together?' she asked in amazement as he unpacked sandwiches, vol-au-vents and other delicacies such as she had not seen since before the war.

'The club where I'm staying do good picnic hampers if you give them enough warning,' he said, easing the stopper off a bottle of champagne. Afterwards they played on the beach, peering into rock pools and chasing each other in and out of the water, till they fell exhausted on the sand. Happy and carefree, Anna rolled onto her back and gazed up at the deep blue sky.

'I'd forgotten what it was like to have such fun,' she said.

He leaned over and kissed her. 'You're so beautiful, Anna. Thank God you happened to come to that restaurant. I could so easily have missed you.'

She laughed up at him. 'You'd have met someone else.'

His eyes were serious. 'No one else would have done. I think we were destined to meet, and now I don't want to let you go.'

She sat up, tossing her hair in the wind and looked across the bay.

'I thought I could hear guns,' she said.

He nodded, watching her.

'Quite likely. The war's not so far away, but don't let it worry you. Today we won't think about it. Only about each other.'

But a change of mood had suddenly gripped her. Tomorrow she would be going back to the war. It was another world, far, far away from all this. Pleasant though it was, this interlude would soon be little more than a memory. There was no room for romance in her life at the moment, as long as the casualties of war demanded so much of her. Nigel was waiting for her to say something. She forced her mind back to the present.

'Nigel, I'm glad I met you, too. I shall often think of this time together. When I get back it's going to keep me sane.'

'I'm not sure that it's going to be enough for me,' he said. 'I must see you again.'

'That's something we can never be sure of. Not with the war.'

He said nothing, but stood up and, taking her hand, led her into the water.

That night, their last, they danced till dawn. In the early hours of the morning as they circled to the music of the Blue Danube, suddenly the lights were dimmed and they found themselves standing in the middle of the floor. He pressed her close and as she looked up at him their lips met and they kissed, lost in each other's arms. When at last they pulled apart, he led her away to a quiet corner on the balcony where they could watch the sun rising over the sea.

'Why are you looking so sad?' he asked her.

'I'm sorry it's over. It's been a wonderful leave, Nigel.'

'There's no need for it to end.' His eyes were tender. 'I don't want to say good-bye, Anna. Not without some hope of seeing you again. What are you going to do when this lot's over?'

'I suppose I shall be going home to a nursing job. What about you?'

'If I survive, I intend to go into banking, overseas if possible.' His eyes rested on her, questioning.'Anna, I'm not usually a reckless person but I've never felt so . . . so positive about a girl before. I don't mind admitting you've swept me off my feet and I want you to be part of my future. What do you say?'

She shook her head. 'I don't want to think about the future,' she said. 'Life's too uncertain. I wouldn't want to make that sort of committment.'

'This blasted war's not going to last for ever. I'm not asking you to marry me now, but when it's over. If I know that you'll consider it, I'll be satisfied.'

That time seemed a long way off. Life could be fun

with someone like Nigel and yes, perhaps she could fall in love with him. She couldn't promise anything, but neither could she refuse him at a time like this.

She smiled at him. 'I'll think about it,' she promised.

When she got back to camp a letter was waiting for her from Jack. It had been written over six weeks ago. Although he was careful not to give away any information, she gathered that he was somewhere in the Far East, or perhaps the Indian Ocean. He referred to the heat and the flying fish which would be seen in the tropics. In spite of the constant danger which must threaten him on the high seas, it was a cheerful letter and set her mind at rest. Jack was obviously enjoying his war.

She was feeling much better herself. The break had done her good and she felt more able to cope with the mangled bodies that were once strong, healthy young men. And when she needed to escape, her thoughts returned to Nigel. Those days with him were still vivid enough for her to recall to memory his face, hear his voice, almost smell his masculinity. If they were both spared it was quite possible that she might marry him one day when this was over.

She was sleeping better these days. It was the sleep of exhaustion but her mind was calm. She had grown used to the discomfort of sleeping under canvas. The nights were as cold as the days were mercilessly hot. Her blanket was full of sand and the flies, which tormented her during the day, settled in black clouds on the canvas at night and gave her some respite.

Psychologically, she felt she was coping better. It had taken her a while to learn to let go of things over which she had no control. She was part of a team and she worked alongside men and women on whom she could rely, whatever was demanded of them. She now felt that she could carry on like this for as long as she had to.

Until one night about a month after she had come back from Alexandria. In the early hours of the morning she suddenly jerked into wakefulness, in a state of terror. She was drenched with sweat. Fear suffocated her. She sat up stifling a cry behind her knuckles.

She knew instantly it had to do with Jack. He was in mortal danger, no question of it. She lay awake till dawn, shivering and biting her lips. As the sun hailed above the featureless skyline, she dressed and went outside. The desert was silent and cool. She felt icy cold. A sentry on duty came towards her, glad of an opportunity to chat.

'Couldn't sleep then?'

She shook her head. 'I had a nightmare.'

She stumbled away from the camp with no thought as to where she was going, trying to reason with herself. Something had happened to Jack, of that she was convinced but this astril link between them did not provide details. She had no means of knowing if his ship had been hit and, if it had, whether he had been picked up. She might have to wait for weeks before news trickled through.

'You'd better come back, Miss. Could be dangerous out there.' The sentry had followed her. Female personnel were not expected to wander off into the desert. Obediently she turned and went back with him to the unit. Perhaps some news had come over the radio. She hurried across to the Signals truck and asked if there was a report of an attack on a convoy.

'Last night, you say? News takes time to filter through, Miss. Worried about someone, are you?'

'Yes. My brother.'

'Don't you worry about it. I'll keep my ears open and let you know.'

'Thanks,' said Anna, turning away.

'You mustn't lose hope,' the operator called after her. 'Some do get hit but plenty survive. Get picked up by other ships.'

Perhaps the medical officer could help her. It didn't occur to her he might think it strange that she knew something had happened to her brother's ship without some official communication.

'When did you hear about this ship?' he asked.

'I didn't hear,' said Anna patiently. 'I just know. We're twins and we always know when something happens to the other even when we're miles apart. There must be some way of finding out.'

Dr Forbes shook his head. He could see that she was badly shaken. 'Sometimes our imagination can play us tricks,' he said gently. 'Especially in war time. You'll hear soon enough. Until then try and put this out of your mind, Anna. You could be worrying unnecessarily.'

She was not to be consoled. 'But I'm absolutely certain that something happened to him last night,' she insisted. 'I must know one way or the other.'

He was a man of about forty with a family of his own, but he was also a soldier. Unless he took a firm line on something like this, he knew how it could get out of hand and undermine the girl's efficiency. He had heard about the closeness of twins and he did not doubt that Anna believed what she had told him. She was not one to indulge in fantasy, indeed she was among the most reliable members of his staff. A practical approach was the best way to help her.

'I'll find out what I can,' he said at length. 'But you must understand you could be mistaken. You're under a great deal of strain, Anna. We all are, and when you're as close to someone as you obviously are to your brother, it's not impossible to imagine something like this. A dream could seem like reality.'

She brushed this aside. 'I know what you're saying but it doesn't help. I know something has happened to him.'

'Give me what details you have and I'll see what I can do, but even the War Office might have no information for a while. Not until those missing have been reported and in the case of prisoners, until the Red Cross are handed a list of names. In some cases that can take a very long time. If anything has happened, the first to hear will be your parents.'

With that she had to be content. The feeling remained with her and the horror of that night did not diminish. Six weeks passed before a letter reached her from her mother . Her fears were confirmed. Jack's ship had been torpedoed. He had been picked up by a Japanese ship and taken to Singapore and was now a prisoner of war.

Chapter Three

Anna was demobbed in the late summer of 1945, soon after the war with Japan ended. After a long stint in the Middle East, she was posted to a nursing unit in Sicily from where she took part in the long Italian campaign. She was glad to be in the thick of it. While she was so deeply involved in nursing the wounded, she had some respite from her constant anxiety about Jack. There was nothing she could do but wait for news. She knew that her parents would be the first to hear anything and it would be relayed to her immediately. Until then, she had to believe that he was still alive, and it was only a matter of time before they would be together again.

Then, at a time when she thought the war would drag on for ever, atomic bombs were dropped on Hiroshima and Nagasaki, causing horrific damage and loss of life. But it brought the war in the Far East to a close, and with it came a real hope that at last they would have news of Jack. Shocked though she was by the devastation caused by the bombs, she condoned the action. It gave the Japanese a taste of the suffering they had inflicted on millions of others. Anna had developed a deep-seated hatred of the race.

In the clearing up operations, the allies saw at first hand the human suffering in the concentration and prisoner of war camps. The survivors of those camps, many of them broken in mind and body, would now be sent home, and Anna wanted to be there when news came through. She applied for early discharge which, after her dedicated service, was granted.

It was a late summer evening when she stepped off the train, along with a few other service personnel. She had not let her parents know when she was arriving. She wanted to make her own way to the house and needed time to come to terms with a home coming without Jack. It was going to be a sad reunion with her parents but she was determined to do her best to make it positive and cheerful.

She had no trouble in finding a taxi and, as they drove along the familiar country lanes, the war years fell away and Jack's presence seemed very close to her.

When they drew up in front of the old house, she sat quite still looking at it, while memories flooded back. She and Jack had lived here since they were four. It had been the scene of many happy family gatherings, tennis parties and boating trips on the river, but now it seemed to her a sad old house that had lost its heart.

The taxi driver came round and opened the door for her.

'You all right, Miss? This is the place, isn't it?'

'Yes thank you,' said Anna. 'It's a long time since I've seen it. I was just remembering.'

'It's like that for a lot of us,' he said. 'I've only just been demobbed myself. Things have changed.'

She paid him and walked towards the house.

'Good luck, Miss,' he called after her.

Her parents had heard the car and came out to

greet her. She went to her mother first and hugged her. She had rarely seen her cry but now Mrs Bradford could not contain her tears.

'We wondered if we would ever see you again, Anna. It's been such a long time. Thank God for bringing you back safely to us.'

Then she went and embraced her father. He looked so much older and had lost a lot of weight. Anna rebuked herself for not taking home leave sooner. She had left them to themselves for too long. Jack would not have approved.

They led her into the house and each room she entered, seemed empty of Jack.

'Have you heard anything?' she asked them.

Her mother shook her head. 'We're still waiting. We must hear something soon.'

Anna took off her service cap and jacket and looked about her.

'It's so good to be back,' she said. She wanted to show her pleasure at seeing them.

'It's been too long, dear,' said her mother. 'Let's take a look at you.' Her eyes scrutinised Anna. 'You look so tired and you're thin. I don't remember you being so thin. It's not surprising though, after all you've been through. You need a good rest. It's your turn now to be cared for.'

Her father stood in front of the fire. He seemed unable to take his eyes off her. 'Four years, Anna,' he said. 'Who would ever have thought it would take so long?'

'Much too long, Daddy,' she said, sadly. 'But I'm glad we had that leave altogether with Jack. When were you last in touch with the Red Cross?'

'They'll let us know as soon as they hear anything, but up to now their lists have been incomplete. The

Japs never recognised international rules concerning prisoners. But I keep in constant touch with the Admiralty. Any news of naval personnel will come through them. As soon as there is news, I shall be the first to hear about it.'

He had a sudden bout of coughing. Anna went to get him a glass of water.

'Isn't he well?' she asked her mother later in the kitchen.

'He hasn't been for some time. The doctors aren't sure yet what the trouble is. They're doing tests.'

'Why didn't you tell me?'

'You had enough to worry about, dear. You had your own war to contend with, and then there was Jack.'

'Isn't there any way of finding out? Must we just sit here and wait?'

Her mother shook her head. Her face was drawn and her hair almost white now. There was such sadness in her eyes.

'None,' she said. 'I often think that one day he might just walk in. I shall never lose hope.'

Anna wished she had her mother's faith. While there was no news there should be hope, but she had lost hers somewhere over the years. There was a bitterness inside her, a deep hatred of the people who had done this to him. But she intended to try and keep cheerful to make things easier for her parents. Jack would have expected that of her.

She devoted all her time to them, taking them for drives in the family car, helping with the meals and answering their numerous questions about her war, but after a month at home she was becoming restless and depressed. She found herself listlessly wandering through the house, unsure what to do with herself. Several times she caught herself snapping at her mother and instantly regretting it. She was here to encourage, not to upset them. They had been through so much already and the least she could do was to be at hand to help with her father. His health seemed to be deteriorating and she noticed that each time they went for a stroll, the distance before he tired became shorter.

Christmas was a dismal affair. Just the three of them. Not that there weren't plenty of invitations, but none of them felt like socialising.

'You should go out, dear,' said her mother. 'It's kind of people to invite you and you should be meeting people of your own age.'

'No, Mum. I'm all right. They'd be strangers to me, and frankly I don't feel like making the effort.'

'It's not right, Anna. You're moping.'

'I don't want to. Don't keep on about it.' She bit her lip, near to tears. 'I'm sorry, Mum, I didn't mean that.'

'I understand, dear. We're all a bit tense.'

'I think perhaps I ought to look for a job.'

'You don't have to, dear. We can manage.'

'I know, but it would be a good idea to keep my hand in. I'll have to go back to nursing sometime. If I found something in Oxford I could live at home.'

After Christmas she started work at the Radcliffe hospital where she had once done her training. She bought an old Morris and drove the half hour journey each day. Most of the staff had, of course, changed. With the exception of one of the pharmacists and a theatre porter, she could remember none of them, but she settled into the routine quickly enough and found it a welcome relief after long days at home with nothing to occupy her mind.

One evening she came home to find her parents together in the sitting room. Her mother held an official looking letter in her hand and she was sobbing uncontrollably.

Anna rushed over to her. 'What is it, darling. Is it Jack?'

'Yes,' said her father. 'News came through today.'

Her mother handed her the piece of paper. 'Two years ago,' she said. 'He died two years ago and we never knew. It seems worse when we've built up hope.'

She had to be strong. For Jack's sake and for them, she had to save her own grief for when she was alone. She sat down beside her mother and drew her close.

'Oh Mum. There was no harm in hoping. I wish I could have done. I tried but so many of them died in those camps.'

'But some survived. Jack was so fit. Why couldn't they have let us know sooner?'

'It takes time for news to filter through,' said her father. 'They weren't going to release news like this until they were sure.'

Her mother shook her head, trying to choke back tears. 'Maybe I was foolish, but I felt certain he would come back. I just couldn't believe that we would never see him again . . . he was so young . . .'

Anna looked across at her father. His face was grey but he, too, was concerned with his wife's grief.

'We must remember the happy times,' he said. 'Jack would have wanted us to face up to this and carry on as best we can. I think it is better to know the truth than to go on living with uncertainty.'

Anna felt a curious emptiness inside her. She had known for so long. It must be worse for her parents.

If only she could lift the burden of their grief, but she didn't know how to do it. She wanted to talk about Jack, but as the days passed it was obvious that her mother found it too painful. When Jack's name came up, as it frequently did, she left the room.

'I want to talk about him, Mum.' said Anna. 'It doesn't seem natural never to mention him.'

'I can't, Anna. We've always shared our thoughts before, but I was sure then he would soon be home. Now it's different. Whenever I think of what he went through I go to pieces.'

She found her father more communicative.

'Will they send his things home?' Anna asked him.

Commander Bradford shook his head. 'I don't expect he had much. The Japs didn't abide by international rules for their prisoners. They took everything, their personal possessions, food parcels, even their mail and we all know how they were treated.'

'I can't help thinking about it. Jack once told me that the one thing he feared was being taken prisoner. He didn't think he could cope with that. I wish I knew exactly what happened however awful it was.' She sat tight-lipped beside her father. Then she burst out, 'God how I hate them. I shall never forgive them.'

'That's war,' said her father gently.

'Shall we never hear how he died?'

'I doubt it. Too many disappeared in those camps. News might trickle through one day. There might be someone who knew him but it's unlikely that we'll ever hear from them. The best we can do is to remember the happy times.'

Her father might be able to but she wasn't good like him. 'I can't,' she said. 'It's harder now I'm back home, Dad. I'm thinking of him all the time. I can't get used to it. Sometimes I can hardly bear it.'

'You will Anna. For his sake you'll carry on and make a good life for yourself.'

One day when her mother was out she went up to Jack's room and closed the door. Everything had been left as it was when he went away. It was the one room that Mrs Baker was not allowed to clean. Her mother looked after it herself. Anna opened the wardrobe and ran her hand over the jackets, remembering the times she had seen Jack wearing them. Then the chest of drawers. The bottom drawer was full of old papers and letters. She sat down on the floor and went through them. There were photographs of school and family holidays, letters she had written to him when he was at Dartmouth. She stayed there, deep in reminiscence for a long time before she put them carefully back and got to her feet. She had found some small comfort sitting there amongst his things. It had brought him closer.

In the early spring her father's health improved. The doctors warned that the remission was likely to be short, but it enabled her to take him about in her car and even go for short walks again which gave her mother a break. She was content with life as it was. She could cope with it. She enjoyed her work at the hospital and had taken to going in at week-ends. Holidays dragged and she was glad to relieve nurses who wanted to be with their families at that time. It seemed that nothing was likely to disturb this uneventful existence, until one day in June she came home to an unexpected visitor.

It was a hot Sunday afternoon and, seeing an unfamiliar car in the drive, she walked round to the garden without bothering to change out of her uniform. In the summer her parents often sat there in the shade of a big maple tree, but today they were not alone. A man's back was towards her. As she drew closer, he turned, a welcoming smile on his lips – Nigel Wainwright! She hadn't seen him since their leave in Alexandria and although afterwards they had exchanged letters, they were few and far between and she had given up any thought of seeing him again. Like so many others, theirs had been a brief wartime encounter and she had long since lost the scrap of paper on which he had written his home address.

He bounded from the deck chair as she approached, his face alight with pleasure.

'Anna. How good to see you after so long.'

He bent and kissed her on the cheek. He hadn't changed. A little older perhaps and he'd put on some weight, but his fair hair was still thick and well groomed and he had that attractive smile that she had almost forgotten. He was wearing a pair of grey flannels and a short sleeved shirt. His arms and face were tanned as though he had spent some time in the sun. She felt hot and untidy. She had been on duty since eight o'clock that morning and she'd had a tough time with one of the patient's relatives. Now she wished she had gone up to her room to tidy up.

'How are you, Nigel, and how on earth did you find us?'

'I've always kept your address. It was only a matter of time before I turned up.' He was holding her hands and smiling down at her. 'I wanted to come before, but I've only been out of the army for a month. Then there were things at home to be sorted out, decisions to be made. But I want to hear about you.'

'Take my chair, dear,' said her mother. 'I'll go and put the kettle on.'

'Let me fetch another,' said Nigel quickly, following her to the verandah. He brought it back but by now Commander Bradford had thought up some excuse to leave them together.

'Where did you finish the war?' asked Nigel.

'Italy.'

'That was a tough campaign. You had more than your share of the fighting.'

'What about you, Nigel?'

'I went on to Sicily and then took part in the D Day landings. Glad to be out of it now. At one time I thought of staying on in the army, but six years in uniform was enough.'

'So what will you do now?'

'I've joined a bank. A few months in London and then overseas I hope.'

'That's what you always planned to do, wasn't it?'

He nodded. 'Not a great career perhaps, but I've had enough adventure to last for a while. Your parents told me that you've gone back to nursing? You're looking very smart in your uniform.'

She put up her hand to smooth her hair. 'I'm sorry. I've just come off duty. I've got a job at a hospital in Oxford. It's convenient and I can help Mum. They probably told you that my father isn't too well?'

He nodded. 'They told me about your brother too. I'm sorry, Anna.'

'That's one of the reasons I want to be here with them.'

'That must be a comfort to them, but it can't be easy living at home again?'

She shrugged. 'Oh, it's not too bad.'

He was watching her closely. 'You deserve some fun, Anna. Now I've found you, we must see more of each other.'

And she did see a lot of Nigel after that. Sometimes he came down at weekends, other times she went up to London to meet him for a show or a meal. On these occasions she often spent the night with a friend and came back the next day. She was surprised to find that she was capable of enjoying herself and she was grateful to Nigel for his undemanding companionship. He had re-entered her life at a time when there was little pleasure in it.

One evening he took her out to dinner in Oxford. He chose an expensive restaurant with a reputation for good food. Nigel liked to do things in style. When she and Jack used to go out for a meal they chose lesser known pubs, and she had always insisted on paying her share. Those had been wonderful carefree days. Now that they were over she never wanted to visit those places again.

That evening they were sitting on the terrace sipping their drinks when Nigel suddenly said 'You've changed, Anna. I suppose I have too. We both had a pretty tough war.'

'I expect we have. I seemed to be able to cope with the war but I can't get over Jack. It gets worse as time goes on.'

'You don't often talk about him. He died some time ago didn't he?'

'Two years now, but it's only recently been confirmed. Time doesn't heal as I thought it would.'

'You'll get over it, Anna. Now the war's finished

you'll be able to put it behind you and make a fresh start.'

She looked at him, surprised. Didn't he understand either? 'I don't think so,' she said slowly. 'I don't think I could ever be as close to anyone as I was to Jack.'

'Not even me?' asked Nigel.'

'I don't think so. It wouldn't be fair on you, Nigel.'

'I'm willing to try. You made a promise. Remember?'

'That was a long time ago, before all this happened. I said I'd think about it. It was war time then. So much uncertainty. We didn't even know if we'd survive.'

'But we did and now I've come to ask you to marry me.'

She stared him as though she were seeing him in a different light. 'Oh, Nigel. I hadn't even thought about marriage – to anyone. Not recently anyway.'

'But you must have. We talked about it. You know I love you.'

'You haven't said so.'

'I wanted to give you time. I felt that something was holding you back. I didn't want to rush you but now time is short. I might be sent overseas any time.'

She wasn't prepared for this. 'Please give me a little longer. I'm worried about Dad and I can't walk out and leave them. Not at the moment. I'd have to talk to them about it.'

'All right,' he said, his expression lugubrious.'But when I go, Anna, I very much want you to be with me. Since I met you there's never been anyone else. I've always been so certain about you and I thought at one time that you felt the same way.'

Perhaps she had been naive. It had been just

too easy to drift through the summer enjoying Nigel's company. 'I am fond of you,' she said.'It's just that . . . well, things have changed with the war and it's difficult to make decisions.'

'You have to face the future though. You can't stay at home for ever and I can offer you an interesting life. You always said you liked travelling and we'd have plenty of that.'

Anna nodded listlessly. 'Where do you expect to be sent?'

'I don't know yet.' He shrugged. 'India perhaps. We don't have a choice. They send you and that's it.'

'It's a long way.'

'You could always fly home if necessary. They're very good about that sort of thing.'

She still hesitated. He leaned towards her and put his hand over hers. 'Anna, can't you see I love you. Please say yes.'

She smiled at him a little sadly. She wished she could be enthusiastic. Perhaps if she married him she could make it work. She would like to try.

She talked to her mother about it one evening after her father had gone to bed.

'Nigel wants me to marry him,' she began.

'He's a nice young man, Anna. Your father and I have been expecting this. You've said yes, of course?'

'Not yet. I wanted to talk to you about it first.'

'It's your life, my dear. We wouldn't want to stand in your way.'

'But there's Dad. He's not going to get better.'

Her mother's face clouded. 'Perhaps not, but I can manage. We have good back-up and you won't be all that far away.'

'That's the point, Mum. Nigel is being posted abroad.'

'Abroad?' Her mother looked startled. 'Will it be far?'

'It may well be. India perhaps. I would be too far away to help you.'

'How long would it be for?'

'A three year tour probably.'

'That's a long time.' She knew what her mother was thinking. It could mean that she would never see her father again. It was a hard decision to make.

'We've talked about it together, Anna. I know your father would encourage you to go. We want to see you happy more than anything. It might even help you to get over Jack. If you're sure that Nigel is the right man for you then you must go ahead.'

She was no nearer a decision. She lay awake at night weighing up the pros and cons and when she woke in the morning she was still far from certain. In the end it was her father who persuaded her, one evening when they were alone.

'Will you join me in a whisky?' he asked, crossing the room to the bar.

'Yes please, Dad. Good idea.'

'Soda?'

She nodded and he brought it across to her before taking his chair by the fire.

'Have you made up your mind yet, Anna?'

She shook her head. 'I find it difficult to make decisions these days.'

'Nigel can't be expected to wait indefinitely. Your mother and I think you should go ahead.'

'I don't want to leave when you're poorly. I want to be near enough to help Mum.'

'I'm all right. By the time you get back I shall be a new man.'

She looked at him fondly. 'That's being a bit optimistic,' she said smiling.

'Perhaps,' he agreed. 'But I'm not dead yet and probably shan't be for years. I don't intend to give up and I don't want you hanging around waiting for it to happen.' Then he became serious. 'The best tonic I could have is to see you happily married, my dear. You know that.'

'Even if we're living overseas?' This was the hard part. The distance from them. She couldn't come home to help them out when they were in difficulties.

He ignored that. 'If we felt you were staying at home because of us we couldn't live with it. We want you to put the past behind you and look to the future. We shan't be here for ever and if we know you're happy, that means more to us than anything. Give Nigel your answer, Anna. Don't keep him waiting any longer.'

The following weekend Nigel took her to meet his parents in Hampstead. She thought them pleasant, easy-going people and immediately felt comfortable with them. On Saturday they came back late from the cinema. The older folk had retired and Nigel took her into the sitting room. He went over to the fireplace and stirred the embers into life, while Anna stood on the hearth watching him.

'Nigel, I've been thinking.'

He put down the poker and turned towards her eagerly. 'Yes?'

'I've spoken to my parents. As I told you, they're my main concern. Anyway, if the offer's still open, I really would like to marry you.'

'Darling!' He took her in his arms then, holding her against him. 'You don't know how much I've wanted to hear this. I've had some fearful doubts over the last few days, almost convinced myself that you would decide against it. I don't know what I'd have done. Oh, Anna, I need you so much.'

'I'm sorry. It was unfair of me to expect you to wait. Had it been straightforward I would gladly have said yes, but I had to consider Mum and Dad. As it was they both insisted on it, so there we are.'

He kissed her then and had any doubts remained, they were swept away by her own response. She needed him too.

They threw an engagement party, attended by a few friends and Nigel took her up to London to choose a ring, a ruby encircled with small diamonds. He slipped it on her finger as they stood on the bank of the Thames, in the shadow of Big Ben. It was evening and the setting sun cast a red glow across the water.

'I've been keeping the good news till now,' said Nigel. 'We've been given a posting. They want us there as soon as possible.'

'India?' asked Anna.

'Japan,' said Nigel.

She stared at him aghast. For a moment, she really thought he was joking.

'What's the matter?' asked Nigel. 'It couldn't be better. Excellent prospects.'

'I can't,' she faltered 'I can't live in that country.'

'Why on earth not? It's a fascinating place with great opportunities. What have you got against it?' He frowned. 'Oh yes, I see . . . the war. It's your brother, isn't it?'

She nodded, speechless. How could she live

amongst people who aroused such loathing in her, people whose cruelty she could never forget? In a way, it would be condoning what they did to Jack.

'You never suggested . . .' she began.

'Japan?' Nigel finished for her. 'Because I never thought of it. The war's over, Anna.' His tone was brusque now. 'Hundreds of people lost loved ones in the war and they don't all feel like you about it. You're not marrying a Japanese. You're marrying me. It doesn't matter where we live so long as we're together.'

She remained silent, twisting her engagement ring round her finger. Her mind was in turmoil. She needed time. Had she known this posting was to be Japan, she thought her answer might have been very different, but how could she explain this to Nigel?

'When will you be going?' she asked.

'In a couple of weeks.'

'We couldn't arrange a wedding in two weeks!'

'It will have to be a Registry Office. We could have some sort of ceremony later perhaps.'

She had to have more time to think about it. In any case she couldn't possibly leave her parents at the moment.

'Dad went into hospital yesterday,' she said slowly. 'He's not at all well. I was hoping we wouldn't have to leave until they've tried this new treatment.'

'Anna, I'm sorry. I understand how you feel but I have to be firm about this. I can't choose when I leave or where I go. It's my job.'

'Nigel, I can't . . . '

'We still have two weeks, darling. I'm sure by then you'll know about your father.'

She shook her head and looked at him miserably.

'Anna, what about us? Surely that's more important than anything? If you love me and I thought you did . . .'

'I do. I couldn't marry you unless I did. Please try to understand, Nigel. Until we know about Dad it would be unkind to leave Mum to face it herself.'

'But you might have to wait indefinitely. Darling, I need you too.'

She looked at him with troubled eyes. 'I know. I don't know what to do.'

'All right then. There is an alternative, one that the Bank suggested, in fact, when I told them we were about to be married. I could go on ahead of you and you would follow as soon as you can. We could be married out there.'

'That would make it much easier for me,' she said. 'Would you mind very much, Nigel?'

'I'd rather we went out together, of course, but this would have certain advantages. It would give me time to get settled in the job. For the first few weeks I might have had to leave you on your own quite a bit, while I learn the ropes.'

'What about the wedding? Are there churches out there?'

'Of course. Or we could be married in the Embassy, followed by some sort of official party. It's not unusual for girls to go out to be married. You could stay with the manager and his wife when you arrive. The Bank would make the necessary arrangements. Would you feel happier then?'

This might give her time to come to terms with it. 'Much happier,' she said, smiling at him.

She accompanied him to Heathrow on New Years Day. Christmas had been a time of uncertainty for her. She dreaded leaving, but Nigel had gone along with her wish to stay in England till arrangements had been made for her father. Now she must overcome her reluctance, and keep her promise. Her parents were right. She owed it to him.

'I'm going to miss you, darling,' he said, embracing her. 'But it won't be for long. You promise you'll join me as soon as you can?'

'Of course. I'll write just as soon as I know and book a flight.'

'I'll start to get things going out there. Find somewhere for you to stay and begin to get the house sorted out. I don't think it has worked out so badly after all.'

His flight number had been called. He took her in his arms and gave her a lingering kiss. 'Bye, my darling. I shall count the days till you come.'

There were tears in her eyes when he released her. She was going to miss him. She needed his reassurance to overcome her misgivings.

Chapter Four

Anna was already in bed when the phone rang. She ran downstairs hoping that it had not disturbed her parents.

'Is that Anna Bradford?' The voice was deep and pleasant with a trace of a northern accent.

'Yes?'

'My name's Hugh Wiley. I'm a friend of Jack's.'

She drew in a sharp breath. 'Jack?' She echoed it almost reverently.

'We were prisoners of war together,' the voice said. 'I have a letter for you from him. I'd like to hand it to you personally. I wondered if we could meet?'

'Well – yes – where do you suggest? Are you local?'

'No. I thought perhaps London. Is that a difficult journey for you?'

'Quite easy.' She paused. Could this man be genuine? It was ages since the war had ended. It could be some sort of a hoax. She played for time.

'When were you thinking of?'

'Let's see. Today's Wednesday. How about Friday?'

She had arranged to do some shopping on Friday. Nigel had warned her that things were short in Japan and she should stock up on essentials and bring them with her. She would have to postpone that.

'Yes,' she agreed. 'That would be fine. Where shall I meet you?'

'How about the Ritz?'

'The Ritz?' It seemed an unlikely rendezvous for such a meeting. She hesitated.

'I have a particular reason for suggesting this,' Hugh went on. 'I'll tell you about it when I see you. Shall we say seven thirty?'

'That suits me.'

'Friday then, at seven thirty,' he repeated.

'Just a moment. How shall I recognise you?'

'Good question,' he said. She could hear a hint of laughter in his voice. 'Let's say I'm an ordinary sort of fellow, a bit on the ugly side perhaps. A beard, greying hair, brown eyes and a limp. If you're still in doubt I could go to the expense of a carnation.'

She smiled at the mouthpiece. 'I don't think that will be necessary. I'm sure I shall have no difficulty.'

She looked out of the window as the train sped towards London, and contemplated the evening ahead of her with some apprehension. Was she doing the right thing? Perhaps she should have suggested that he come home first, though on reflection she dared not risk inviting him without first hearing what he had to say. The meeting would surely be upsetting and she must protect her parents from unnecessary distress. She had told them that she was going up to town to meet a friend.

She took a taxi to Piccadilly. It was almost dark and beginning to rain. She could see the fine drizzle in the reflection of the lights on the damp road. People were hurrying along the pavements and putting up their umbrellas.

The taxi drew up outside the Ritz. It had escaped

serious bomb damage, but they were still working on repairs. It was a large old fashioned building which had managed to retain some of its pre-war splendour. She went through the revolving doors and into the thickly carpeted foyer. Guilt-edged chairs in faded red velvet and heavy brocade curtains gave the place an air of opulence. She looked about her. People were standing about in groups engaged in animated conversation or waiting for friends. Most of them were in evening dress. Others still in the services wore uniform.

Almost immediately a man came over to her. He was tall with thick brown hair, tinged with grey and a well trimmed beard, exactly as he had described. His eyes were warm and friendly. Smiling, he held out his hand as he introduced himself.

'Hugh Wiley,' he said. 'Thanks for coming. I hope you had no difficulty in getting here?'

'None at all,' said Anna. 'It's not far, and for once the train was on time.'

'How about a drink?'

He led the way to the bar and found a quiet corner where the waiter brought their order.

'How did you know me?' she began.

'You're like your brother,' he said. 'Startlingly similar, in fact.'

'People always used to say that. We were alike in every way.'

'To be expected with twins, I should think.'

'Jack told you about me, then?'

'Yes. He talked a lot about you. But first I think I'd better explain why I chose this place for our meeting.' He picked up the glass in front of him and drank slowly as though considering where to begin.

'As you can imagine, life in camp was pretty grim

and to help pass the time we sometimes talked about what we'd do when the war was over. Jack used to say that if we came through we would celebrate by having a slap-up meal at the Ritz. Anyway, you were always included in these plans and Jack once said that if he didn't make it, I was to bring you here myself. So you see, this evening is for Jack.'

Anna had never cried for her brother. She wished she could. It might have relieved the pain, brought about some kind of healing but there was only this tight bitter anger gripping her. Hatred had been her antidote to grief, a deep indelible hatred towards the people who had been responsible for Jack's death.

She felt Hugh's eyes resting on her as she looked at him, dry-eyed. Even now she could not disguise her anger.

'I had hoped,' he said quietly, 'that by now it would have been a little easier for you, but I can see that it isn't.'

'It never will be,' she said. 'I know Jack's dead, but I can't accept it. Please tell me everything you can about him. You don't have to spare me. I won't make a fool of myself here.'

'How much do you already know?' he asked gently.

'I knew that something had happened to him.'

'A telegram?'

'No,' she said, pausing. Would he understand how it was between herself and Jack? Nigel couldn't, but there was something about this man that gave her confidence. 'I knew when his ship was sunk. We always knew when one or the other was in trouble. I think I knew when he died. I was serving with an ambulance unit in Italy at the time. We had a lot of casualties and I had little time to think of Jack.

Then, one evening, when I was on duty in the field hospital, I suddenly knew with a flash of certainty that he was dead. It was terrible. I couldn't tell anyone not even my parents because they wouldn't have believed me. It wasn't official you see.'

She experienced again the agony of that moment and struggled to control herself. She looked at Hugh and, seeing the compassion in his eyes, felt encouraged to go on.

'I never imagined it was a peaceful death, a kind of slipping away.' She moved her hands gently apart as she spoke, to give emphasis to her words. 'I couldn't imagine Jack lying down and dying. He was too alive, too strong. He would have fought death like he used to fight all discipline. I was sure that he had died violently. Was I right?'

'It's incredible. You know without me telling you.'

'I expect it's difficult for you to understand this. No one can imagine how close we were. So long as Jack was around, I felt safe. I didn't need anyone else.'

Hugh nodded. 'I can understand that,' he said.

She had never spoken to anyone like this about Jack before and, having begun, she had to continue. It was as if by talking about him she could momentarily alleviate her anger, and in Hugh she had a sympathetic listener.

'Even when we were older,' she went on, 'and Jack went to boarding school, there was a kind of telepathy between us. We actually knew what the other was feeling and when one of you has gone, it's like losing a part of yourself. You can never be the same again.'

'And it becomes no better as time passes?' suggested Hugh gently.

Anna shook her head. 'I'm told it does but I don't

believe it.' She paused, trying to come to terms with the pain of speaking about Jack and struggling to control her voice. 'I remember the first time I went on holiday with my parents without Jack. He was at boarding school. I was about twelve and I remember looking down at the water flowing under a bridge and, suddenly, I don't know why, I felt desperately sad. I was missing Jack terribly. I think I realised then that we wouldn't always be together and that already he was growing away from me. At that moment I felt as though I'd lost all my security.'

'Uncanny,' said Hugh. 'Jack often spoke of this closeness he had with you. In fact he used the same sort of words to describe it. When did you last see him?'

'Five years ago now, when we were on leave together. We had a wonderful time but I never saw him again after that.' She tucked an errant strand of hair behind her ear and regarded Hugh earnestly. 'Tell me about him, ' she said. 'That's what you came for, wasn't it? I've done all the talking.'

Hugh responded with a reassuring smile. 'Let's go and find something to eat and I'll tell you about the camp.'

He led the way, limping towards the dining room. It was decorated in Regency style, and from each end of the high ceiling hung two enormous chandaliers. The waiter showed them to a table with a reserved card prominently displayed, and held a chair for Anna to sit down. Having ordered the meal, Hugh asked for the wine list. He relaxed back in his chair and smiled at her.

'This place is a far cry from the camp,' he said, 'and I don't want it to be a solemn occasion. Jack was greatly looking forward to this and I know that he would want us to make the most of it. I think, in a way, it's an appropriate place to meet and talk about him, don't you think so, Anna?'

She met his gaze. 'It was a good choice,' she agreed.

'It makes it easier for me because from what you've told me, you've already shared many of Jack's experiences, in spirit anyway. Besides, you must have read and heard about conditions in those Japanese prison camps. No words can describe them accurately, but anyone living through the experience will remember it for the rest of their life.'

Anna listened to his story without interruption. Besides the hardship and suffering, he spoke of moments of humour and courage and the concern of the men for their fellow prisoners.

'Jack never allowed conditions to get him down you know, Anna. He refused to be bullied, nor would he stand by and watch the guards ill-treat a fellow prisoner without some sort of protest.' He paused while the waiter removed their empty plates. Then he said quietly, 'In the end, he suffered for his courage.'

Anna, watching him closely as he spoke, tried to picture him in the scenes he was so vividly describing. It seemed to her that he had just stepped out of that camp, fresh from his friendship with Jack. She could understand why these two had been so close. Then she asked the question that had been on her mind for so long.

'How did he die, Hugh?'

He hesitated. 'I'll tell you more about it over coffee,' he said finally.

When they had finished eating they found a secluded corner in the lounge and Hugh continued.

She was glad he did not try to spare her the horror of it. He had shared a part of her brother's life from which she had been excluded and she wanted to hear it all.

'It all began over a tiny radio,' said Hugh. 'It was our only contact with the outside world, and every evening when the guards changed for the night watch, we tuned into the world service. There were only a handful of us who knew where that radio was hidden and we always took the precaution of posting a man to warn us if a guard was coming. On this particular evening, the radio operator, a young Scot called Sandy, had just tuned in. It was the time of the D-Day landings and for the first time since our imprisonment, we saw a ray of hope. Each one of us there was straining his ears to hear how the battle was progressing. Even then we believed that if the Allies could establish a foothold in France it could mean that the end of the war was in sight.'

Hugh's cheek muscles tightened as he stirred his coffee with a quick agitated movement, slopping it over into the small saucer.

'Suddenly the warning was given that guards were approaching. We managed to hide the radio but the guards went straight to Sandy and marched him off to the commandant. Somehow they must have got hold of information that he was the radio expert. Jack and I sat up all night waiting for him, and fearing the worst. They had cruel means to force a man to answer questions and even someone like Sandy could weaken under torture.'

Hugh paused deep in reflection for so long that Anna thought he had forgotten her. It was a long time before he made a visible effort to bring himself back to the present.

'Go on, Hugh,' she prompted him gently. 'I want to hear it all.'

He cleared his throat before resuming, with obvious reluctance, his tale.

'The next morning we were lined up as usual for roll call. The guard room door opened and Sandy was marched out between two guards and made to stand in front of us. He was in a shocking state, but despite his severely lacerated back, he managed to walk firmly. A rock was placed in front of him and he was told to pick it up and hold it high above his head while the pervert of a Commandant questioned him. The guards strutted up and down the lines, yelling questions and bashing out indiscriminately at anyone who refused to answer. This was the stage when prisoners with information could be made to blurt it out.'

'And did he?' asked Anna.

Hugh shook his head. 'By now Sandy was swaying. The Commandant knew he'd be useless to them unconscious and shouted to the guards to bring water. When our daily ration was minimal you can imagine that Sandy couldn't believe he was being offered a whole jugful. But he wouldn't give in. He stood there silent and stubborn. The Commandant was working up a fine old rage and finally he ordered Sandy to drink and go on drinking till he could stomach no more. Then they knocked him to the ground and tied him to posts as one of the guards placed his army boots on Sandy's stomach and slowly began to stamp.'

Hugh wasn't looking at her any more, but at some point beyond her, as though he were watching the scene unfold before his eyes.

'I anticipated Jack's reaction and put out a hand to

stop him, but it was too late. He was standing beside me and I could feel the tension mounting when he broke rank and sprang at the guard, slamming a fist into his face. There was a stunned silence as the man sank to the ground with blood trickling from the corner of his mouth.'

Anna held her breath. She could see it all. Jack would never tolerate such inhumanity.

'They shot him then?' she asked softly.

'They set upon him with their bayonets. It was all over in a moment.'

Hugh had finished. She could see that it had cost him a great effort. His face was drawn and there was bleakness in his eyes.

'Was the radio ever found?' she asked.

'No. Thank God the secret was kept. It was our life-line and the Japs were prepared to kill to take it from us.' He was looking at her again, a worried frown on his face. 'Anna, forgive me. I meant to spare you the more harrowing details.'

'I didn't want you to. I wanted to know exactly what happened.'

'Well then. You have the story now and you're entitled to it.'

'Thanks for telling me, Hugh. I know it wasn't easy.'

'Now for the letter.' She watched as he drew a scrap of tattered paper from his wallet which he handed her. 'This is it. It's been with me a long time – all the way to Australia in fact. I went there on my way home. You may find some of it difficult to read. It was written about a month before he died. I'm sorry I've kept it but it could have been lost had I posted it. I wanted to wait till I could deliver it personally. I believe that was what Jack wanted.'

She took it from him, this scrap of paper on which her brother had written his last words to her. She unfolded it and read it slowly, taking in every word.

'Dear Dad, Mum, Anna. I'm giving this note to Hugh. If he survives and I don't, he'll see that you get it. Conditions are hard here but I have good friends and much to be thankful for. In fact there are some things about life in camp that I wouldn't have missed. If I don't turn up when this lot's finished don't be sad. I think of you every day and feel very close to you. I'm grateful for all you have given me. Happy memories help to keep us going. Hugh too has been a tower of strength. I hope one day you'll meet him. God bless you, Jack.'

Anna felt the tears pricking her eyes. It was ironical that all this time she had been unable to cry and now in the Ritz coffee room she couldn't help herself.

'Perhaps I should have sent it,' said Hugh. 'I hope your parents are still alive?'

'Yes,' she whispered, thankful that Hugh made no attempt to console her. 'What does he mean when he says there are some things he wouldn't have missed?'

'I . . . I'm not sure that you'll be able to understand this, Anna, but quite a few of us found a faith of sorts in that camp, though I don't know about Jack. Something kept him going and he set himself high standards which affected a lot of us who were close to him. The chaps had a very high regard for him and he had a deep concern for their welfare. I think it sprang from his faith though he rarely spoke of it.'

She forced herself to look at him. 'I don't think Jack was religious,' she said, her voice tight. 'I can't believe that anyone could be under those circumstances.'

'That's understandable, but nevertheless it's true.

In those early months our morale was very low. Conditions were appalling and men were dying every day. We were a sick, unhealthy bunch and we seemed to have lost all sense of pride and human decency, but gradually things changed.'

'You mean conditions improved?' she asked, hopefullly.

'Not conditions – rather our attitude towards them,' said Hugh thoughtfully. 'The guards' treatment of us remained the same. They were just as ruthless, but because we began to understand why they acted the way they did, we no longer feared them. I know now that benevolence can overcome the most adverse situations and turn them into valuable experiences and I think this is what Jack is saying in his letter. All the time we looked for revenge we were limiting our ability to understand and to love. Jack always used to say that fear walks hand in hand with hatred. A few of us began to realise that we had to free ourselves of bitterness if we were to retain any shreds of self-respect.'

'Sounds a bit moralistic, and I think rather impractical.'

'No,' said Hugh firmly. 'Not if it enables you to understand the Japanese. Sacrifice and bloodshed are part of their history. They have an utter contempt for death. No self-respecting Japanese would allow himself to be captured. He would prefer to die and they despise a man who has surrendered to the enemy. I'm not excusing their behaviour but we began to understand why they acted in ways which to us were nothing less than barbaric.'

'But what difference did that make to the prisoners?' Anna was having difficulty in following his train of thought.

'As we began to understand our guards,' he went on, 'we no longer feared them and this gave us a tremendous advantage over them. Jack had always been very keen to keep our men occupied, and we organised activities for them. For instance, some who were musicians, made instruments from bamboo and odd bits and pieces they'd collected, and soon we had an orchestra of sorts. Other men started language classes or bible study, anything to occupy our minds. In other words we were trying to make the best of an intolerable situation and gradually we began to think less about our own troubles and looked for ways of helping the other fellow.'

Anna began to see why this man was Jack's friend. He obviously had some of the attributes he had given Jack. She wondered how he was making out in this country now it was all over.

'You must be thankful to be home,' she said. 'What are you doing now?'

'I'm going into the church. I think there's a need for us here. In a different way perhaps, but a need just the same. What about you, Anna? Has the war affected your plans?'

'I'm living at home with Mum and Dad. Finding it difficult to settle down again. You can't put the clock back and it's hard to live with parents again once you've left home and I find it specially hard without Jack. He had such a wonderful sense of humour. There are so many memories and I know Mum and Dad find it difficult too, and I expect they think me impossible at times. Dad's not at all well either and as I'm a nurse, I can help Mum with him, for a little longer anyway.'

'Are you going away, then?'

'I'm engaged to be married.'

He nodded knowingly. 'I noticed a ring on your finger. Who's the lucky fellow?'

'Nigel Cartwright. He was a captain in the Royal Artillery. I met him during the war.' She was silent for a moment, twisting the ring on her finger. She wondered whether she should tell Hugh, but there was something about him that inspired confidence. She looked across at him with troubled eyes.

'Hugh, I believe I might be making a terrible mistake. I'm going out to Japan shortly to marry Nigel. I shall be living amongst people I hate. Do you think I'm mad?'

'Does your fiance know how you feel about this?'

She shook her head. 'I don't think he understands.'

'Have you given him the chance?'

She paused while the waiter refilled their cups with coffee. 'No,' she said slowly. 'It's something I have to work out for myself. After what you've just told me, I don't know that I ever shall.'

'Had I known, I would have kept quiet. As it is I've only fuelled your anger.'

'You would still have told me. You said yourself I was entitled to know.'

'On the other hand perhaps it's the best thing you can do,' said Hugh. 'Living in Japan may help you to come to terms with Jack's death. You'll be able to judge the people for yourself and inevitably you'll come across a lot of decent ones.'

'I'm afraid that doesn't help my personal feelings. It's going to be difficult to like any of them when I think of what they did to Jack and Sandy.'

'War brings out the worst in people as well as the best. It's what we make of the peace that matters now, isn't it?'

'I'm not likely to have much influence in that

respect. There'll be other British people where I'm going, and I suppose I shall be spending most of my time with them. I don't expect to meet many Japanese.'

'Is that why you agreed to go?'

'When we got engaged, Nigel had no idea he would be posted to Japan. I couldn't break it off just because I loathe the Japanese.'

'Not if you love him.'

Silence fell between them. Hugh shifted his leg and stretched it out in front of him. A spasm of pain passed across his face.

'Is that a result of your time in camp?' she asked.

'I broke it stumbling over some rocks when we were working on the railway. It never set properly.'

'What bastards they were.'

'I was one of the lucky ones. I came out alive.'

She looked across the room. People were gradually leaving and soon she would have catch her train. She was reluctant to go. She felt that she had been privileged to share in a small part of Jack's suffering.

Hugh dropped her off at the station and got out to open the door for her. They stood looking at each other in the dim light of the entrance and she wondered if she would ever see him again.

He thrust his hand into his coat pocket. 'I nearly forgot,' he said. 'Do you recognise this?' He handed her a small penknife, and as she looked closely at it she remembered.

'I gave it to Jack for his tenth birthday,' she said.

'It went through camp with him. Somehow he always managed to keep it hidden. It was amongst his things and I think perhaps it should come back to you.'

'I'd like to keep it,' she said, fingering it

affectionately before slipping it into her handbag. She looked up at him. He was watching her. For a moment in the soft light, he could have been Jack. He had been so close to her brother, had suffered with him, had grown to know him so well and had watched him die. Jack had in some way made this man what he was.

He seemed to be waiting for her to say something. Perhaps he, too, was remembering Jack, the things that he had said about her. Her thoughts were too confused to put into words.

'One day would you be able to go and see my parents?' she asked. 'My father can't get about these days and I know they'd appreciate it.'

'I'd be pleased to,' he said. 'I hope they'll understand my reason for keeping you to myself this time. The important thing was to deliver the letter.'

She smiled at him. 'Thank you for this evening and for all you've told me.' It sounded trite but it was the best she could do.

'In spite of everything, make up your mind to enjoy Japan, Anna. I shall be thinking of you.'

When Anna came down to breakfast the next morning both her parents were already there. She sat down and waited while her mother poured out the tea.

'Did you have a good time, dear?' she asked.

'Yes thanks. I met a friend of Jack's.'

'Jack's?' Her mother put the teapot down carefully and looked at her. Anna thought she detected a flicker of hope in the soft blue eyes. She hurried on. 'His name was Hugh Wiley. He was a prisoner too. He was with Jack when he died.'

'Why didn't you tell us? You just said you were

meeting a friend. You didn't say he had anything to do with Jack.'

'Let me explain, Mum: I had a phone call from Hugh some days ago. I wanted to hear what he had to say before I told you about it. I didn't want you to be upset.'

'But why didn't you ask him here? Surely whatever he told you concerned all of us.'

'He brought a letter to me from Jack. He wanted to deliver it personally.'

'But Jack died long ago. Why did it take so long?'

'Hugh went to Australia at the end of the war and has only recently arrived in this country.'

'I don't understand, Anna,' her mother's tone was accusing.' You must have known how much we would want to see any friend of Jack's.'

Anna accepted her mother's frustration. She had to try to make it clear to her.

'He wanted to meet me in London,' she said. 'He had a special reason.'

'You should have insisted. After all we had a right . . .'

'Let's listen to what Anna has to say, dear.' Commander Bradford interrupted her. 'There must be a good explanation.'

'There is.' Anna looked at him gratefully. 'Hugh and Jack often talked about having a meal at the Ritz after the war and Jack had made him promise that if he couldn't be there himself, Hugh was to take me. He was keeping that promise. But he did say that he would like to see you.'

'You gave him our address and telephone number?' asked her mother.

Anna smiled. 'Yes, of course.'

'You said he gave you a letter,' Commander Bradford interrupted. 'There must be a good explanation.'

'I have it here.' She passed the envelope to him. Her father drew out the piece of paper and read it, then he passed it wordlessly to his wife. Her hand trembled as she took it from him. It was some moments before she could bring herself to look at it. When she did, she read it several times before laying it on the table.

'I must go and find a hankerchief,' she said, getting up and leaving the room. Anna would have followed her but she knew that her mother hated to be seen crying. She considered it a sign of weakness.

'She'll be all right,' her father assured Anna, after his wife had left. 'It's come as a shock. Brought it all back again.'

'Perhaps I should have told you I was going to meet Hugh,' said Anna. 'It was a brief unexpected call and at the time I was worried whether it was genuine.'

'You did what you thought best at the time,' said Commander Bradford. 'What else did he tell you? Now we're alone you can speak freely.'

She was glad her mother had left them together. It gave her the chance to tell him some of things he would want to know, and which would have been too painful for her mother's ears. It was hard to speak of it. The bitterness and hatred that she had harboured for so long had been beginning to recede; now it returned to haunt her. She looked across to the cabinet on which stood Jack's photograph, and to her surprise she found that she was crying.

'It's hard for you, I know,' said her father, 'but you mustn't let it affect your life with Nigel. Once you reach Japan you'll find things will be different.'

She dabbed her eyes with a hankerchief.

'I still wonder if I'm doing the right thing.'

'Nigel will help you. He'll understand.'

She shook her head. 'I can't speak to him about it. He thinks I should have got over it by now.'

Commander Bradford leaned towards her, forcing her to look at him.

'Grief affects us all in different ways, my dear. Being a twin the loss for you has been more traumatic. But Jack wouldn't want you to grieve or bear grudges. You have a chance now to make a new life for yourself. You'll need courage to live in Japan but then you have that in good measure.'

She was less sure. After speaking to Hugh last night her world had once again crumbled about her and she had lost all sense of direction. She wondered whether she was even being fair to Nigel in agreeing to marry him.

'Your mother and I have been discussing your departure,' her father was saying. 'We don't think you should delay any longer. It's not fair on Nigel. I'm on the mend now and your mother can manage with the extra help available.'

'All right,' she said reluctantly. Then because she wanted to reassure him, 'You don't have to worry, you know. I'll manage.'

A thin smile lighted his face. 'That's what I was hoping to hear. It's some time since I've felt enthusiasm for anything but then when Jack died, it seemed to knock the stuffing out of all of us.'

Yet when she rang to book a flight to Tokyo and they offered her one the following week, she was assailed by a new indecision, and turned it down. It was too soon after her meeting with Hugh. She needed a little longer, time to absorb it. She made a reservation for a month ahead.

Chapter Five

When Anna caught sight of Nigel's tall figure standing at the arrival barrier at Tokyo's Haneda Airport, the anxiety that had dogged her over the last few months faded. As she waited to push her luggage trolley through she was aware that now she was standing on Japanese soil and was actually glad to be here.

The next moment Nigel was beside her, smiling at her and, then she was in his arms. Everything was going to work out all right.

'Anna, it's so good to see you. How was the journey?'

'Fine but I'm glad it's over.'

He kissed her and then held her away from him, searching her face.

'I can't tell you how thankful I am you're here. Sometimes I thought you'd never make it.'

'That's all over now. Dad's better and here I am.'

'That's great news.' He took the trolley from her. 'Let's get your luggage together. The car's outside.'

He sat close to her in the back as the driver skilfully negotiated the crowded streets, weaving his way between the trams, rickshaws and three-wheeled trucks which cluttered the road. The constant blaring of horns made little impression on the pedestrians who went about their business with a complete disregard for traffic. Open fronted stalls lined the route, and business was brisk, but Anna had expected to see more bomb damage.

'The Japanese wasted no time once the war was over,' said Nigel. 'Most of the damage was in the back streets of Tokyo where incendiary bombs started fires among all those wooden buildings. There are vast areas, of course, which have been demolished in Yokohama and Kobe, but the Japs have done an enormous amount of reconstruction already. They're an industrious race.'

She peered out of the window. She had, to her knowledge, never seen a Japanese before. Their flat faces and slanting eyes intrigued her, but they all looked alike.

'I'm taking you straight to the Browne's house,' Nigel said, 'so that you can settle in. You'll be staying with Jean and Stan until we're married.'

'I know. Jean wrote me a nice letter offering to help with the wedding arrangements.'

'You'll have a lot to discuss with her. I'm afraid we had to go ahead with some things without consulting you. Time was getting short and they knew we'd want to be married as soon as possible.'

'It's kind of them to have me to stay.'

'They're looking forward to meeting you. You'll like Jean. I'm afraid I have to get back to the office this afternoon but I'll pick you up later and take you out for a meal. I can't wait to have you to myself.'

She leaned towards him. 'I'm really happy to be here Nigel.'

'I've been keeping the really exciting news until you arrived,' he went on. 'We're being sent to Osaka. Stan wants me to open up a new branch there. It means promotion, so that's one of the reasons for getting married as soon as possible amd then we can move straight up there.'

'How far is that from Tokyo?'

'About four hundred miles. Takes five hours by train. At the moment there aren't a lot of foreigners there but they're beginning to move in. The banks are among the first, followed by insurance companies and the odd trader or two. There'll be a lot of competition from other banks to get in with the Japanese firms.'

He slipped an arm round her waist and pulled her closer to him. 'You're going to like it here, darling. We've been allocated a nice little house in the hills between Osaka and Kobe together with a car and driver and we'll arrange for someone to help in the house. All on the company, of course.'

After the uncertainties of the last few months, it was a relief to feel that at last she was free to get on with her own life. Now she was actually here it was hard to believe there had been times when she had seriously thought of writing to Nigel to tell him she couldn't go through with it.

'I shall be working right up to the time we leave,' Nigel was saying. 'I'm afraid you'll have to bear with long office hours till I get things sorted out. You'll find plenty to do though and once you get to know people, you won't have a moment to yourself. There's a busy social life among the foreigners here and you won't be lonely. It goes without saying that I'd much rather spend the time with you, but for the present the job's paramount. You do understand, don't you, darling?'

'Of course. Being on my own has never been a problem. I'll be glad to have time to settle in and enjoy getting the house in order.'

'Oh Anna,' he said, gazing at her, 'I'm lucky to have someone like you to share this with. A lot of the chaps here will be wishing they were in my shoes.'

'You'll have a good view of Mount Fuji from here,' said Jean as she opened the bedroom door. She was a tall, attractive brunette with hazel eyes. She spoke with a slight Scottish accent.

Anna crossed to the open window. Far in the distance like a great snow capped cone, the mountain rose against a clear blue sky.

She had seen pictures of it and now she could hardly believe that she was looking at the real thing. It was ethereal, something of immense beauty and significance. She thought perhaps it might be an omen for the future.

'I've always wanted to climb it,' said Jean, 'but I'm told it's better viewed from a distance. When you actually get there, you'll find it's nothing but a giant slagheap which thousands of people scramble up each year. The Japanese regard it as a holy mountain and people of all ages make the pilgrimage at least once in their lifetime.'

'I would like to climb it one day,' Anna said.

Her luggage had already been brought to her room and piled neatly in a corner. She was feeling hot and sticky after the flight and longed for a shower.

Jean, sensing her need, said, 'I'm sure you'll want a little time to yourself to unpack and settle down. Have a bath if you like and any washing put into the linen basket. It'll be ready the next day and if there's anything you need just let me know. I'll wait for you in the garden. Come down when you're ready and we'll have a cup of tea.'

Anna turned to her with a grateful smile.

'It's very good of you to have me to stay, Jean, and to help with the wedding. We're both so grateful to you and Stan.'

Jean gave her a smile which lit her eyes and dimpelled her cheeks. 'It's the least we can do when you're so far from home. We want to make it a really happy day for you both, Anna. We'll discuss the details later. I'm just sorry it's such a rush. I expect Nigel told you that you're being sent to Osaka?

'Yes, he did. It sounds exciting.'

'I'll tell you more about that later. Just now I expect all you want is to relax. Take your time.'

When Jean left her, Anna sank into a chair and looked about her. The room was cool and spacious with pale green walls on which hung a series of Japanese prints. A floral counterpane covered the bed which matched the curtains and on the dressing table stood a bowl of purple iris. It was so much better than she had expected. She had dwelt too long on her dread of this country and she had given little thought to the pleasant things that awaited her. Jean had obviously put a lot of thought into her visit and tried to make everything as easy for her as possible.

She went over to her suitcase and shook out the dresses which she hung in the wardrobe, selecting a floral cotton to wear with a wide belt. Then she undressed and ran a bath. Standing naked on the cool tiled bathroom floor was delicious. She posed for a moment in front of the long mirror, gazing at her slim, perfectly proportioned body and long shapely legs. A small waist accentuated the curve of her breasts and her thick auburn hair fell about her neck. Grey green eyes stared back at her. Was it really her, Anna Bradford, here in *Japan*?

Pinning up her hair, she stepped into the water and lay back, allowing her thoughts to wander. It was good to see Nigel again and she was touched that her coming had meant so much to him. She was glad that they were to begin their married life in Osaka. It would be on an equal footing, starting a new life together and meeting new people.

Clean and refreshed, she stepped from the bath and towelling herself dry she went to her room to dress. Sitting down at the dressing table, she brushed out her hair allowing it to hang loose. She remembered that Nigel had once remarked that it was her hair that turned him on.

When she was ready she went across to the window and looked down on the garden below. A narrow stone footpath led between ornamental shrubs to a small pool nestling among rocks. Mount Fuji had disappeared into a haze. This was a humid heat, different from that of the Middle East as she remembered it. The sound of cicadas filled the air.

She could hear children's voices at the bottom of the garden and wondered if it were too early to put in an appearance. She waited a little longer and then went downstairs. There was no one about so she wandered outside following the path in the direction of the voices. She found Jean on a bench seat in the shade of a pine tree.

'Come and sit down, Anna.' Jean patted the bench beside her. 'It's so hot inside, and there's a breeze here. The children have just gone swimming so we have peace and quiet for a while.'

Almost immediately a little Japanese maid came tripping down the path carrying a tray. She was dressed in a kimono and wore her straight black hair cut in a fringe. She placed the tray carefully on the table before bowing to Anna and murmuring something in Japanese.

'This is Eriko-san,' said Jean. 'The san means honourable and is affixed to all names. She's welcomes you to her country.'

'Thank you,' said Anna, smiling at the girl.

When she had departed Jean said, 'Eriko-san has been with us since we first came here. Then there's Nishio-san, the cook, and we have a young girl who helps with the children. Stan has a driver and there's also a part-time gardener. Quite a good staff, which certainly makes life easy for me.'

'There can't be anything left for you to do,' said Anna. 'How do you spend your time?'

Jean laughed. 'That's one of the advantages of living overseas. We have a busy social life with lots of entertaining to do. I'm not sure what sort of a set-up you'll find in Osaka, but I'm sure Nigel will have organised something similar.' She reached for the teapot and began to pour. 'It's a pity you'll be leaving Tokyo before you've had time to explore but you'll be back. Nigel will be coming on business and he'll bring you with him.'

'He's very enthusiastic about Osaka. It sounds a fascinating place.'

'Stan thinks very highly of Nigel and expects him to do well there. It's a big industrial city, not far from Kobe which was badly bombed by the Americans, of course. There's plenty of scope there for business, but you'll be living in the country. Apparently the house is in the hills and I've been told it's very beautiful there.'

'How long have you lived in Japan?' asked Anna.

'About eighteen months. We were among the first to come out after the war. Stan was in the Bank before he joined the army and we were married on one of his leaves. Soon after war broke out Edward was born and later on Sophie. Stan and I didn't see much of each other until it was all over so when we were sent out here I had to try and get used to married life again, this time in a strange and devastated country. Rather like you and Nigel now.'

'Did you find it difficult?'

'Let's say it wasn't easy at first. Stan was completely absorbed in his work and in the evenings he often had to meet Japanese businessmen socially. I rarely went on those occasions as the Japanese don't bring their women to social functions nor do they expect foreigners to. You'll find it's the same in Osaka. How long have you known Nigel, Anna?'

'Since the war. I met him when we were both serving in the desert. He was in the Gunners and I was attached to an ambulance unit. We met on a short leave in Alexandria and didn't see each other again till after the war.'

'That was a long separation.'

'There was too much going on for us to miss each other. We were both in the thick of it. When eventually we did meet up again it was all rather rushed. Nigel came to see me in Oxfordshire. He had already joined the Bank and we were just getting to know each other again when he was sent to Japan.'

'Not long enough,' said Jean firmly. 'Besides you must have both changed over that time, what with all you went through in the war. It's inevitable.'

'I still feel that we have a lot to learn about each other. When eventually Nigel came home – I was the first to be demobbed – my father was seriously ill and I was helping my mother with him, so we didn't have a lot of time together. Nigel wanted to get married before we came out but I couldn't leave with Dad so ill, so the best thing seemed to be to come later.'

'You had some difficult decisions to make, Anna. Has your father fully recovered?'

Anna shook her head. 'No. I don't think he will. He's certainly better and Mum has a lot of good help with Home Care nurses and friends.'

'Hard for you to leave him though.'

'It was all the harder because they'd lost my brother during the war and so there was only me left. They insisted that I should come though. Dad said it was unfair to keep Nigel waiting any longer.'

'They'll be sad to miss the wedding but we'll have some good photographs taken for them. I must tell you what arrangements we've made so far. Time being short we had to go ahead and have the invitations printed. As it's to be a Bank wedding there were some people we felt we ought to ask as well as Nigel's friends. After discussion with him we got together a list. We've also arranged for a marquee to be put up here in the garden, and the caterers are booked. So all that remains now is for you and Nigel to decide whether you want to be married in a church or at the Embassy.'

'Have you fixed the date yet?'

Jean turned to her, her face showing concern. 'I'm so sorry, my dear. It's your big day and I omitted that vital piece of information. We've fixed it for two weeks today. I know it doesn't give you very long but Stan insists that he wants Nigel in Osaka as soon as possible. That's why we felt we must go ahead with the arrangements. I do hope you'll be happy about this, Anna?'

She felt detached as though they were discussing someone else's wedding, but she managed a smile.

'I'm grateful to you for thinking of everything,' she said. 'So long as I don't have to do anything but turn up.'

They were still in the garden talking when Nigel arrived. He'd changed into a pair of starched white cotton trousers and a long-sleeved shirt and was wearing a tie.

'Hello there!' he said, coming straight to Anna and kissing her.

'Hello Nigel,' said Jean.'We've been going over the wedding arrangements and I think we've covered everything. I'll get the invitations off as soon as you let me have the list then all that remains is to decide where you want to be married.'

Nigel looked at Anna. 'What do you think, darling? Do you want a church wedding or shall we go for the British Embassy? Same sort of thing as a Registry Office and less fuss perhaps.'

'The Embassy is fine by me,' Anna said. She was watching a tall, good-looking man with greying hair, coming from the house. As he arrived before them, Nigel stood up and introduced her to Jean's husband, Stan.

'So this is Anna,' he said, looking at her intently; she felt as if she was being sized up. 'Good to see you, my dear. Welcome to Japan.'

'It's nice to be here,' she said.

'All well at home? Nigel told us your father was ill.'

'He's better, thank you.'

He glanced at Nigel. 'You have a pretty impatient bridegroom here and I must admit I've been anxious, too. We want to get Nigel up to Osaka as soon as possible.'

Was he blaming her for the delay? She felt guilty that she had put Nigel under this sort of pressure.

Jean stepped in. 'She's here now, Stan, and everything's going according to plan. The date's fixed and you'll be able to open the new branch on schedule. Don't make Anna feel uncomfortable. I'm sure she came just as soon as she could.'

'I wouldn't want to do that,' said Stan, with an apologetic smile. 'You must forgive me. We men are inclined to think of everything in terms of business. There's keen competition here and the Japanese keep us on our toes. Isn't that so, Nigel?'

'True. I think I'm extremely fortunate to have been posted here.'

Later that evening Nigel drove Anna into town. He took the main route into the centre, pointing out places of interest like the Imperial Palace, Meiji Park, and the Diet, the Japanese Houses of Parliament. The pavements were crowded. There were a lot of GIs about with Japanese girls, dressed in kimonos, hanging onto their arms. The streets were well lighted and as they approached the centre, neon lights advertised restaurants, beer, baby foods, every conceivable thing.

'I have in mind a tempura restaurant,' he told her. 'The ideal introduction to Japanese food.'

'Sounds exciting. I can't believe I'm here, you know, Nigel. Jean has been so kind. She's thought of everything.'

'I knew you'd like her, Stan too. They're both first rate. I must say though, that I shall be glad when the whole thing's over and we can settle down to our own lives.'

Anna murmured agreement.

'I'm glad we're going to a place that's new to us both so that we can set up home together. I'm sure

Jean would do everything she could to help, but it will be fun discovering things for ourselves.'

'I shall have to leave most of that to you, I'm afraid. It's going to take all my time to get the new office launched.'

'That's all right,' Anna said.'I shall find plenty to do when you're busy. Will the house be furnished?'

'Basically, yes. You'll want to add a few bits and pieces and we'll have an allowance for that. Stan's been quite generous about it.'

'He seemed a bit annoyed that I was so long coming?'

'He was. To be honest, Anna, I expected you much earlier. As soon as I arrived, I was up to my eyes in work. Trying to get a grasp of the job, attending meetings, talking to people who were starting up businesses and trying to assess whether or not they justified loans. Banking is a very different business here. Quite frankly, I haven't had time to give much thought to the wedding.'

Anna stiffened at his accusing tone. This was a side of Nigel she had glimpsed once before. She had put it down to stress and hoped it might pass.

'You know the reason, Nigel. I didn't feel I could leave Dad just then.'

'Had we been married you'd have thought nothing of it. As it was, you took a dickens of a long time to make up your mind. In fact, sometimes I wondered if you intended to come at all.'

She glanced at him. The muscles of his face were taut, his hands gripping the steering wheel white-knuckled.

'You yourself suggested it as an alternative,' she pointed out. 'In fact at the time you seemed to think it a good idea, as I recall.'

'I was thinking in terms of weeks not of months. I was pretty desperate at times. I needed someone to talk to and you weren't there. I couldn't understand why it was taking you so long.'

She was taken aback by his attitude. She blamed herself that she had given little thought to Nigel's position. It had been all she could do to cope with her own problems.

'I'm sorry, Nigel. Maybe I did take longer than necessary. I hadn't realised that it was that urgent.'

'Not when you knew I was waiting for you?'

'Ann made a placatory gesture. 'Don't let's argue, darling. Not now I'm here.'

'I think it's something we need to talk about.' His voice was brusque. 'At one point you weren't even writing. I didn't know what the hell to think. Did I have a wife coming out or not? What was I to tell the Brownes? It was damned difficult for me.'

'I'm sorry. It wasn't an ideal situation by any means. I wanted to come, of course I did, but it would have been insensitive to leave Mum to cope on her own. Don't let's spend our first evening together arguing, please, Nigel.'

Nigel frowned. 'All right. We'll let it pass.' He was concentrating on overtaking a motor trishaw. She was relieved that his attention was once again on the road.

'Those jeeps are the military police,' he remarked presently. 'The Yanks are all over the place attempting to keep law and order.'

'With success?'

'Oh yes. The Japanese are orderly people. They understand discipline. If they know what's expected of them, they'll comply.'

At that moment Nigel slammed on the brakes,

narrowly missing a pedestrian who had stepped off the pavement. Anna smothered a gasp. Slowly they moved forward again and presently turned onto the Ginza which ran through the entertainment area.

'There must be an awful lot of accidents,' she said.

'There are. You can't drive anywhere in this country without a horn, which they ignore anyway. They reckon that if you hoot at them you've seen them and will therefore avoid them. Sometimes it's impossible to.'

'What happens if you hit someone?'

'If they're still alive they'll probably stagger to their feet and bow and apologise for getting in your way.'

'Anna's eyebrows shot up. 'What strange behaviour.'

'They're strange people. Quite unlike any other race.'

She disliked the derogatory way he spoke of them. If you're going to do business with them, surely you have to try to understand them.'

'The Japanese,' went on Nigel, as he negotiated another side turning, 'are scrupulously polite and quite impossible to fathom.'

He parked the car in front of what looked like a coffee house. A Japanese girl in a kimono stood outside bowing and smiling at them. Ignoring her, Nigel took Anna's arm and steered her towards a small restaurant on the corner of the street. A red lantern hung over the doorway painted with black characters indicating the name of the place.

'Tomi's Tempura Bar,' said Nigel, translating.

As they entered, two girls in kimono bowed low murmuring greetings. The place was dimly lit and in a far corner a young American couple were studying a menu, otherwise most of the customers were

Japanese men. Somewhere a radio was playing oriental music. Anna found the thin high-pitched voice strange and tuneless to her ears.

'We'll sit up at the bar and you can watch the food being prepared,' Nigel suggested, leading the way.

She followed him between the tables, feeling herself to be the object of the men's curiosity, something she would no doubt have to get used to. Then as she reached Nigel, she glanced at the man behind the bar. He was tall for a Japanese and clad in a chef's white apron and hat. His face was round and dark with wide flat nostrils and thick sensuous lips. At that moment he looked up and his black expressionless eyes met hers. A shiver swept through her and suddenly she felt icy cold.

Nigel was staring at her. He had pulled out a stool for her to sit on. Beside him stood a waitress, holding a bowl with steaming hot towels. Anna stood rooted to the spot, unable to drag her eyes away from the man behind the bar. She was seeing, not the chef, but a Japanese soldier, dressed in the peaked cap and uniform of a guard in a prisoner of war camp.

She had to get away from him. She turned quickly and looked round the room, searching desperately for an empty table, anywhere but at the bar where Nigel still waited, a puzzled expression on his face. She felt that everyone in the room was watching her and slowly she moved towards the stool. Nigel helped her onto it, as if she were an invalid, and now she was only a few feet away from the chef. He was holding a long pointed knife with which he sliced vegetables into long strips, before plunging them in boiling fat. He ignored her as he picked up a pair of chopsticks and selected some prawns and chopped vegetables which he dipped in batter, before placing them in a hot skillet.

The moment passed but she still could not control the trembling of her limbs. Nigel was watching her anxiously.

'What's the matter?' he asked. 'Aren't you feeling well?'

'Just a bit tired,' she said.

'Dozo?' A waitress with short frizzy hair after the current fashion of foreign women, held out the hot towels to her.

'Take one,' said Nigel. 'Coming off the street, it's a good idea to freshen up.' He took one himself and rubbed it over his face, finishing off by wiping his hands and replaced the towel in the waiting basket. Automatically she followed his actions without thought and realised too late that she had wiped off most of her make-up.

Two small china containers were placed in front of them and filled with a hot liquid from a china carafe.

'Sake,' said Nigel. 'You hold out your cup to be filled and it will be recharged as soon as it's empty. Be careful, Anna, it's quite potent.'

The chef now placed the cooked food on plates in front of them. Anna surveyed the food with dismay. Lightly fried pieces of lobster, octupus, prawns and vegetables. She had no appetite for it but concentrated on manipulating her chopsticks. Glancing at Nigel, she was relieved to see that he seemed to have noticed nothing amiss. He was already dipping a morsel of lobster into one of the sauces. She played with the food in front of her.

'Eat up, Anna. Don't you like it?'

'I'm not very hungry.'

'Are you all right, darling?' he asked, solicitous now.

She put up her hand to her forehead. 'I suddenly felt strange. Probably after the long flight.'

'Would you like me to run you home?'

She shook her head. She must make some attempt to overcome her fear. If she could avoid looking at this big Japanese who at times was only inches away from her as he leaned across the bar to put pieces of food on her plate, if she could avoid meeting his cold eyes, she'd be all right. She had to get through this meal with some appearance of enjoyment. Nigel was telling her something about a maid he had employed who would be coming to Osaka with them. She tried to concentrate.

'I was going to take you on a quick tour of the city after this,' he went on, 'but pehaps we should leave it till another night?'

'Would you mind very much? I do feel rather tired.'

He looked at her, his eyes anxious. 'Sorry, darling. I've been rushing you. There'll be other opportunities to see the sights.' He asked for the bill and brought out his wallet.

Thankfully she followed him to the door. Outside he took her hand and led her to the car as she took deep gulps of the cold night air to steady her nerves.

In the main street the traffic was as bad as ever. People were now coming out of the places of entertainment, a lot of them American servicemen with Japanese girls tottering on unaccustomed high heels, clinging to their arms.

Presently they left the main road and soon they were driving towards the quieter residential area. She was thankful that he didn't attempt to talk and before long he turned into a drive and pulled up in front of the Browne's house. No lights shone at the windows.

'Eleven-thirty,' he said, looking at his watch. 'It looks as though everyone's in bed.'

The front door was unlocked and without waiting for an invitation, Nigel entered and closed it behind him. The shutters were closed in the sitting room and the standard light had been left on. Anna kicked off her shoes and went over to the couch. Nigel followed her.

'We have to make up for lost time,' he said and, drawing her towards him kissed her long and passionately. He had lost none of his skill in arousing her and she gave herself up to the enjoyment of his embrace, relaxing in the security of his arms.

'Darling, I've waited so long for that,' he murmured. 'You don't regret coming, do you?'

She drew away and looked at him. 'Why do you ask?'

'I don't know. This evening you suddenly became quite withdrawn. I felt I'd lost you. You had such a strange expression on your face, almost as though you were afraid. Then it passed. What happened to you in that restaurant?'

'I don't know. But you're right. Something strange did happen when that chef looked at me. Just for a moment I had a vision of a Japanese soldier standing in front of me. His uniform was so clear and I saw the cruelty in his eyes. It was like something out of the past happening here and now.'

'But you've never even seen a Japanese soldier.' His eyes narrowed. 'It's because of your brother, isn't it?'

'I suppose it is.' She had to admit it.

'Anna, come and sit down.' He led her to the couch and sat close to her. 'That's all in the past now. You must forget it. I know the Japanese treated their prisoners abominably but you can't judge them all by that. They weren't the only ones to treat prisoners badly.'

He didn't understand. He wasn't involved. Her resolution to keep her feelings about Jack a secret, was forgotten. She turned to face him, anger in her eyes.

'I'm not talking about any prisoner of war. I'm talking about my brother and I know what sort of life they led in that camp where he died. One of his friends who survived gave me the whole story. It was appalling what they did to their prisoners. If you had lost someone you loved like that, you wouldn't forgive them. I can't either.'

Nigel stared at her, suddenly a stranger. His eyes were hostile, his face white and drawn. Why couldn't he try to understand how she felt? She had no idea what to say to diffuse the situation. Then, to her horror, she began to cry.

'I'm sorry, Nigel,' she sobbed as he passed her a handkerchief. 'Maybe I'm tired. I don't know. I had no idea this would happen.'

Nigel's voice was cold. 'Perhaps then, you did make a mistake in coming. Perhaps, after all, it's something you won't be able to come to terms with.'

She struggled for control. 'It's too late now. I'm here. Just give me time.'

'We haven't got time,' he said. 'I came here to do a job. I've been given promotion within a tour of duty. That's unusual and offers me a great opportunity which I intend to make the most of. I'm not going to let them down. I simply haven't the time nor the inclination to work through the psychological problems of my wife.'

'I see I can't expect you to understand, Nigel,' she said, her tears drying up. 'I won't disappoint you, I promise. You can be sure I'll keep to my part of the bargain.'

'Bargain!' Nigel spat out the word. 'Is that all our marriage means to you?'

He got up and stood with his back to her. 'Something of an anti-climax after all these months, isn't it?' Without looking at her, he went to the door and opened it. 'I'm going home now and I'll give you a ring tomorrow.'

She didn't call him back. As the sound of his footsteps faded, she followed him through the door. Outside, the beam of the car's headlights swept briefly across the ceiling as Nigel drove off. She mounted the stairs, slowly, wearily, wrestling with her thoughts, trapped in a situation over which she had no control.

Chapter Six

Stan had already finished breakfast and the children had left for school when Anna came downstairs the next morning. Jean, hearing her, came into the hall.

'Hello, my dear. I hope you had a good night?'

'Yes, thank you.' In fact Anna had spent most of the night hot and restless, drifting between dreams and reality. 'I'm sorry I'm late. Has everyone finished breakfast?'

'Stan always goes off to the office early and the children start school at eight in the summer but you and I can take our time.' She looked at Anna closely. 'You're looking tired, Anna. Are you all right?'

'A bit of a headache, that's all, Probably the journey.'

'I'll get you an aspirin,' said Jean. 'A cup of coffee will put you right, or do you prefer tea?'

'Coffee, please. Strong and black.' Anna followed her into the dining room where Eriko-san was tidying the table.

'If you're feeling up to it I thought we might go shopping later,' said Jean. 'There may be a few things you need and I'll take you to the American Women's Club for lunch. They do quite a decent meal there. I don't want you to feel confined to the house while you're here, Anna. If you need transport, we can always arrange for an office car to take you.'

'There's no need for that. I can walk or take public transport.'

'You'll find it difficult to get around unless you speak the language,' said Jean, pouring the coffee. 'Very few Japanese speak English as yet and it's really easier to use the car.' She gave Anna a reassuring smile. 'It won't take you long to get used to the life. One can even learn to enjoy it.'

'I'm sure I shall. Just the same I love exploring and finding my way around. It's quite safe, isn't it?'

'Absolutely. You don't have to worry about that. It's just that in the heat it's a good idea to spare yourself. You'll find plenty of other outlets for your energy.'

'Such as?'

Jean picked up her cup and sipped her coffee thoughtfully, then she said, 'I'm really speaking of the role of a bank wife here. In Japan a wife takes second place. In fact the Japanese word for housewife is oku-san, meaning the inner part, or you could say out of sight and it's not so different for us. We have a certain amount of freedom when our husbands are at work, but I've come to the conclusion that my real function is to support Stan and that means that I have to be available at all times.'

'More involved in the job than you'd be at home then?' suggested Anna.

'Exactly. In a way an artificial sort of life but nevertheless interesting. I often think that I play as important a role for the bank as does Stan. At any rate, I like to think so!'

The telephone rang and Jean went to answer it. When she came back she said, 'It's Nigel. He wants to speak to you. Don't forget we're having a dinner party this evening, Anna. I forgot to remind him. Tell him eight o'clock.'

Anna went into the hall and picked up the receiver.

'Hello.'

'Anna? I hope you're feeling better? I don't know how we got ourselves into that situation last night. It seemed pointless.' His voice was cheerful, dismissing her misgivings as trivial. She couldn't be so light hearted about it.

'It wasn't pointless, Nigel. It was a very real problem. I lay awake all night thinking about it.'

'We'll talk about it again when we're in a calmer frame of mind. You mustn't worry. It was silly of me to get so upset when you'd only just arrived. Forgive me, darling?'

'I am worried, Nigel.' She lowered her voice. 'How can we marry when we don't see eye to eye about living here?'

'Once we get to Osaka, we'll have all the time in the world to sort it out.' His voice changed, suddenly concerned. 'You're all right, Anna, aren't you? You sound so serious.'

'I wish there was more time to talk. There's a dinner party tonight. Jean wanted me to remind you. She said eight o'clock.'

'Damn. I'd forgotten. We can do without that.'

'It's kind of them,' Anna protested.'Jean thought I ought to meet a few people.'

'Could we meet for lunch?'

'Jean's taking me shopping and to lunch at the American Club.'

'Shall I never get you to myself?'

She wanted to be with him. Time was running out and she had to talk to him, try to get him to understand her misgivings before it was too late.

'I have to go now,' said Nigel, abruptly. 'I've got a meeting. See you this evening, darling.'

She put down the receiver and returned to the dining room.

'It was about something we were discussing last night,' she told Jean.'I reminded him about this evening.'

'I know you'd rather be alone together,' said Jean, 'but you'll have time for that later. Now, if you're feeling up to it we'll go into town. I just have to see the cook about the meal this evening, then I'll be ready.'

The car was waiting outside. Jean spoke to the driver in English and asked him to drop them at the Daimaru, a big department store in the main shopping area.

'We're going via the Imperial Palace,' said Jean. 'That's where the Emperor lives.'

'Still?'

'Oh yes. The Allies need him. The Japanese are far more likely to be amenable to his orders than they are to the Americans. He's a kind of go-between.'

They drove through the park where cherry blossom hung heavy on branches. Through the trees Anna could see white stone walls hiding a substantial Japanese style building, the whole edifice being surrounded by a wide moat.

'Once a year on New Year's day, the public are allowed across the bridge to the courtyard when the Emperor appears. They come in their hordes to see him.'

They continued towards the shopping centre and the driver pulled up outside the department store. Young girls wearing navy blue uniform and white gloves bowed them in and directed them towards the lifts.

Jean waved them aside. 'We'll walk round first to give you an idea of what they sell and the prices,' she said. 'You'll find things are quite cheap but not such good quality as at home.' She reached for an exquisite porcelain doll dressed in rich brocade. 'These are collectors' items,' she said. 'As you see well out of reach of children. Some Japanese women have very valuable collections and exhibit them on special occasions.'

In the kimono department they examined the brocades.

'Japanese women wear these round their waists to keep their kimonos in place but we find a different use for them,' said Jean. 'The lengths are just long enough to make into cocktail dresses. My dressmaker could run you up one in a few days.'

After the assistant had folded the material carefully in gift wrapping and tied the parcel with colourful ribbons, Jean led the way to the lift. 'I'm dying for a long cool drink,' she said. 'Let's go up to the roof restaurant.'

They walked out into a cool garden where shady trees and waterfalls gave the impression of careful landscaping. Close by the restaurant, toddlers played happily in a paddling pool while their mothers took a well earned rest.

'It's incredible,' gasped Anna. 'I've never seen anything like it.'

'They're ingenious people. They brought an elephant up here once. Slung it up in a sort of crane. I doubt whether the elephant enjoyed it.'

Jean gave their orders to a waiter and sank gratefully into a chair. Anna looked at her anxiously.

'Are you all right?'

'Yes. The heat sometimes gets me down and I think I should let you into a secret. I'm pregnant. It was unexpected but now that we've got used to the idea, we're delighted about it.'

Anna was immediately concerned. 'Is it wise to traipse round in this heat, Jean? Shouldn't you be resting?'

'I'm all right. I don't intend to stay at home all day getting bored. The doctor says everything's fine, but the heat always affects me. I'm getting on for forty you know, and sometimes I do feel a bit anxious.'

'You look so well. You had no trouble before, did you?'

'None, perfectly straightforward. Now, what about you? You're looking better. Has the headache gone?'

'Completely.'

'By the way, I forgot to tell you, a couple of parcels were delivered to the house this morning for you and Nigel. Wedding presents, I expect.'

Anna fell silent as she watched two small children filling their buckets.

'Anna, did you hear what I said? Everything's all right, isn't it? I mean about the wedding?

Anna forced herself to meet Jean's enquiring gaze. 'Of course,' she said. 'It's just that this is a different world and it's taking me time to get used to it. I can't believe I'm about to be married.'

Jean's eyes were sympathetic. 'That's understandable,' she said. 'We have rather rushed you into it, but once you get to Osaka, you'll have plenty of time to settle down.'

'I know. I'm looking forward to it. You've been very patient with me, Jean.'

The waiter delivered their drinks, ice tinkling in the glasses. Anna was glad of the interruption. She had a feeling Jean suspected that all was not well and she doubted whether she had reassured her. She preferred not to answer any more questions.

When Stan came home at six-thirty, Jean was upstairs changing for dinner. She put on a long black evening dress which fell from the waist in soft folds, disguising her thickening waistline.

'I shan't be able to wear this much longer,' she lamented, and was studying herself in the mirror when Stan walked in.

'How are you?' he asked, giving her a brief kiss. 'Not overdoing it in this heat, I hope?'

As he spoke he began to strip off his clothes, leaving them in a heap at his feet.

I'm rather tired today,' Jean admitted. 'Going shopping is always exhausting.'

Stan grunted. He gathered up his clothing in a bundle and dropped it in the linen basket.

'What do you think of Anna?' he asked, reaching for a towel and tucking it into his waist. 'Seems a nice girl.'

'I like her very much but I have a feeling that she's not altogether sure about Nigel.'

Stan's thick eyebrows shot up. 'Then she ought to be. She's had enough time to think about it.'

'I know, but she's only just arrived and she's suddenly being rushed into this wedding. She hasn't seen Nigel for months, and I don't think he's taken much trouble to put her at ease.'

'What makes you say that?'

'It's just a hunch. He's inclined to be a bit self centred.'

'He's a bright fellow. He'll do well and she should see that.'

'There's more to marriage than that. You should know.' She smiled at him affectionately. 'To tell you the truth I'm worried about her. To my mind she isn't behaving like a girl whose heart is in this marriage.' She sat down at the dressing table and started on her make-up. 'She has reservations about it.'

'Nonsense. She's not a child. She's a mature woman. She's had more than enough time. I want Nigel up in Osaka within two weeks and I'm not waiting any longer. I've already postponed his transfer so that he could be here for Anna's arrival.' There was a note of irritation in his voice. 'Nigel has his career to consider and Anna should be willing to co-operate.'

Jean was silent. She walked out of the bathroom. She wasn't going to argue with her husband, and in part she felt he was right.

'I don't want you worrying about it.' Stan said from the bathroom. 'You've got the baby to think about. The sooner this wedding's over and we can settle down to our own lives again, the better.'

'Just the same, while Anna's with us I feel responsible for her. She has no relatives or friends here, except us.'

'She's not the first woman to come out to marry. In the old days they used to come by sea and often hadn't seen their men for months. What gives you this idea, anyway?'

'Did you hear them come in last night?'

'No.'

'They were talking for ages downstairs and it sounded to me as though they were having an argument.'

'A lovers' tiff, more likely' said Stan from under the shower. 'I think you're letting your imagination run away with you, my dear.'

She left him to it and went downstairs to inspect the table. Everything had to be supervised. The servants were excellent, but if she showed lack of interest, standards could quickly drop.

Nigel had arrived. She could hear him talking to Anna in the sitting room and she went to join them. He was wearing a white dinner jacket and black trousers, the approved dress for a formal dinner party. Anna had changed into a long skirt and cream blouse. She wore her hair up, revealing her elegant neck and features. Jean thought it made her look older. She was really very lovely with her unusual colouring. If only she looked happier. She'd be good for Nigel if she was strong enough to stand up to him. He'd be a fool if he didn't show that he cared about her.

'You look lovely, my dear,' she said, sitting down beside Anna. 'Stan will be down in a moment. Meanwhile I'll tell you a little about the people who are coming this evening. To begin with, there's Deidre and Alan McCall, a couple from the Embassy. Deidre's a good friend of mine though a trifle outspoken at times. Then there're the Wissers. He's Stan's opposite number in the Dutch bank, and Harry Mears is coming. He's sharing a house with Nigel until the wedding, but I expect Nigel's told you about him already. I think you'll find them quite an entertaining lot.'

When dinner was announced, Jean led the guests into the dining room. Anna was seated between the Dutchman and Alan McCall with Nigel opposite. He looked across at her and there was a chill in his expression that bothered her.

'So you've just arrived?' asked Alan McCall, and Anna turned to him with relief. 'You must feel quite confused pitched into a situation like this.'

'I am a bit but I'm sure I shall enjoy it. Just at the moment I find it hard to hold on to reality though. It seems more like a dream.'

'I wonder what we can talk about to bring you down to earth?' he said, a smile crinkling the corners of his brown eyes.

'Tell me about Japan,' Anna said eagerly. 'I know very little apart from what we read in the newspapers at home, and Nigel's letters of course. Do you speak Japanese?'

'I'm learning,' he said with some amusement. 'I think it's a good idea for anyone who expects to be here for any length of time.'

'Once we get to Osaka, I must have lessons.'

'I heard you were going there.' Alan looked at her with interest. 'It'll be an interesting experience for you. Not such a strong American presence as here. That may well lead to problems for Nigel. He'll have to start from scratch. One of the biggest difficulties in this country is to understand the people. They're inclined to tell you what they think you'd like to hear, even when it bears little relation to the truth. It's not surprising that our races have different attitudes, but if we're to live together we have to arrive at some sort of compromise.'

'Difficult to do business though?' suggested Anna.

'It certainly is, but to give these people their due, they're trying to toe the line.

'Surely they should. After all, they lost the war.'

'True but if we're to have their co-operation, there has to be a bit of give and take.'

'How do they feel now it's over?'

Alan picked up his wine glass and drank thoughtfully before answering. 'It's a complex subject. They've never been occupied before. Throughout the whole of their history they've always been the victors so this is an entirely new experience for them. Even before the war, very few foreigners were allowed into the country. The Japanese have always been suspicious of them, added to which they looked on their Emperor as divine and their country as unconquerable so it was a shattering experience when they were told to surrender.'

'It must really have dented their pride.'

Alan nodded. 'They didn't know what to make of it. Their own history is made up of barbarism and bloodshed and they expected the same treatment from the Americans. It was a pleasant surprise for them to find the army of occupation behaving in such a civilised way.'

'What do the Americans intend to do here?' asked Anna.

She was aware that the other guests had fallen silent and were listening to their conversation. She glanced across the table and saw that Harry, Nigel's messmate, was watching her intently. Did he disapprove of her? She wondered how much Nigel had confided in him.

'A good question,' said Stan, coming into the conversation. 'I see you want to familiarise yourself with the set up, Anna, but in the end we probably know little more than you, although we like to think we do. Let's say that the aim of the occupation is not to hold the enemy down or demand restitution but to help the Japanese back on their feet by giving financial aid and teaching them new technology. The Americans are keen to teach them democracy. They think that's the answer to everything. What they don't seem to realise is that democracy is quite alien to Japanese culture. It's causing quite a few problems.'

'I'd like to add a little more to that,' said the Dutchman, with barely a trace of an accent. 'Surely one of the most important aspects of the occupation is to make damned sure that they never start another war.'

'That goes without saying,' Stan agreed.

'It seems extraordinary to me,' said Deirdre, 'that some people think the Japanese retrograde. It's simply not true. They don't have a sense of humour, that's for sure and some people might think them devious but they're certainly not stupid.'

'No one's suggesting they are,' said her husband.

'I think what Deirdre means is that they can be very stubborn when it suits them,' suggested Jean. 'Personally I don't think we have to worry too much about how the Japanese are faring under the Americans. They're shrewd enough to seize all the opportunities that come their way. The occupation won't last for ever and once free of it, they'll streak ahead with their newly acquired knowledge and it won't be long before they're a very competitive force in the world.'

No one was prepared to argue against this. In the silence that followed, Deirdre said, 'I think it's only after you've been here for a while that you can begin to make sense of it. How did you feel about coming here, Anna? A lot of people are hostile towards the Japanese. After all they were pretty brutal towards their prisoners.'

Before Anna had time to reply, Alan McCall cut in, 'That's best forgotten, Deirdre. If we take that attitude, we can't do our jobs properly. It's up to us to build bridges of reconciliation. Anna probably agrees with you that many people at home do feel that way, but if they do, they shouldn't come to Japan. Don't you agree, Nigel?'

Anna glanced across the table, waiting for his reply. He was looking at her with a wry smile. 'I think you'd better let Anna answer on her own behalf,' he said.

'My brother died in a Japanese prisoner of war camp,' she said, 'so obviously I'm biased.'

An awkward silence fell on the guests. Then Jean said,'I think it's very brave of you to come, Anna. It must have been a difficult decision for you to make. I'm sure all of us sympathise with you and will do our best to make you happy here.'

Chapter Seven

As each day brought the wedding closer Anna's anxiety deepened. Sometimes she felt Jean looking at her with a puzzled expression. She wished she could confide in her, but Jean's loyalties were to Stan and the Bank and she couldn't expect her to have patience with what Nigel termed her 'psychological problems'. Indeed she hardly understood them herself.

In spite of Jean's kindness, she felt very lonely. These days her thoughts often returned to Jack for spiritual comfort and she found herself remembering things she had not thought about for years. She would have given anything to have his cheerful guidance now.

In her lonelier moments Anna sought the company of Sophie and Edward. They had taken a liking to her and sometimes when they came home from school she went with them to the park to sail their boats.

'I wish you weren't going away,' said Sophie. sitting beside her on a bench and watching Edward trying to recover his boat. The engine had puttered to a stop and the little craft was slowly drifting away from the bank.

'The battery's finished,' said Anna, going to his aid. 'You'd better bring it out otherwise you'll lose it.' She watched as he manoevoured it towards him with a long stick.

'I wish you weren't going away,' Sophie repeated, coming to stand beside Anna and holding her hand. 'Couldn't you live here? Nigel's got a house.'

'Your father wants him to work in a different part of Japan so I'm going with him,' said Anna, smiling down at her.

'Could we come and see you sometimes?'

'It's a long way, Sophie. Four hundred miles. It takes hours.'

'Perhaps just sometimes?'

'Perhaps.'

'Do you love Nigel?'

'Of course. Why do you ask?'

'You don't get close to each other, kiss and all that.'

'Sometimes we do. We wait until nobody's watching.'

Edward managed to get hold of the boat and lifting it out of the water, brought it to show Anna.

'Can you see if it's the battery?' he asked.

She tried switching the starter button on and off. 'There's no way of telling without special testing equipment, but I'd say that's certainly the cause. I'll get you a new one tomorrow.'

'Can I borrow your sailing boat?' he asked Sophie.

'No.'

'You're not using it.'

'No.' She turned her back on him, her way of ending the conversation. 'Nigel's house is just over there,' she said to Anna, pointing to the other side of the park. 'I'm bored with boats. Shall we go and see him?'

'No,' said Edward. 'It's miles. It's too hot.'

'I'm thirsty,' said Sophie. 'He'll give us something nice to drink.'

'He's still at the office.' said Anna.

'I suppose he has to work late, like Daddy.'

'A lot of men do. It's not like school where you finish at the same time every day.'

She looked across the park to where Sophie had pointed. In the distance she could see a group of houses.

'It doesn't look miles away to me, Edward,' she observed.

'It is, but only by road,' Edward admitted. 'If you cross the park, it only takes about fifteen minutes.' Edward spoke with the air of one wise in local knowledge.

'So can we go there?' Sophie asked eagerly.

'There isn't time now, Sophie,' Anna said. 'It's nearly your supper time.'

Sophie put on a resigned expression. 'Okay,' she said. 'We'll take you there another day.'

Anna didn't see Nigel again until the following evening, when he took her to the Imperial Hotel for dinner.

'It's the only building in Tokyo which is earthquake proof, or so they say. It's not yet been severely tested.'

He seemed very cheerful. She looked at him across the table. I should be enjoying this, she thought. Everything's so normal. What's the matter with me?

'You look nice,' he said. 'Been to the hairdresser?'

'This morning. Jean introduced me to her dressmaker, too. She's running me up a few dresses.'

'We'll have to come to some arrangement about an

allowance,' he said. 'As soon as we get to Osaka, I'll let you have so much a month for housekeeping plus a personal allowance, whatever you feel you need.'

'That's generous of you, Nigel, but I have some money of my own. Enough anyway for my personal use.'

'You'll need to buy quite a few things and that's the easiest arrangement. Gives you some independence. I want my wife to do me credit.' His tone was teasing.

Did he see her as a possession? She felt he was weighing her assets and liabilities, and recently the latter had been predominant. There were things she wanted to discuss with him. She longed for his reassurance, but they were half way through their meal and there had been no opportunity. Now, as they waited for their dessert course, he was talking about his work.

'I shan't have a big staff, at least to start with. I'll have to see how it goes. A couple of clerks, an office boy and a secretary and of course a driver. We'll have to arrange for you to have the car sometimes. The house is about half an hour's drive from Osaka and there's a station quite close. I don't want you to feel isolated when you're on your own all day.'

'Nigel, the other evening when I got so upset . . .'

'Darling, the other evening we were both tired. Let's forget about that, shall we? There's nothing more to be said.'

Unspoken questions hung between them. She couldn't get close to him.

'You're looking so much better than you did, much more relaxed. You're beautiful, you know, Anna.' He smiled at her, admiration in his eyes. 'Just like the girl I used to know.'

'She's not the same, Nigel. Neither of us are. A lot of water has passed under the bridge since Egypt and we need to talk about it. It's no good pretending we're the same people.'

'Of course we aren't. We all move on. The important thing is that I still love you and I hope the same goes for you?'

He waited. Why did she hesitate? It was true, wasn't it? Whenever he took her in his arms and kissed her, she had no difficulty in responding.

'Of course,' she said, lamely.

'You don't sound very convincing.'

She was silent. Perhaps the fault lay with her. They had been through a bad patch and she had expected too much of him. It wasn't an unusual condition between engaged couples and most of them seemed to go ahead and make a success of their marriage. She should try to take more of an interest in his work.

'I thought one evening, when the cook's out, I might come over and fix a meal for you,' she suggested. 'I would enjoy doing the shopping and preparing it.'

She immediately sensed his disapproval. 'There's no need to do that,' he said. 'Jean has said on more than one occasion that if we don't want to go out for a meal I'd be welcome to come and join you.'

'But it would be fun. If Harry's in he can eat with us, otherwise we could have the evening to ourselves.'

'I think that might upset the cook. Even if I give him time off, I don't think he'd like to feel you were using his kitchen. It'll be a different matter when we're in Osaka. It will be your own place and you can do what you like.'

She let it go at that. When at the end of the

evening, he dropped her off and kissed her good-night, she said 'I'll see you tomorrow then?'

'Yes, but not till later. In fact, probably not until after dinner.'

That meant she would have to spend the evening with Stan and Jean. She tried to avoid that. Besides Jean would want to know what Nigel was up to. She disapproved of him putting in long hours at the office that she thought should be spent with Anna. She decided to skip supper and told Jean that she was going out.

It was a lovely evening as she wandered towards the park. There were a lot of people about, family groups admiring the cherry blossom, young men with their bottles of beer sitting on the benches, children feeding the ducks.

She paused on the bridge to look down on the little lake below. Purple and yellow iris flowered in profusion and deep red water lilies bloomed on its surface, in contrast to the murky water beneath. As she watched couples wandering along the paths, hand in hand, sometimes pausing to take a photograph, she felt excluded from their love and was suddenly horribly depressed and lonely.

The lake was fed by a stream; a path followed one of its banks, disappearing into a group of weeping willow trees where branches swept the water. Another path ran down a gentle slope to join it by the lake, and along it a couple were strolling hand in hand. The girl was dressed in a kimono and much like the others – above average prettiness perhaps, but otherwise unexceptional. It was the man who drew her attention: European, tall, fair haired and devastingly familiar as her husband-to-be.

She turned her back towards them, her heart

suddenly pumping. It couldn't be! Not Nigel. Surely her imagination was playing her tricks. The couple passed by the bridge, deep in conversation. Watching them go, Anna knew she was not mistaken; even from the back. Nigel was all too obviously Nigel. She tried to still her fluttering heart by taking deep breaths. The implication of what she had just witnessed overwhelmed her. Was this liaison common knowledge? Surely the Bank would frown on such a relationship. If Stan knew about it, he would be only too anxious to rush the wedding through and move Nigel out of the area. This might, in fact, be the very reason for all the hurry.

Anger possessed her now. How could Nigel do this to her? Only yesterday he had told her that he loved her. What a fool she'd been to believe him. She should have trusted her intuition and had the courage to break off the engagement there and then.

She had to speak to him. There was no time to be lost. She must go to his house and wait until he came back, with or without the girl. This resolved, she set off along the path Sophie had pointed out the other day, retracing the steps of Nigel and his companion. She walked quickly, deep in thought.

It wasn't till she'd almost reached the house that it occurred to her she wouldn't be able to get in unless Harry was home. If that was the case, she would wait. It was out of the question to put it off till the next evening.

She rang the bell and to her relief Harry appeared.

'Hello, Anna. Nigel's out, I'm afraid.'

'Would you mind if I waited? He said he'd be working late and I thought I'd wander over to see him when he comes home.'

Harry hesitated. 'Does he know you're coming?'

'No.'

'He might not be back for some time and I'm afraid I've got to go out.'

'Anna was determined not to be put off. 'I'd still like to wait. There's something I need to talk to him about.'

'All right. Come in and I'll get you a drink.'

'Thanks. Something long and cold please. Non-alcoholic.'

Presently he came and put a tall glass of orange in front of her.

'Harry?' she said tentatively.

'Yes?'

'Have you got a girl friend?'

He looked at her, surprised. 'No. Why?'

'I just thought it must be a bit lonely sometimes?'

'There's not exactly a great choice of unattached girls in this place.'

'The local girls are very pretty.'

'Maybe. But relationships of that kind are frowned on by the Bank. It's one of the things we're warned about. There's nothing against going to geisha parties and night clubs with the chaps though. There's no lack of entertainment here. Just don't get involved. That's what they always say.'

'Fair enough, I suppose.'

'A chap could get himrself into all sorts of trouble,' Harry went on. 'Now, if you'll excuse me, I'm off to play squash. Sure you'll be all right? It might be a long wait.'

'Yes thanks.'

She heard him close the door and then the car starting up. She decided to let Jean know where she was in case the wait proved a long one. She picked up the phone.

'Jean, it's Anna. I'm at Nigel's. I'm just ringing to let you know I might be late.'

'That's all right. Is Nigel there?'

'Not at the moment. I've just spoken to Harry. He doesn't think he'll be long.' That should put Jean's mind at rest.

'Are you all right, dear? If Nigel's anything like Stan, not long can mean an hour or more.'

'Please don't worry about me. I'm fine.'

They said their goodbyes. Anna went back to the sitting room and sipped her drink. She was shaking. She must try and pull herself together and think how best to handle this.

An hour passed. She got up and went over to the window. It was beginning to get dark and the street lights had come on. She watched as an elderly woman passed by holding a small boy by the hand. She was dressed in a dark kimono and her wooden getas clip-clopped as she tripped along.

She drew the curtains and turned away with a sigh. Perhaps after all she should go home and confront Nigel tomorrow when she felt calmer. No, dammit, she was going to get an explanation if it meant waiting all night.

Soon after ten she heard a car pull up outside and the front door slam. Nigel came into the room and seeing her, stopped dead. Thankfully, he was alone.

'Anna! What in heaven's name are you doing here?' There was an edge to his voice, as he stood frowning down at her.

'Waiting to see you.'

'How long have you been here? I told you I'd be late.'

'About an hour and a half. I walked through the park.'

He stared at her. 'Why didn't you tell me you were coming?' His eyes were twin accusations.

'I wanted a walk and decided to come and see you. I knew you might be late but I was quite happy to wait. Harry let me in. We talked for a bit and then he went to play squash.'

'What was so urgent? You could have rung me.'

'Is there any reason why I shouldn't come to see you?'

'None at all.'

Enough of prevarication. 'I thought I saw you in the park,' she said.

'I told you I was working,' he said coldly.

'I saw you walking in the park with a girl, a Japanese girl. Nigel, don't tell me it wasn't true. I wasn't making a mistake.'

'Very well. What if I was?'

'Who is she?'

'Nothing more than a friend. For goodness sake, Anna, don't read something into this that doesn't exist.'

'I'm not reading anything into it. I just want an explanation. I think I'm entitled to it.'

'If you want the truth, I'll tell you, but you won't like it.' He raised his voice. 'I was bloody lonely waiting for you. What did you expect me to do? Not to look at a girl all that time?' He glared at her.

She ignored that. Instead she said, 'It seemed to me that you were quite fond of this girl.'

'So you were spying on me?'

'No. I was on the bridge and you came down the path holding her hand and then went off in the direction of the trees. I couldn't help seeing you.'

'We were saying goodbye. I won't be seeing her again.'

'I think you should have done that before I came. You haven't been honest with me.'

'There wasn't much point in upsetting you unnecessarily. We'll be living in Osaka anyway.'

'Does she mind?'

'She's a little upset but she'll get over it.'

'Did she know we were engaged? Did you tell her that?'

'It wasn't necessary for me to tell her. There was no question of marriage. She knew that.'

She was on her feet now. 'Then I think you've behaved despicably.' She was sick of the whole business. She wanted to get out of this house, anywhere away from Nigel.

He crossed to the door and leaned against it as though he had read her thoughts.

'I understand now,' he said, facing her. 'It's because she's a Japanese, isn't it? You're so obsessed by your brother that you just can't think rationally.'

She stared at him in silence, hatred in her heart. It had begun to rain. She could hear the patter on the windows and the wind stirred the curtains. She was going to get wet walking home.

'Nigel, I don't really care what interpretation you put on this. As far as I'm concerned, I'm breaking off the engagement.'

His face froze. 'What are you saying? Can't you see it's too late to change your mind? You can't call it off now, not after the Browne's have gone to all this trouble over the wedding arrangements. There's less than a week to go.'

'Time enough. Jean will understand.'

His attitude suddenly changed. He stepped towards her, his eyes now pleading. 'Anna, you won't tell them? Something like that would finish me. Stan couldn't take it. Look, let's sit down and talk this over calmly. We can sort it out.'

'I've tried to sort out a lot of things since I've been here. I've wanted to talk to you about them but you're never interested. Only now when you think your job's threatened are you willing to listen to me. It's too late, Nigel. If you told me about the girl before, I would have tried to understand, but there's more to it than that. If we go ahead with this marriage, it will end in disaster.'

He stood looking at her, his hostility tinged with uncertainty.

At last he spoke. 'What are you going to do then? Go home?'

'I don't know. I might find a job.'

He stared at her in utter astonishment. 'You're crazy! Jobs aren't that easy to come by, not for a foreigner. Besides where would you live? You can't stay with the Brownes indefinitely.'

'I wouldn't dream of imposing on them. I'm a nurse,' she reminded him. 'There must be hospitals. In the American sector perhaps, and I could probably live in.'

'How long have you been thinking about this? You've obviously got it all worked out. It looks as if you were just waiting for such an opportunity to put it into practice.'

She regarded him coldly. 'I've thought about it several times since I've been here, times when I thought you'd never understand how I felt. Perhaps the first night I arrived.'

'The first night? You mean that nonsense about the Japanese cook? Surely that didn't mean so much to you?'

'It meant a great deal, and I'm sorry you didn't appreciate that.'

He went over to the cabinet and poured himself a strong whisky. 'Do you want a drink?'

'No thanks.'

He came and sat down, putting the glass on the table in front of him. His hand was shaking.

Presently he said, 'This is final then, Anna?'

'Final is a strong word. I certainly need to think.'

He shook his head in bewilderment. 'After all this time. Where did it begin to go wrong?'

She had asked herself the same question many times.

They talked until past midnight, but only went round in circles.

'I'm going home now,' Anna announced eventually. 'I'll walk.'

'Don't talk rubbish.' He picked up the car keys. 'I'll drive you.'

She was too tired to argue.

'What are you going to tell them?' he asked as they got in the car.

'Stan and Jean?' She shrugged. 'I don't know yet. I won't say anything about the girl if that's what's worrying you. I'll have to make up some excuse.'

'I'll tell Stan in the office tomorrow. When you've definitely decided what you're going to do, let me know.'

'There's one more thing, Nigel. You'd better have this back.'

She slipped the engagement ring off her finger. He took it and she felt him looking at her. She was glad it was dark because she couldn't bring herself to meet his eyes. Somehow returning the ring was the part that hurt most.

* * *

It continued to rain all night. Anna, lying awake, listened to it lashing the windows. Far from feeling miserable, a burden had been lifted from her. It was as though she was following a pre-ordained path, with no knowing where it would lead, yet now she had no fear in taking it. She could, of course, return home, but she felt strangely reluctant to do so at the moment. If her future was not to include Nigel, then she must find another direction.

She rose early and had a shower. As soon as she heard Stan and the children leave the house, she came downstairs. Jean was in the dining room reading a newspaper. She looked up when Anna came in and sat down beside her.

'What would you like to do today, my dear? I thought of taking you to Kamakura, but in this weather it would be miserable. Perhaps a relaxing day at home?'

'Jean, there's something I have to tell you,' Anna said, coming straight to the point. 'Last night, Nigel and I broke off our engagement.'

Jean put down the newspaper. 'I thought there was something in the wind,' she said gently. 'Do you want to talk about it?'

Anna hesitated, then went on slowly, weighing her words.

'I want you both to know that it's my decision and I'm very sorry because I've caused you all a lot of trouble. I'll try and explain it to you though I can hardly expect you to understand.'

'Try me,' said Jean.

'Since I arrived, Nigel and I haven't been getting along too well. We've had a lot of disagreements which remain unresolved. I think some of these stem from the fact that my brother was killed by the Japanese in a prisoner of war camp and I'm finding it very difficult to come to terms with it. Nigel can't understand this. It happened a long time ago, you see. Perhaps he's right and I should have got over it by now, but it's got to the point where I'm no longer sure of my feelings for him.'

She was acutely aware that she was talking to the wife of Nigel's boss and any criticism of him must be avoided. In her efforts to do this she probably over-emphasised her own failings, knowing that she would be the one least likely to be affected if accusations had to be made. But when she searched Jean's eyes for condemnation, she saw only sympathy.

'Don't you think,' said Jean gently, 'that it requires more thought. You haven't really had any time alone together to work through this. Once you're married and you get used to living in this country, you might find that a lot of your problems will disappear naturally. They often do.'

Anna made a dismissive gesture. 'I don't think we can be married just on the chance that it might happen. It's something that has to be worked out beforehand because once you've taken that step, it's too late to change your mind.'

'You could be wrong about Nigel,' suggested Jean. 'If you call it off now without giving yourselves time to resolve your differences, you might regret it. Why don't you just postpone the wedding for a while?'

'With Nigel going up to Osaka? No, Jean. Nigel's given me long enough to make up my mind.'

'How did he take it?' Jean asked.

'He thinks I'm being unreasonable. I must admit my excuse seems a lame one and that when I search for a more valid reason, I'm at a loss.'

'It seems simple to me,' said Jean. 'If you really loved him, you'd want to give this every chance of success. You obviously don't love him enough and quite rightly you can't marry him without that essential ingredient.' She paused for a moment, then went on, 'What I can't understand though, is why you agreed to marry him in the first place?'

Anna thought for a while, then she said, 'It was during the war when he asked me and I promised to think about it. It progressed from there. I was fond of him and I thought it was enough. Perhaps it still is, but there's a lack of understanding between us that convinces me that I can't go ahead with it. I suppose you'd called it incompatibility. It's something I've only discovered recently.'

'Then you really have no alternative. It's going to be hard on Nigel, but I dare say he'll cope. He's got his job and he's used to being on his own. But what about you? What do you propose to do now? Go home?'

'I'm not sure. I'd like to stay on for a while. I have some money of my own, so I can manage for a month or so. I'll move out of here as soon as I can find a room in a hotel.'

'Then what?'

'I'm a trained nurse so I might try and look round for a job.' She paused and smiled at Jean, a rather wintry smile. 'Jean, I really am grateful to you and Stan for all your kindness. Please don't think too badly of me.'

'Of course I won't.' She spoke for herself. She could not include Sam in this. 'I'm only sorry it's turned out like this, but I hope we can still be friends, my dear. You could be lonely in this country on your own. Besides I shall be interested to know how you get on.'

'I'll keep in touch but I don't want you to feel responsible for me. I can look after myself.'

'I admire your courage,' said Jean. 'I'm not sure I could have done it. Have you any ideas about a job?'

'Not yet. I intend to look this morning.'

'You could try the International Hospital,' Jean said. 'They might well recruit locally. It's run by nuns and has a good reputation.'

Chapter Eight

Anna joined the queue to wait for a bus to take her into the centre of Tokyo. She was glad that Jean had not offered the use of an office car. At some point in the future, she would have to depend on public transport and she might as well get used to it.

When the bus arrived, order went by the board and she found herself carried forward by the sheer pressure of people. Once on board she saw there was no hope of a seat and clung to a strap, jammed against her fellow travellers. It gave her some satisfaction that apart from an occasional glance they appeared to accept the presence of a European amongst them as perfectly normal.

She alighted in Shinjiku where only the other day she and Jean had been shopping. Now as she stood on the curb, part of the teeming humanity of this over-populated city, she felt very vulnerable. The noise confused her. An American car glided past. From inside a man, a westerner, looked idly at the passing scene, his gaze resting briefly on her as he was swept on into the traffic.

She stopped a trishaw and gave him the scrap of paper on which was written the address of the hospital. Once installed in her seat Anna was paralysed with fear as the rider wove his way through the maelstrom of traffic, narrowly missing other vehicles and sworn at by drivers. At times it seemed impossible to avoid a collision yet within ten minutes he delivered her safely outside the hospital.

It was an austere looking building surrounded by high walls. More like a prison, she thought. She joined a stream of visitors through the heavy doors and found her way to Reception.

The Japanese woman behind the desk was on the telephone and Anna waited until she finished an interminable conversation and put down the receiver.

'I'd like to see Mother Superior.' She would start at the top. If the woman was unavailable she would have to settle for a lesser being.

'Name please?' The receptionist looked at her through thick glasses.

'Anna Bradford.'

'Have you an appointment?

'No. I've come about a job.'

'Please wait,' said the woman, indicating a chair. Anna sat down and picked up one of the magazines. It was in Japanese. Fifteen minutes passed and she thought that she must have been forgottten. The receptionist was on the phone again.

'Miss Bradford?' She looked up to see a young Japanese nurse with straight bobbed hair standing beside her. 'I take you to Mother Agnes.'

Anna followed the girl along endless corridors and was shown into a room which bore the doctor's name. The woman sitting at the desk wore a nun's white habit which left only her face visible. She was a European. She looked up as Anna came into the room, her keen blue eyes sweeping over her.

'You've come about a job?' she asked.

'Yes. I didn't know where to apply, so I thought it best to come personally.'

Mother Agnes smiled at her. 'It's probably the best way. Won't you sit down?'

Anna took the chair on the other side of the desk.

'Are you English?'

'Yes.'

'Then perhaps you'll begin by telling me something about yourself. What sort of a job are you looking for?' She spoke with a foreign accent, probably Dutch, thought Anna.

'I'm a trained nurse. I have my diploma with me here. I was hoping to find a nursing job where I can live in.'

She handed her qualifications to Mother Agnes who studied them carefully.

'You're well qualified I see.'

'I finished my training during the war and was posted to a casualty clearing station in North Africa.'

'In the army?'

'Yes. I was attached to an nursing unit.'

'How long have you been in Japan?'

'Nearly two weeks.'

'Two weeks? That's a very short time. May I ask what brought you here and how long you propose to stay?'

Anna gave a concise and honest account while Mother Agnes leant back in her chair with her hands folded in her lap. She listened without interruption. At last Anna fell silent. She had said more than she intended but the quiet attention of the nun had encouraged her to pour out her heart.

'So you want to stay on in Japan?' asked Mother Agnes. 'May I ask why?'

'I'm not ready to return home yet. It was a long way to come and I'd like to live here for a while.'

'I may be able to help you,' said the nun, 'though

not in the way you wish. I have no vacancies on the wards at present but I am short-staffed on the administrative side. I need someone to help me in the office. Can you type?'

Anna hesitated. She really wanted to nurse. Her secretarial experience was practically nil, and if she accepted this offer she might find it difficult to transfer. On the other hand, she needed a job and somewhere to live and this seemed a possibility.

'A little,' she said.

'My assistant is on sick leave and we are under more pressure than usual. It would be a good time for you to learn something about the way the hospital is run. What do you think?'

'I'd be willing to try but I'd like to transfer to nursing later on. Would I be able to do that?'

'I'll certainly bear it in mind. We do need qualified nurses from time to time but for the present, it would have to be office work. If you decide on this when would you be able to start?'

'Tomorrow?' suggested Anna.

'Very well. I'll see that a bedroom is prepared for you. It'll be a small, simple room. When you arrive give your name at the reception desk and someone will take you there. When you're ready come and see me. As far as meals are concerned, you'll be able to use the nurses' dining room which is open twenty four hours a day. Would you be happy with these arrangements?'

'Perfectly,' said Anna.

'Now, there's the matter of salary to be discussed.' Mother Agnes went on, outlining some figures which Anna, knowing little about the cost of living, thought quite acceptable.

'You'll find this rather different from what you're

used to,' said the nun. 'This is an old-fashioned hospital. We are gradually making improvements but it takes time. We work closely with one or two of the Japanese hospitals as well as the American army hospital. They're very co-operative and allow us the use of their equipment in emergencies. They also take our patients when special treatment is required. We're an independent hospital, which enables us to make our own decisions and cuts out a lot of formality.'

'What about the staff?' asked Anna. 'Are they mostly Europeans?'

'A mixture. I myself am a doctor and other nuns in our Order are nurses. We have five European doctors working full time on the staff and the services of an American and Japanese surgeon, both excellent and highly skilled men. Also we have some fine Japanese consultants. It works very well provided we organise things carefully. As for the nursing staff, they are Japanese and Europeans. Quite a few of them live at home and come in daily.'

'And your patients?'

'They are drawn mainly from the foreign community but we take quite a number of Japanese, particularly children, who are referred to us by local doctors.'

'I like the sound of it,' Anna said, 'and I look forward to working here. I hope I'll be able to help a little on the nursing side whenever you're short-handed.'

'I think you will fit in very well.' Mother Agnes got up and opened the door for her.'I'll see you tomorrow then,' she said 'and I'll bear in mind your nursing skills. When circumstances allow we may well be able to transfer you to the wards.'

* * *

Anna looked about the small hospital room. It was painted white and along one side stood a single iron bedstead with a pink cover. A small chest of drawers with a mirror stood against the wall, and in a corner was a metal rail with a few battered coathangers, screened by a thin curtain. A couple of worn rugs covered the floor and on the wall was a rather poor woodblock print of Mount Fuji.

She went down the corridor to explore the washing facilities and found a door marked 'Bathroom'. She looked inside and was dismayed to see a Japanese style bath, half the normal length and a wooden stool on the tiled floor. The Japanese, she had been told, did their washing outside the bath and only used it for relaxation afterwards. Another door was marked WC. Inside was a basin at floor level on either side of which one placed one's feet and squatted, a balancing feat which she had so far managed to avoid. Pulling the chain, a torrent of water cascaded over the floor, forcing her to jump clear. Unnerved, she set off to find something more familiar.

A Japanese nurse was coming along the corridor.

'Excuse me,' said Anna. 'I'm looking for the *benjo.*'. It was one of the few Japanese words she had learnt, deeming it to be an important one.

The girl smiled at her. '*Hai*. This way,' she said, leading the way down yet another corridor. 'Here also a bathroom.' She opened the door to reveal a good sized western style bath and a wash basin. 'Plenty hot water,' the girl assured her with a small bow.

Thanking her, Anna returned to her room. She went over to the window and looked down on a narrow street. The rain was still falling, and the humidity was high. A group of men were unloading stores from a truck and wheeling them into the hospital shouting instructions to the others as they hurried back and forth. Opposite was a warehouse which darkened the room and would effectively keep out the sun, possibly an advantage on a hot day.

She thought of the comfortable room she'd just left overlooking the shady garden and the view of Mount Fuji. She glanced at the picture on the wall, thinking that in future, she would have to make do with that.

The little room was hot and stuffy but in spite of this, she was undismayed. It was her own and from now on she was accountable only to herself. The strain of the past days had been heavy and now she was out of the way, she was sure the Brownes would breathe a sigh of relief. They had been very decent about the whole business. She had sensed some restraint on Stan's part and he had avoided her the previous evening, but Jean was genuinely concerned for her.

Anna felt no hostility towards Nigel. He had given her the excuse she needed to end their relationship and for this, in some perverse way, she was grateful. Now it was over. If she had any regrets, they were only for what might have been.

She opened her suitcase and took out a few dresses which she hung in the small space behind the curtain. Her undies she put in neat piles in the chest of drawers. At least the room was spotlessly clean. She brought out the photograph of her parents which she placed on a small table by the window. Soon she must write and tell them of her decision.

At the bottom of her suitcase she came across Jack's picture. She had not taken it out since her arrival in

Japan. Now she picked it up and studied it closely, this photograph of a good-looking naval officer with the care-free smile. The steady eyes gazed into hers and gently she touched his face. She felt a loneliness so sharp it was akin to a physical pain. The years had in no way dulled that. Now that she was in Japan, his presence was somehow more real, and so overwhelming that she swung round to make sure she was alone. Of course, there was no one – only the memories.

'What's happened to you, Jack?' she whispered. 'Why is it that after all this time you are still as real as life itself? I don't even know if memories are true any longer. Were you ever the person that I now think of as you?'

With a sigh she positioned the picture carefully on the chest of drawers.

'I wonder,' she said to the photograph, 'if you understand that without you I'm only part of the person I'm meant to be.'

She looked at her watch. Eleven o'clock. She must go down and report for duty. She was wearing a plain navy skirt and white blouse and she had twisted her hair neatly into the nape of her neck. She wanted to look business-like.

Outside the door of Mother Agnes' office, she made some final minute adjustments to her clothing and knocked twice. A voice inside called her to come in.

'You've arrived at a opportune moment,' Mother Agnes told her; she was sorting mail. 'There's a lot to be done. Come and sit beside me and we'll look at this together.'

The nun gave Anna a notebook and immediately launched into dictation of some letters. Anna's shorthand was rusty but she got by, blending it with her own particular brand of longhand.

That done, Mother Agnes went over to the filing cabinet. Briefly she described the system.

'You'll soon find your way about,' she said. 'You may well find that you can improve on our way of doing things, and you're quite welcome to try.'

'The typewriter?' asked Anna.

'Over there.' Her heart sank as Mother Agnes took off the cover to reveal an ancient model. 'It's time we upgraded this,' she said. 'Do you think you can manage with it?'

'I should think so, but I could do a more professional job on a modern machine.' Glancing at Mother Agnes, she caught an amused twinkle in her eye.

'The stationary's in that cupboard,' she said. 'I'm afraid I have to leave you now for a meeting, but I should be back within the hour. If the phone rings please take a message and say I'll ring back.'

Left on her own, Anna opened the cupboard and selected some sheets of headed paper. She sat down in front of the typewriter – an American Brickenslender – and, rolling in a piece of scrap paper, typed out some notes. The machine seemed to work but the ribbon was faded. She rummaged in the draw and found a new one which she put in. After that she went through her notes and began on the mail. It was one o'clock before Mother Agnes returned, by which time she had got through most of the letters and put them in a neat pile on the desk.

Finding them well set out in dark print with envelopes attached, she smiled her appreciation. 'A good start,' she said. 'You're obviously a very organised person. Now . . .' She went to a chart on the wall. 'If you look at this, you'll see the lay-out of the hospital. It will give you an idea of the wards and treatment rooms. This afternoon you may like to accompany me on my rounds but first it's lunch time. Do you think you can find your way to the dining-room?'

The place was full of people and the noise of plates and cutlery being cleared against the constant hum of conversation took Anna back to her training days. There was a strong smell of cooking, some sort of spice mingling with the smell of coffee.

She looked round for a place to sit. Across the room a friendly looking fair-haired girl in a nurse's uniform was sitting alone. Anna carried her tray across.

'May I join you?'

'Please do,' the girl said. 'I haven't seen you before, have I?'

'No. My name's Anna Bradford and I'm helping Mother Agnes in the office.'

'Helen Wills,' the girl said. 'I'm a staff nurse on the children's ward. What brings you to this hospital?'

'I wanted a job. Actually I'm a nurse myself, but at the moment there are no vacancies on the wards. Mother Agnes said she might be able to transfer me later.'

'If she said so, then she will,' said Helen. 'What are you doing in Japan?'

'I came to be married but it didn't work out. I wanted to stay on for a while so I decided to look for a job.' She saw Helen looking at her left hand. 'I gave the ring back,' she said.

Helen coloured. 'I'm sorry. I didn't mean to be rude. I'm rather conscious of rings at the moment because I've just become engaged myself.'

'Congratulations.'

'Thanks. I'm awfully sorry though that it didn't turn out well for you. I'd like to hear about it some time but I guess it's painful talking about it.'

'What about you?' asked Anna. 'How did you come to be here?'

'I came on my way from Singapore after the war. I'm a New Zealander but I don't have any close family ties. It seemed a good idea to stay for a while.'

'And your fiance. Is he a doctor?'

'Yes. A New Zealander, too. I don't know how long we'll stay. It rather depends on what he wants to do. We like it here, so I guess we'll be around for a while.'

'When are you thinking of getting married?'

'We haven't decided yet. We've got to find somewhere to live first.' Helen looked at Anna with interest. 'Had you known this guy long?' she asked. 'It's an awful long way to come only to discover you've made a mistake. Do you think it will work out eventually?'

Anna shook her head. 'I shan't change my mind. I'm sure we've done the right thing. I'm still glad to be here.'

'You're very brave.'

Anna shrugged. 'Not really. I did what I wanted to do. Selfish really.'

'You don't seem the selfish type to me. I just hope you won't find it lonesome on your own. Look, if there's anything you want or you feel in need of company, don't hesitate to get hold of me. I've got a room in the hospital – number fifteen.'

'I appreciate that, Helen. I suppose now I'd better get back to the office. There's so much to do, but I hope to see you again soon.'

She was about to leave but Helen stopped her.

'Just before you go, Anna, Dave and I are having an engagement party here in the hospital on Saturday evening, about eight o'clock. Do come along and meet a few people.'

'Thanks a lot,' said Anna, genuinely grateful. Meeting Helen had lifted her spirits considerably.

The afternoon was spent doing the rounds with Mother Agnes. The long dark corridors and stairs leading to wards and treatment rooms seemed endless. Small hospital windows allowed little light and air into the place and overhead fans did nothing to relieve the heat.

'This place was built in the twenties,' Mother Agnes informed her, 'to service the increasing population of foreigners. Bits have been added on from time to time, making it a very awkward place to run. These big rooms with their high ceilings are cool in the summer, but take a lot of heating in winter. In a way it's a pity it wasn't bombed and then we might have had a nice modern building in it's place.'

Or no building at all, Anna couldn't help thinking.

When they reached the wards, Mother Agnes made a point of introducing her to the staff.

'This is my new assistant,' she said, and, busy as they were, the nurses all exchanged pleasantries with Anna. As soon as they were alone again Mother Agnes spoke to Anna about the patients and their treatment. There might be drawbacks to the building, but it seemed to Anna that their approach to patients was right up to date.

Back in the office, the telephone rang and while Mother Agnes dealt with the calls, Anna jotted down notes to remind her what she had learnt that afternoon.

At six o'clock Mother Agnes firmly closed the office door. 'That's enough for one day. We begin at eight tomorrow.'

Anna went up to her room utterly exhausted. She flung off her clothes and, putting on a cotton dressing gown, headed for the bathroom. She'd got through the day all right, but she had a feeling it wouldn't be long before Mother Agnes would be leaving her to run things on her own. She just hoped she'd be able to cope.

Feeling much refreshed, she returned to her room and sat down to write to her parents.

'Dear Mother and Dad,

Since my last letter telling you of my safe arrival, there have been unforeseen changes. You'll be sorry to hear that Nigel and I, after much thought, have decided to break off our engagement. I know you'll find this hard to understand. Sometimes I do myself but I can assure you that I have done the right thing. When we got together again we realised that it wasn't going to work out. Perhaps given more time together we might have resolved our differences, but Nigel is shortly going to another part of Japan to open a new branch.

The Brownes couldn't have been kinder. They had already made most of the wedding arrangements and of course these had to be cancelled. I felt very badly about this but I could see no alternative. Nigel will now go to his new posting on his own.'

It was terribly hot. Her hand was sticking to the paper. She got up and went over to the window. Not a breath of air. The sound of traffic drifted up to her. It was dark now and the sky was clear. She was surprised to see The Plough and found the familiar constellation comforting. Turning back to the letter, she picked up her pen again.

'You'll be wondering why I'm not returning home immediately. Having come so far, I want to see something of the country so I've decided to take a job in a hospital which is run by an Order of nuns. Fortunately, I brought my credentials with me and although there isn't a vacancy on the wards at present, the Mother Superior has promised to transfer me when there is. Until then I'm helping in the office and finding my secretarial skills very rusty!

'I've just finished my first day's work and feel very tired. I'm a little homesick and wish you were close. It would be wonderful to talk to you.

'I hope Dad is improving and that you'll write and give me good news soon. With all my love,

'Anna.'

Sealing the envelope, she wrote a short note to Jean, thanking her for her kindness and assuring her that she was perfectly all right and enjoying the work. Then she took the letter down to the post box in the main hall. On the way back, she passed the dining room. It reminded her she hadn't eaten, but she had no appetite and decided to skip supper and go to bed.

She slept fitfully, tossing on the hard, lumpy mattress till the early hours of the morning. When she finally awoke from troubled dreams at daybreak, she had a shower and a cup of coffee before making her way to the office.

'My diary's on the desk,' said Mother Agnes before she left for a meeting. 'Please make any appointments for me when you see I'm free. One more thing:

I'm meant to be seeing Dr Egawa at eleven this morning. Could you get a message through to the children's ward with my apologies and ask if he could postpone the meeting. Make sure he gets the message. Time's too precious to waste on fruitless assignments.'

During the morning she tried several times to contact Dr Egawa but was told that he had not yet arrived. Another hour passed during which she got through the mail and took some telephone messages. With time on her hands, she resolved to find this elusive doctor.

Finding her way to the children's ward, she espied a tall Japanese wearing the usual doctor's white coat, and a stethescope round his neck. He was talking to a young patient, accompanied by the Ward Sister. If this was Dr Egawa, she thought, watching their slow progress, she would have to curb her impatience. She popped into the Sister's office to wait.

When at last the doctor and the sister came into the office, she stepped forward. 'Dr Egawa?' she asked.

'Yes?' His voice was curt. He was a good looking man of about forty. His features were more prominent than those of the average Japanese, his eyes less slanting. His black hair was oiled and well brushed. Like most medical men, he disliked interruptions when he was discussing a case.

'I have a message for you from Mother Agnes. She's sorry but she had to go to a meeting this morning and asked if you could postpone your appointment with her till later?'

He nodded. 'Very well.' His eyes, brown and penetrating, lingered on her for a moment before he asked in good English, 'I haven't seen you before, have I?'

'Probably not. I'm working for Mother Agnes.'

'Ah so? Then please tell her I'll be there at two thirty.'

He turned back to Sister and Anna, assuming she was dismissed, returned to the office.

She was kneeling on the floor that afternoon trying to sort out the filing system when there came a tap on the door and Dr Egawa entered. Embarrassed, she scrambled to her feet.

'Mother Agnes has just gone to the path lab. Shall I tell her you're here?'

'I'm early,' he said. 'I'll wait.'

He was holding some X-rays. There was no chair to offer him other than her own which was piled high with files. She made to move them.

'Leave them, please. I prefer to stand.'

She carried on working, aware that he was watching her. She picked up the files from the floor and with her back to him continued to work at the desk.

'You're American?' he asked. His voice was deep and he spoke with a pronounced accent.

She shook her head. 'No. I came out from England a few weeks ago.'

'Ah so. You came to Japan to work in this hospital?'

'No. I came to stay with friends.'

'And you decided to find a job? An unusual holiday.'

'It's a good way of getting to know people.'

He seemed taken aback by her brusque reply and fell silent.

Mother Agnes came in. 'Yoshi, I'm sorry to keep you waiting. Shall we go into the X-ray room? You've met Anna, my new assistant?'

'We've introduced ourselves,' he said, but already his attention was on the patient they were to discuss.

'This X-ray shows lesions,' he was saying as they left the room.

Why, she thought, as she wrestled with letters which had been incorrectly filed, did she feel no animosity towards this man? He must have played his part in the war and yet in spite of his somewhat abrupt manner, she did not find him disagreeable. Being a doctor he would presumably have taken no part in the fighting, yet the fact remained he was a Japanese and she should be hating him. Could her attitude towards the Japanese already be softening?

She paused in her task, stabbed by a feeling of disloyalty to Jack. She could never form a friendship with any Japanese.

Anna didn't really want to go to the party. At the end of the day the last thing she felt like was socialising, but Helen had insisted that she must come and meet Dave. The two women had become good friends and the New Zealander often came to Anna's room for a chat. Consequently Anna felt she must make the effort. She changed into a soft navy and white cotton dress, leaving her hair to hang loose on her shoulders, thick and lustrous.

The party was held in one of the staff rooms and had been going for some time when she arrived. She made her way to where Dave and Helen were talking to a group of people. Dave was a tall, red headed Kiwi with blue eyes and an easy manner.

'Good to meet you, Anna,' he said, shaking hands with her.'Helen's told me a lot about you. How are you getting on?'

'Settling in gradually.'

'Takes time, doesn't it?' he said with a grin. 'What

part of England do you come from? I was over there myself during the war.'

'In the services?' she asked, suddenly interested.

'The New Zealand Navy.'

'My brother was in the Navy. Which ship were you on?'

'A small frigate by the name of *Wallaby*. You wouldn't have heard of it.'

'Jack was on a cruiser. He was torpedoed.'

His eyes held sympathy. 'Was he one of the lucky ones?'

'He was picked up by the Japanese ship that hit them.'

'So they took him prisoner?'

Anna nodded.

'That must make it hard for you here,' said Dave.

She was about to answer when they were joined by Dr Egawa.

'I've already met Anna,' he told Dave. 'I have an apology to make to her.'

'Then we'll leave you to make it while we circulate,' said Dave, taking Helen's arm and steering her away.

'I left the room rather abruptly the other day,' said Yoshi Egawa.'You must have thought me rude. I was concerned about a patient.'

'There's no need to apologise.'

'Mother Agnes told me that you're a nurse. What brought you to Japan? Surely there's plenty of work in your English hospitals?'

'Actually I came here to be married,' she said quietly.

'So you won't be working here for long then? It's what you call a temporary job? If you're shortly to marry . . .'

Anna shook her head. 'Circumstances changed. I hope to work here for some time.'

He was puzzled and she was grateful that he didn't pursue it.

'We're always in need of skilled nurses,' he said. 'Did you train in England?'

'At the Radcliffe in Oxford', she said.

'A very fine hospital.'

She was surprised. 'You know it?'

'Yes. I've visited it on several occasions. Were you there during the war?'

'Yes. Then I joined the Services and was sent to North Africa.'

'You're too young to have been in service.'

She shook her head. 'No. Most of the women my age were either in the Services or working in factories or on farms.'

'Few of our women were in uniform,' he said. 'I don't think Japanese women have the right temperament to make good soldiers.'

She felt that the remark was in some way critical and was at a loss for a reply.

Sensing this, he said, 'Forgive me. I didn't mean to be impolite. Western women have many fine qualities.' He took her empty glass. 'Let me find you another drink.'

'Fruit juice, please.' She waited hoping that no one would claim her attention in his absence. She watched him move confidently through the crowded room and return with the drinks. He handed one to her.

'Here's to your visit to Japan,' he said formally. 'It's a beautiful country and I hope you'll enjoy it.'

She smiled at him. 'I'm sure I will.'

'Have you known David and Helen very long?'

'I met Helen here. She's been very kind.'

'She's a charming girl. Beautiful as well, and David's a fine doctor. I hope they won't be leaving us yet. David has made a valuable contribution to our work here, particularly in the field of research.'

'Tell me, Dr Egawa, where did you learn to speak English so well?'

'I'm working with patients who are suffering from radiation. I travel abroad a lot attending conferences and I do a certain amount of lecturing in America and Europe. English is the universal language and if we're to understand one another, it's essential to speak it.'

She was silent, fingering her glass and wondering if she dare ask him about something that was bothering her. Feeling his eyes on her, she decided to risk it.

'How do you feel about working with the people who dropped the bomb?' she asked.

'That's a profound question,' he said thoughtfully, sipping his drink. 'I don't know that I've ever given much thought to it, but then I'm a doctor, not a politician. I'm not so much concerned with who dropped the bomb as to what to do about the effects of it. To see that it never happens again is something which concerns us all.'

'And none of us are ever likely to forget it.'

'I hope not,' he said with feeling. 'I think that we, as a nation, have a responsibility to make sure of that. We owe it to our people who suffered from it and still do, of course.'

'Such terrible effects. How long will they last?'

He shrugged. 'For our lifetime and perhaps into the next generation. It's not only the physical effects of radiation, terrible though they are, but the personal tragedies that have left scars and caused serious social problems. Children deprived of their parents and their security and, at the other end of the scale, old people who would normally depend on their sons and daughters to look after them in their old age. Many of them have been left homeless and without relatives. Whole families were wiped out.'

'Many countries suffered tragedies through the war,' she pointed out.

'Of course,' he said gravely. 'But we were talking about the effects of the bomb, were we not? That was mass destruction of the most terrible kind with unforeseen and far reaching consequences, and Japan was unique in that respect.'

She let it pass, but she felt an anger surging within her. Doctor Egawa was concerned only with the plight of his own people. She could have spoken of individual acts of cruelty, of brutal treatment inflicted by his race on other – innocent – beings.

But in spite of her emotional antipathy, this man intrigued her. His compassion was shown in his work with the suffering. While she was trying to come to terms with her own particular tragedy, he was concerned for the whole.

There was much more she would like to have asked him and she felt unreasonably irritated when Helen touched her on the arm.

'Yoshi, please excuse me, but Anna said she wanted to learn Japanese. I think I've found someone who would teach her. Come and meet her, Anna.'

Chapter Nine

The heat was draining. There was no relief from it. The overhead fan provided some movement of air, but blew papers in all directions. Anna switched the fan off and gathered them up off the floor.

Mother Agnes had closed the office two hours ago, but after hours was the only time she had to catch up on work without interruption. She was thankful she had been given a free hand to sort out things in her own way.

The jangle of the telephone startled her.

'Is that you, Anna?'

'Nigel! How did you know where to find me? I'm not usually working this late.'

'The girl on the switchboard put me through. I'm off to Osaka tomorrow, but I couldn't leave without speaking to you. It didn't seem right.' His voice was cheerful, as though nothing untoward had occurred between them. And why not? she thought. Now we know where we stand with each other, there's no reason why we shouldn't be friends.

'I hope everything goes well for you there,' she said.

'I wanted to make sure you were all right.'

'I'm fine.'

'And the job?'

'I like it.'

'You've only been there for a short time. What happens if it doesn't work out?'

'Don't worry about me, Nigel. I'm quite capable of looking after myself.'

'I'm sure you are, but I'm still concerned. After all, if everything had gone according to plan we'd have been married by now. I still want you. The whole thing seems crazy to me.'

'But it isn't. Under the circumstances it was the sensible thing to do.'

'How long do you intend to stay in this job?'

'I don't know yet. Perhaps a year. Now I'm here, I'd like to see something of the country.'

'We could have done that together and in comfort. We'd have had our own home and a car and plenty of time to get around, but you turned it all down.'

She was exasperated. 'Don't go on. I think we've said all that needs to be said on that subject.'

'You'll never stand it, Anna. You'll get desperately lonely. You can't have many friends and you'll have to work long, unsocial hours. I can't bear the thought of you on your own.'

'I knew what to expect when I took the job on. It's not the first time I've worked in a hospital.'

'I wonder what your parents must think of me?'

'They have nothing against you. I've told them that it was by mutual consent. I'm staying in Japan by choice.'

There was a long pause at the other end of the line, then he said, 'Look Anna, why don't we see how it goes? I'll have to come to Tokyo now and again. I'd like to see you. I'll give you a ring.'

She had to be firm even at the risk of hurting him. She was not prepared to go through the last few months again.

'I don't think there's much point. What we've done is right. I shall remember the good times we've had together and forget the rest. Go and enjoy the job in Osaka. I know you'll make a success of it.'

'It's going to be lonely without you,' he admitted. 'I've got used to the idea of having you there with me.'

She didn't remind him that he'd seemed to have found the answer to loneliness. Almost as though she had transmitted her thoughts, he went on, 'I'm not seeing Michiko again. I was telling you the truth when I said we ended it that evening.'

'That has nothing to do with me any more.'

'I wanted you to know, that's all. If you don't want to see me, there's nothing more I can do about it. It just seems, well, a bloody shame, that's all.'

Afterwards she couldn't settle down to work. She tidied up in the office and went to the dining room, the conversation with Nigel still in her mind. An uneasy thought was bothering her. She had done what she had wanted to do, but was she being fair to Nigel or was she being altogether selfish?

She had little appetite for food these days, but she needed company. She looked round the dining room for Helen but there was no sign of her. She hadn't seen her for days. She opened her book and started to read.

'Hello there. Do you want to be on your own, or can I join you?'

She looked up, her face brightening. 'Helen! I was hoping to see you. Where've you been?'

'I'm sorry, I forgot to tell you. I was on night duty and out of circulation. How are things, Anna?'

'Busy. I really want to get back to nursing though. I

hope Mother Agnes doesn't find me too useful and keeps me in the office.'

Helen sat down, placing a cup of coffee before her.

'She won't. We're short of staff nurses. Actually there may be an opportunity for you in the near future. I haven't had a chance to tell you but we're leaving Japan.'

It was a moment before Anna was able to absorb this. She had taken it for granted that Helen would be here for months at least. Without her, life would indeed be very lonely.

'But I thought you'd decided to stay on after you and Dave were married?'

Helen shook her head. 'There's been a change of plan. Dave's been offered a houseman's job in Wellington. Too good an opportunity to turn down. I love it here, but now we're going back to New Zealand and that's that. Actually I'm thrilled about it.'

'When are you leaving?'

'Not for a while yet. Dave's staying on until they've found a replacement for him here, which shouldn't prove too difficult. Lots of doctors want to work here. I'm worried about you though. Are you going to be all right?'

'Why shouldn't I?' Her laugh had a forced ring.

Helen looked at her closely. 'You are happy, aren't you? I mean I'm so besotted with Dave that if we suddenly broke it off I don't know how I'd manage. I know it's none of my business. I just can't help wondering how you really feel. I must say you put a good face on it, but after all you came out here to be married. You must have loved him. You could have had a good life style with a house and all that goes with it here. And what do you do? Chuck it all up and come to this place to work. Why?'

Anna considered her remarks. She couldn't expect Helen to understand the agonising she'd been through before she came to this decision.

'You don't mind my asking, do you?' Helen reached for the sugar and spooned a generous helping in her coffee.

'Of course not. It wasn't until I got to Japan that I realised that it wouldn't work out. It might have done in England, but not here.'

'Then it's the place, not the man?'

'Both.'

'Then why don't you go home?'

'Several reasons. To lay a ghost perhaps. You see, my brother was killed in a Japanese prisoner of war camp.' She looked at Helen. 'It might sound unreasonable to you, but I loathe the Japanese.'

Helen's blue eyes were wide with sympathy. 'So that's it! Then you must go home. I just can't grasp why you want to live among them. It must add to the pain.'

'I have this idea that it's only here that I can come to terms with it. It may be crazy, but I have to see it through.'

'Dave told me that you'd had a brother in the Navy. His ship was torpedoed, wasn't it? What happened to him after that?'

Anna was silent for a few moments. She didn't want to talk about it. She wanted to keep her grief to herself, keep it alive within her. It was a tangible thing, her last link with Jack and she could so easily lose it.

'Don't tell me, if it's too painful,' Helen said sympathetically, 'but sometimes it helps to talk, you know.'

Reluctantly Anna began, and as Helen listened, was surprised to see tears well in her eyes. But she ploughed on until finally she had told all she knew about Jack's internment and death.

'No wonder you feel the way you do. I'd feel the same. But again, why torment yourself? If you're not going to marry Nigel, I think you should go home, find someone you could be happy with and start afresh. Forget the past.'

Anna smiled. 'More easily said than done. If only one could tidy things up like that, but I know this is where I must be for the present. I don't really know why, but I must.'

Helen drank her coffee in silence. Then she asked, 'How did you get along with Yoshi the other evening? Do you hate him too?'

'Of course not. He's different somehow. I've been wanting to thank you for inviting me. It was great.'

'What did you talk about – to Yoshi – I mean?'

'His work, the bomb, that sort of thing. He wanted to know what I did during the war. I rather liked him.'

'He's a brilliant doctor and very modest. Have you never heard of him?'

Anna shook her head. 'Only so far as he works in this hospital and is a specialist in burns and radiation.'

'He's a leading authority on it and he lectures all over the world. He's got Dave really interested in the subject. I think if we were staying here, Dave would have gone over to that branch of medicine.' Helen glanced at the clock on the wall. 'Speaking of Dave, I've got to meet him soon. We're going out for a drink. Like to come?'

Anna shook her head. 'Not tonight, Helen, thanks.

Tell me, why does Doctor Egawa work here? Why not in a Japanese hospital?'

'He works in a number of hospitals, but he likes to keep in touch with the foreign doctors here. It's an important part of his work. He wants to discuss new techniques with them and in a way build bridges, so that they can prevent anything like that happening again.'

'Mother Agnes thinks very highly of him.'

'We all do. He's one of our best consultants and a really nice guy. Perhaps,' she added thoughtfully, 'someone like that might help you to overcome your dislike of the Japanese.'

Anna finished her coffee hardly noticing it was stone cold. 'I don't think anyone can,' she said. 'Only me.'

The heat was unbearable. Anna threw off the sheet and lay naked. The persistent buzzing of a mosquito intruded on her thoughts and, switching on the light, she tracked it until it lay dead between her palms. When eventually she drifted off to sleep, she dreamed Jack was coming across a field towards her through a mist. He was wearing a short sleeved open necked shirt and she could smell the newly-cut hay. The grass was wet underfoot. She could feel the dampness on her bare feet. He came to her eagerly, as though this was their first meeting after a long separation, but as she ran to him with outstretched hands, he suddenly faded from sight. She cried out to him to come back to her but he'd gone and nothing remained but the empty field with the grass lying there.

She woke in a sweat, still calling his name.

'You're looking pale.' Mother Agnes looked at her

closely the next morning. 'You're working too hard Anna. How long did you stay on last night?'

'Not late. I can get through a lot when there are no interruptions.'

Mother finished signing some letters, then looked up. 'You're not lonely here, Anna, I hope?'

'No. That's never been a problem for me.'

'Sometimes I think you're working late for want of something better to do. It's not right for someone as young as you. You should be having fun.'

'Time enough for that.'

'Have you made friends here?'

'I like Helen very much.'

'I'm glad to hear it,' said Mother Agnes, laying the letters aside in a neat pile. 'There are times when everyone needs a friend.'

She sounded wistful. There must be times in her own life, thought Anna, when she knew loneliness. In her position there could be few people in whom she could confide. But then she had her religion to console her.

'You've told me that you went through a difficult time with your engagement,' said Mother Agnes. 'Even when we think these things are resolved, they have a habit of returning to haunt us. Then we wonder if we've made the right decision.'

Anna waited.

'What I'm saying, Anna, is that it's not good to brood. Should you find yourself in need of a listening ear, you'll find one here.'

Anna was moved by the woman's perception. She looked up and saw the concern in her eyes. 'Thank you,' she said, 'I'll certainly bear it in mind'.

Having said what she had to, Mother Agnes was all briskness again.

'I haven't lost sight of the fact that you want to get back to nursing, my dear. I may well have a place for you soon and though I shall be sorry to lose your administrative skills, I won't stand in your way.'

Anna valued her time off. Most days after work she walked in a small park not far from the hospital, and at weekends she went farther afield, exploring areas that had, in some parts, suffered badly from bomb damage. Nevertheless many old timbered houses remained, and the owners had decorated them with tubs of flowering shrubs. Caged birds hung from the windows singing their hearts much to the enjoyment of passers-by. Here she found people sitting outside working at their crafts. A man painting a sprig of cherry blossom on a lacquer bowl attracted her attention. At his invitation she went inside to inspect a display of his work and bought a small lacquer tray. As she walked away with her purchase, she was aware of his gaze following her. Away from the city, a foreign woman on her own was an object of curiosity.

She felt she must master the language. She was missing so much. Her young teacher was good, but she was desperately shy and too much time was wasted on lengthy explanations.

One weekend she went to Kamakura. The train was packed with families laden with water sport equipment. She enjoyed the proximity of the cheerful crowd and was sorry when, on arriving at Kamakura, they went off laughing together in the direction of the beaches, leaving her to find her way to the old part of the town.

Finding the park, she sat down on a bench and opened her guide book. In the twelth century, during the Kamakura period, this town had apparently been the residence of the Shoguns, the ruling classes in Japan.

She discovered most of the famous sites before returning to the park to see the giant Buddha. According to her book, it was built in 1252 and housed in a temple which was later destroyed by a tidal wave. Now the statue stood in the open, a huge and solitary figure looking down on the crowds below. She joined them and recorded its presence by taking a picture, along with hundreds of other photographers.

Wandering under the shade of the trees she welcomed the coolness of the sea breeze after the oppressive heat of Tokyo. She sat down on a grassy slope to eat some fruit she had bought at the station. A small girl with a short fringe and rosy cheeks came slowly towards her and paused a few yards away. Anna smiled and held out her hand, feeling a special warmth as the child gazed round-eyed at her and ventured closer, a solemn expression on her face. Then, suddenly taking fright, she ran back to her mother who was seated on a rug nearby. The woman smiled shyly and gave a small nod of acknowledgement. Anna felt herself accepted and made welcome by the smile. It seemed of immense importance to her.

Through the pines she glimpsed the bright vermillion of torii gates. A pair of Buddhist priests dressed in safron robes and deep in conversation were strolling towards them and she followed them along the stepping stones. Ahead of her now was the Shinto shrine set high on a concrete base and sheltered by a sloping roof. A priest stood by the great bell ready to summon the Gods by pulling the thick crimson and white bell rope. It seemed strange to Anna that the Buddhist and Shinto religions were so closely interwoven. She made up her mind to find out more about it.

The sudden, deep boom of the bell startled her and she shivered, but her spirits lifted as she came out into the warmth of the sun and looked towards the distant mountains. Coming down the steps she came upon a beggar dressed entirely in white. She supposed this was one of the war wounded who depended on the generosity of his countrymen for his living. Hearing her approach, he held out his hand for alms. Taking a few small notes from her purse, she put them into his hand and looking into his eyes, she saw that he was blind. Perhaps it was as well he couldn't see that it was his erstwhile enemy who had shown compassion on him. Nonetheless she felt glad that she had made the gesture.

When Anna returned to the hospital she asked at Reception if there was any mail and was handed a letter from her mother. She waited until she reached the privacy of her room before tearing it open.

Dearest Anna, she read. We received your letter telling us of your decision. Is it really all over? You gave the matter such careful thought before you left and we can't understand your sudden change of heart. Is it fair to Nigel or to the people in the Bank who were making all the wedding arrangements? We feel that something very serious must have happened to cause this complete reversal of plans, something that you seem unwilling to share with us.

If, however, you're sure you've done the right thing, why don't you come home? You will be so lonely living by yourself in a foreign country and so long as you are there, Nigel must feel in some way responsible for you.

Perhaps you simply need more time, dear, to think it through and you might find even now that you can work things out between you. Nigel's a nice fellow and we feel sorry for him. Please write more fully next time and set our minds at rest.

You remember Hugh, Jack's friend? He telephoned the other day to enquire after your father. He has been offered a place at the theological college in Oxford and asked if he could come and call on us sometime. Of course we're delighted. He enquired after you and sent good wishes.

Good of Hugh to go and see them. Maybe she should write to him sometime. Now he was close to her parents perhaps he'd make a regular thing of keeping an eye out for them.

Your father seems to have picked up lately and is stronger,' her mother went on. 'I can manage quite well but we are anxious to know more of your plans. Take care of yourself, my dear. We both send our love, Mother.

Anna held the letter in her hands as she thought it over. Her explanation to her parents had been brief but whatever she had written would have been unacceptable, at any rate to her mother. Her father would have been more understanding.

Her thoughts were interrupted by a knock on the door.

'Ah, you're back,' said Helen, coming in and sitting down on the bed. 'I've been looking for you all day.'

'I've been to Kamakura.'

'You really get around, don't you? You've explored

parts of Tokyo I shall never see. I wish we could have gone together, Anna, but I've come with a much more exciting suggestion.'

'Oh?'

'How would you like to climb Mount Fuji?'

'I couldn't. I'm nowhere near fit enough.'

'Neither am I, but Dave and I have always wanted to. If we're going to do it before we leave it's got to be soon. We're planning to go sometime next month. Why don't you come with us?'

Anna hesitated. 'I'd hold you back.'

'I don't think so,' said Helen. 'It's a long, hard slog but you're as fit as I am. Yoshi said he might come, too.'

'Dr Egawa? Hasn't he climbed it already?'

'He climbs it most years and he'll act as our guide. The idea is to arrive on the summit at dawn in time to see the sun rise. Do come, Anna. You could ask Nigel, too, if you thought it a good idea. I suppose you're still friends?'

'He's already left for Osaka,' said Anna quickly, thanking her stars.

'I'd enjoy it much more if you come along too,' said Helen. 'We'll climb together, and if we can't make it, we'll turn back and wait for them at the bottom.'

'I shall lose an awful lot of face if I have to admit defeat.'

'If anyone gives up it's sure to be me. Anyway, I'm going to tell Dave you're coming. I'll let you know later about the time. We three will travel there together. Yoshi wants to come in his own car so that he can get back if he has too.'

In spite of her reservations, the challenge excited Anna. Ever since she looked out of the bedroom window after she arrived and saw the mountain, she felt drawn to it.

'All right,' she said, decisively. 'I'd like to have a go. I'll make a point of exercising regularly over the next few weeks and get into trim.'

It was another two weeks before Mother Agnes told Anna that she could transfer to the children's ward, and do nursing full time.

'Helen will be leaving soon,' the nun said, 'and we need someone to take her place. She'll be able to show you the ropes.'

'What about the office? Will you have help here?'

'The girl who worked here before has fully recovered and wants to come back so it all fits nicely. I'm very grateful to you, Anna, for bringing order to the system. Now we must try and keep it that way.'

'I've enjoyed it. When do you want me to start?'

'Shall we say in a week's time? I've just had a word with the Ward Sister. She's Japanese but speaks excellent English and she's delighted to have a fully qualified nurse to replace Helen.'

That was the weekend that she had promised Helen she would climb Mount Fuji with her and Dave. Mother Agnes noticed her hesitation.

'Are you happy with this arrangement?'

'Very. It's just that Helen had invited me to climb Mount Fuji with them that weekend.'

'In that case, you can start on the Tuesday.' Mother Agnes looked up from her work with a twinkle in her eye. 'Don't knock yourself out, will you. You'll find the climb quite exhausting.'

'I'll be careful.'

'No other questions then before you begin?'

'Only the language. I'm having Japanese lessons

but I know very little as yet and nearly all the children are Japanese. How am I going to communicate with them?'

'That won't be a problem. The nurses are Japanese. You'll find it a good way to pick up the language. Don't worry, Anna. I know you're going to be very useful there.'

Things were going better than she could have expected. In her euphoria she decided to write to Hugh. She had never thanked him for taking her out to dinner that evening or for delivering Jack's letter.

She wrote fluently, covering several pages. She told him of her broken engagement, her indecision, her impressions of Japan and even the incident in the tempura bar. She mentioned Doctor Egawa and his concern for the victims of Hiroshima. She wrote the sort of letter she would have written to Jack, her thoughts spilling over the pages. She only paused before signing her name. Then, after a moment's hesitation, she wrote simply 'Yours, Anna'.

She posted the letter in the main hall. She was on her way back when she met Dr Egawa. He was carrying a briefcase and appeared to be in a hurry, but seeing her, he stopped.

'Ah, Anna, I hear you're going to join us on the climb?'

'Helen suggested that I should.'

'You have climbed before, of course?'

'I've done a bit in Scotland.'

'You'll find this very different. More like a test of endurance. It's hard going. But I expect Helen warned you.'

'She did. I shall do my best not to hold you back.'

He was silent for a moment, and she wondered if

he were going to advise her against the climb. Then he appeared to think better of it.

'I can see that you're determined and that's what counts. It's most important that we reach the summit before dawn breaks. It's a magnificent sight.'

'I wouldn't want you to wait for me. If I can't keep up, I shall come back.'

'We walk as a party,' he reminded her. 'A leader is responsible for everyone in his group.' He cast a critical glance at the high-heeled shoes she was wearing. 'May I suggest you wear sensible shoes. More accidents are caused by unsuitable footwear than for any other reason.'

'I'll be sure to do that.'

She was beginning to regret that he was to accompany them. She would have preferred to have a local guide who would set a steady pace for Helen and herself. Now she was going to feel under pressure. She suspected that Doctor Egawa had a low opinion of western women and little faith in her ability to cope with the climb. Nettled by his attitude, she made up her mind to prove him wrong.

His next remark was reassuring. 'Good,' he said with a curt nod. 'Then we will meet in Hakone and climb together.'

Chapter Ten

The road to Hakone ran along the rocky coastline. Anna looked across at the clear blue water of the Pacific where gentle white-crested waves broke on the small islands cluttering the shore. Twisted pines bent by incessant wind clung like sentinels to the rocks.

The road was clear except for an occasional car or lone cyclist, but Dave drove cautiously to avoid the potholes. When they came to villages where children and animals wandered freely over the highway he was forced to wait patiently until they moved out of the way.

'Isn't it beautiful?' said Helen, sniffing the salty tang of the sea. 'I'm so thankful that we came on this trip and with you, Anna. This is one experience that we'll always remember sharing. You know, in a way I envy you staying on, but you must find time to get around. Why don't you think about buying a car?'

'I can't afford it. Besides I probably wouldn't use it much. What's the point when the public transport's so good?'

'A car gives you independence.'

'Unless the thing breaks down,' said Dave who was having trouble engaging second gear; the old vehicle was making heavy weather of the hill. 'This damned clutch seems to be packing up.'

'You should have had it looked at, Dave.'

'Not worth it now. We'll be getting rid of it soon.'

Helen was watching ominous clouds gathering out to sea. 'I hope that doesn't mean rain,' she said.

'It isn't only rain that might stop us reaching the summit,' said Dave. 'If the cloud comes down suddenly – and that can happen any time – the guides won't let you go any further. You'd see nothing anyway.'

'So you have to be sure before you start that you're going to be able to make it?' asked Anna.

'You can never be that certain. If the cloud settles, there's nothing for it but to turn round and come down as fast as you can. If you don't and visibility drops to a few yards, it's only too easy to lose the path and get totally lost. That's why everyone climbs in mid-summer when the weather is likely to be good.'

The road was climbing steadily now, through cryptomeria trees rising tall and black on the mountainside, and further on they came upon forests of bamboo, strange shapes bending and rustling in the wind. Taking it slowly, they reached the Atami pass at two thousand feet and began the descent through maples and dark green pines. Their fragrance hung on the clean air, reminding Anna of Scotland.

'The Japanese know how to look after their forests,' said Dave. 'They're dependent on them. Wood is used for everything here, all their buildings and most of their every day articles. We could learn a lot from these people.'

At the toll Dave handed some notes to the policeman who was passing the time of day with a hiker. They drove on, flanking a wooded mountainside towards the Hakone pass. Ahead of them the gulf of Saruga opened up with new promontories in the distance. Then suddenly, rounding a bend, the majestic outline of Mount Fuji burst into full view.

Anna drew in her breath sharply at the sight of the summit tinged with blue. On this serene summer day, it's conical beauty rising from the haze of the plain seemed unreal, as though suspended in the sky.

'It's like the meeting of heaven and earth,' said Helen with awe.

'Twelve thousand feet,' Dave told them. That's what we're about to climb.'

'You can go some of the way by car,' said Helen, as if to reassure Anna.

'Trust you to find that bit in the guide book,' said David. 'You're out of luck though. We're doing it properly.'

'I think you might have consulted us.' Helen sounded petulent.

'Yoshi wouldn't hear of us taking the easy way. He's our guide and we go along with him.'

'I hope to goodness I don't let you down,' said Anna. 'I don't mind you two witnessing my lack of stamina, but Dr Egawa is another matter. I don't think he has much faith in my climbing ability.' She was still smarting from the reservations he'd expressed.

'Don't worry about Yoshi,' said Helen. 'He promised to take it steadily with plenty of time for rest. I'm not going to kill myself either.'

Dave had no difficulty in finding the hotel. Their arrival was awaited and as they drew up an entourage came to greet them.

'Irashai,' the girls chorused with low bows.

As Dave took the luggage out of the car, his gentle teasing in their native tongue delighted the maids, reducing them to helpless giggles. Leaving him to make arrangements for the car, Helen and Anna followed the girls along the stepping stones to the entrance of the inn and up a short flight of steps. At the top were numerous pairs of slippers.

'You have to leave your own shoes outside and take a pair, whichever fits you best,' Helen said. 'The idea is that you don't take the dirt from the street into the hotel.'

They were taken through the narrow polished hallway, down a corridor where the maid opened sliding paper doors, to a room with tatami matting. It opened onto a garden where a waterfall cascaded into a small pond. The maid bowed as they entered and produced freshly starched *yukatas* for them to change into.

'We thought you wouldn't mind sharing a room,' Helen said, 'It's nicer than being on your own and we'll only use it for a few hours before and after the climb. We can rest here and have a meal before we start.'

Dave came in as the maid brought a tray with green tea and small pink and green soy bean cakes.

'There's a garage attached to the hotel,' he said, biting into a cake. 'I've asked them to have a look at the car and ordered a taxi to take us round this afternoon. We might as well see what we can while we're here.'

Yoshi had turned up when they got back to the hotel.

'Sorry I'm late,' he said, reserving a nod of greeting for Anna. 'I got held up, but if we start at six it will be time enough. Right now I need a bath. I suggest a light meal before we set off. What do you think, David?

'I'll order it,' said Dave.

By six o'clock that evening a long line of hikers were already zig-zagging their way up on the north side of the mountain. A peculiar chant drifted down to them.

'What's that they're singing?' asked Anna.

'With each step they chant "Rokkon Shojo",' said Yoshi. 'It means purify the body and mind of evil. The rhythm makes it easier to keep a steady pace.' He looked at Anna. 'You can try it yourself as you regulate your breathing.'

Glad that he seemed in a relaxed mood, she followed the others into the base hut to collect their climbing sticks.

'At each stage you'll have a chop put on your stick and at the summit it will be marked in red, as proof that you really have climbed Fuji-san,' said Yoshi. 'See this stick—' he struck the ground sharply with it. '—it's an important part of our equipment and we use it to support the conscience as well as the body. So you see we're well equipped for all eventualities.'

He led them to where people were queueing to start the climb.

'I never thought I'd be climbing a mountain at night,' said Anna. Now they were on their way, she was glad she'd said nothing more about her hesitation in coming. She was aware of Yoshi throwing her anxious glances from time to time, but she saw that both old and young were tackling the climb quite cheerfully. If they could, so could she.

Yoshi was moving forward to take his place and the others fell in behind him. Slowly they moved up the foot of the mountain.

'Keep together,' he instructed. 'That way we can encourage each other. Right David?'

'Sure,' said Dave. 'We'll take our pace from the girls.'

Yoshi went ahead, closely followed by Helen. Anna paced herself behind her. She was wearing strong canvas shoes but the loose cinders made it difficult to grip and she kept sliding back until she discovered she did better when she took shorter steps. She noticed that Helen was having the same trouble.

At the next bend in the zigzag path, they paused for a while.

'Go on behind David,' Yoshi told Helen. 'I'll stay with Anna.'

'Take your time,' he told her. 'You'll soon find your own pace.'

After a while, she settled into a steady rhythm, but her breath was now coming in short gasps. How long, she wondered, could she keep this up?

'Ten minutes rest at the next hut,' said Yoshi, ahead of her. 'How are you doing?'

'All right,' she lied, moving over to make room for a couple overtaking them. Both climbers were dressed entirely in white.

'Members of Fujiko,' said Yoshi, as the pair pulled ahead. 'They're an organisation of Mount Fuji worshippers making their annual pilgrimage. Fanatics, of course. Most people climb it for pleasure or just to prove that they can.'

'What's your reason?'

'A little of both , but I don't take it too seriously,' he said. 'Neither must you.'

'I'm deadly serious,' Anna assured him. 'I wouldn't be putting all this effort into it unless I was.'

'Ah yes,' said Yoshi, a flash of amusement in his eyes as he looked back at her. 'I've heard it said that the English take their pleasures seriously.'

'You also made it clear that you didn't want to be held back by an inexperienced climber.' She said it deliberately lightly, with a hint of laughter in her voice.

'That was only common sense,' he said seriously. 'I understand Helen invited you to join the party and she herself has never climbed Fuji-san. She had no idea what it involved. It's up to me to assess the ability of anyone coming with us for safety's sake. I didn't intend any criticism of you.'

She simply had to take a break. Her leg muscles ached intolerably.

'Please go ahead,' she said. 'I'm holding you back.'

'Just take it at your own pace,' he said, but she was relieved when he hurried on to join Dave. When she was able to continue, she found Helen waiting for her.

'All right?' the New Zealander asked.

'I think I'm doing fine till I see whole families ahead of me. One fellow just passed me with a baby on his back. It's demoralising.'

'Driven by their determination to reach the summit,' said Helen, 'or religious fervour. I used to do quite a bit of climbing in New Zealand when I was a child. We were taught to regulate our breathing by numbers, four in, hold for two, and four out. That way you make use of the whole of your lung capacity. Are you sure you're okay?'

'I've broken through the pain barrier several times,' Anna said grimly. 'It does seem to get easier as you go on, though.'

'You're doing better than me. Actually I'm finding it pretty hard going.'

'When I look up and see how far we have to go, I'm paralysed, said Anna. 'The only way is to keep plodding, take it one step at a time.'

'I've got to make it. I shan't have another chance. You will though. Anna. I wonder if you'll still be in Japan this time next year?'

'I've no idea. At the moment I'm living one week at a time or rather, one step at a time.' She grinned. 'Like climbing this mountain.'

'Look we're almost at the next station. Now for a rest.'

The men were already waiting outside for them. Anna sank thankfully onto a bench.

'Let me take your sticks,' said Yoshi. 'I'll get them branded for you.'

He returned with each stick marked with a Japanese character. 'Five more to go,' he said. 'Ten minutes here, then we move on. Does that suit everyone?'

'I suppose so,' said Helen, reluctantly.

'This isn't a holiday,' said Dave, who seemed unaffected by the climb. 'It's a challenge.'

It was beginning to get dark and the first bright stars were appearing in the limpid blue sky. Far below them the lights of the villages twinkled by the lakeside as a small boat chugged across the dark water.

Dave took Helen's hand and they went on together.

Yoshi waited for Anna. 'Don't worry about people passing you,' he said.'You'll probably overtake them later on.'

At that moment someone ahead of her slipped and sent a pile of shale cascading down in front of Anna.

She would have fallen too had not Yoshi put out a hand to save her. It took her a moment to regain her balance and continue. She seemed to have lost control of her legs. She glanced up at him expecting to see annoyance, but there was only concern in his face and she was glad to have him there. She needed his reassurance.

'Are we up to schedule?' she asked him.

'A little behind perhaps, but nothing to worry about. We should reach the top station by one o'clock and we can rest there before starting on the final haul. Another couple of hours after that to reach the summit, if we're to see the dawn.'

Three o'clock in the morning.

'Another five hours,' she said with dismay.

'At the next station we'll have some refreshment,' Yoshi consoled her.' It's surprising how much energy a little food can generate.'

There were a few people coming down the mountain now, having given up the struggle. Anna could see the relief on their faces. Just for a moment she was tempted to join them, but Yoshi was already striding on ahead and she forced her legs to a quicker pace. He was tall for a Japanese and moved with the ease of an athelete. So long as she kept her eyes fastened on his back she felt she could draw some strength and determination from him.

Dave and Helen were already at the next rest hut and had ordered cold drinks and small sweet cakes. Anna had never tasted anything so wonderful. Long before she was ready, the men were picking up their sticks, now marked with six chops and then they were on their way again.

'How did you get along with Yoshi?' asked Helen, matching her pace to Anna's.

'I was seriously thinking of giving up at one point, but I didn't have the nerve.'

'I meant after what you said the other day. You found it hard to like these people.'

'I shouldn't have told you. I should have kept it to myself.'

'Then you don't feel like that about him?'

'No. Strangely enough, I don't, but it's probably because I'm getting used to living here. I've met so many nice people. How long have you known Yoshi, Helen? As a friend, I mean.'

'Quite a time. We had to work hard at it. I don't think it ever occured to Yoshi that we liked him and wanted to be his friends. To begin with he was so formal. We tease him about it now and he doesn't mind. I just wish he'd bring his wife along sometimes.'

It hadn't occurred to Anna that he must be married. She had thought of him as a man dedicated to his work with little time for a personal life. It came as something of a shock.

'Why doesn't he?' she asked.

'Japanese women don't like leaving their homes, except perhaps to visit friends.'

Anna found this hard to accept.

'None of them?'

'Not many. The wife's place is in the home with the children. That's how the men like it. Women don't expect to be invited out. I think perhaps with the occupation it might change but I can't see that it will ever work because hardly any of them speak English. It's impossible to communicate with them.'

'I can't think why they would want to mix with us, anyway. We probably wouldn't have much in common.'

'You're right. It isn't just the language. They're afraid they might make all sorts of social blunders. It wouldn't worry us, but it would be a disaster for them.'

'If they don't want to change their ways, you can hardly blame them.'

'Yoshi's different though,' said Helen. 'He's used to us so you'd think he would encourage his wife to make friends, but whenever I ask him to bring her he always makes an excuse.'

'Have they a family?'

'Two boys and a girl. Boys are more important because they carry on the family name. They're spoilt silly and are brought up to feel superior to their sisters.'

Anna didn't like the sound of that.

'Don't the girls resent that?'

'It's always been like that. They don't know any different. Just because we don't have the same traditions, we can't say it's wrong for them.'

'You'd think the women would revolt,' said Anna. Having always valued her independence, she found the Japanese way hard to imagine.

'They seem quite content with their lot. They're charming and gentle and proud of their place at the centre of the family. It's not surprising that our men love them.'

'And sometimes marry them?'

'Rarely. There was once a man called Lafcadio Hearn in the last century who fell in love with a Japanese girl. He married her and spent his life here, but he was never accepted by the Japanese though he lived here till he was an old man.'

'I think that's a very sad story.'

Talking to Helen had taken Anna's mind off the

climb. She was surprised to find that they were now a good deal higher. Glancing up, she saw that Yoshi and Dave were waiting and from their expressions they were none too pleased.

'You'll have to do better than this,' said Dave. 'or we'll never make it. We thought you'd given up.'

'Sorry,' said Helen, looking abashed. 'We were talking.'

'You can do that when we get down again,' said Dave. 'We wondered what the devil you were up to.'

Anna glanced at Yoshi. He was already moving on and Dave went after him.

'See what I mean?' said Helen. 'It's a man's country. Women tolerated so long as they toe the line. Dave's picked up some bad habits here. I'll have to take him in hand.'

The higher they climbed, the steeper became the path and although every muscle protested, Anna was now confident she would make it. She paused for a moment to look back down the mountainside. It was dark and a long procession of climbers were making their way steadily up the zigzag path holding lighted torches. The moon threw shafts of silver across the lakes far below.

'Beautiful, isn't it?' said Yoshi softly at her side.

'It's one of the most beautiful sights I've ever seen.'

'Wait till you see the dawn breaking,' he said, leading the way into the hut. 'We have an hour's rest here before the final climb.'

Padded benches had been provided where exhausted climbers could relax before making the final assault. Most of the places had already been taken, but they found two spaces for the girls. Taking off her shoes, Anna sank onto a mattress and immediately fell into a deep sleep. She was awoken by Yoshi gently shaking her.

'Time to go,' he said and to her shame she saw that Helen and Dave were already booted and ready.

'We gave you as long as we dared,' said Helen. 'There are a few clouds about, so we want to get up there in case a mist comes down. You looked so peaceful we hated to wake you.'

Forcing her stiff limbs into action, Anna eased herself off the bench and pulled on her shoes.

Outside the air was chilly as the climbers set out to tackle the last long haul to the summit. The route was very steep now and they were forced to slow pace until at last with shouts from Yoshi and Dave, they topped the summit and stood looking down at the colourless landscape below. Away to the west was a range of snow-capped mountains.

'The Alps,' said Yoshi. 'One day you must go there.'

Then, as they watched, a streak of brilliant red appeared as the sun crept up behind the mountains, covering the surrounding plains with suffused light. Anna was spellbound. If for no other reason, she was glad she had come to Japan to see this.

Some of the climbers had broken into a chant, others were praying. The four of them stood together talking quietly and picking out landmarks along the coast.

'That little cluster of lights is Hakone, and there's our hotel,' said Dave. 'The one with the row of fairy lights.'

Gradually the day brightened, revealing some unwelcome sights in the immediate area: all about them lay discarded bits of rubbish, an odd straw sandle and wooden boxes which had once contained refreshment. Turning his back on this man-made refuse, Yoshi pointed towards a building.

'One of our most important meteorological stations,' he said.

After taking their fill of the view, Yoshi led the way to a souvenir shop. While the men waited for the final chops on their sticks, Helen and Anna selected postcards to send home.

'Let's take a look at the crater,' said Dave. 'It's been dead for years. Quite safe.'

They walked over and looked down into a deep pit. Dark rocks plunged into its sinister depth. Around its edges lay small piles of stones.

'There's a legend,' said Yoshi, 'that the souls of dead children have the task of filling the crater with stones, so the pilgrims make it easier for them by collecting them in heaps.'

Anna shuddered. 'It sounds like a horror story!'

Yoshi looked quickly at her. 'Not all legends are beautiful. Like real life, some are happy or amusing, others are deeply sad. They reflect our customs and our history. We're a superstitious race, wouldn't you agree, David?'

'More than most, I'd say, but sensitive too. I've always found thoughtfulness and kindness here.'

'I would hope so,' said Yoshi. 'If it were otherwise, we would be failing in common courtesy.'

Anna, listening to their conversation, wondered at the respect that these two men had for each other. Not so long ago they were mortal enemies. How could they forget so quickly? She supposed they must be united by their work.

'We'd better start back,' declared Dave. 'We're all going to need hot baths after this – I'm anxious about the car, too. If they can't fix it, we might have to beg a lift from Yoshi.'

Exhilerated by her success, Anna followed closely behind Dave. They began the descent, sliding and stumbling as they tried to control their limbs. To her surprise they reached the bottom in a couple of hours. By then her legs were shaking and she sank down on a rock to rest.

'You'll be all right in a moment,' said Yoshi, watching her with some amusement. She stood up shakily, shamed by his apparent lack of fatigue. Several minutes passed before she felt able to continue the final lap.

Back at the hotel, the girls went off to their bathroom.

'Wasn't that fantastic!' said Helen, lowering herself into the piping hot water of their shared Japanese-style bath. 'Aren't you glad you came?'

'I wouldn't have missed it for anything. To think I nearly gave up.'

'At what point?'

'When I was with Yoshi. Some people were coming down and I was tempted to join them. I just hated to admit defeat to him.'

Breakfast was waiting for them when they got back to their room: fried eggs and bacon with salads, rice and Indian tea.

'Bad news, I'm afraid,' said Dave, tucking in. 'The car won't be ready. They've got to send for a spare part and they won't have it fixed till tomorrow.'

'Tomorrow!' exclaimed Anna. 'But I'm on duty tomorrow.'

'I have to leave soon,' said Yoshi. 'If you don't mind an early start, I can offer you a lift.'

'Would you really?' said Anna. 'That would be a great help.'

Yoshi drove fast and Anna was surprised when they reached the top of the pass and he suddenly pulled off the road.

'I think we should have one more look at the mountain we've just climbed,' he said.

The mountain stood majestically, capped with white mist.

'It's so much more beautiful from a distance,' said Anna.

'We were lucky. The mist is a bad sign. If it thickens no one will reach the summit. That happened last time I came.'

'To think of all that wasted effort,' remarked Anna, as they got out of the car.

'Not wasted,' said Yoshi. 'It's an achievement even if you don't reach the top. You did very well. You have every reason to be proud of yourself. I must admit that when Dave told me you were coming, I had reservations, but you've proved me wrong. You must be quite fit.'

She was pleased with the compliment.

'Must be my army life,' she said.

He looked puzzled but she did not elaborate.

Returning to the car, they drove on, the road dipping and curving its way downhill. Anna settled herself low in her seat and once or twice felt her eyes closing.

'Tired?' asked Yoshi. 'Sleep if you wish. It will take us three hours to reach Tokyo and you've had an eventful night.'

She shifted her position. How was it that he seemed to be able to do with hardly any sleep? He'd been on the go for the last twenty-four hours and from his comments, he still had work ahead of him.

'Are you going straight to the hospital?' she asked. 'If not, please drop me off wherever convenient. I can easily catch a bus.'

'I'm going there so I'll take you all the way. I want to visit one of my patients, a little girl I'm worried about.'

'What's wrong with her?' asked Anna.

'A case of radiation. Her mother was caught in the blast when she was pregnant. It affected the unborn child.'

'Will she die?'

'Yes, though perhaps not just yet.'

'Is she on the children's ward?' she asked.

'She is.'

'I'm starting work there tomorrow. Mother Agnes wants me to take Helen's place when she leaves.'

'Have you had much experience with children?' Yoshi enquired.

'Not for some years but I'm looking forward to nursing again.'

'You may find some of the cases distressing,' he mused. 'Many of them come from poor homes and in some cases their parents resist hospital treatment. When eventually the children come to us, it's often too late to do anything.'

'I'm a nurse,' she reminded him. 'I've seen terrible scenes on the battlefield. I think I'll be able to cope however distressing it is.'

'Ah yes, the war,' said Yoshi softly. 'You were very young to be involved in all that.'

'But not too young to to be with men who were dying or maimed for life. Not too young to sit beside them holding their hands as they died.'

'I'm sorry. I wasn't in any way underrating your experience.'

An uneasy silence fell between them.

Presently she asked, 'What were you doing during the war, Doctor Egawa?'

'My name's Yoshi,' he said. 'Helen and Dave use it and so can you. I was in the Dutch East Indies for a while, then I worked in a hospital in Singapore.'

'My brother went through Singapore.' Anna paused, then added. 'As a prisoner-of-war.'

Yoshi glanced at her. 'Then it must have been very unpleasant for him.'

'It was. He died in a camp in Thailand.'

'The Railway?'

Instinctively she stiffened. 'Yes.'

'Then you must have very strong feelings against us.'

'I do. I shall never forget what happened to him. I shall always hate the people responsible for his death.'

Yoshi was silent, concentrating on a sharp bend. Presently he said, 'What made you come to Japan then – curiosity? You wanted to see first hand what monsters we are?'

'I never wanted to come here.' Her voice trembled. 'Nigel, my fiance was sent here after we got engaged.'

'And when there was no marriage, you decided to stay on?' He sounded surprised.

'I felt it was important to stay for a while. I've never been happy since Jack's death. I just can't accept it. He was my twin brother, you see. I thought perhaps I might find some sort of reason for his death if I stayed on. Some kind of understanding to make it more tolerable.' She sighed. 'Now I know I'm hoping for the impossible.'

'We can't always find reasons for tragedies. We can only learn to accept them.'

She found Yoshi's complacency infuriating.

'Have you any idea what it was like in those camps?' she demanded. 'Men dying of starvation, deprived of medical care. Do you know they were tortured and murdered?' Her voice was strident.

Yoshi had become quiet again. She looked across at him. The muscles of his face were taut, his lips tightly pressed together.

'Did you know about those things, Yoshi?' she insisted.

'It's something we are not proud of,' he said at last. 'The men in charge of those camps were not of high calibre. They were ordinary men, frustrated that they couldn't play a more glorious role for their country. You must try to understand that they despised their prisoners. It has always been a disgrace for a Japanese to be taken prisoner and many men committed suicide rather than allow themselves to be captured. It might help you to learn that most of those guards paid a high price for their cruelty. Some were executed, others who did return home found themselves scorned by their own people.'

She was suddenly depressed. She had no right to blame him personally, to make him a scapegoat for her frustration. Yet he could not shrug off some of the responsibility for his countrymen's behaviour.

'I'm anxious to get back to the hospital,' Yoshi said, 'but I think we need a break. Would you like a drink of some kind?'

'If you've time.'

At the next village, he pulled up in front of a small open fronted stall. Under the shade of a tree stood a table and some benches.

'We'll see if we can find something here,' he said, getting out of the car. 'What would you like?'

As soon as the order was brought, she said, 'I'm sorry, Yoshi. I had no right to attack you.'

He looked at her with sympathy. 'You might not believe me but I do understand how you feel. You must have been very close to your brother.'

'I knew when he died. We were as close as that.'

'Then I think it was brave of you to come to Japan,' he said, 'and I hope in time that your opinion of us will change. You must remember that we are products of our culture, though first and foremost we are of course individuals and responsible for our actions.'

'You think that our culture can affect our behaviour?'

He seemed surprised that she should ask.

'Naturally. What I'm trying to say is that in order to understand why people act as they do you have to take everything into account – culture, religion, education, upbringing. It all contributes to the whole. Too often we judge a person solely by what we know about him, which often isn't very much.'

He took a long drink and put his beer on the table in front of him.

'You must forgive me for asking, Anna, but do you think your country is blameless?'

'Of course not. We have much to answer for. You're thinking, of course, of the atom bomb?'

'It killed thousands of innocent women and children and maimed others for life, as did all the other bombing. You couldn't have been ignorant of the consequences. We believe that the reason for its use was to bring the war to an end quickly, so perhaps ultimately it did good by saving life. I don't think our

Emperor or his generals would ever have conceded defeat otherwise, but that still doesn't excuse the use of such a cruel weapon.'

She looked away. Yoshi had a calm and matter of fact way of putting his arguments. Whatever the provocation, she felt ashamed of her outburst.

'I'm sorry to hurry you,' he said getting up, 'but we shall have to move on.'

'I'm ready,' said Anna, taking out her purse.

He brushed it aside. 'It's not a large bill.'

She didn't press it. She had no idea what the custom was here. In her ignorance she had felt she had to make the offer.

Soon they reached the outskirts of Tokyo and were slowed down by the thickening traffic. His concentration was fully on his driving and he no longer spoke.

When they reached the hospital, she waited while he got out her small suitcase from the boot.

'Thank you for bringing me back,' she said.

'It may have been a controversial journey,' he said, looking at her gravely, 'but I'm glad you've been honest with me. It's sometimes necessary to talk about the past if we're to learn from our mistakes. Don't you agree?'

His brown eyes searched for her reaction.

She nodded. She was tired – too tired to discuss it any more. 'You're probably right,' she said.

'Resentment is a luxury few of us can afford,' he went on. 'You have a lot to forgive, but I think that one day you'll find that you can.'

She had no reply to that. Picking up her bag, she went into the hospital.

Chapter Eleven

It was late when Yoshi left the hospital for his house on the outskirts of Tokyo. The drive home took a good hour and although he would have preferred to live nearer to his work, his wife, Tama, liked it here and the children had settled well in the local school.

He had promised Tama he would be home before the children went to bed and already dusk was falling. It always happened like this. Once he arrived on the children's ward it was difficult to get away. He had been there most of the day and having had no sleep the night before, he was now desperately tired.

His young patient's condition had stabilised but he would not allow himself to be over optimistic. Too often, just when he had seen definite signs of recovery, the situation was reversed and he had lost the patient. He found this particularly painful when a child's life was at stake and he could never accept it without re-examining every aspect of the treatment to find where it might have been improved.

Now he turned off the main road into a residential area. The narrow winding street was lined with high bamboo fences which hid large houses and gardens owned by wealthy Japanese.

He had to pull in to the side to allow a car to pass. The traffic was becoming impossible these days. When they bought this house at the end of the war, few people owned cars but with the arrival of the Americans, everything was changing and not always for the better.

Once over the bridge the road widened. He drew up under the dim light of a street lamp. Leaving the car, he entered through the garden gate, brushing against the bell to announce his arrival. He followed the flagstone path towards the house, pleased to see that Tama had ordered the candles to be lighted in the stone lanterns. Flickering shadows fell on the azalea bushes and the little stream.

Michiko had laid out his slippers ready for him and now he sat down on the step and took off his shoes as the maid came to welcome him with a low bow.

Weary and glad to be back, he entered the peace of his home and went in search of Tama. She was sitting on the balcony with the sliding doors open to the garden. Ichiro, their seven year old son was sitting on a rug beside her, deep in a book. On hearing his father, he got to his feet and bowed, murmuring a welcome.

Tama also rose to meet her husband with a bow, somewhat less deep than Michiko-san's. He acknowledged this mark of respect with a slight movement of his head. Tama was beautiful, with the pale skin and finely chiselled features of a Japanese woman of high birth. She was dressed in a dark blue kimono and wore her shining black hair twisted to the side of her head exposing the nape of her neck, a part of the body which he found particularly attractive.

She smiled at him, her eyes tender with the pleasure of seeing him. 'How did the climb go?' she asked.

'The weather was good and we made it to the top. I'm afraid I'm late. I've been at the hospital all day.'

'They telephoned to tell me. Thank you for your message,' she said.

'I had hoped to be back at mid-day but once on the ward there's always something.'

Her expression softened in sympathy.

'You must be tired Yoshi. Go and take a bath and then tell me about it.'

'Where are Kumo and Chieko?'

'Michiko is putting them to bed. We weren't sure when you'd be home and they were fractious. I'll go and tell them you're here.'

But they had already heard him and came into the room dressed for bed. Kuma led the way, closely followed by his little sister, Chieko. At four, Kuma was a sturdy child with wide alert eyes. Chieko was a dainty little girl with an impish face and short dark hair. She was expected to keep a respectful distance behind her brother but now it was too much for her and she ran the last few steps to her father with a big smile. He picked her up and held her close before setting her down carefully and asking them in turn about their day. He made a point of doing this whenever he could, because so often they were asleep before he reached home. Even weekends could be curtailed when he was working.

Presently Michiko came to claim them and took the three of them off to bed, leaving him free to take his bath. Tama was right. He was tired.

In their bedroom the futon had been laid out on the tatami in readiness for the night. He stripped and, wrapping a towel round his waist, made his way to the bathroom at the back of the house. Having washed and rinsed himself, he got into the tub and submerged himself in the steaming water.

It was good to be home. He had much to be

thankful for. Not all men were as fortunate as he in having an understanding wife. Tama rarely questiond his long hours at the hospital nor his trips abroad. She was content in her home and on his return, showed her affection in numerous small ways. There was, he thought, much to be said for an arranged marriage, though these days some youngsters were determined to make up their own minds about their future partners. But he had been brought up in an orthodox family and had been happy to go along with his parents' choice for him.

He had been born in Osaka, the son of a surgeon, with two younger sisters. As a boy he held a superior position in the family and it was decided that he should follow in his father's footsteps in the medical profession. When he was twenty-eight and qualified as a doctor, a marriage was arranged for him with the daughter of a rich landowner. Shortly after Ichiro was born, war broke out and he was drafted into the army. Tama spent the war years with her parents in the country, and it had been a relief for him to know that she and the child were safely away from the city, which had undergone major air attacks.

He lay there for some time while his thoughts wandered from one thing to another. Then he got out and towelled himself and, putting on his yukata, went to join Tama on the balcony. Relaxing in the cushioned chair, a new western style acquisition, he gladly accepted the whisky his wife poured for him.

'I was later than I intended,' he explained in his precise Japanese, 'because of this child. She's suffering from leukaemia. Most of her life has been spent in and out of hospital. She would benefit from another spell at home but I'm not sure the family can cope.'

'Surely her parents would want to look after her?'

'That's the trouble. Her parents are dead. Her father was a Kamikaze pilot, killed over Singapore, and her mother died within a few weeks of the bomb on Hiroshima. It was a premature birth and the child was damaged while still in the womb.'

Tama drew in a sharp breath of anxiety. 'Then who will care for her?'

'She lives with her aunt, but she has her own children to worry about. I'm not sure whether she can be relied upon now Suzu is so ill.'

'Then perhaps she should remain in hospital,' suggested Tama.

'She frets when she sees the other children going home,' said Yoshi, sipping his whisky, thoughtfully.

Tama understood his need for quiet. She continued her embroidery, waiting for him to speak, while his mind wandered over the events of the last twenty-four hours.

Presently she said, 'Tell me about the climb.'

'It went well but the pace was slow. A foreign woman came with us.'

'You mean your friends from New Zealand?'

'Yes, but this woman was a friend of Helen's, a nurse at the hospital.'

'Does she also come from New Zealand?'

'She's English. A strange, rather unhappy person.'

Tama looked up at him. 'Why is she here? Is it difficult to find work in her own country?'

'She came to marry someone in a foreign bank but the wedding was cancelled. I don't know why. So now she's working at the hospital.'

'Perhaps there was some disagreement,' said Tama.' No wonder she's unhappy.'

'That's not the main reason. Her brother was killed

in one of our prison camps. She seems unable to accept it and it's made her very bitter.'

'How sad for her. Did she speak of this when you were climbing?'

'Dave's car failed to start and I brought her back to the hospital. She spoke of it then. She was extremely forthright and I think she held me responsible, at least in part.'

Tama's eyes widened in surprise. 'You? Why should she hold you responsible? You've helped so many people.'

'Obviously because I belong to the race that killed him. In me she saw her brother's murderer. I can understand it, though it's hard to see how a foreigner's mind works.'

'I've often heard this, but I have no experience of them,' said Tama. 'I think she was being very unjust.'

He smiled at her. 'Would you like to meet my New Zealand friends?' he asked her. 'When I make excuses, they think I have some strange reason for keeping you hidden.'

She laughed at him. 'No, Yoshi. I wouldn't understand them. I don't have your intelligence and I can't speak their language. I'd be afraid of making some social blunder and that would embarrass you.'

'You please me the way you are,' said Yoshi. 'You understand, don't you, Tama, that it's important for me to mix with foreigners because of my work? Besides I like David and Helen. As for the others, I don't care greatly for them.'

'It's easier to make friends when we're younger,' Tama reassured him. 'We're not so critical then, and we accept new ideas without question. When we're older we become set in our ways and we think we have all the answers.'

'We Japanese have always been an insular people,' sighed Yoshi, 'but we must make sure that our children mix freely with Westerners so that they feel at ease with them. One day the world will belong to them, but our experiences are of value and we must pass on the lessons we've learnt.'

'If they remember what we've taught them, only good can come from it,' said Tama calmly. 'We have the burden of the war to carry, Yoshi. It has affected all our lives and influenced our thinking. We have to overcome many of our old prejudices. It will be different for our children, won't it?'

'You're not only beautiful,' observed Yoshi, 'but wise as well.'

That night when they had turned off the light, he lay stretched out beside her listening to the rasping sound of the geckos, the giant lizards that made their home somewhere behind the summer house.

Tama was already asleep. He turned onto his side and watched the pale outline of the trees in the garden. He was thinking again of his patients and it disturbed him that the foreign woman intruded on his thoughts. She had a strange beauty, unlike the delicate grace of a Japanese woman, but there was spirit about her. She spoke as frankly as a man, demanding answers to questions which rarely concerned other women. In a way her brashness repulsed him. In his country it was considered extremely bad manners to impose one's grief upon others. We prefer to keep it to ourselves, he thought, hidden from the world. But did that make it right?

Anna had started her nursing duties on the children's ward. Sano-san, the Sister in charge, was a Japanese woman of about forty and under her were three staff nurses, including Anna. Japanese probationers and auxillery nurses together with the domestics, made up the complement of staff.

Anna found it hard to come to terms with the nursing standards. At home hygiene was a priority, cases were well documented and relatives admitted under control. Here they came and went, helping to feed the children and entertain them. She had to admit, however, that though administration left a lot to be desired, the concern of doctors and nurses for their patients was excellent. One thing did concern her though and she spoke to Helen about it.

'It seems that they discharge the patients as soon as there are the slightest signs of recovery. I'm sure it's much too soon,' she said.' Is there any supervision when they get home?'

'There simply aren't enough beds,' said Helen. 'The best we can do is to treat emergencies and put them on the road to recovery. Sometimes they have to be discharged to make room for more serious cases.'

'Then you must get a lot of them back again?' suggested Anna.

'A few perhaps. It's not ideal but it's a system that seems to work. There's no alternative. As it is the place is overcrowded.'

It accounted for the children on makeshift beds, lying in the corridor waiting for a place on the ward. They suffered from a variety of illnesses. Some were casualties of road accidents, others had broken bones or infections of one kind or another. The consultants came daily to see their small patients, Yoshi's concern being solely with the children suffering from radiation and burns. There were many of these.

Since she had been on the ward, Anna had spoken

to him on several occasions concerning the patients. He had made no reference to the Fuji expedition and she took this as a silent rebuke. She was troubled by their conversation on the way back and deeply regretted her outburst. Now, she watched him as he moved about the ward, taking time to talk to each child as they eagerly awaited his attention. She had been wrong about him. He shared few of the characteristics she attributed to Japanese people in general. With his patients he was a gentle caring man and yet . . . She felt that there was a certain arrogance about him, an agression almost. It was not a trait she cared for.

At the end of the day Anna was exhausted. Frequently late off duty, she forced herself to open her books and work at the exercises, to be ready for her next Japanese lesson. She found that her limited knowledge was sufficient on the ward. The children enjoyed her amateurish attempts at Japanese, and she was surprised how quickly they grasped her meaning.

She had grown deeply attached to Yoshi's small patient, Suzu. She was a frail child of five, with a round olive coloured face and deep-set eyes. When her fever was high and she became fractious it was for Anna that she looked. One day she had been particularly restless, and Anna stayed on to be with her. She picked up a picture book and slowly began to read to the child, stringing together the few Japanese words she knew. Presently she became aware of someone standing by the bed. She looked up to see Yoshi watching her.

'So you're learning our language?'

'I'm trying, but it's difficult.'

'It's worth persevering. I can see, like the rest of us, you're fond of the child.'

'I love them all,' said Anna, 'But there's something special about this one. Is she going to recover, Yoshi?'

'I can't tell. There are so many things that we still don't understand about the disease. We might not be able to save this little one. All I can say is that we're learning more about the effects of radiation all the time, but as yet there is no cure.'

A nurse came to tidy the bed, and Anna lifted the child and cradled her in her arms, so small and frail. Suzu studied her, her eyes bright with fever. Anna, filled with tenderness, smiled down into the small pinched face and whispered softly to her.

'She responds to you,' said Yoshi. 'You may be able to help her to hold on to that thin thread of life.'

Anna heard his words but her attention was not diverted from Suzu. Rocked gently in her arms, the child was soon asleep. Anna laid her on the bed and put a cover over her.

'Her aunt hasn't been to visit today,' she said.

'She can't always manage it. She has the other children. She knows Suzu's well cared for here.'

'What about her husband? Couldn't he help so she could come and see her?'

'He works night shifts in a factory and sleeps most of the day. The woman gets little help or sympathy from him.'

'What will become of Suzu then?' asked Anna.

'If she survives this phase of the disease, she might live a few more years but she'll never be as strong as the others.'

When Anna arrived on duty the next morning, she found Yoshi already there talking to Sister Sano. He must have spent last night at the hospital, a thing he frequently did when he was anxious about a patient. Suzu was very weak and her breathing was shallow. Her tenuous grasp on life seemed to be slowly slipping away.

'We're going to try a transfusion,' Yoshi said, including Anna in the conversation. 'Unless we do, we shall lose her.'

For the next twenty-four hours, Suzu remained critically ill and then she began to rally.

'Try her with a little soup,' said Sister.

Anna was kneeling by her bed feeding her small spoonfuls when Suzu's aunt arrived. Happy with the improvement in the child's condition, Anna smiled at the woman and was surprised to see hostility in her eyes. Speaking in Japanese, Suzu's aunt took the cup from Anna and waving her away, continued to feed the child herself.

Suzu's eyes followed Anna and she reached out her hand. Hurt and bewildered, Anna turned away and busied herself with another patient. She could see no reason for the woman's hostility.

So absorbed was Anna with hospital life and her young charges that when one evening she was told there was a telephone call for her, it was like a communication from another world.

'Hello, Anna. It's Jean. It's been so long since we've heard from you, How are you?'

'Fine. I'm working on the wards now. We're very busy but I love it. What about you, Jean? Everything all right with the baby?'

'I'll be glad when these last few weeks are over. I get so bored.'

'It'll all be worth it when it arrives.'

'I rang to ask if you could tear yourself away from the hospital to have a meal with us?'

Anna hesitated. It was so long since she'd stayed with them. She could think of no reason why they should want to keep in contact. For her part, she had no particular wish to meet her countrymen. She would have nothing to say to them, geared as she was to hospital life now. She felt nervous at the mere thought of it. Besides, she preferred to avoid anything that would remind her of Nigel.

'Do come,' said Jean. 'A break in your routine would do you good. I'll put on a nice dinner specially for you. A change from hospital fare.'

'It's kind of you, Jean. I can't believe though that Stan would want to see me.'

'Nonsense. That's all finished with. Don't think we're going to try and persuade you to change your mind about Nigel. We won't mention him, I promise.'

She had no real excuse and she didn't want to offend Jean.

'Thanks, Jean. Then I'd love to come.'

She came off duty one evening and was making her way to the dining room when she met Yoshi striding along the corridor in his white coat. It seemed that his hours were considerably longer than hers.

'Finished for the day?' he asked her.

'Yes.'

'You're looking tired. The children's ward is our busiest and demands total concentration. It's a hard way to begin your nursing duties.'

He seemed to have something more to say, so she waited.

'I've been meaning to speak to you.' He looked at

his watch. 'How would you like to get away from the hospital for a change and we'll find a restaurant somewhere? I haven't eaten myself yet.'

'I'd like it very much.'

'Good. You may want to change and I must make a phone call to my wife to say I'll be late. I'll meet you in the main hall in twenty minutes.'

She had to take a shower. She felt exhausted and keyed up after her six hour duty. Yoshi was right. Working with children drained one of energy and emotion more than any other type of nursing. They demanded round the clock attention.

Flinging her uniform on the bed, she went across to the bathroom, wondering what Yoshi wanted to see her about that couldn't be discussed on the ward.

In ten minutes she was back and put on a cool green dress she had brought from home and a pair of high-heeled sandals. Then taking the pins from her hair, she shook it loose and put on a little make-up. It was all she had time for. When she went downstairs Yoshi was already waiting for her.

He took her to a restaurant not far from the hospital, where the customers were all Japanese. The place was softly lighted and they were offered a table near the window. Yoshi was dressed in a dark suit and tie, his hair thick and sleek.

'What do you feel like, Anna? Have you tried sushi yet? It's a special raw fish. Delicious.'

She shook her head. She didn't feel she could cope with that right now.

'You'd prefer something cooked then?'

'I'm not very hungry. Please would you choose something?'

He gave the order and then turned his attention to her.

'I asked you to come because I have a favour to ask you. Perhaps I should't even suggest it on top of your other work so I shall understand if you feel unable to accept. I want you to be honest about it.'

'Has it to do with Suzu?' she asked.

'Yes.'

'Then you know I'll do what I can.'

'Let me tell you what I have in mind. It seems that the present treatment is suiting her and has given her another span of life, but how long it will last, is impossible to tell. I think a change from the hospital environment would be good for her and might make things easier for the family. She'll be under a doctor but there could be problems in sending her home. They're a very poor, uneducated family.'

'Where does she live?'

'Not far away. Within walking distance of the hospital. It's a primitive, overcrowded housing area with few modern facilities.'

Anna frowned. 'Then is it right to discharge her?'

'I believe it is. I think the child needs to be with her family in familiar surroundings for a while. It's sad for her to see other children leaving hospital to go home while she has to remain. We don't have the facilities here for recuperation that you do in England, so we have to make the most of what we have.

'But is it worth the risk? If she loses ground . . . ?'

'If that happens, it won't be because we've sent her home. She's more likely to fret while she's in hospital. There's more to a patient's treatment than just medical care. I'm sure you would agree with that?'

'Indeed I do,' said Anna.

'Of course there's a risk,' Yoshi went on, 'but one I'm willing to take, but only if she's closely supervised.'

'Is there any chance of improvement, Yoshi?'

He shook his head slowly. 'In the long term? I'm not optimistic.'

He was warning her gently of what she already knew. Her heart was heavy, yet she had to believe that a miracle could happen.

'Surely there's always hope?' she pressed.

'I never give up hope,' he said. 'The important thing at the moment is to keep her happy, and that in itself will improve her chances. I shall visit her from time to time but what I want to ask you is this, Anna. Would you be willing to supervise the care she has from her aunt, Yasuko?'

She stared at him in dismay. 'But I'm working at the hospital. I can't give that up.'

'I'm not asking you to. I want you to go and see her whenever you can spare the time, if possible once a day. There's no need to stay long. It's important to check that Suzu is properly cared for and that she is being given her proper doses of medicines. If the family expects you from time to time, they'll take more care. They need this support.'

'I don't think her aunt likes me,' said Anna. 'She rejects any help I offer.'

'That's natural. She'd want to look after her niece herself while she's with her.'

'No,' said Anna, firmly. 'She allows the other nurses to help her. I wish I knew the reason.'

'Then it might be that Yasuko thinks you're an American. It was the Americans who killed her sister, and now she is about to lose a niece.'

'And she holds me responsible? That's unfair.' Then she remembered the accusation she had thrown at Yoshi, and said no more.

'She's a simple woman.'

They ate in silence for a while, then Yoshi said. 'It's not an easy thing I'm asking you to do, I know.'

She wanted to, but if Yasuko thought her responsible for Suzu's illness then how could she possibly intrude?'

'We're not speaking of the family,' said Yoshi, 'but the child. She has taken to you. I think you'll be able to overcome any problems, and for the sake of Suzu, they'll accept you.'

Still her reservations persisted. 'I don't speak the language,' she said. 'How can I communicate with them?'

'You'll find ways. The fact that you visit and support them will encourage them.'

Yoshi's manner was professional. The easy manner he adopted with Helen and Dave and even herself in Hakone had been dropped. She had no idea what he was thinking behind that inscrutible mask, but she had an uneasy feeling he was assessing her, wondering whether she cared enough for the child to do what he asked.

'Perhaps you want to think about it?' he suggested

'No. I'd like to try but if the family reject me, I don't think it would help Suzu if I continued.'

'That's agreed, then,' said Yoshi, relief in his voice. 'I'll make arrangements to take you to the house myself and explain to Yasuko why you're coming. I must warn you again though, that conditions there are primitive. You won't mind that?'

'I think I know what to expect.'

'There's one more thing,' he said, his voice sharply impersonal. 'I'm afraid we shall be unable to offer you payment for this. We have not arranged anything quite like this before and as it's not official, there's no money to cover it. The family are poor and cannot afford to pay.'

She was indignant. Surely he didn't think that this was a condition of her agreement?

'I wouldn't expect any such thing,' she said, making no attempt to hide her anger. Sometimes he got it completely wrong.

He looked away. 'I'm grateful to you then. If there are any problems, you must let us know.'

Two days later he took her to Yasuko's house. Walking from the hospital, they turned into an alleyway behind some motor works. They came into a narrow street with open fronted shops and dilapidated wooden houses. Rotting vegetables and rubbish had been thrown into an open drain which ran down the middle of the street. The stench was terrible. Anna picked her way through the debris and wondered how Yoshi could consider allowing Suzu to go home under these conditions. It appalled her that children played barefoot in such filth. As she struggled to keep up with him, Yoshi told her what he proposed to say to Yasuko. 'I shall explain that you have agreed to supervise Suzu's care,' he said. 'Yasuko must understand that Suzu tires easily and must be given time to rest. Her friends will be running in and out all the time. She'll want to see them of course, but her aunt must be firm about sending them away when Suzu needs to sleep. I will impress this upon her and want you to do the same.'

'If Yasuko decides to do things her own way, how am I going to dissuade her?'

Yoshi brushed her fears aside. 'Don't worry. She'll do as we say or she knows that she won't be allowed to keep Suzu.'

'And the medicine? You'll go through that?'

'Of course. I'll explain about that. Leave it to me.'

She couldn't imagine it working. A sick child sent home to a place like this, and she, Anna, was going to be responsible for her. In spite of her assurances to Yoshi, none of her training had prepared her for this. Alone and with little knowledge of the language how was she going to manage? Yet Yoshi trusted her.

'This might well be her last visit home,' said Yoshi. 'It's very important that the family should have this time together.'

He stopped in front of a row of wooden buildings. Patched with boards and strips of tin, it bore little resemblance to a home.

'This is the house. Don't forget to remove your shoes,' he reminded her.

Yasuko was waiting and came out to greet them. With a low bow she invited them inside. Suzu was already installed on a futon where she could see what was going on in the street. Surrounded by a group of children each trying to outdo the other for claims on her attention, she was flushed with excitement.

'See what I mean?' said Yoshi. 'She's happy.'

Yasuko sent the children scampering. Seeing Anna, Suzu held out her hand and smiled. She sat down on the floor beside Suzu and began to talk to her quietly while Yoshi outlined the treatment to her aunt. The woman seemed in a good frame of mind this morning, but Anna felt that this was in deference to Yoshi. Only time would tell whether she would be accepted by the family.

Yoshi had brought the medicines with him and

now went over them carefully, afterwards placing them on a high shelf well out of reach of the other children. Then he examined Suzu.

'You're doing nicely,' he told her. 'Carry on like this and we'll have you up again soon.'

In spite of his words, Anna saw that his expression was grave. Not even to Yasuko did he convey his real thoughts. Often it's only the doctors and nurses who know the truth, she thought, and they have to bear the suffering for the family. How many times during the war had she been in the same situation with the young men in her charge who had fought so bravely for life. You have to encourage hope. Often it's all that they have to cling to.

When he left, Anna stayed on with Suzu for a while. She'd brought with her some gifts of fruit and trinkets for the children which she distributed. They were received with exclamations of pleasure while Yasuko stood by, her face impassive.

Presently Suzu drifted off to sleep and Anna rose stiffly to her feet. She spoke to Yasuko slowly in Japanese.

'I must go now. Tomorrow I'll come again.'

The woman followed her into the street. '*Arigato gozaimasu*,' she said, thanking her.

Anna acknowledged the bow murmuring, '*Sayonara*.'

The letter was waiting for her on her return to the hospital. The writing was unfamiliar and she took it with her to the dining room. She'd had nothing to eat since breakfast and she was famished. Sitting down at a table by herself, she tore it open and turned to the last page. It was from Hugh.

Dear Anna, she read. *I was delighted to receive your letter. It took me straight back to that evening we had together.*

I was sorry to hear of your decision to break off your engagement though not altogether surprised. I can understand and sympathise with your resrvations. You were none too certain that you were doing the right thing when you left.

I'm sure you're right to remain in Japan for the time being. It would have been a wasted experience had you come straight home and I can reassure you on one point. I've been to see your parents several times. They will have told you, I think, that I'm not far from them in Oxford. I enjoy their company and although I'm no doctor, I think you father is stronger. We enjoy long conversations and as you can imagine a lot of it concerns Jack. Rest assured that you are not needed here at present.

Now you have this unique opportunity to mix with Japanese people on equal terms. This might be difficult as the wife of a businessman, but a nurse is trusted in any country! I shall be interested to hear how you get on.

As for myself, I'm enjoying the training though it's hard to put the brain to work again after all this time. I'm out of practise but I think I can cope and I'm certain I made the right decision to enter the priesthood. It's something which Jack and I often discussed in camp and he encouraged me though he never thought it was for him.

I always felt though that he was a better Christian than most of us. As you well know, Jack had a strong will and in the early days in camp he was rebellious and found it harder than most of us to take the guards' brutality. Eventually though, he came to terms with it in the most extraordinary way. In spite of everything, he seemed to find peace of mind. I hope you'll be able to do the same one day, Anna.

I must close as I'm meant to be working on a thesis which is overdue. I look forward to hearing from you and hope that you'll enjoy Japan. Jack would have wished it.

Sincerely Yours, Hugh.

She folded the letter thoughtfully. She was encouraged that Hugh understood her decision over Nigel. He was the only one who did. When she spoke to anyone else about it, she got the impression that they thought she had treated Nigel unfairly. Indeed there had been times when she had to ask herself that question.

Chapter Twelve

The next evening after work, Anna walked to Yasuko's house. She was glad of the exercise, but as she picked her way along the filthy alleyway she wished it could have been taken in more salubrious surroundings.

When she arrived the smell of cooking wafted towards her. Yasuko was preparing the evening meal. Sliced vegetables and bean curd had been put in a metal container and were now sizzling over a charcoal fire.

Seeing Anna, she rose gracefully to her feet and invited her inside. Her hostility seemed to have subsided a little as, in rapid Japanese, aided by gestures, she gave a lengthy report on Suzu's health. Anna had difficulty in following the words, but she gathered that the child was stronger and had spent a good deal of time sleeping. She went across to where Suzu lay looking at a picture book which she had been given at the hospital.

'Come and sit by me,' Suzu said, patting the cushion beside her. She had learned to speak slowly so that Anna could understand. 'Will you read to me?'

Anna lowered herself onto the cushion. 'Happy to be home again?' she asked.

'I like the hospital,' said Suzu. 'But I'd rather be

here. If they allowed me to leave, I must be better, mustn't I?'

'We all hope so, Suzu.'

'I'm glad you came. Will you stay here with me now?' said Suzu.

'I must go back to the hospital. I'll come again tomorrow.'

The child seem satisfied with her reply. She looked at Anna, affection in the dark eyes that seemed larger than ever in her thin pinched face.

'My auntie says I shall be better soon,' she said. 'Then I'll be able to play with my friends. Do you think so?'

Anna hesitated. Had she understood correctly? Surely Yasuko didn't really believe that? Or was it that like herself, she couldn't bear to face the truth?

'Let's see how you get on, shall we?' she suggested, taking a thermometer out of her bag and placing it in Suzu's mouth.

'You're doing well,' she said presently, noting that her temperature had settled just above normal. 'But I think you'll have to be patient a little while longer.' She spoke partly in Japanese and partly in English. Suzu was learning a few English words and somehow they grasped the gist of each other's meaning. Often the effort made them smile.

'I shall never be well like the others,' said Suzu, wistfully. 'Auntie says it to make me feel better.'

Anna was saved from having to reply by Yasuko who came in with a bowl of green tea which she offered to Anna.

'She's happy to see you,' she told Anna. 'She asks for you all the time.'

Anna had her fingers on Suzu's wrist. 'She's all right, isn't she?' Yasuko asked anxiously.

'Yes,' said Anna, struggling with her Japanese vocabulary. She had taken the precaution of bringing a dictionary, and she now referred to it. 'She has a slight temperature. Perhaps she's excited. Have her friends been?'

'All the time,' said Yasuko. 'I have a problem keeping them away. She keeps asking them to come.'

'Doctor Egawa said she must not tire. It is very important.'

'I have told the children,' said Yasuko. 'It's hard for them to understand how ill Suzu really is.'

'Perhaps now we can wash her?' Anna suggested, bringing out some towels and soap she had brought from the hospital. Yasuko disappeared for a moment and came back with a bowl of water.

Slipping a macintosh sheet beneath the covers, Anna showed her how to wash Suzu quickly without getting the bedding wet, and then helped the child into clean clothes. When they had finished, Anna asked where she could dispose of the dirty water. Yasuko took her to a small wooden structure at the back of the house where she poured the water into a bucket which also served as a privet. The smell of urine was strong and attracted a multitude of flies, but at least it was outside the house. Suzu had her own little pot from the hospital and was not required to go out to the toilet.

On her return, Anna noticed a man sleeping on a mattress in the back room. Remembering Yoshi's remarks about the family, Anna assumed that it must be Yasuko's husband recovering from the nightshift. There was little enough room in this tiny house for the family, let alone having to nurse a seriously ill child. Yet Yasuko managed to keep the small rooms clean and neat. Somewhere in the street a transister was blaring, and smoke from a hibachi drifted through the room causing Suzu to cough. Far from ideal circumstances, but it was home to Suzu. Anna's heart went out to Yasuko for her valiant efforts to care for her sister's child. She felt privileged to be asked to help.

Anna indicated that she wanted to check the medicines and Yasuko took them off the shelf and handed them to her. All was correct and as Anna put them back, her gaze fell on a picture in a silver frame. It was of a young woman with long straight hair and serious eyes. Beside it was a vase with a single red carnation and a small Buddha image. A lighted candle burned in a glass jar.'

'Suzu's mother? asked Anna. 'Your sister?'

'*Hai*,' said Yasuko, bowing her head. '*So desu*. Hiroshima.'

'*Sumimasen* – I'm sorry,' said Anna.

As Yasuko lifted her head, their eyes met and Anna saw no bitterness, only deep sorrow and she knew that her apology had been accepted.

'I go back to the hospital now,' she said. 'Doctor Egawa will call tomorrow.'

'*Wakarimasu*,' said Yasuko. 'I understand.'

Now that the barriers between them were lowered, perhaps Yasuko would be able to trust her. But how long would it be before Yoshi would be forced to take Suzu back into hospital? For her part, Anna was willing to continue for as long as her visits helped Yasuko and made it possible for Suzu to be with her family.

It was Saturday, the day that Anna had promised to go to Jean's dinner party. She felt desperately tired and thought about making some excuse to cry off. In the end she discarded the idea as inconsiderate.

At seven she took a taxi to Shibuya. She was the last to arrive and as she entered the room, the men rose to their feet. Jean introduced her to an American couple, Liz and Bud Dixon, and Ralph and Hilary Collins, a young English couple who had recently joined the British Embassy. A bachelor called Don who worked in an insurance firm made up the party. Anna was introduced as a friend who nursed at a local hospital. She was relieved that no reference was made to Nigel, thus making further explanation unnecessary.

As Jean had promised, the meal was good and Anna, who had little interest in food these days, tucked in unashamedly. The talk was of China. The Communists under Mao Tse-Tung had ousted the Chinese Nationalists who had fled to Formosa.

Anna, listening, knew nothing of the situation. She rarely saw a newspaper or listened to the radio and if she was starved of news she managed to live without it. Perhaps, she thought, she was subconsciously insulating herself against the outside world.

'Can you bring me up to date?' she asked Bud, sitting on her right. 'I seem to be hopelessly out of touch with everything. A hospital is a world in itself.'

'I don't know that I can,' he said. 'All we know at the moment is that there's a change of government in China and this could develop into a serious situation, and threaten the stability of the whole of the Far East. We Americans have our hands full here, but I'd guess your people in Hongkong are feeling a little uncomfortable too. They ought to be building up their forces there.'

'You mean the Communists might decide to take Hongkong?' she asked.

'Could happen. Communism is a powerful force and they might have a go at extending their territories while everyone here are recovering from the effects of the war.'

'Surely the memory of war is still too fresh for anyone to start another, specially after the atomic bomb?' suggested his wife.

'China wasn't involved in that and no one doubts that Communism is spreading,' said Stan. 'I'm very thankful that you people have a presence here in Japan, Bud. It's my opinion that there are going to be some unwelcome changes out here in the near future, particularly in Korea. That's going to be the trouble spot eventually, I think. At the moment we have no idea what China has in mind, but they're not to be trusted.'

'You're right, I guess,' said Bud. 'The Japanese are thankful to have us around just now. They're in no position to defend themselves, nor their people in Korea and it might, in the end, be up to us. I don't know if you'd agree with me, Stan, but I reckon we have a good man in MacArthur?'

'I'd go along with that,' said Stan.

'So where does Japan fit into all this?' asked Hilary. Anna was glad that she was not the only one to appear politically ignorant.

'Japan has no say in it,' said Bud. 'The West are determined to make sure that Japan will never again be a military threat, not in the foreseeable future, anyway. So if there's going to be trouble in Korea, as Stan seems to think, we shall certainly be involved.'

Anna was depressed to hear this. 'So hardly have we finished one war when we could be precipitated into another?' she asked.

Bud nodded. 'With all the implications of modern warfare.'

'Surely they'll never use the bomb again?' suggested Hilary.

'Let's hope not, but it's no use burying our heads in the sand. The bomb exists and if we're in a tight spot, someone might be tempted to press the button.'

Anna shuddered. 'It doesn't bear thinking about,' she said.

'It did the trick last time, didn't it?' said Stan.

What would Yoshi have made of this conversation, she wondered. He would have been shocked to hear these men talking glibly of another war. He had spoken of trust and learning from mistakes. He couldn't conceive of anyone contemplating the use of that horrendous weapon ever again. All his work now was directed towards peaceful co-existence. Was it such an impossible dream?

'Conversely, the bomb could work as a deterrent,' Ralph pointed out. Comparitively new to the diplomatic service, he believed that everything could be settled round a table. 'It's unlikely that China has it yet, and the mere threat might be sufficient to keep them in their place.'

'Japan would never use it, even if they had it,' said Anna.

Don gave her an enquiring glance. 'I guess you're right,' he said. 'They're making damned sure that the rest of the world knows what it's like to be at the receiving end. We must hope that China is ready to listen and that in the end, as Stan suggests, the bomb will prove a strong force for peace.'

The conversation was dominated by the men, and Jean suggested that they should be left to it. Over coffee, while Hilary and Liz chatted together, Anna had an opportunity to enquire after Nigel.

'He seems to be settling down very well,' said Jean. 'He's been in Osaka for less than three months, and Stan's pleased with what he's achieved there already. I expect you know he's coming down sometime next month?'

Anna shook her head. 'No.'

'You'll be seeing him, I expect?'

'I don't think so. We've made no plans to meet.'

'You're still friends though?' asked Jean with a small frown. 'You've known each other for a long time, Anna. Surely there's no reason to avoid each other?'

Anna shrugged. 'Nor is there any particular reason to get together again.'

'Perhaps you'd like me to arrange something?' Jean suggested gently.

'No.' Anna spoke louder than she intended. Her freedom was vital to her, and she was finding a purpose to life again. She was healing and she wanted to be done with the past. If Nigel put her under pressure, all that she had gained by her independence, could be lost. She couldn't risk it.

'Don't think me rude, Jean,' she said, steadying her voice, 'but I'd rather you didn't. My hours are irregular and I wouldn't be able to commit myself. I'd love to meet you for lunch one day though.'

'We'll do that then, and as far as Nigel's concerned I won't press you. But if ever there's anything I can do to bring you two together again, I'd like to help.'

Anna smiled. 'Thanks, but that won't happen.'

'No regrets then?'

'None. I love the work and I'm getting to know a few Japanese people.'

Jean raised her brows. 'What about the language? Isn't that a disadvantage?'

'I'm having lessons. I understand quite a bit now.'

'And the social life? Don't you find it dull?'

'No. I've made a few friends. A nice New Zealand couple who took me to climb Mount Fuji.'

'You amaze me,' said Jean, looking at her with frank admiration. 'You don't let the grass grow under your feet, do you?'

'It's a different life but it's a rewarding one.' Anna paused and looked across to the other women. She didn't want to monopolise Jean but it was good to talk to her again. 'I know it must seem to you as though I used Nigel as an excuse to come out here only to ditch him, but it wasn't like that at all, I promise. I had thought it through very carefully. It's only now I realise how wrong I was.'

'You don't have to convince me, my dear. I understand.'

'I want you to know why I don't think there's much point in trying to get together again.'

Jean sighed. 'Then I must let it rest.' she said. 'I promised I wouldn't try to influence you. I'm not keeping my word, but I have to admit that I hoped it would be different.' She searched Anna's eyes to reassure herself that she really meant what she said. 'Let's keep in touch though, Anna. I shall want to know what you're getting up to.'

It was late when Don and his wife dropped her back at the hospital. Helen was in the entrance hall, having been out with Dave.

'My, you're looking glamorous,' she said. 'Where've you been?'

'Out to dinner.'

'Anyone interesting?'

'With Jean. The people I stayed with when I arrived here.'

Helen was immediately interested. 'Did you see Nigel?'

Anna shook her head, smiling. 'No.'

'Pity. I thought you two might get together again. Actually I've been wanting to see you. I have something to tell you.'

'Come to my room then. I can offer you a glass of sherry.'

Helen settled herself on the bed and accepted the glass Anna offered her.

'Dave and I are leaving in two weeks time,' she announced.

'Two weeks! That's awfully soon.'

'I know. There's been a change of plan. They've found someone to replace Dave here and he's anxious to get cracking on this new job. His family wanted us to have the wedding there anyway, so it makes sense.'

'I'm going to miss you, Helen.'

'Me too, but you must come and visit us.'

'Maybe. It's a long way though.'

'You know, Anna,' Helen said slowly, sipping her sherry, 'I hate leaving you on your own here.'

'I'm not on my own. I'm getting to know people. I'm happy here.'

Helen looked at her closely. 'Are you really? It doesn't strike me like that. There seem to be so many unresolved problems in your life.'

Anna laughed. 'I'll get them sorted out sometime,' she said lightly.

Helen looked towards the dressing table.

'Is that your brother?' she asked.

'Yes.' Anna picked up the photograph and handed it to Helen.

'There's an incredible likeness.'

'Well, we were twins. That was taken the last time I saw him. Mum and Dad wanted us both done, so reluctantly we went off to the photographers. Had he lived, I expect he'd have been very different now.'

'After his experiences, yes,' said Helen, slowly, then, 'They shall not grow old as we that are left grow old . . .'

'Exactly. But I expect they would have liked the chance.'

Helen got up and put the photo back. Then she turned to face Anna. 'Are you getting over it, Anna? Now you've been here some time, it must be easier?'

'I think it is. I don't want to carry a vendetta for Jack and he certainly wouldn't want me to. Sometimes though, it seems that's what I'm doing and I can't help myself.'

'It'll pass,' said Helen reassuringly. 'Now the war's over we should be trying to build bridges. It won't help if you keep looking back. I do want you to be happy, Anna.'

Anna sighed. 'I know, and let's say most of the time I am.'

'There's something else I want to ask you,' said Helen. 'How's Suzu?'

'Back home again. Yoshi thought that it was best for her and I think perhaps he's right.'

'Yoshi's very wise. He told Dave what you're doing for her. I think it's just great.'

'I'm glad to do it.'

'But Yoshi's concerned about you. He feels that he asked you to take on more than he should have done.

He wanted me to talk to you about it. You do look awfully tired, you know.'

'Hardly surprising. I've been to a dinner party and I found the experience rather shattering. They were talking politics and I was completely out of touch. I'm an awful ignoramus.'

'We do get involved here, don't we? Probably to the exclusion of everything else.' She hesitated and then went on slowly. 'Anyway how do you feel about Suzu? Can you cope?'

'Of course. I'm glad he asked me to keep an eye on her. I get on all right with her aunt now so that makes it easier.

Helen's blue eyes rested on Anna thoughtfully. 'I don't think I could have done it, you know. I'm not sure Dave would even let me.'

'That's the great advantage of being independent. You can do as you like.'

'I'll reassure Yoshi then. It's funny, but even with his authority he's not at all sure how to handle foreigners, or let's say foreign women. But I think you should take it as a compliment that he chose you for the job rather than a Japanese girl. I wonder what the real reason was?'

'I can't imagine. Perhaps he thought it would be good for me.'

'Does he know how you feel about the Japanese?'

'Oh yes. On the journey back from Hakone, I made it abundantly clear. I'm afraid I got really angry.'

Helen was startled. 'You didn't! But it wasn't his fault.'

'I don't think he's aware how awful it was in those camps. He tried to explain it away logically, and I lost my cool.' She hadn't meant to tell Helen. She knew it would only upset her.

'So what happened?'

'He was quite calm about it. But he did ask if I thought his was the only country to blame for what happened during the war. It's all right, you know. We spoke frankly and perhaps it was no bad thing.'

But she could see that Helen was still troubled.

'Please don't worry, Helen. I apologised and I think he knew why I got so angry. If he hadn't done, he would never have asked me to look after Suzu. In fact this might have been the reason why he did.'

'Perhaps,' said Helen. 'I'm glad you told me anyway, because Dave and I want you to come to a little dinner we're having at our favourite restaurant before we leave. Dave's asking one of his medical friends along and his girl friend, another New Zealander, a staff nurse. Yoshi's coming too, so perhaps you two can make it up. There'll just be the six of us.'

'Is it a sort of farewell party?'

'Not really. There'll be a general one at the hospital for all our friends. This is special for close friends, and we want you to come.'

'Thank you, Helen. Of course, I'd love to.'

'We've booked a table for Saturday week.' Helen got up and stretched. 'I must let you go to bed. You look exhausted.'

She started towards the door, then paused and, turning, came back and kissed Anna. 'You know, I'm going to miss you terribly.'

Anna visited Suzu every day the following week. Her routine was always the same. She checked Suzu's pulse and took her temperature, which could be erratic. She had bouts of sickness and listlessness. At other times she perked up and drank the soup that

Anna brought in a flask from the hospital, reinforced with vitamins. Yasuko always had hot water ready and together they washed the child and changed her clothes and Anna took the dirty linen back to the hospital to wash. Sometimes she stayed on for a while to read Suzu a story or, as she became more fluent, chatted in her slowly improving Japanese, to Yasuko.

The following Sunday she was off duty and visited in the morning. On the way she stopped at a stall to buy fruit and vegetables, also sweets to hand out to the children in the alleyway as she went along. They waited for her to come now and ran after her, practising their smattering of English. A few of the older people, recognising her, bowed as she passed. She was never quite sure how she should respond. Social intricacies were quite beyond her, and she thought it safer to stick to an inclination of the head and a smile. Their curiosity had changed to a kind of approval. It might be that they'd heard from Yasuko that she was trying to help. The thought pleased her.

It was a pleasant day and her spirits were high. Far from these visits becoming a burden, she was enjoying them. She felt she was visiting friends, and her affection for Suzu and her family deepened. It really seemed that against all odds Suzu was coming through this phase of her illness and was at last growing stronger.

But as soon as she entered the house she saw there had been a sudden reversal. Suzu's eyes were closed and her breathing was fast and shallow. Anna, feeling her forehead, ascertained that she had a high fever. Yasuko hovered nearby in agitation.

'We must get her to hospital immediately,' Anna said. 'I'll go and arrange it.'

She hurried back to the ward and spoke to Sister Sano. An ambulance was sent and in a short time Suzu was once again installed in her hospital bed.

Anna remained beside her all day. She was afraid to leave even when Suzu slept. She waited impatiently for Yoshi, confident that he was the only one who could halt the rapid deterioration. They had been trying to phone him all day, but there was no reply from his house. Then, towards evening, he came on the ward and went straight to Suzu. Anna had never seen him so upset.

'I blame myself,' he said, examining her. 'I should have come sooner, but I took the family out for the day. When did you bring her in?'

'I went to see her about eleven this morning and arranged an ambulance immediately. Yasuko said she had been up all night with her.'

'Have you been with her all day?'

Anna nodded and turned away. She felt near to tears and knew that Yoshi would disapprove of this unprofessional display of emotion.

'We'll have to give her another transfusion,' he said. 'It's the only chance.'

Soon the equipment was set up and Suzu fell into a quiet sleep. Not until then did Yoshi drag his attention away from her to look at Anna. His expression was no longer inscrutible. His concern for her was clear and meeting his gaze she saw something else, something besides concern, which quickened her heart.

'Have you not eaten?' he asked her.

'I had something at lunch time.'

'There's nothing more we can do at the moment. She'll sleep and we won't know till the morning whether she's going to rally. You must go to bed, Anna. You look exhausted.'

Reluctantly she left the ward, but not till the early hours did she fall into a troubled sleep. She was certain that Suzu would wake and ask for her yet she dare not return. Yoshi would almost certainly be spending the night on the ward. She longed to be there with him, but she had to comply with his orders.

The next morning there was little change in Suzu's condition. Yasuko came early and stayed all day. Anna divided her time between Suzu and her other duties. Sometime during the morning Yoshi called in to check on Suzu and then left.

Mid-afternoon, Sister ordered Anna to take a break.

'I don't want to see you back here till the evening,' she told her firmly. 'The child is rallying and there'll be little change before then.'

Anna forced herself to eat something and, feeling the need for fresh air, walked towards the park which was a favourite place of hers. She sat down on a wooden bench beside the lake and watched the branches of the weeping willow stroking the water, rippling the smooth surface.

Her thoughts turned to Yoshi. If anyone could save Suzu, he could. He would never give up until he had tried everything, but she knew that even he would eventually come to the end of his resources. She feared the child would not recover this time. It was only a matter of hours and, anxious though she was to return to the ward, she was almost afraid to do so. Again and again she looked at her watch. Finally, unable to stay away any longer, she got up and walked back.

Suzu was sleeping peacefully, Yasuko by her side. Her breathing was easier and Yasuko said she had taken a little soup. Hearing Anna talking to her aunt, she opened her eyes and reached out her hand. Anna took it and smiled at her, finding comfort in this physical contact. Contented, Suzu lay back on her pillow, a high unhealthy colour in her cheeks.

Presently Anna was aware of a difference in the rhythm of her breathing. Her eyes were closed and the hand in hers was limp. Anna bent her head to the child's cheek and listened, willing her little heart to beat. Nothing. Suzu had given up her struggle for life. Choking back her tears, Anna looked across to Yasuko and saw that she already knew: she was weeping silently. Anna got up and went around the bed, putting a hand on her shoulder.

'I'll take you home now,' she said, gently.

Yasuko shook her head. 'Let me stay,' she whispered. 'Just a little longer.'

Anna left her with her grief. There was a procedure to follow, and she went into the office to put it in motion. Sister Sano came and a screen was put round the bed.

'I'm going to take Yasuko home now,' Anna said presently. 'She can't be allowed to go alone.'

They walked together, Yasuko still blinded by tears. Anna took her arm and guided her along the crowded pavement and when they turned into the street and neared the house, people seeing them understood that the news was bad and that Suzu would not be returning. They stood silently, their heads bowed in respect and sympathy as they passed.

Anna left Yasuko in the care of her family. When she returned to the ward, Suzu had been taken away.

Chapter Thirteen

As a nurse, Anna was far from unfamiliar with death. Any death always left her with a sense of bereavement, but with Suzu she felt a deep personal loss unlike anything she had felt since Jack's demise. Her heart ached with a physical pain which remained with her for days, and at night she lay thinking about the child and wondering if she had resented the tragedy that deprived her of a mother and resulted in her own illness. She saw no evidence of this. She believed that Suzu had known she was going to die. Children like animals, were uncomplicated and receptive to the truth. There was an innocence about them, their spirits as yet unaffected by life.

In her experience she found that people faced death in many ways. Some with resignation as a release from pain or anxiety, others with a deep faith met it with trust, but some she had known had fought it with a terrible fear.

Had Suzu been afraid? She didn't think so. It rather depended on what Yasuko had told her about how her mother had died, whether she had softened the harsh reality for her. In any event it was seen in a different light in Japan, where death was accepted as inevitable as life itself. These people have a wisdom, thought Anna, enabling them to accept tragedy in a way that we in the West have lost.

Anna searching for relief found it in writing to Hugh.

I have grown so fond of this child and now she's gone I feel bereft. I went to her funeral yesterday. She was cremated and her ashes interned in a Buddhist cemetery in a lovely spot under pine trees. Here in Japan most people are both Shintoists and Buddhists as the two religions are inter-related. They believe that it's only the ashes of her sick body that lie there while her soul is very much alive. Once a year, quite soon in fact, they have a special festival when the souls of the departed come back to visit them so the family are not devastated.

The sorrow I feel for Suzu is not the same as when Jack died. I feel no anger or bitterness but a kind of acceptance and relief that she's no longer suffering though I'm not at all sure what replaces this in the next world, if there is one.

She paused thoughtfully. It was strange that she had little difficulty in believing that Suzu's spirit was even now homing towards her mother yet she could not accept that Jack was existing somewhere out there in limbo. He was dead and she would never see him again. That was the end of it. All that remained were memories that grew fainter as the years passed. Yet there were times as in those dreams, when his presence was so real. She picked up her pen and continued.

I've been dreaming about Jack recently. Sometimes his image is so clear that I can almost believe that he is alive. In one of my dreams he was one of a working party in the jungle, breaking up rocks. I could feel the heat and hear the screeching of jungle birds as the men worked under the blazing sun. A guard was standing over Jack with a bayonette urging him to work faster, yet he could barely lift the pickaxe. He looked so old that I wondered for a moment if it really was him. I saw the anguish, the hatred in his eyes. It didn't seem to fit in with what you called his peace of mind. It's troubled me ever since. I can't understand why I should be having these dreams when I haven't seen Jack for so long.

Perhaps you'll be able to make some sense of it all, Hugh? I look forward to hearing from you.

Sincerely, Anna.

She read the letter through again and then put it in an envelope and addressed it to him at the theological college.

The next day she was on duty supervising the drug round when Sister Sano told her that Dr Egawa wanted to see her in his office.

'Now?' she asked. The morning was the busiest time on the ward and they needed all the staff available.

'It's all right,' said Sister. 'I'll carry on here.'

Anna went downstairs to his office and knocked on the door. As she entered, Yoshi looked up from the papers strewn about his desk.

'Thank you for coming,' he said. 'Please sit down.'

She thought how tired and pre-occupied he looked.

'I want to thank you for what you did for Suzu and her family,' he said. 'We failed to save her, but thanks to you she was able to be with her family for those last few days. It meant a lot to them and to her.'

'I wish I could have done more.'

'It's always sad when a child dies,' he said gently. 'I

went to see her aunt afterwards. She wanted me to thank you for what you did.' He was speaking slowly, choosing his words carefully. 'She asked me to explain to you that at first she found it hard to accept your help. She not unnaturally associated you with what happened to Suzu and her mother, but she now realises that she was wrong and asks for your forgiveness.'

Anna was moved by his words. She was still feeling emotional and found it hard to control her feelings.

'There's nothing to forgive,' she said, listlessly.

'You mustn't be upset,' said Yoshi, watching her. 'Had she lived, she would never have been well and active like her cousins. These things are often for the best.'

'That's hard to believe.'

'Nevertheless we have to accept it and concentrate on the work ahead. It's the living who need us, not the dead.'

There was something more she wanted to tell him. The conversation at Jean's dinner party the other evening rankled with her. The price of war seemed to have been too readily forgotten. She struggled to put her thoughts into words.

'I'm beginning to change my mind about the bomb,' she said, hesitating before going on. 'I'm coming to the view that I don't think it can be justified under any circumstances.'

He brushed this aside impatiently. 'I don't want to go into the political implications of that now,' he said, 'I suggest you take Yasuko's words as they were intended. It was her peace offering to you, in memory of Suzu.'

She was hurt by his brusqueness. Of course she understood what Yasuko was saying.

He relented a little. 'You should try and go to our O-Bon festival next week, Anna. It might help you to understand the way we feel about death. You can be sure Suzu's family will be taking part. If you go down to the river on that night, you might see Suzu's candle floating down, guiding her back again to the spirit world.'

'I'd very much like to go,' said Anna.

'I would come with you but it's a family occasion and I must go home. If you cared to join them, I'm sure Suzu's family would welcome you.'

'I couldn't impose on them at such a time,' she protested.

'They would feel honoured that you wanted to be with them. Believe me.'

When the time came, she thought she would go alone to see the festival, after first going to Suzu's house. Though she had no intention of intruding on the family, it seemed important to make this short pilgrimage before going down to the river to watch the festivities.

It had been raining and she picked her way through the puddles, past the rows of poor dwellings where tonight families were coming together to celebrate. The glow of the lanterns lighted her way down the street.

A small boy, recognising her, ran up and stopped in front of her. He held a bean cake in his fist which he offered her. She accepted it with a smile.

'You go to Suzu's house?' he asked her.

'I'm going to the river,' she told him.

'Tonight we light a candle for Suzu,' he said. 'Please wait a minute.'

He ran off to fetch his friends and they accompanied her until they reached the house, where they went in to tell Yasuko of her arrival. Anna waited outside wondering whether to slip away unnoticed, but it was already too late. Yasuko came out and, bowing low, murmured, 'You are welcome. Please come in.'

There was nothing for it but to follow her. The small house was full. Silence fell as Anna was introduced to each one as Suzu's friend, the nurse from the hospital. Though she sensed their unease at her presence, she felt obliged to accept the delicacies they offered her.

'You'll come with us to the river?' asked Yasuko.

Anna shook her head. 'I think this is a special time, just for your family.'

'Please come.' Yasuko smilingly pressed her.

Afraid of giving offence, Anna nodded and the cavalcade made their way down the street, intermingling with other families. In the distance she could hear the bands playing and as they reached the bridge the scene was lighted by the flames from the bonfires. People clapped their hands and danced to the rhythm of the music. Some of the men, stimulated by liquor, staggered from one group to another, clasping bottles. Anna, standing on the bridge with Yasuko, looked down on the calm water and saw hundreds of little lights passing under the bridge and floating away into the distance.

They moved on, andYasuko led her to a stall where they bought two small floats.

'One for Suzu and one for my sister,' she said.

But Anna wanted to launch her love for Suzu in its own little craft and purchased one herself. These they carried to the water's edge and Yasuko told the children to take a taper and light the tiny candles.

The floats were then put onto the water and they stood close together to watch as they were caught up in the current and began their journey towards the ocean.

'Each one represents a soul,' explained Yasuko. 'Suzu is on her way to her mother now.'

With a corner of her kimono sleeve, she wiped away a tear. Then she smiled.

'We must remember that this is a happy occasion,' she said, but whatever they believed, Anna suspected that the gaiety of the festival could not relieve the pain of those more recently bereaved.

'Now we go home and have something to eat,' said Yasuko. 'Will you come with us?'

Anna shook her head. She had intruded long enough on the family's grief.

'But we are honoured that you're here to share this special time with us,' Yasuko insisted.

'I have to go to the hospital,' explained Anna with a regretful smile, and Yasuko accepted this.

She walked back alone, pondering the evening events. She was glad she had come and felt strangely happy that Suzu and her mother were united far beyond the limits of death held by her own culture.

Yoshi had not been on the ward for three days. A younger doctor had taken his place and was looking after his patients. Anna searched for him with a sense of urgency. She wanted to tell him about the evening she had spent with Suzu's family while it was still fresh in her mind.

Helen might have known where to contact him, but she had already left the ward and was now staying with friends until she and Dave left for New Zealand.

'Do you know when Dr Egawa will be back?' Anna asked Sister.

Sister Sano shrugged. 'We never know where he is,' she replied. 'I believe he is attending a conference, in which case he could be away for a week or more.'

'And if there's an emergency? Surely he leaves an address where he can be contacted?'

'The ward is adequately covered by the other doctors. They can cope with any emergency. If it's important that you know you could ask Mother Agnes.'

She had no reasonable excuse for asking, but the days seemed endless when Yoshi failed to make his daily visit to the ward. Why had he become so important to her? She admired him, certainly. He was a brilliant doctor and she valued his friendship. There was more to it than that though. She was after all a mature woman in control of her emotions and it worried her that she seemed unable to prevent her thoughts constantly returning to him.

She wondered whether he'd be back in time for Helen and Dave's farewell dinner on Saturday. If he was absent the evening would lose a great deal of it's appeal for her.

On Saturday, she took special care with her appearance. She had been to the hairdresser and now wore a new dress which she'd had made in a cream silk, its soft folds flattering to her figure. Putting the final touches to her make-up, she viewed herself in the mirror with approval.

When she arrived at the restaurant, Dave and Helen were already sitting at the bar with Max and Holly. Anna had met them both before in the hospital and they exchanged greetings. There was no sign of

Yoshi. Her heart sank. So it was as she thought, he had been unable to make it. The eager anticipation with which she had looked forward to the evening evaporated.

'We've settled for *saki*. Are you happy with that?' Dave asked her. 'Or would you prefer something else?

'She had developed a taste for the hot rice wine.'That's fine. Thanks, Dave.'

'We don't know if Yoshi's going to make it,' Helen said, confirming her fears. 'He's been away all week, but he promised he'd try and get back in time.'

'Where did he go?' enquired Anna.

'He had to go to Kobe. He's giving a series of lectures there. You can never be sure with him. Yoshi never says no when people ask him to do something. He stays as long as he's needed.'

'If he doesn't turn up, we'll have to make the most of it without him,' said Dave. 'Apart from the hospital party, it's the last opportunity we'll have to see you, Anna, because Helen and I are off next Saturday.'

Anna's back was to the door, but she sensed it the moment Yoshi walked in.

'Sorry I'm late,' he said, joining them. 'I had to call in at the hospital after I got back from the Kansai.'

His gaze dwelt on Anna a moment longer than was necessary. Meeting his eyes, she felt a surge of pure happiness. The evening had been saved after all.

'We're used to that, Yoshi,' Helen teased him. 'We know patients take priority. We're just thankful you turned up at all. We half expected you to say you were too busy.'

'I wouldn't do that,' said Yoshi. 'I've been greatly looking forward to it. I must say,' he said, looking round, 'you've chosen a very exclusive restaurant. Not a place I would normally come to.'

'We wanted something special,' said Dave. 'It's the last time we'll be together.' He led them to a reserved table overlooking a lake, and the waitress brought the menus.

'This has to be in lieu of a trip to Nikko, Anna,' Helen said. 'We were hoping to arrange that, but it's something you'll have to see another time. You must get to the Alps too and Kyoto, the old capital. Whatever you do, don't miss that.'

'Perhaps you'll come with us sometime,' suggested Holly.

'I'd really like to. There's so much I want to see before I leave.'

'Sounds as though you could do with a few weeks off,' said Dave. 'Not a bad idea before you go home. Hotels are no problem these days, are they Yoshi? They're not expensive and always spotlessly clean.'

Yoshi turned to Anna. 'Are you returning to England soon then?' he asked.

'Not just yet. I promised Mother Agnes I'd stay on for a while.'

'We'd be sorry to lose you, especially with Helen leaving us,' said Yoshi. 'Tell me, did you go to the O-Bon festival?'

'Yes. I went with Yasuko and her family.'

'That was a nice idea,' said Yoshi. 'I'm sure she appreciated it.'

'It wasn't intended.' Anna felt that some explanation was needed because Holly and Max were not to know what she was talking about. 'I went to the O-ban festival with Suzu's family,' she explained to them. 'The little girl died in the hospital. I was walking to the river when I met some children who insisted on coming with me to Suzu's house. Yasuko saw me and invited me to join then. It was kind of her.' It still upset her to talk about it.

'And why not?' said Yoshi. 'You were Suzu's friend. It was the natural thing to do.'

She felt better about it now Yoshi had stated his approval. She hoped he would let the matter drop, but he seemed to have forgotten the others, and addressed his remarks to her.

'Do you agree that the festival is a happy occasion?' he asked.

'Yes and no. The concept is a happy one. Yasuko and I lit candles for Suzu, but of course she was feeling sad – so was I.'

'I'm not surprised,' said Holly. 'I think it was very brave of you to go.'

Yoshi looked at her and smiled. He obviously knew these two.

'Grief passes all the sooner when it is unaccompanied by anger,' he said, giving Anna food for thought. Helen glanced at Yoshi, then at Anna but she said nothing.

The soup bowls had been taken away, and their cup refilled with *sake*. The next course was brought to the table with sauces and small portions of radish.

'When are you and Helen getting married?' Yoshi asked Dave.

'Two weeks after arriving in New Zealand,' said Dave. 'We'll spend that time with the family and meeting friends and house hunting. There's a lot to be done before I start work again.'

'You'll come and see us, Yoshi, won't you?' Helen urged him.

He smiled at her. 'I think it's unlikely in the foreseeable future. It would be difficult to find the time.'

'I'm keen to fix up a conference once I find the necessary contacts,' said Dave. 'I think there're a lot of people in our country who would be very interested to hear what you have to say. Don't you think so, Holly? Once Holly gets back, you'll have two medical contacts in New Zealand, Yoshi.'

'We'll be coming on leave in a few months time,' said Holly. 'I don't know how long we'll be staying though.' She threw Max an enquiring glance.

'We're thinking of getting married,' said Max.

'We were wondering when the announcement would be made,' said Dave, with a grin. 'It's been a long time coming.'

'We couldn't decide where we wanted to live,' said Holly.

'It seems if I want Holly, I'll have to settle for her country,' said Max.

'There you are then, Yoshi. Plenty of contacts. If we could line up some lectures for you, Yoshi, would you be willing to visit us?

'That would certainly be a very strong incentive for coming,' Yoshi agreed, 'and with the added pleasure of seeing you all again, I could hardly refuse.'

'Perhaps you could persuade Tama to come too?' suggested Helen. 'You could bring the whole family.'

'That would be a problem. Tama doesn't like travelling.'

'We've never met her, Yoshi,' said Helen, gazing at him with her searching blue eyes. 'I wish we had. You've been such a good friend to us and we don't even know her.'

'You understand the difficulties. She's happy at home. She doesn't speak your language so she feels there would be no point in meeting. You could only smile at each other.'

'You could translate for us,' pressed Helen.

'I wouldn't enjoy that,' said Yoshi, brushing the idea aside. 'Perhaps next time you visit Japan, she'll be speaking English.'

The small cups had been frequently recharged as course after course was brought to them, and Anna was feeling pleasantly relaxed. Perhaps it was the wine too that made Helen so bold in her questioning of Yoshi.

'Doesn't Tama mind you coming out with us, Yoshi?' she asked. 'I would resent David showing some foreigners round New Zealand and leaving me at home.'

'Helen, don't keep on,' said Dave. 'There isn't the same language problem, is there? If you go on about it, Yoshi will go home. You'll make him feel guilty.'

Yoshi laughed. 'Of course she doesn't. I don't feel at all guilty. Helen's entitled to ask and it gives me the opportunity of explaining. Tama and I have an understanding. She's happy with the children and her friends and wouldn't enjoy international gatherings.'

'But isn't she interested in your work?' Helen pressed.

'Of course she is, and I often discuss it with her but that doesn't mean that she wants to come to the hospital and meet my medical friends, not even the Japanse ones.'

Dave was getting hot under the collar. 'Surely you know Helen, things are different here. You can't judge everything by the way we do them at home.'

Helen was contrite. 'Sorry, Yoshi. I didn't mean to be critical but I wish I knew Tama. I'm sure I'd like her.'

'I know what you mean,' said Yoshi. 'I'll tell

her you were asking about her and see if I can persuade her to learn English. I'm sure that if she understood your language, nothing would give her greater pleasure than to socialise with people like you. The language is the problem.'

Dave cut in quickly. 'I think what Helen's trying to say is what we both feel and probably Anna as well, that we have enjoyed living in your country and wanted to get to know as many people as possible. We've met with kindness and courtesy here and you've made us most welcome, Yoshi. That's one of the purposes of tonight, to say thank you for your friendship.'

The conversation drifted on with the men having some digs at the Americans.

'It could have been a lot worse for you Japanese,' said Dave. 'Now, if the New Zealanders had been in occupation . . .'

But Yoshi brushed aside the joke. 'The Americans have done a lot for us. They're helping to put us on our feet again, and I believe we will be able to build on that.'

'When we get home we'll follow events here with great interest,' said Dave. 'I think this country has a great future. Your people are industrious and conscientious and they're determined to take advantage of the opportunities offered. One day I bet we'll find you leading the rest of the world in the economic field. If we want to compete we can't afford to rest on our laurels. We're going to have to work hard to keep pace with you.'

'All of which will be of little use unless we work together for peace,' said Yoshi seriously. 'None of us can afford another war. Our planet simply won't sustain it.'

'I've already heard people speaking of the possibility of a war in Korea,' said Anna.

Yoshi nodded. 'Now there's a Communist government in China, I can understand their fear. It's certainly a threat and we're helpless to intervene or even protest. We have no say in the political arena these days.'

'But is another war a real possibility?' pressed Anna.

'We have a lot of people in Korea,' said Yoshi, "but there's little we can do about it. We can only hope that the leaders will talk through every alternative before resorting to force.'

So Yoshi already knew how tenuous was his dream for peace. Anna felt sure he would never give up working for it nevertheless.

'If the worst comes to the worst,' said Max, 'it would be localised, I suppose?'

'One never can tell,' said Yoshi. 'But I trust the Americans – and of course – yourselves,' he added with a smile.

'Japan will never seem the same to me again,' said Helen. 'When we leave here a part of me will always remain.'

'You have the mind of a Japanese,' said Yoshi. 'Perhaps you could write a *haiku*.'

'I've written several. I love Japanese poetry.'

'I'm afraid I won't be able to come and see you off,' Yoshi said. 'Our good-byes will have to be said at the hospital.'

'It's as good a place as any,' said Dave. 'That's where we first met, after all.'

'I'd like to come to the docks,' said Anna. 'May I?'

Holly turned to her. 'If you like we'll go together,' she said, 'and bring plenty of hankies.'

'That would be great,' said Helen, nodding. 'And don't be sad. We'll meet up again one day.' She looked towards Yoshi. 'You will keep an eye on Anna for us, won't you? Sometimes I don't think she knows how to look after herself.'

'Helen!' Anna remonstrated. 'Of course I'm all right and perfectly capable of looking after myself. Don't take any notice, Yoshi.'

'I'll do my best,' said Yoshi. 'Anna's done a great deal for us and we must take care of her.' He was smiling at her. She felt the colour rising in her cheeks.

'Thank you,' said Helen, suddenly serious. 'I feel better about leaving her now.'

When the day of departure came, Anna was at the quayside with Max and Holly and many others, to see Dave and Helen off.

Kissing Helen good-bye, she couldn't control her tears.

'Thanks for everything, Helen. I'm really going to miss you both.'

'Come and see us, if you can,' said Helen, hugging her. 'Perhaps on your way home. And Anna, be happy. Make the most of your time here. There's so much that's lovely about this country and the people. Please try and forget the past.'

'I'm working on it,' Anna reassured her. 'I'm very fond of Japan.'

'You know,' said Helen, taking a long look at her, 'I have a strange feeling you might be here for quite a long time.'

'I doubt that, but long enough to lay a few ghosts perhaps.' She spoke lightly because she didn't want Helen to see how utterly lost she felt at that moment.

As she watched the ship leaving the quay and

slowly make its way out to sea, dragging with it a tangle of multi-coloured streamers, Holly came close and took her hand. Silently they stood, watching. Anna's thoughts went back to the time, six months ago now, when she arrived here and Nigel had been waiting to meet her. She had never dreamed the course her life would take. It could have been so much simpler but then life rarely was.

The ship was making its way out of the port now and she could no longer see Helen and Dave standing among the passengers still waving to their friends on the quayside. The streamers were floating forlornly on the muddy water, the ship's last link with land severed.

'Come back and have a snack with us,' suggested Holly.

Anna thanked her, but just now she needed to be alone. 'Could I make it some other time?' she asked Holly.

'Of course. I understand how you feel. Don't ever feel lonely, will you, Anna? Helen might not be here, but I am.' She went off in search of Max.

Anna found a trishaw to take her back to the hospital. She went up to her room and looked out of the window. Just at this moment, everything looked as bleak as the view and the absence of her friends was a dull pain in her heart.

Chapter Fourteen

'I'm thinking of moving you to another ward,' said Mother Agnes when she called Anna into her office.

Anna received this with dismay. Wasn't her work satisfactory? Had Mother disapproved of her involvement with Suzu? She had taken over from Helen on the children's ward and had only been there six weeks.

'May I ask why?' she asked. 'I love that ward.'

'This is something of an emergency. Sister Ito is to have an operation and I'm looking for someone to take on the women's general ward in her absence. There are a number of foreign patients there and we need someone in charge who speaks English. It means promotion, Anna, and you'll be gaining experience. I'm asking you to take on the responsibilities of Ward Sister.

She didn't want to move, not even for promotion. She loved those children. Everyone on the ward had been affected by Suzu's death though not perhaps as deeply as she had. They needed to recover from it and they could help each other in this. It was important for her to remain there at least for the time being.

'How long would it be for?' Anna asked.

'Until such time as Sister Ito is fit again. Possibly some months, perhaps longer.'

Anna hesitated. She had an idea that her personal reasons might not be acceptable to Mother Agnes. She would have to offer something more practical.

'I don't think I've had enough experience yet to take charge of a ward,' she said.

'I think that's for me to judge. I know you were very fond of Suzu, Anna, and felt her death keenly. Is that the reason why you want to stay?'

'Wherever I am I shall miss her. Mother, did you mind me visiting her outside the hospital? I thought Dr Egawa . . .'

'Dr Egawa consulted me before he asked you to supervise Suzu. We appreciate what you did for her, Anna but I feel it might be no bad thing for you to have a change at the moment, at least a temporary one. Losing a young patient can have a devastating effect on the carers, but that is not my main reason for asking. We need a European in charge of Women's General to take the place of Sister Ito. I've had some very good reports of your work and you're the one who comes to mind. You'll have a good supporting staff working under you.'

Anna was silent. There was another reason which she couldn't disclose to Mother Agnes. It meant that she would see less of Yoshi. At the moment with the loss of Suzu as well as Helen leaving, she felt she couldn't cope with it. Perhaps this astute woman might suspect she was becoming too friendly with the Japanese doctor, but Anna could think of no reason why she should. There was no possible way she could know what was in her mind.

'You're hesitating, my dear.' Mother Agnes was waiting for her reply, her eyes questioning Anna. 'I don't understand why?'

'I shall miss the children terribly.'

Mother Agnes tapped her pencil thoughtfully on the desk.

'You are happy with us here, aren't you, Anna?'

The question was unexpected. 'Yes. I love the work,' she answered guardedly.

'Now Helen's left us, you must be lonely at times?'

'I miss her certainly.'

'But you're not thinking of returning home yet?'

'Not yet. I'd like to stay on for a while.'

'I hope you will. You have become a valuable member of the nursing staff. You'll let me know when you are thinking of leaving, won't you?'

'Of course. The only problem might be if my father's health deteriorates again. I think then I'd have to go home and it could happen quite suddenly.'

'I understand that, of course. Now, tell me, what is your real objection to moving to another ward?'

'I'll miss the children. I expected to be on their ward a lot longer.'

Mother Agnes' voice became business-like. 'You must know from experience that when you're asked to take on further responsibility, unless you have a very good reason against it, it's almost an obligation, a duty, to accept. So few people are able to take responsibility. You are capable of it and we need your co-operation over this.'

She could prevaricate no more. 'I'm sorry, Mother. Of course I'll go.'

'I'm glad to hear it. I gather you're making good progress with the language now?'

'Yes. I'm having lessons. I'm learning a lot from the children, too. They enjoy correcting my mistakes.'

'The nurses and patients appreciate the fact that you're taking the trouble to learn their language.'

'I'd be missing a lot if I didn't at least try to communicate with them.'

'Well then,' said Mother Agnes, briskly. 'They'll be expecting you on the ward first thing Monday morning. See how it goes, Anna, and let me know.'

It took Anna a while to settle down on Women's General. The ward itself was small but included half a dozen private rooms, all of which were occupied by foreigners. All the patients were in for short term treatment and were supervised by two doctors – a Japanese consultant and an Australian. Anna had been right in thinking that none of Yoshi's patients were here which meant there was no reason for him to visit. She hadn't seen him for days.

She missed the children and longed to be back with them. Occasionally she found some excuse to visit the ward. She wanted to keep in touch and it was an opportunity to practise her Japanese. Her brief visits never coincided with Yoshi's rounds, which were made at the busiest times of day when she was required on her own ward.

More and more often, when she got back to her room in the evenings, usually tired and despondent, she was overwhelmed with loneliness. She missed Helen more than she had thought possible. No more dropping in for a chat. No unexpected invitations for the week-ends. She had met up with Holly one lunchtime in the dining room, and they had talked about an outing together, but so far nothing had come of it. Anna felt she did not know her well enough to broach the subject again. It had to come from Holly. She had been with her Japanese teacher to the Bunraku theatre to see the famous puppet plays, but she found the girl formal and uninteresting and she preferred her own company. Keen to experience another aspect of Japanese life, she enrolled on a course of flower arrangement, sitting cross legged on the floor and endeavouring to imitate the displays demonstrated by a Japanese who looked more like a Sumo wrestler than a flower arranger.

As the days dragged by she questioned whether she was right in staying on at a time when her parents would have welcomed her return. She had received no letters from them recently and this worried her. Sensibly she told herself that, had there been a sudden change in her father's condition, her mother would have written or cabled. Nonetheless she felt restless and depressed.

She also had to face the fact that it was unlikely that she would see much more of Yoshi. Perhaps it was just as well. There were times when her wish to see him was so intense, that she wondered if she were in love with him. Then she pulled herself up sharply. How could she even consider it with Jack ever present in her thoughts? In the past, her hatred of the Japanese had fuelled her grief and sustained her. Now she saw them in a very different light, and counted some of them as friends. But to even consider that she might be in love with Yoshi, was gross disloyalty to Jack. Yet it was something over which she seemed to have no control.

She wondered, when Helen had suggested that he might be the one to help her over her prejudices, if she had given any thought as to where it might lead? What did she have in mind when she so innocently suggested that Yoshi might keep a friendly eye on her? Certainly someone as honest and ingenuous as Helen would have no hidden motives. If anything her fault lay in lack of thought before speaking. It was purely a spontaneous request out of her concern for Anna. She knew Helen thought highly of Yoshi and would expect Anna to be mature enough not to entertain romantic thoughts about a married Japanese consultant. In any case, such a relationship was impossible to contemplate. Yet such reasoning did nothing to quell the longing within her.

One morning she had just come off duty when she was told that she had a visitor in Reception.

She made her way there, wondering who it might be. Few people knew where she was working. It could, of course, be Jean, she thought hopefully. But her visitor turned out to be male. As she approached the desk, she immediately recognised the tall figure who stood with his back to her.

'Nigel! What are you doing here?'

'Came to see you. But it seems as though you're working.' He looked her up and down critically. 'Shall I come back later?'

'I've just come off duty.'

'Then how about having something to eat with me?'

She hesitated. She had to admit to herself that she was pleased to see him, but she was wary of his motives for this visit. She must be careful not to give the impression that she might reconsider her decision.

'What's the matter?' he asked. 'Surely we're still friends?'

'I hope so, Nigel,' she said with a smile. 'All right then – a quick lunch. But first I need to change.'

She went upstairs, freshened up and put on a linen dress and jacket, leaving her hair loose.

'That's better,' said Nigel, taking her arm and

leading her to his car. 'You were looking rather tired and despondent. I hope I'm wrong?'

'Tired, possibly. Despondent, no. Where are we going?'

'Where do you suggest? You know the area better than me.'

'I don't eat out much.'

'Then get in and let's explore,' said Nigel. As they drove down the main street towards the centre, he asked, 'How's the job going?'

'Fine. Hard work but I'm enjoying it.'

'So no regrets?'

She shook her head. 'What about you? How do you like Osaka?'

'The job's interesting. A real challenge and I live in a delightful house between Osaka and Kobe. It's a little village in hills that are covered with wild azaleas in the spring. Quite a lot of foreigners in the area. You'd love it up there.'

'I'm glad it's turned out all right for you.'

'I don't know that it has. I was counting on you, Anna. I wish you were there with me.'

She said nothing.

He parked the car in a side street. 'We'd better walk from here and find a nice restaurant.'

'I saw Jean the other day,' she told him. 'She invited me to a dinner party. She said how well you were doing.'

'Not bad really. I've made some good contacts, but it was important to get up there in good time. Foreign companies are moving in fast and they need banks. Competition's keen.'

'How long will you be in Tokyo?'

'A couple of days. It's all I can spare. I'm staying with Harry.'

They had come to a small restaurant with bamboo curtains. Nigel stopped to look at the menu.

'How about this place?' he suggested. 'There's a good choice.'

'Suits me,' Anna said.

Sitting in the cool of the interior sipping a beer, she had to admit it was good to be with him again.

'How much time do you get off?' he asked presently. 'Any local holiday?'

'Odd bits here and there. Not usually more than three days at a time.'

'I was just thinking, there's a lot to see where I am. We could explore the area together. But we'd need a few days. It takes five hours by train to Osaka. Could you manage a bit longer?'

'Where would I stay?' she asked.

He frowned. 'For goodness sake, Anna. With me, of course. Surely the fact that we've postponed the wedding doesn't prevent us seeing each other from time to time, does it?'

'Postponed? It wasn't postponed, Nigel. You know that. It's final.'

'Oh come on, Anna. We've been through quite a bit since we met in Alexandria, lots of ups and downs and looking back, I can see that I was rushing you. But now we're both in Japan it would be ridiculous not meet occasionally. I'm still fond of you, you know.'

She eyed him across the table. His fair, handsome face was smiling at her, and for a moment she was tempted to forget their disagreements.

'You've lost an awful lot of weight,' he said. 'You look as though you haven't had anything to eat for weeks.'

It was true. Her hospital diet wasn't particularly

well balanced perhaps, but she never felt hungry anyway.

'I'm certainly enjoying this,' she admitted. 'I must say I do get fed up with canteen food.'

'So what do you say to taking a few days off and coming up to the Kansai? You'd love the house, and the staff are first rate. I have a driver, then there's the maid and a cook. They look after me well and would welcome a visitor.'

It was tempting. She'd like to see more of Japan and she was due for some leave. It would fill her time and Nigel could be an amusing companion. But then how could she when she had no intention of changing her mind about him? She'd be putting herself in a compromising situation. Him too, for that matter.

He watched her, waiting for her to make up her mind. He looked confident, happy to be with her and yet she couldn't commit herself. She'd have to think about it, play for time.

'Maybe Nigel. I've just been put in charge of a new ward and I can't take time off for a while.' That at least was true.

'I wasn't thinking of it just yet. I'm pretty tied up myself at present, but in a few week's when things have settled down. Perhaps a long weekend. We could go to Kyoto, the old capital. I've been there already and it's beautiful city, some lovely old temples and gardens. You'd enjoy that.'

She felt some of the old excitement returning that she used to feel when she was with him. He was looking at her across the table and his eyes were tender.

'God, I've missed you, Anna. Maybe we needed this separation to make me realise how important you are to me.'

'The situation hasn't changed. Please remember that. I like my job at the hospital. I shall probably stay there for another six months or so and then I'll go home. Dad's still far from well and I want to see him.'

'But you like Japan. If you didn't you wouldn't be working here. That was one of the things you were worried about, whether you could live here after what happened to Jack. Perhaps you're over that now?' There was an edge of sarcasm to his voice.

'I shall never get over it and it has nothing to do with you and me.'

'Look Anna, I have to go back tomorrow evening on the overnight train. Have dinner with me this evening. Just for today let's forget any disagreements. We might still be able to sort something out.'

'I can't. I'm on duty this evening.'

'Then cancel it. Say you're not well.'

She stared at him. He couldn't be serious, but his face was flushed and suddenly his eyes were hostile.

'Of course I can't,' she said heatedly. 'I'm amazed you even suggest it.'

'What I meant was, couldn't you find someone to take your place. Surely it's possible to swap with someone?'

'Not at short notice and I'd only resort to that if I was ill. Nigel, I honestly don't think we ought to see each other again. We always end up arguing.'

His expression changed quickly. 'Silly of me,' he said contritely. 'Of course you can't. It's just that it means a lot to me. What about lunch tomorrow then?'

They had finished the meal and were drinking coffee. She shouldn't have allowed herself to be persuaded. She thought she had put all this behind her and that Nigel had accepted her decision, in which case no harm would have come by having a friendly lunch together. But it seemed she was wrong. She had forgotten how determined he could be and it worried her that he still seemed to be in love with her.

'I'm afraid I can't,' she said. 'I'm on duty until two tomorrow.'

'It seems to me you always have a ready excuse, Anna.' He shrugged. 'Very well. I'll accept it but it rather looks as though I've wasted my time here. I came down specially to see you, to try and patch things up, but you're having none of it.'

'It wouldn't have been waste of time had you accepted the situation. I thought I'd made that perfectly clear.'

'It's not easy to put you out of my mind. You seem to forget that we were very close once and you can't just wipe that off the slate. I believe you loved me. You made me wait a long time for you, Anna, but I thought it was worth it. I still do.'

She looked at him silently, wondering yet again if she was the one to blame. She couldn't rid herself of the feeling but neither could she marry him out of a sense of guilt.

'That wasn't the only reason I came,' Nigel went on. 'I wanted to satisfy myself that you were all right. I still feel responsible for you, you know.'

'There's no need.'

'Then there's nothing for it but to take you back to the hospital, I suppose.'

They got up and walked out to the car. The short drive back to the hospital took place in silence. Not until they drew up before the main entrance did Nigel break it.

'Let me know then if you want to come to Osaka.'

He handed her a card. 'My telephone number's on this.'

'I will,' she said.

She stood there waiting but he seemed in no hurry to go. He sat looking at her, a puzzled expression on his face.

'I can't understand you, Anna.' He sounded exasperated.

A car drove by, just managing to pass Nigel and parked in the place reserved for doctors. She saw with dismay that it was Yoshi. He could hardly failed to have seen her.

'You'll have to move, Nigel. You're blocking the way for doctors and ambulances.'

He shrugged. 'Good-bye then. But don't think I'm giving up that easily.'

Without waiting for her reply, he drove out of the hospital gates at the speed of an ambulance answering an emergency.

Anna, ignoring Yoshi, went up the steps into the hospital. She paused at the desk to ask if there was any mail and was handed a letter from her mother.

'Hello, Anna. We've missed you on the ward.' Yoshi stood at her elbow. He was wearing a dark suit and was carrying a briefcase. She was conscious of the colour rising to her cheeks which must surely be visible to him.

'I'm in Women's General now,' she told him, not knowing what else to say.

'I know. Weren't you happy with us?'

'Mother Agnes asked me to take over temporarily because Sister Ito is on sick leave. I couldn't really refuse.'

'Well, I hope you'll be back with us soon. Actually I

wanted to see you. If you have a moment would you come to my office?'

She followed him. On entering his office, he put his case on the desk and opened it, going through the contents as though searching for something.

'Sit down,' he said, indicating a chair. He appeared ill-at-ease.

'I was about to speak to you outside, but I saw you had a friend with you.'

'Yes. That was Nigel. He's in Tokyo for a short time and we went out to lunch.'

'The man you're going to marry?'

'No. He's the man I came out to marry. I'm not going to marry him now.'

He still seemed preoccupied with the contents of his case and hardly listening to what she said.

'But you're still friends? Is this an English custom?'

She had to laugh. 'Not necessarily. We've known each other quite a long time, and as he's in Tokyo for a few days he wanted to know how I was getting on. Nothing more than that.'

He looked at her then. 'You must forgive my questions. I find it mystifying. Perhaps you're still fond of him?'

'I'm not in love with him any more. There's a difference.'

Abruptly he changed the subject. 'I've heard from David and Helen. They've arrived in New Zealand.'

'I had a card as well.'

He had found what he wanted in the case and now snapped it closed. He sat down at his desk, his full concentration on her.

'I'm wondering if you would like to come with me to Nikko next Saturday. My wife is taking the children to visit her mother and will be unable to come.

The colours are very beautiful in the autumn, and I usually make a trip at this time of year. Perhaps you remember that David and Helen said you should go there one day?'

'Is that the reason you're asking me?' She said it with a hint of mirth.

He smiled then. 'I'm inviting you because I would enjoy your company.'

'In that case, I'd like to come with you,' she said.

'Good. We shall go by car. We must make an early start if we're to have plenty of time there. I'll pick you up outside the hospital at seven.'

'I'll be ready,' said Anna. 'And thank you for inviting me, Yoshi.'

For the remainder of the day, her spirits soared. Even the memory of her meeting with Nigel no longer disturbed her. If she felt any moral concern about accepting Yoshi's invitation, she ignored it. The ethics of such an invitation according to the Japanese code of conduct were beyond her. Yoshi's questions about Nigel suggested that he wished to reassure himself she really was romantically unattached.

In any case it was more than likely that he was simply responding to Helen's concern that she should see something of the country, his way of thanking her for what she did for Suzu. Anyway what did it matter? Enough that on Saturday she would have a whole day in his company.

That night she dreamed again of Jack.

Chapter Fifteen

It was a crisp autumn morning when Anna waited outside the main hospital gates. High clouds moved slowly across a blue sky and a gentle breeze brushed the branches of trees. Yoshi turned up on time and leaned across to open the door for her. Once out of the hospital grounds he drove fast, and soon they were clear of the traffic and heading north. The wind blowing through the open car windows ruffled his usually neat hair giving him a carefree boyish appearance. Anna glanced at him and saw that his usually controlled expression had lifted and he looked relaxed and happy. They chatted desultorily about nothing in particular.

She welcomed the coolness after the enervating humidity of the summer months. Autumn had renewed her vigour and she found her energy returning. That morning she had sprung out of bed with a sense of joyous expectancy. She pulled on a pair of cotton trousers, with a shirt and light pullover. She had no idea what Yoshi's view on women in trousers might be, but she felt comfortable in them and decided to risk it. He looked at her with approval.

'You're looking very nice today,' he said suddenly, turning his head to smile at her.

'It's a relief to get out of uniform for a while,' she admitted, relieved at his approval. 'Thank you for asking me to come with you today, Yoshi. I really appreciate it.'

'Good for you to get away from the hospital for a while. It's only too easy to let work rule our lives. I notice you do that yourself.'

'Only when I was nursing Suzu.'

'There've been other times, I think. I hope you're taking all the holiday due to you, Anna. You must make full use of your time here. It's a beautiful country and I agree with Helen when she said you must see all you can.'

'I'm not doing too badly. Mount Fuji and now Nikko.'

'You must get to Kyoto sometime. That's obligatory.'

'I might well be going to Osaka. I can reach Kyota from there, can't I?' She frowned, wondering whether she dare risk more complications with Nigel if she were to go there with him.

'It's only a few hours away. You could easily do it in a day. When are you thinking of going?'

'Not yet. Mother Agnes wants me on the ward full time at the moment, but I hope to get there eventually.' She didn't want to follow the trend of that conversation and changed the subject. 'Where do you live, Yoshi?'

'About an hour's drive out of Tokyo, towards Yokohama.'

'Quite a long way for you to come each day, specially in the rush hour. The traffic here's worse than in London.'

'I avoid it. I often sleep at the hospital if I'm working late. It's nice where we are. My wife doesn't want to move and the children are settled at school. It suits us all.'

'Tell me about your schools. At what age do the children start?'

'The system is similar to yours. They go to primary school at six until they're twelve. Education is compulsory until fifteen but many of the children stay on, of course, for higher education. They learn the usual subjects like science, mathematics and music, but we put more emphasis than you do, I think, on things like art and physical education. The biggest problem for the children is the language.'

'Japanese? But why?'

'They have to learn ninety-six characters called Katakana and Hiragana before they're nine. Then another set of characters called Kanji which look rather like pictures and show a meaning. At the end of primary they're expected to be able to read and write eight hundred and eighty of them as well as handling their other subjects.'

'Poor little things.' Anna was secretly horrified.

'We have one of the highest standards of education in the world,' Yoshi said with some pride. 'Mind you, I think we're inclined to push our children too hard. Like parents everywhere, Tama and I are anxious they should do well in their examinations.'

They were coming to a village with straw-thatched roofs. Yoshi slowed down and waited patiently for a group of children to run across the road after a ball. Chicken and oxen had to be avoided too, but once clear of the community, he picked up speed until the road began to climb through bamboo groves and pine forests. A delicious fragrance drifted through the window and Anna gulped in deep breaths of mountain air. She felt a great sense of well being. It was sheer bliss to be driving through the countryside beside Yoshi. She wanted to hold back time to prevent it passing too quickly. It was as though this was the first day of a new beginning.

There was a strong breeze up here, bending the bamboos till they swept the ground. Yoshi drew her attention to them.

'The bamboo represents resilience, one of the qualities we most admire in people,' he informed her. 'In an earthquake, a bamboo grove is the safest place to be. The branches may bend, but they rarely break and will spring back again.'

'It would be an amazing stroke of luck if I happened to be in one when an earthquake happened.'

He chuckled. 'Yes, it would.'

'Some people have small patches in their gardens. Hardly sufficient, I agree, to give shelter in a bad quake.'

'I've never been in one,' said Anna.

'You will sooner or later. Most of the quakes are mere tremors but we've had some terrible ones with loss of life.'

As they approached the National Park high in the hills, the traffic became congested. People were arriving by all means of transport and Yoshi wended the car slowly between pedestrians, bicycles and buses, searching for a place to park. When he came across a space he backed skilfully into it and, getting out, locked his door. She noticed it didn't seem to occur to him to open her door or even wait until she was ready. Japanese custom, she supposed.

'First I'm going to take you to the Toshogu shrine,' he announced, guiding her towards a wide avenue of cypresses. It was deliciously cool in the shade beneath them. They walked along as far as a bright vermillion bridge, where they paused for a moment.

Anna looking down into the clear water, thought of a sadder time.

'It reminds me of O-ban,' she said. 'I stood on a bridge with Yasuko, watching the little floats on the water.'

'I hope this is a happier occasion,' said Yoshi, watching her closely.

Anna turned to him, smiling, and found herself arrested by the expression in his eyes, at first unfathomable. Then, as she searched their depths, she saw something more which awoke a response from her own heart. Afraid that he might read her secret, she looked away, embarrassed.

'Of course it is,' she said, lightly. 'This is very different.'

She looked across to the shrine which was surrounded by maple trees, at this time of year covered by a riot of bronze and red leaves. Was it her imagination, or did Yoshi too feel some of the emotions she found so disturbing? If he did, it was unlikely that he would ever acknowledge them, even to himself. The Japanese were not a race given to emotion.

'We're coming to the Yomeimon Gate' said Yoshi. 'We believe it's the most beautiful part of the shrine. The name means a lovely place where one lingers to absorb beauty.'

He pointed out to her the intrincial carving on the latticed panels – dragons and Pekinese dogs intertwined with demons. She was fascinated by the exquisite detail and would have spent much longer examining it.

'I don't want to rush you,' said Yoshi presently, 'but we must move on. There's a lot to see.'

They passed through the white Chinese Gate and between moss covered walls, up a flight of two hundred stone steps to a small chapel. Yoshi led the way and took the steps at such a speed that she had difficulty in keeping up with him and soon had to stop to get her breath.

'Let me help you,' he said, holding out his hand.

She took it. The touch was electric, as though a current had raced up her arm to her heart, increasing the already rapid beat. Strength sprang into her limbs and suddenly the climb became easy, as it had when he went ahead of her on Mount Fuji. When they reached the top, he promptly released her hand as though it had been no more than a functional gesture. Could he really be unaware of the sensations he had aroused in her? It surely wasn't possible.

But he had already opened his guide book and was studying it.

'This chapel,' he said, 'houses the tomb of Ieyasu, one of the greatest leaders of our country and a brave shogun. Now for the Rinnoji Temple. This is much older, built in 848. Let's go and take a look at the giant Buddhas.'

She was grateful to Ieyasu. The tomb itself was hardly worth the effort but it had prompted Yoshi to take her hand in his. They descended the long flight of steps.

'Yoshi, how is it that the Buddhist and Shinto religions are so closely connected?' she asked him.

'You must have noticed then that many Buddhist temples are marked by Shinto shrines. Generally speaking, our people are married by Shinto rites which has to do with our ancestors and what has gone before, but we are buried by Buddhist rites which concern the present. In other words if we faithfully follow the teaching of the Buddha, a better life awaits us in the next world. There's a lot more to it than that, but that's putting it simply.'

'Do you believe in these religions then?'

'I suppose I do. I've been brought up on them and my children as well. My belief is based more on tradition than personal conviction though.'

He waited for her to come out of the temple. 'Now we have to return to the station and take a cable car across to Lake Chuzenji where we can see the Kegon waterfall. It takes about ten minutes.'

There were already long queues, and Yoshi grumbled about the waste of time, but it was not long before their turn came to board the cable car. Suspended high above the dense forest, they had a spectacular view of the autumn colours and far beyond, the lake.

They were packed together in a small cabin, everyone talking and pointing out things of interest. After they had swung along the cable for a few minutes the car seemed to lose speed and some of the younger girls turned away from the window, squealing in fear. Anna, pressed close to Yoshi, had already noticed the apparent fragility of the mechanism that kept them on the cable and drew comfort from his presence.

He smiled at her reassuringly. 'All right?' he asked.

She nodded and looked away, not wanting him to see how terrified she really was. The car gradually picked up speed and they were on their way.

Arriving at the cable station, they got off and followed the crowd to a platform where they had a fine view of the waterfall. Anna caught her breath at the sheer beauty of it. Mount Nantai rose high in the distance and below them, lay the lake. Mist rose above the cascading water of the fall like a curtain of lace.

Far above them, she spotted a bridge spanning the gorge. On it stood a solitary figure – a man as far as she could tell – looking down on the rocks below. Something struck her as odd about his attitude as he peered over the railings and she drew Yoshi's attention to him.

'How did he get there?' she asked.

Other people had noticed him now and gradually silence replaced the light-hearted chatter of the crowd. Then, even as they watched, the figure jumped and the next moment was falling like a rag doll, down, down, until spreadeagled, it disappeared from sight.

Anna gasped. 'He'll be killed.'

Yoshi seemed unmoved. 'People come here to commit harakiri. It's not uncommon, but I'm sorry you were here to see it.'

'But what can we do?' She was appalled by Yoshi's bland acceptance. Surely a doctor should hurry to the scene?

'There's nothing we can do,' he said. 'No one falling from there ever survivies. It's what he intended.'

Anna was silent for a moment, appalled.

'But it's such a waste.'

'Yes indeed. Quite probably he was only a student who had failed his exams and couldn't face the disgrace.'

'Failed his exams! You mean he'd commit suicide just because he failed his exams?'

'It's a matter of great importance,' said Yoshi, matter of factly. 'He would know that his family expected better of him. The burden's unbearable.'

'Supposing he didn't kill himself. What would his family do?'

'They'd make excuses for him to cover their shame.'

'Does it really matter that much?'

'Yes. It does.' He sounded curt.

She followed him as he turned away, but she felt that a shadow had fallen over them and for her the day was spoiled.

When they reached the cable car she looked back to see if there was any sign of the fallen figure, but the scene was hidden by trees.

'Will someone go to him?' Anna asked, unable to hide her anxiety.

'They'll have difficulty reaching him but someone will send for an ambulance. His family will be informed and asked to identify him but sometimes it takes time. You mustn't let this upset you, Anna.'

'How can I help it?' she protested. 'It's a dreadful thing.'

'It's sad but we must accept it. If a person feels that he's bringing disgrace to his family or to his country and he's unable to live with it, what he does is his choice, not ours.'

To Anna's Western values this was incomprehensible.

'But doesn't he think of the sorrow it will cause his family?'

'He sees it as the honourable thing to do. Sometimes you hear of couples dying together. Perhaps their family disapproves of their union and, rather than be separated, they choose to be united in death and together in the next world. Perhaps that's hard for you to understand?'

'Yes, it is,' said Anna, bluntly. 'Life is precious and

anyway some people believe that death is the end.'

'And you?' He turned to her, his tone harsh. 'What do you believe? Aren't you a Christian?'

'I'm . . . I'm not sure,' she said slowly. 'I suppose I am. Nominally anyway.'

'That surprises me. In Japan we have a very positive attitude towards death. Life is a temporary affair and we put more emphasis on the hope of something better beyond. I thought this is what Christians believe, too.'

'Yes, they do though personally I have doubts about it.'

'What did your brother believe, Anna?'

'I'm told that he became a Christian in the camp.'

He looked at her with surprise. 'By all accounts and your own assessment of it, it was an appalling place. How could it happen there?'

'I don't know but it did. Jack had a friend in the camp who came to see me later in England. He told me that some of the men did become Christians and that it changed their lives. They weren't afraid any more. They seemed to be able to forgive their guards bcause they understood why they acted as they did. I don't think they could do that unless they were helped by their faith.'

'Forgiveness is the most difficult thing that Christ demanded of his followers, isn't it?'

'You seem to know a lot about it, Yoshi. How's that?'

'It's something that has always interested me. A long time ago, many Japanese were converted to Christianity by Portuguese missionaries, but others were tortured and many of them died for their faith. It must have a strong appeal if people are willing to go that far for it.'

'It's because Christians live in the power of the Spirit rather than by their own strength. They discovered that in camp. Once they committed themselves to Christ, forgiveness followed naturally.'

'And is that faith easy to find?' Yoshi asked, intrigued now.

She shrugged and turned away. 'I don't think I have it. If I had I suppose I wouldn't still feel so angry about Jack.'

She'd never given much thought to it before. She'd surprised herself by explaining to Yoshi what she herself had been unable to accept.

'We all need something believe in,' said Yoshi. 'Personally I think we have to learn about many religions before we find one on which to build our lives.'

They were walking towards the restaurant where a long queue was already forming.

'It's time we had something to eat,' said Yoshi 'and then we'll walk a little in the park before we go back. Would you settle for a snack? I can't tolerate queues.'

'I'm not hungry,' said Anna. 'I'd be quite happy with an apple.'

He made the purchases and they found a vacant bench under a pine tree. A few yards away an old woman was sweeping up fallen leaves. She wore dark blue baggy trousers and a large conical straw hat. Patiently she gathered the leaves together only to lose them as a flurry of wind teased them from under her broom. Unperturbed, she retrieved them and added them to a pile she was making in a sheltered corner of the grassy slope. She whistled under her breath as she worked, swinging the broom back and forth.

Yoshi sat close to Anna and unwrapped his

sandwich. 'Ah,' he said, settling back, 'this is what I enjoy.'

She was feeling calmer now. Yoshi had in some way been able to convince her that the tragedy was in keeping with the Japanese way of life, but she still found his attitude hard to accept. She was grateful that they had moved away from the subject but something of the day had been lost. She tried to reach him by expressing her pleasure at being with him.

'I'm so glad that I've seen this place with you. Don't you think that when you share something beautiful with a friend, it deepens one's awareness of it?'

He studied her thoughtfully. 'You're beginning to think like a Japanese,' he said.

She laughed, enjoying the compliment. 'Thoughts aren't the perogative of a nation, surely? They're universal. Language is the difficulty.'

'That perhaps is our own fault,' said Yoshi. 'As a nation Japan has been isolated too long. You know, it's good to see you so happy, Anna. Usually I find you very serious.'

She thought about this. 'Perhaps it's because we discuss serious subjects,' she said presently. 'Besides, I'm not always sure how you'll react to what I say. I never know what you're thinking and I wouldn't want to risk offending you.'

'Or is it because we work together and you can't forget our roles when we're off duty?'

'That may be,' she admitted.

'A pity. David and Helen found no difficulty once we were away from the hospital.'

'You've known them longer than you've known me. I still think of you as an eminent physician.'

He threw back his head and laughed. 'Am I such a formidable person then?' he asked.

'Not really,' she said, smiling, 'but you are eminent and I am a little in awe of you.'

'You never fail to surprise me, Anna. Just when I think I'm beginning to understand you, you come out with something quite disconcerting.'

Suddenly a flood of school children poured along the path past them, the girls dressed in white blouses and dark skirts and spotless white socks, the boys in white shirts and dark trousers with peaked caps. Not so different from schoolchildren back home, Anna thought. They moved along the path decorously, chattering and laughing together, but with none of the racing about and yelling that Anna associated with English children on an outing. Several small ones paused in front of their bench and stood staring at them with their wide, slanting eyes, mouths slightly open.

'They still aren't used to foreigners,' Yoshi excused them. 'Specially when they're accompanied by a Japanese. You must forgive them. They're only small children.'

'I don't mind in the least. It gives me the opportunity to study them too,' said Anna.

He looked at his watch. 'Shall we take a look at the gardens before we start back?' he suggested.

They wandered across the lawn and through trees that opened to an area where rocks and small shrubs were landscaped to form a natural looking garden. Old stone lanterns had been placed among the rocks so that their light would filter through the leaves, and small waterfalls had been designed to disgorge into a lake. Across the lawn Anna noticed a small square building with a thatched roof.

'That's where the tea ceremony is performed,' explained Yoshi. 'It's a long procedure. They say it's good for the soul, but being a man of little patience I find the whole thing tedious. My wife is very fond of it though.'

Reminded of his wife, Anna unwillingly considered her. What was his family doing at this moment? What had he told them about this day she was spending in his company? She wondered if he had found it necessary to lie to his wife, or had she little interest in what he did when he was away from home? There were so many unknown factors, and Anna had to make do with the little information he was willing to impart. There was much of his life she would never know about and he shared only a very small part of it with her. She felt a surge of unreasonable resentment that he knew so much more about her than she about him.

In the car going home, she sat quietly beside him. The man on the bridge was still on her mind. For someone so compassionate with his patients, it was surprising how easily Yoshi could put it from his mind.

'You're not still thinking about that man on the bridge, I hope?' He interrupted her thoughts as if he could read them.

'I was thinking about his family. Perhaps by now they'll have heard about the accident. They must be heart-broken. In a way it's a reflection on their love for him.'

'I don't think so. What makes you think we have the right to make other people's decisions for them? Surely it's enough to try and make the right ones for ourselves?'

'This was so violent though. It was shattering.'

'To a Westerner it might seem uncaring.' His voice was suddenly gentle. 'Perhaps in your country suicide is more of a social problem and can be blamed on society at large. It makes people uncomfortable because they all feel a share of the responsibility. I like to believe that we are all in charge of our own destiny. What's your opinion on that, Anna?'

'Of course it happens at home. It happens everywhere, but not in such public places. It seemed that the man was advertising his tragedy, and it was all the more shocking because the sun was shining and everyone was enjoying themselves.'

'Sometimes it's on beautiful days like this when we feel isolated and sad. It's useless to waste our compassion on something we have no control over. Better to put our efforts into things that we are able to change.'

'Like Hiroshima? At least we can all see that that never happens again.'

'We can try, but we can't be sure.'

'I'd like to go there one day, Yoshi.'

He frowned. 'Why would you want to go there? There're much better places to visit. You'd see little of the damage now. Most of the city has been rebuilt although there are museums which would give you some idea of what it was about. But do you really want to see it? Wasn't nursing Suzu enough?'

'It's because of her I need to go.'

'I shall have to go there myself shortly,' he admitted, sounding reluctant.

'Then could I come with you?' she asked eagerly. 'I know you'd be able to explain it to me so I'd understand.'

Startled by her frankness, he glanced at her. The breeze through the open car window was blowing her thick auburn hair back from her face and for another moment their gaze met and held before he looked back to the road. Then, almost abruptly, he said, 'I can't take you. I shall be in conference. If you really want to go, you must arrange something for yourself.'

'Yes, of course. I just thought . . .'

'I'm sorry, Anna. I'd like us to go together, but it isn't possible. You mustn't forget that I'm well known in medical circles and a married man. I don't know what the custom is in your country, but here we have appearances to observe. If I arrived in Hiroshima with you, it would be a matter for speculation. I wouldn't want to hurt my wife.'

'And today?' she asked, a spark of mischief creeping into her voice.

'Today is different. There was talk of going with Helen and David. As that wasn't possible, I thought you might like to come along with me.'

She was contrite. 'I'm sorry. I shouldn't have asked.'

'You're right though. It's not a trip you should make on your own. You'll find it too disturbing. Haven't you a friend who could go with you?'

She shook her head. 'Not really.'

'You said you might be going to Osaka. It's not far from Hiroshima. Have you friends there?'

'Only Nigel. He wanted to take me to Kyoto.'

'You shouldn't miss the opportunity. You must be due for some time off?'

'That's not the problem.'

He was silent for a moment, then he said. 'I think I understand. If you see your fiance again, he will naturally try to persuade you to marry him?'

'That has something to do with it, but in any case he wouldn't want to go to Hiroshima.'

'Many people are fascinated by the place, perhaps because of what it symbolises. If you have to choose between Kyoto and Hiroshima though, I would suggest you go to Kyoto.'

'I hope I shall have an opportunity to see them both one day.'

'I have some books about Hiroshima that you're welcome to borrow.'

They had reached the outskirts of Tokyo and he was silent now, concentrating on the traffic. She was surprised when he stopped the car some distance from the hospital and waited for her to get out.

'Thank you so much, Yoshi. It was a wonderful day.'

'You mustn't thank me.' He looked at her for a long moment and then he said, 'Nikko has never seemed more beautiful to me than it did today.'

She saw nothing of Yoshi over the following days, but she was content to think about the day they'd spent together. Yoshi had said nothing about seeing her again, but she felt certain it wouldn't be long before he made some excuse to seek her out. Each day she woke with a sense of anticipation.

Her relationship with Yoshi had no future. She accepted that. But she was beginning to enjoy life again, to experience long forgotten emotions. She was afraid that her new found happiness might slip from her grasp and she would sink back into the shadows of depression. She recognised that she had come dangerously close to it before. If this was being in love, then however painful it might be, it was preferable to being out of it. If it was to be unreciprocated, she would learn to live with it. She had no right to expect anything more.

Chapter Sixteen

Tama studied the branch of pine she had brought from the country yesterday and started snipping. With deft movements she began to create an autumn arrangement which was already taking shape in her mind to blend perfectly with the scene on the kakemona that hung in the alcove.

It was a peaceful time of day, just before the children returned from school and as usual, her mind turned to Yoshi, causing her a sense of unease. She tried to analyse why it was she felt like this and she had to admit it stemmed from what he had told her about the foreign woman.

He had often spoken of this woman recently. He had told her how she had helped to look after the sick child and had gone to her home to nurse her. He had related too, how upset she had been when the child had died and that now her New Zealand friends had left, she would be lonely.

'Would you like to invite her to our home?' Tama had suggested.

He shook his head. 'How could we, when you don't speak the same language? It would be an impossible situation. She still has friends, the people she stayed with in Tokyo when she arrived in our country.'

'We could give her a nice meal and she could meet

the children. Perhaps she would like to see a Japanese home.'

'You should know by now, Tama, that I like my home to myself. I work hard and when I get home, I like to be with my family.'

She accepted that, but she was glad she had made the offer and was relieved that Yoshi had not thought it necessary.

Yoshi always told her everything about his work, but she had never wanted to be part of it. It was enough to be his wife, to bring up his children and keep a nice home for him to come back to. She was proud of his reputation and felt that she shared his honour. She was a very fortunate woman to have won the love of a man like Yoshi. He worked hard and being a doctor, was away from home for long periods at a time. From experience she knew she could never expect him to keep regular hours. This rarely worried her until recently. It was the day she took the children to see her mother. She had expected Yoshi to be home before her, but it was later than usual before he returned.

'I spent the day with a colleague,' he told her. 'You know how it is. We were working together on a series of talks we have to give. It took time and later we went out for a meal.'

She was getting the children's books together ready for school at the time and wasn't paying much attention.

'Was it Dr Moshi?' she asked.

'No, no. You don't know this fellow. He comes from Nagasaki.'

'You should have invited him here,' she said. 'The children and I were away and you would have had the house to yourselves. Michiko would have prepared a meal.'

'Not on this occasion.' She wondered why he sounded so upset about it. 'I know what's best, Tama. I don't invite just anyone to our home.'

She let the matter drop. It was of little importance. Afterwards though, she thought it over. Only rarely did he discuss work with a colleague on a Saturday. The only thing that kept him from his family at weekends were his patients. The trouble was he was overworked and she must expect him to get impatient at times. Sometimes she couldn't help wishing that life was as it used to be, when there was less pressure and more opportunity to be together as a family. It was years since they'd had time to really enjoy each other's company in a relaxed manner.

Unlike many of his friends, Yoshi was not expected to attend the kind of business functions that went on long into the night, often culminating in a party, and the men returning home drunk, having had a happy time with a geisha girl or a bar hostess. Her friends had often told her stories of how they had waited up to help their husbands to bed after such a party. In Japan such occasions were also opportunities to discuss business and anyone who left early was thought to be uninterested in the affairs of their firm, and promotion might even be withheld.

Yoshi came and went as he pleased for he was under no one's authority. He had always insisted that he would rather be with her than attending geisha parties. He had told her often that he did not expect her to meet his medical colleagues and even though foreigners lived in their country in great numbers, there was no need for her to learn English simply to accompany him on social functions where she would have suffered from shyness and embarrassment. Some of her friends were exposed to this, and she knew how they disliked it.

Yoshi was not a man to go off to find some light relief in the pleasure bars or geisha houses but had he done so, she would have accepted it. Any demonstration of jealousy would be demeaning and uncharacteristic of her. So why now, did she feel uneasy about the English woman?

Nothing that Yoshi had actually said implied he was attracted to her. Tama thought it unlikely he would pursue a relationship such as this because of his position in the medical world. A geisha might have been acceptable, a foreigner, never. Tama argued with herself that the woman was only in Japan temporarily and would return to England one day. But Yoshi was an attractive man. Her friends had told her so, and even after ten years of marriage and three lovely children, he was still capable of arousing deep sensual feelings in her.

Yoshi was used to meeting people from all over the world and was eager to exchange ideas and put forward the views of his own countrymen. This woman was a nurse and they would have much in common. Tama had no idea if she was beautiful. Yoshi had not mentioned her appearance, nor had he given any indication of her personality, other than to mention that she was unhappy. But Tama's heart told her that there was danger here, perhaps something that Yoshi had not yet even admitted to himself.

She heard the children's voices as soon as they entered the garden. They came scampering into the room, carrying their yellow school hats and their satchels.

'I did well at school,' Kuma informed her. 'The teacher said so. I was top of my class.'

'I did well, too,' said Chieko.

'You always say that,' accused her brother, 'but you're with the little ones. It isn't real work.'

'But it is,' said Chieko. 'I learned ten hiragana characters today.'

'That's nothing. I already know all ninety six and soon I shall start Kanji,' said Kuma.

Chieko gave up the uneven contest, and her mother said gently, 'I'm very proud of you both. Show me your books.'

Eagerly they pulled their writing books out of their satchels and opened them at today's lessons. Their work was neat and correct and after encouraging them, Tama suggested they should go into the garden and feed the fish. They ran out, followed by Michiko whose job it was to keep an unobtrusive eye on them when they returned home from school.

Tama went to take a bath. She wanted to be ready when Yoshi came home. Having put on a blue starched yukata with a design of white chrysanthemums, she called to Chieko and drawing the child close to her on the balcony, she opened a picture book.

It was eight o'clock before Yoshi came in and the children were already preparing for bed. Tama could tell by his manner that he had something on his mind, but he was looking so tired that she didn't question him.

Instead she said gently, 'The children are waiting for you, Yoshi. Say good-night to them and then go and take a bath. You'll feel better then.'

When he returned half an hour later, he was

looking much more relaxed. He sat down opposite her and sipped his drink.

'The children seem to be doing well at school,' he remarked, smiling at her. 'They wanted me to see their work.'

'They work hard. Sometimes I think they don't have time to be children, but they seem to thrive on it.'

'They must be encouraged,' said Yoshi.

Michiko had already set the table and presently she brought in the evening meal, some broiled eels with a shoyu sauce, a selection of raw vegetables and boiled rice. They moved to the table and Yoshi set about the meal with relish.

Opposite him, Tama ate slowly and waited for an opportune moment to tell him her news.

'I had a letter from your mother today,' she said presently. 'She's had one of her bad spells again. I think perhaps we should try and see her some time.'

'What have you in mind?' asked Yoshi, lifting a bowl of rice and deftly using his chopsticks.

'You said you were thinking of going to Hiroshima. When will that be?'

'It hasn't been decided yet. In a week or two perhaps.'

'I was wondering whether I would take the children to visit your mother in Osaka at the same time,' she suggested. 'We could travel together and the children and I could get off the train there while you carry on to Hiroshima. Then, perhaps, after the conference, you might be able to join us and spend a day with her there?'

Yoshi glanced at her and helped himself to a radish which he chewed thoughtfully.

'What do you think?' Tama went on. 'It's some time

since we saw Mother and she is getting on, you know.'

'Perhaps you're right,' said Yoshi. 'It's a matter of timing and I can't restrict myself. After my lecture, the delegates will want to talk things over. I can't say how long it will take. I may stay there another night so that we can discuss things the next day.'

'We could stay with Mother until you come,' suggested Tama.

Yoshi frowned. 'I can't commit myself,' he said. 'Perhaps it would be better if you just take the children along sometime. In any case, I may possibly stop off on the return journey, just to see Mother.'

Tama was disappointed. She had another plan which she wanted to introduce but she was unable to bring up the subject while he was in his present frame of mind. He was decidedly testy at the moment.

Michiko brought in clean plates and fresh fruit together with a pot of green tea. Tama told her she could go to her room and that she would clear the table herself presently. They ate in silence. Tama thought her plan was a good one. Yoshi could do with a few days off work and there was still a chance that he might agree to it.

She watched a lizard crawl across the ceiling, then she said, 'I had thought that if it could be arranged, you might take a few days of your holiday and we could go on to Kyoto with the children. It's so beautiful there in the autumn.'

'Don't press me, Tama. Work must come first and I'm unable to think of a holiday at the present time.' His voice was unusually sharp but now she had started on the subject she was determined to see it through.

'You work too hard, Yoshi. Last year you failed to take your full holiday. We only had that one week by the sea. The children hardly see you at all these days.'

He looked at her, a cold glint in his eyes. 'I have this lecture to work on,' he said, getting up. 'We'll discuss this some other time.'

He pulled back the sliding doors and went into the room furnished in western style with a table and upright chairs. She could see him through the gap of the half open doors. He opened his brief case and sitting down, took out some papers and began to write.

With a sigh she cleared away the rest of the meal. She tidied up in the kitchen, taking time to decide what they needed to buy in the market the next day. When she returned to the main room she noticed that Yoshi was still working.

Feeling melancholy, she picked up her embroidery and began to sew.

It was unlike Yoshi to be so irritable and she was sure that it had to do with pressure of work. Not only was his expertise sought by leading hospitals all over the country but he was constantly approached to give lectures. Moreover, he was a Consultant at two hospitals as well as looking after his own patients. He was not a man to spare himself.

These days he had no time for golf which he used to enjoy, nor any other recreation. It wasn't surprising that he was exhausted. It was useless for her to remonstrate with him though. Yoshi was a determined man and he would decide for himself when he would take time off. It was so when he climbed Mount Fuji this year. He suddenly found the time and she was glad that he did, but she felt anxious that he saw so little of the children. These days they often asked if he would be home before they went to sleep and why wasn't it as it used to be? They didn't understand that someone as knowledgeable as their father was always in demand.

It was no good waiting up for him. He might work through until the early hours of the morning. She put away her work and went across to slide open the shoji doors to tell Yoshi that she was going to bed.

She lay awake for a long time and when he came to bed an hour later, she feigned sleep. He turned off the light and settling down with his back to her as he did so often these days, fell asleep immediately. Or seemed to.

The next day his dark mood had passed. Tama having spent a restless night, felt washed out and she was greatly relieved to find that Yoshi had recovered his spirits.

At breakfast he said to the children in a light-hearted way, 'Your mother tells me I'm working too hard. She's right. I think we should go for a trip to the country next Saturday.'

'Hai, hai,' chorused the two younger ones. 'What a great idea!'

Tama glanced at her eldest son. In his quiet way she could see that he was just as delighted as the others. She knew Yoshi would rise to the occasion in the end. Catching her eye, he smiled at the children and gently teased them.

'Well then, where shall we go?'

'To the sea,' cried Chieko.

'No,' said Kuma. 'Let's go to the hills and explore.'

A heated argument ensued between the three of them until Yoshi broke it up.

'How about taking our fishing nets and we'll find a

stream,' he proposed. 'Your mother will pack us a picnic.'

As Tama gently acquiesced, she thought that perhaps now she had his mind running along the right lines, the trip to Kyoto might still materialise. She would wait a while yet before resurrecting the sugject though.

As soon as Yoshi reached the hospital he went to the children's ward and checked on some of his young patients. From there he walked briskly to Mother Agnes' office to tell her of a decision he'd come to concerning the treatment of a patient who had been causing concern. By the time he sat down at his desk to write out some reports, it was midday and he had to be at a hospital on the other side of Tokyo by two o'clock. Lunch would have to be skipped today.

He found it difficult to concentrate. He was feeling very badly about his brusqueness the evening before. Tama was a good woman and thought only of what was beneficial to the whole family. The problem was that his conscience was troubling him. The other day he had told her a downright lie. He'd never done that before and it made him feel worse when she had believed him unquestioningly. Yet he saw no way round it.

How could he expect her to understand that prompted by Helen's suggestion, he had taken Anna to Nikko because at times she looked so sad and he felt she must be lonely, more so after losing Suzu. However, he'd have to be careful in future. It wouldn't do to be seen in the company of this attractive Western woman too often. People might start talking and if it reached Tama's ears, she'd be upset.

He got up and went across to the window in an effort to bring his mind to bear on the report. The thought of Anna returned to trouble him frequently these days, often at the most inconvenient moments. He could picture her face so clearly: the smooth texture of her skin and her beautiful mouth tantalisingly smiling at him. He'd never seen such green eyes, so expressive that he could read her thoughts. He tried not to dwell on them but he was flattered by the warm way in which she responded to him that day in Nikko. He had been wrong in his earlier impressions that she was a somewhat gauche, outspoken woman, the sort that rarely appealed to him. Far from it, he was finding great difficulty in resisting her.

He looked at his watch. Ten minutes wasted. He started writing and managed to get through some of the work. He would have to leave the rest and come back to it later if he was to be in time for the meeting.

By the time he got back to it again it was five o'clock and he managed to finish the report in half an hour.

After putting away his papers, he looked at his watch. He wondered if Anna was on duty that evening and was fleetingly tempted to think up some excuse to visit the ward. Instead, he picked up his case and closed the office. On his way out, he passed the dining room and looked in. There was just the chance that Anna was having an early meal but the place was almost empty.

With a sense of disappointment, he got in the car and drove home. It was not unusual, he thought as he stopped by the traffic lights, for men to form an alliance with a woman other than their wives, but he had never felt the need for such a relationship. Had he considered it, he would have discarded the idea for he wouldn't wish to hurt Tama and had no intention of doing so now.

Before he reached home, he had made up his mind that he would avoid Anna except under strictly professional circumstances. He would completely put her out of his mind. Perhaps, then, he would be able to rid himself of this ridiculous obsession. By the time he reached home, he had thrust all thoughts of her aside. His family now claimed his whole attention.

Anna wondered if Yoshi was avoiding her. It was two weeks now since their expedition to Nikko and she had seen nothing of him. She had been over their conversation many times, wondering if she had offended him. Perhaps she had been precocious in asking him outright if she might accompany him to Hiroshima. If she saw him by chance, she would try to put matters right, but she wouldn't deliberately seek him out. Unfortunately he never had any reason to come to the women's ward.

She had met up with Holly again at a lecture and had arranged to go with Max and her for a walk round a lake some miles north of Tokyo. She had enjoyed the trip and appreciated the invitation, but it wasn't like being with Dave and Helen. She still missed Helen dreadfully.

She was worried because the last letter from her mother brought the news that her father had not been so well, and she wondered if she might have to go home sooner than she'd planned. On the other hand, her mother said she was managing and had good support and told her not to worry. If the time came when she felt Anna should come home, she'd let her know.

Since seeing Nigel, she had decided against ringing Jean to suggest meeting for lunch. In spite of Jean's overtures of friendship, she still felt that, as his boss's wife, her loyalties must lie with Nigel, and that she would avoid saying anything that might reflect badly on him. Instead, she left a message with the Sister on the maternity ward, asking to be informed when Jean came in.

When the message came, two weeks later than she expected it, Anna went over one afternoon to see her. Jean was sitting up in bed with the baby in a cot beside her. She was looking pale but cheerful.

'It's good of you to come over, Anna. I was wondering if I'd see you. How's everything?'

'Fine. But how about you?' She went across to where the baby slept peacefully. 'What's his name?' she asked.

'Guy. Do you think it suits him?'

'Few names suit a baby, but it'll be a nice name when he's older. Stan must be pleased.'

'He is. Thank goodness we have help. I don't think I could face looking after him myself as well as the other two.'

'Are they all well?'

'Yes. They often speak of you. You must come over and see us one week-end Anna. You look as though you could do with a break. Don't you ever get leave?'

'I'm due for some but I've recently been moved onto another ward to take the place of the Sister. I'll have to wait for a bit.'

'Promotion then?'

'Yes, but I preferred the children's ward where I was before.'

'You've done awfully well, Anna. All credit to you.

Nigel said he saw you the other day when he was down.'

'Yes. He took me out to lunch. I'm afraid it wasn't a very happy event.'

'I know he hoped you might change your mind. He just can't understand why you should want to work in a hospital when you could be having a good time together in Osaka.'

Anna smiled wryly. 'It might not turn out to be such a good time.'

'But there must have been a time once when it was all right. I'm sorry to keep on about it, but I'm sure you could do worse than marry Nigel. He's ambitious and he could give you a good life. He's madly in love with you, you know.'

'I wish he wasn't. It makes me feel guilty.'

'Then you might change your mind?'

'I don't think so. I'm happy as I am. I'm just sorry I gave everyone all this trouble, more so because you were having this lovely baby.'

'I wouldn't have met you otherwise, would I?'

'I've brought him a present.' She had wanted to find something Japanese and after searching the shops, had alighted on a baby's silver spoon and pusher with the Japanese chrysanthemum emblem engraved on them. She watched Jean unwrap them and knew from her expression that she was pleased.

'Oh how lovely, Anna. These will always remind him of where he was born and he can pass them on to his children. You are kind.'

'Glad you like them. I was rather pleased when I found them.'

'Tell me,' said Jean, laying them aside. 'What do you do with yourself in your time off? I often wonder.'

'I went to Nikko the other day.'

'Not on your own?'

'No. My New Zealand friend left to get married. I went with one of the doctors.'

'Oh? English?'

'No. A Japanese but he speaks good English.'

'Good grief! You do surprise me. Is he married?'

Anna laughed. 'Yes. I think he suggested it because he thought I was lonely. You don't have to worry. He's very fond of his wife.'

'What a pity.'

'Jean, I don't need romance so don't read anything into it.'

'Every girl needs it.'

'I want time to recover from my disastrous mistake with Nigel. I can do with a cooling off period.'

'So there's no future in this . . . this doctor?'

'None. It isn't always necessary to have a future, is it? Not all relationships are happily resolved, yet at the time they can be very valuable. I think we must be able to relinquish them or they can be damaging. I'd never want to involve this man in anything that might jeopodise his career or his private life. I think too highly of him for that.'

'But if it weren't for these reservations, would you be willing to enter into a relationship with a Japanese?'

Anna was thoughtful. 'I don't know how far I'd want to go down that road. Not far, I think but I value his friendship deeply.'

'I wouldn't think it would ever be put to the test,' said Jean. 'What I know about the Japanese is that they never show their feelings, least of all to a foreigner, however attractive. But heaven knows, you're attractive enough so he must be tempted.'

Anna was silent. She was regretting that she had spoken about it to Jean. It was a mistake to confide in anyone.

'Don't worry,' said Jean, sensing her reluctance to continue the conversation. 'You can trust me. I discuss most things with Stan, but this I will keep quiet about, I promise. I appreciate that you've made me your confidante, Anna.'

'Thanks.' Anna put her hand over her friend's. 'I had no intention of telling you and I don't know why I did, but it was a relief to talk about it.'

On her way back to her room Anna stopped in the main hall to look at the notice board. Lectures were usually held at the end of each month and some of them were in English. The one listed for tomorrow caught her eye: 'Children of the Atomic Bomb.' In small letters underneath, she saw that Yoshi was to be the speaker. She was free tomorrow evening.

Although she arrived at the lecture room in good time, the hall was already packed with foreigners as well as Japanese. She found a seat beside one of the Australian nurses in the fourth row. The lecture was to be illustrated by slides, so that even if there was a language problem with some of the younger nurses, they would be able to understand the gist of the lecture. Clearly it was a subject of enormous importance and to hear an authority like Yoshi Egawa speaking was a great attraction.

Promptly at eight, Yoshi walked onto the platform and took his place at a table along with some other doctors. He was dressed in a dark suit with a collar and tie and appeared completely at ease.

An elderly Japanese got to his feet and spoke in Japanese. He introduced Yoshi, emphasising his special interest in the effects of radiation in relation to the bombs at Hiroshima and Nagasake. He explained that the lecture would be given in English and illustrated by slides so that everyone should be able to get something out of it. However a Japanese version would be available for those who wanted it.

Then the microphone was adjusted and Yoshi himself stood up. He explained that some of the photographs which would be used to illustrate the talk would certainly be disturbing. He then launched into his talk.

'It is estimated that four thousand children were made orphans when the atomic bomb fell on Hiroshima. Three days later another bomb fell on Nagasaki. Many of these children were found alone in smoldering ruins and did not know their own names. It was impossible to list them all because so many records were lost.

'In Hiroshima a centre for lost children was opened in one of the primary schools which had escaped destruction. School personnel and neighbourhood mothers took turns in caring for them day and night, but nevertheless child after child died calling out for its mother. The situation was the same in Nagasaki. Religious Orders and other charitable organisations sprang up and were financed by various philanthropists but in spite of these, they could not hope to care for all the children. Many depended on the goodwill of individuals and as a result, some were fostered.

'Then there were the unborn children. Many babies in utero in Hiroshima and Nagasaki at the time of the bombing suffered mental retardation, deformities and tumours and continue to do so.'

Here Yoshi launched into medical details, such as

periods in gestation and the effect of radiation according to the distance from the centre of the explosion. Such statistics could only be estimated and it would be years before the full toll of damage was known, as many more were expected to die or develop symptoms in the future.

Every now and then he paused as a picture came up on the screen, illustrating the devastation. There was a picture taken from an American plane, a few minutes after the bomb had been dropped. It showed the cloud, the brilliant light and the black smoke.

Yoshi went on to speak of the contamination caused by the 'black rain' which fell from the north to the west of the centre, distributing the radioactivity over a wide area. He spoke briefly of the damage done to the soil and animal life.

Then he continued, 'These victims are dependent on us to concentrate all our medical knowledge to help them. But for the vast majority, it's too late. There is little we can do for them, except to ensure that their suffering is not in vain. We must not keep these facts to ourselves. They must be made available to the world, for only then will people understand that this is too high a price to pay for victory.

'I have chosen to speak of children, not because the horror was confined to them, but because theirs is a special kind of trauma, dependent as they were on their parents and the special need of every child for security. These two essential needs were taken from them, and it concerns all of us because their lives will always be affected by this deprivation and everything possible must be done to try and compensate for it.'

Doctor Egawa sat down. The chairman invited questions. There was a pause while the audience seemed to be trying to digest a subject that was too strong for them. Then the questions began. Yoshi dealt with each succinctly and clearly. Speaking in a language other than his own, he clarified a badly put question and gave his answer. He stressed that his remarks in many cases could only be speculative. It was too soon yet to assess the full damage. They were treading new ground, learning from experience. No previous medical knowledge had equipped them for the holocaust of those few seconds. It was new medical territory.

Anna was profoundly moved by his words, especially his compassion and the absence of blame. As people got up to leave she made her way towards Yoshi. He was speaking to a group of doctors but she was content to wait unobserved until he had finished. Presently he saw her and walked over to her, smiling.

'I wondered if you'd come,' he said quietly.

'I wanted to hear about it,' she explained. 'I'm only just beginning to understand how terrible it was. Thanks to you.'

'It needs courage to admit that,' he said, looking at her seriously. 'But then I would expect that of you. I haven't given you those books yet, have I? Do you still want to read about it?'

'Yes please. '

'Then come to my office. I have several which may interest you.'

She followed him out of the hall and along the corridor to his room.

'Sit down,' he invited. 'It might take a little time to find them.'

He scanned the bookcase, selecting a few books. 'I keep my English books here. The Japanese medical books are at the other hospital. I don't expect your Japanese is up to those yet?'

She laughed. 'By no means.'

She waited, watching him thumbing through the books before passing them over to her.

'I think those two will answer most of your questions. One is medical and the other is an account of personal experiences.' He handed her another small volume. 'Perhaps this will appeal to you too. It's a short novel, quite well written, a translation from the Japanese. I think you'll like it. There are others, but this is enough to go on with.'

Anna thanked him. 'I don't know how you find time to do all that you do and keep abreast with medical developments,' she said.

'At the expense of my family and private life. I went to Hiroshima last week-end. My family came with me as far as Osaka and I met them there after the conference. I'm sorry I couldn't take you.'

'I intend to go one day. I wanted to be with you because you are about the most unbiased person I've met, and you come close to the truth.'

'Only close?'

'I don't think anyone can be completely truthful all the time. Sometimes the truth has to be fabricated slightly to make it more palatable, otherwise it's too painful.'

He thought about that. 'Perhaps you're right. I've been told that the Japanese are great ones for that. We like to tell people what they want to hear, but that's a national characteristic and cannot be interpreted as lying. As for myself, I tend to lean the other way. I hate deceit, but we all use it in some form or other, even to ourselves.'

She looked at him and saw in his eyes that he

wanted to say something more, something that he could not perhaps put into words? She felt that it may be best left unsaid and to make it easier for him, she picked up the books and turned towards the door.

'Anna?'

She turned to face him. 'Yes?'

He hesitated, then said, 'I'd like to spend more time with you, but it's impossible. You understand, don't you?' In that instant his eyes reflected more feeling than words ever could.

'Yes,' she said softly. 'I understand.'

She closed the door behind her and went upstairs. She knew now why she rarely saw him. Why in fact, he was avoiding her. He had nothing to offer her and if he followed his inclinations, he might not be able to withdraw. She knew he would never commit himself to that extent. Neither would she want him to. Or would she?

Chapter Seventeen

In spite of the demands made on her as nurse in charge of the ward, Anna was restless. Since speaking with Yoshi that evening after the lecture, the expression in his dark eyes returned frequently to taunt her, intensifying her longing to see him again.

The women's ward did not give her the same sense of satisfaction she had derived from working with the children, and she wondered how much longer it would be before Sister Ito was back. In response to her enquirires she learned that she was expected to be away for some weeks yet.

There had been a time, not so long ago, when she was convinced that she was doing the right thing by staying on in Japan, at least for a while until she was sure what her next move should be. Now, however, she seemed to have lost her sense of direction. It was like crossing a bridge over a raging torrent that would destroy her if she fell. Too late now to turn back, and although the far bank was shrouded in mist, she believed that if she could reach it, she would have come through the most difficult period of her life. At the moment she felt that she lacked the confidence to move that short distance to safety. She had no idea what to do about it.

It was at a time when she was feeling incapable of

coming to any sensible conclusion about the future that Hugh's letter came.

Dear Anna, It was good to hear from you again. Your letters are full of interest and I can see that you're finding answers to your questions which will encourage you to continue your search. Our anxieties and inferiorities are natural emotions but they must be balanced by a spiritual understanding if we are to grow.

Your experience with Suzu was valuable and it's good to hear of the work that Japanese doctor is doing in the field. It makes one realise how wrong it is to judge a nation by the crimes of a few.

I've recently met up with two friends from the camp, both of whom knew Jack and we talk a lot about those times. I was interested to hear about your dreams. Jack would be very much in your mind now you're living in Japan and that would account for them. It seemed remarkable though that the jungle scene which you described was so typical of life in the prison camp. There is something that perhaps I should have told you before. Jack had become very restless and one day he made an unsuccessful bid for freedom. He was discovered and taken into solitary confinement. He never spoke of what they did to him there but it seemed to be a turning point for him. When at last he was released, near to starvation and suffering from diseases of malnutrition, there was an extraordinary change in him. He no longer seemed afraid of the guards and was quite free of the resentment which dogged the rest of us. He set about encouraging and helping the other prisoners. In fact he became a source of inspiration to the rest of us. Personally I think during that time, he had come to rely on spiritual help.

Anna stopped reading and looked across to Jack's photograph. She wasn't surprised to hear that he'd tried to escape. It was consistent with everything she knew about her brother, but the religious streak was something quite new. He had never shown the slightest interest in anything like that and she thought that Hugh, with his leanings in that direction, might have been reading more into Jack's change of attitude than was actually there. Far more likely that Jack had decided that resistance was useless and it was only sensible to accept the situation.

She picked up the letter and went on reading.

Hardly a day passes when I don't think of him and I sometimes wonder what career he would have followed. Perhaps he would have stayed in the Navy as he loved the life. He once told me that living in close contact with the sea convinced him that there was a power for good at work in the world. Another expression of his faith perhaps?

I think of you often and pray that you'll find peace and happiness in what you're doing.

Yours ever, Hugh.

She read the letter through again and felt encouraged. He had put into words some of her thoughts, and given her more confidence in the future. She decided that she would go to Hiroshima soon. She had three days leave due to her, just enough to make the long journey there and back.

She thought again about ringing Nigel. She didn't want to give him the idea that she might be changing her mind about him, but it would be a friendly gesture, to tell him of her intention. It was unlikely he would want to come with her, but at least she could offer him the opportunity. She rang his office that afternoon.

'Nigel?' she said crisply, when he came on the line. 'It's Anna.'

'Anna! Is everything all right?'

'Yes. Everything's fine. I'm ringing to let you know I've got a few days off and I'm going to Hiroshima.'

'Hiroshima! What the devil for?'

'Because I want to see the place. I'm taking the overnight train to Osaka on Saturday. I wondered if you'd be interested in coming?'

'How long are you staying?'

'Till Monday. I'm on duty Tuesday morning.'

'Couldn't you come up on Friday and spend a day here?'

'I'm afraid not. I have to fit in with the rest of the staff. I've just this minute made arrangements with the ward.'

'Then you'll have to go alone. I've got a meeting on Monday which I can't cancel. There's not a hope in hell that I can get away at such short notice.' He sounded exasperated.

'I understand that, but unless I go now I might not get another chance. Dad's still not well and I might have to go home suddenly.'

'What do you want to go to Hiroshima for anyway? It's a gloomy place. You'd do much better to give up that idea and let me take you to Kyoto. We could do it easily in a day.'

'Another time perhaps. I want to go to Hiroshima.'

He sighed. 'If you've made up your mind, there's not much I can do about it. Couldn't you stop off for a couple of hours on the way?'

'There's not enough time. I want a whole day there and I'll stay overnight and come back the next day.'

'Anna look . . .'

'The situation hasn't changed,' she interrupted him. 'I rang just in case you wanted to come.'

'You're driving me crazy, you know. One moment you don't want to see me again and the next you're ringing me as though we're still good friends. What am I supposed to think?'

She had a vision of him running his hands through his hair.

'Just that. Nothing more. I thought if I was coming your way you would want me to let you know. After all, you did suggest it. I'm sorry but I must go now.'

She put down the phone abruptly, before the conversation degenerated into an argument. She had expected it might and it very nearly had. She should perhaps have given it more thought and, in the event, she was greatly relieved that he couldn't come. She had wanted to get back on a friendly footing with Nigel before she left Japan. But perhaps it would have made their relationship worse, not better.

Anna caught the overnight train, arriving in Osaka at six in the morning, just as dawn was creeping over the hills. She had an hour before the train left for Hiroshima, so she took herself into the station restaurant. Early though it was, the place was crowded with weary travellers. Some of them looked as though they'd been there all night, which in all probability they had, coming by bus from remote country districts.

She ordered a cup of tea and a sweet roll and carried them to a table that was already occupied by a young couple. She asked if she might share it with them. They bowed and smiled. Foreigners were still an unusual sight in this part of Japan, so she must expect to attract some attention, more so as a young woman travelling on her own. The girl stole the occasional glance at her and Anna knew that she'd be the subject of much discussion once she had departed. She looked at her watch. Still another forty minutes to wait. She left the table and went outside to stroll up and down the platform.

The air was crisp on this clear autumn day and she felt a sense of excitement, though she was in no doubt that what she was about to see would be deeply distressing. She was glad now that she was going alone or it might have become simply a sight-seeing trip. Yoshi had remarked with some sarcasm in his voice, that the place these days was overrun with tourists.

'Anna!'

She swung round to see Nigel striding down the platform towards her.

'Just in time. I was afraid I was going to be too late. I couldn't miss the chance to see you.'

He reached to take her hands in his. Against her better judgement she let him.

'Whatever time did you get up?' she said.

'About five. It takes about an hour to get here. I hoped I could persuade you to change your mind. Come with me to Kyoto instead?'

'No.' For a moment she panicked. She hoped desperately that he wouldn't get angry about it. 'I'm going to Hiroshima and that's that. I've got my ticket. If you want to, you can come.'

'I've no desire to, not even with you. Why do you want to go, Anna?'

Was there any point in telling him? Would he understand?

'I'm going because I nursed a little girl who died as a result of the bomb and because I know a Japanese doctor who is working with people suffering from radiation. It was such a terrible thing to watch that child die. I want to know what it was like on that August morning in 1945. I want to feel part of it, however small.'

Nigel was listening to her as though intent on hearing what she had to say. Normally he would have brushed it aside as if it were of no consequence.

'It has something to do with Jack, too, hasn't it?' His voice was gentle now, compassionate.

She was encouraged to go on, to try to explain.

'I think perhaps it has. It's made me realise that we weren't blameless either. We caused suffering as well on a far greater scale.'

'It brought the war to a close. It could have dragged on indefinitely.'

'But I'm afraid that one day it might happen again. People seem to forget so easily.'

'It's not likely to. I don't think you can take responsibility for that, Anna. Anyway, does it make you feel any better about Jack?'

She looked up at him, surprised by the question. In the past he had always been reluctant to mention Jack.

'Perhaps not. But I have noticed how these people accept personal tragedy without bitterness. I wish I could feel the same way.'

'I don't believe you can learn anything from the Japanese. Not when you blame them for Jack's death. It doesn't make sense.'

'Strange, isn't it?' Her smile was tinged with sadness.

People were gathering on the platform. Among

them were vendors displaying their wares, soft drinks, cigarettes and fruit. There was a brisk trade in bento boxes containing neatly packed lunches.

'Have you got anything to eat?' Nigel asked her.

She shook her head.

'Let me get you something.'

As he was buying her some fruit and a can of juice the train drew into the station.'

'Have you a reservation?' he asked.

'No. I'll take my chances.'

'I don't think you'll have much choice. You'll find it's all one class. You'll have to push your way on. There'll be a rush.'

The passengers were not immediately allowed to board the train. Attendants had to first clean away the debris from the last contingent of travellers. But at last all was ready and Nigel propelled her forward with the pushing, excited crowd and found a window seat for her.

'I hope you'll find what you're looking for in Hiroshima,' he said.

'Thanks Nigel, and for coming to the station.'

'Next time give me more notice,' he grinned at her as he left.

She watched him, grateful that he had taken the trouble to come and glad that after all she had rung him.

The carriage was filling rapidly, all manners forgotten, people scrambling to find places, children to the foremost. Some had already staked their claim and had taken off their shoes and put up their feet on the seat opposite, reluctant to move them to make room for fellow travellers. It was a complete reversal, Anna thought, of the characteristic Japanese politeness.

The train jerked forward. They were off. Anna stared out through the window at the dreary suburbs of Osaka. The countryside was scarcely more prepossessing. They stopped at Kobe. Beyond it the train ran alongside the coast for a short time before moving inland through paddy fields where strange volcanic cones rose abruptly out of the earth.

Anna studied her fellow passengers. Some of the women had pulled their feet up onto the seat and sat on their heels as they would in their own homes; others had opened their kimonos and were suckling their babies, quite unselfconsciously. The men occupied themselves opening the food boxes and sampling pieces of red sausage, fish and pickled vegetables. Having taken the greater part for themselves, they offered small pieces to their wives and children before finishing off the contents.

She was horrified by the amount of litter that was dumped on the floor, with a complete disregard for the litter container. The meal lasted for the duration of the journey, interspersed with brief periods of sleep. By mid-afternoon they were passing through a fruit growing area where women were harvesting oranges. They wore dark blue cotton trousers and jackets with white scarves tied over their heads, and some had babies strapped to their backs. Surely their small legs must become deformed, confined in this position for hours on end. Approaching Hiroshima, she caught her first sight of the hazy city, backed by hills to the east. As the train drew to a stop, she thankfully prised herself off her hard wooden seat and, picking up her suitcase, made her way through the debris.

Time was not to be squandered. She had already

decided on a plan of action. A row of taxis waited outside the station and immediately one drew up in front of her and a small man with a shock of untidy hair opened the door for her. In her best Japanese she asked him to take her to an inexpensive hotel. He nodded and smiled at her, exposing a row of uneven teeth as he clamboured back into the driver's seat. There he sat and waited.

'We go now,' said Anna, impatient at the unnecessary delay.

'We wait husband?' he asked in English.

'No. I'm on my own.'

'Ah, so? Then we go.' He coaxed the reluctant engine into action and drove off smartly.

As they progressed through the newly built city, the tall concrete office blocks and department stores, she saw him studying her in the mirror.

'You American?' he asked.

'English.'

Presently they came to the Peace Park laid out in the centre of the city.

'Big museum here,' said the driver, slackening speed and pointing to a building in the centre of the park. 'Peace Memorial Museum,' he said. 'You like see?'

'Not now. Later, after you take me to the hotel.' The man seemed to speak adequate English and Anna abandoned her attempts to struggle with Japanese.

'Hills very beautiful,' he went on. 'You like go there, see everything, town, sea?'

'Maybe later,' said Anna. 'I don't have too much time.'

'I take now. OK?'

'OK.' It wasn't a bad idea to get a view of the whole

before she started her exploration of the town. He threw her a broad grin over his shoulder. 'My name Koji. OK?'

His cheerful spirits were infectious.

'I'll call you Koji, then,' she said.

He turned off the main road and took a narrow street that led up a steep hill. This was a part of the city that seemed to have escaped the bombing. Children playing between old wooden houses, stopped to stare at the taxi with its foreign passenger. Koji had his hand perpetually on the horn which the children ignored until he leaned out of the window and scolded them, whereupon they dissolved into laughter.

They climbed on up through the pine woods, the car protesting at the demands made on it as it bounced from one pothole to another, until they came to an area of rocks and scrub. Here Koji stopped the car and invited Anna to get out and look at the view. By now the car was steaming in an alarming manner, and it seemed imperative that the engine be allowed to cool.

The day had become bright and clear, and the city sprawled below them over a wide plain with hills rimming it. Tall skyscrapers rose from the area of ruin amidst a forest of naked twisted girders. Near the sea, giant cranes were loading goods onto ships bound for other lands and in the centre of this hideous landscape lay the green area of the Peace Park, with its memorial amongst the trees.

'Park beautiful,' said Koji. 'Over there is Inland Sea. Also beautiful. You go to Inland Sea?'

Anna shook her head. 'No. I don't have enough time. I have to go back to Tokyo tomorrow.'

Koji took in a sharp breath through his teeth. 'Pity.

I take you see many interesting things. You live in Japan long time?'

'Only six months.'

'Is that so? When you go home?' Koji's curiosity knew no bounds and she thought this should give her a certain freedom to learn something of this cheerful little man who had taken her under his wing.

'I'm not sure,' she answered. 'How long have you lived in Hiroshima?'

'Many years. I born here.'

'So you were here when the bomb fell?'

'*Hai*. I work that morning. We hear planes and see great red flame. Then bang!' He clapped his hands together and then put them over his ears. 'Like fire. Then black rain fall and many people die. River full of black mud and dead peoples. My baby, she die.'

Anna gave a murmur of sympathy. 'And your wife?'

He shook his head. 'Wife also, but not for many months. Slowly – slowly. All hair come out and very much sickness.' He smiled, the kind of smile which comes naturally to Japanese people when they speak of grief. It was their way of making light of sad news for the listener.

'Were you with her when it happened?' Anna asked gently.

'No. I work in docks. Long way from bomb. When I come home, house gone.' A vigorous headshaking and clicking of teeth. 'Many, many people die, but finished now. No more bombs. You go to museum and see.'

'Yes,' said Anna, thankful that Koji had managed to stay happy and even philosophical when he spoke of it. 'Shall we return to the town now?'

'You like to stay in mountains?' asked Koji.

'I would like to, yes, but there are no hotels here.'

'Yes. Special hotel. A place where women can go. Convent.'

'Do they take guests?' she asked, surprised.

'*Hai*. I bring many peoples to this convent. Very peaceful place. You like it. Very cheap.'

Anna considered. It sounded ideal, but how was she to see Hiroshima if she was stuck up a mountain.

'I take you down and up again. I take you anywhere you want,' said Koji. 'You pay me two thousand yen.' It was ridiculously cheap.

Anna nodded. 'Thank you, Koji. I accept.'

'OK. We go now.' This time Anna sat in front beside him. Not only had she got herself transport but a guide as well and she wanted to make the most of it.

They continued slowly up the hill, the car giving warning that it might stop at any moment, and turned in an entrance where a grey stone slab bore the words Convent of Peace – Carmelite, and underneath were Japanese characters. The drive was lined with cryptomeria trees and at the end of it stood a tall grey house. They drew up in front of a heavy wooden door and Koji brought out her suitcase and rang the bell. The door was opened by a nun and Koji, having spoken to her, told Anna that he would wait outside. She followed the nun along a corridor to a small room in which was a bed and a small chest of drawers.

'I hope you'll be comfortable.' The nun spoke English. 'We eat at six. Vespers are at seven and mass at six thirty in the morning.'

When she had left, Anna walked across to the window and looked out on the cloisters. What a fantastic place to have found, and all through the little Japanese who was so anxious for her welfare. She found him outside, a broad grin on his face.

'First we go to Peace Memorial Museum,' he said, starting up the engine and driving at a reckless pace down the hill. In no time at all he had stopped outside the entrance to the park.

'What time you like me come back?' he asked.

Anna looked at her watch. It was already three o'clock.

'Four-thirty?' she suggested.

'OK. I come then.'

She went into the bright, well-lighted building and paused to read an account of that morning seven years ago.

On the morning of August 6th, 1945, the weather was fine and calm. People were already at work and children had gone to school. Suddenly at eight fifteen an atomic bomb exploded over the city in a gigantic fireball. The temperature of this fireball – often referred to as a miniature sun – is estimated at 300,000 degrees centigrade. Black sticky liquid like raindrops fell. The river water was black like ink. In the mud radioactivity was strong and all the fish died. Fires broke out over the city centre. More than 200,000 people were killed or injured. Of 45 hospitals, only 3 were left standing and only 28 of the 290 doctors in the city were unhurt and left to cope with the people as they struggled through the burning city to reach help.

Anna had already read an account from the books Yoshi had lent her but this made a much deeper impression on her. She went on to read stories of individual tragedies until she herself began to feel the pain of it. She looked at a picture of a young soldier bleeding from the pores who died two hours later, the scorched blazer of a thirteen year old schoolboy, one of 6000 who had been taking part in an air-raid defence programme and who stood unprotected in the street when the bomb fell. She saw the photo of a man stone-dead, sitting on his bicycle as it leaned against the railing; dead people floating down the river and a baby seeking the breasts of her dead mother. Charts hung on the walls of the thermal radiations, and there was a full sized model of the bomb that was dropped on Nagasake a few days later.

When Anna emerged into the sunlight she felt emotionally shattered and took deep breaths of fresh air, conscious of its purity and life-giving qualities. For the next half hour she wandered through the trees looking at the Children's statue and the ruined dome of the bomb that had been preserved as a memorial. For a while she sat on a bench under the shade of the tree. It was there that Koji found her.

'You see enough?' he asked.

'Yes.'

'Then we go look at town. I take you see my house.'

She shook her head. 'No thank you, Koji. I'd like to go back to the Convent.'

'You no want see more?' he asked, surprised. 'I take you see peoples sick from bomb.'

'No more, Koji. Sorry, I've seen enough.'

'Many peoples want see,' he said, 'but they not feel. You feel, so you have seen enough.'

Anna took this to be a kind of compliment and smiled at him.

'How do you feel about the bomb, Koji? Do you hate the people responsible?'

'Sure. When it happen, I am angry. I want kill those people, but no more. I love my family. Hate spoil beautiful memories.'

'I believe you're right,' she said, amazed that a taxi driver should speak so profoundly.

'OK,' said Koji, cheerfully. 'Tomorrow we see more. Train go to Tokyo every six hours, eight, two and eight at night. What time you go?'

'You know everything,' said Anna.

He shrugged, drawing in his breath sharply to express his pleasure.

'I take many people see Hiroshima. If people want see terrible things, we make good living. We make new life now.'

'I'll catch the two o'clock train, then. Will you take me to the station?'

'*Hai*.' He gave a small bow, and climbing into the ramshackle car again, they set off up the hill.

'Do all taxi-drivers in Hiroshima speak good English, like you?' Anna asked.

He shrugged. 'All speak some English. Sometimes people ask for driver who speak good English and I get job.' He grinned.'I get married soon and maybe one day I get teaching job. Are you married?'

'No. I'm a nurse.'

'Ah, *so desu-ka*? You sympathetic person. But why you not get married? You pretty. All girls marry.'

Anna laughed. 'Maybe I will. One day.'

'I think you have some trouble,' he said presently, showing remarkable perception. 'Maybe you speak to nuns.'

'You think they can help me?' said Anna dubiously, wondering if he were joking.

But Koji was in earnest. 'Very wise peoples. They understand many things. Often I bring peoples to them because they sad, afraid. Many peoples like that and I bring them to the nuns. Nuns help.'

'Is that why you took me there?' asked Anna, suddenly interested.

'I think you try find peace,' he said. 'That's why you come here.'

They were high above the town now. The car gamely wound its way round the hairpin bends. They came to a plateau, and the road levelled off. Koji crouched over the wheel, encouraging his car, and it gradually picked up speed.'

'How do you know so much about the nuns, Koji?

'I know they good people. They help us after bomb. They help us now.'

'Are you a Christian then?'

'Of course. You too?'

She was spared having to answer because at that moment the car began to splutter and came to a halt. The radiator was boiling.

'We stop here,' said Koji. He got out and peered under the bonnet. 'I put water in the radiator.' He scampered round to the boot of the car and brought out a large can.

'Not yet,' said Anna, alarmed. 'Wait till it's cool.'

'I know. I know,' said Koji with a grin. 'But you in hurry?'

'No, but I think, if you don't mind, I'll walk the rest of the way. It's not far. Then you can go back to town and have it fixed.'

'OK then,' he said cheerfully. 'I come tomorrow.'

Leaving him to deal with the engine, she started on her way up the hill, walking slowly. The air up here was delightful, a slight breeze coming off the sea. Soon she was out of sight of the car and came to an area of rocks and scrub where occasional stunted oaks and lacquer trees grew. Wild azaleas grew in abundance, and Anna thought how beautiful it must be in spring.

Rounding the next bend, she saw the figure of a nun ahead of her. She was walking slowly, pausing every now and then to look at the view below. Anna maintained her pace, drawing closer and the nun, hearing footsteps behind her, looked back. Seeing Anna, she made a small gesture of greeting, and waited for her to catch up.

'It's beautiful, isn't it?' said Anna, drawing level.

'Very,' the nun agreed, in English. 'You're going to our convent?'

'Yes. I'm staying the night there.'

'You haven't walked all this way, surely?'

'Oh no. The car broke down.'

The nun laughed. 'Then you must have come up with Koji. How he keeps that old machine going, I will never know.'

Now she was close to her, Anna saw that there was something different about the features of this nun.

'Are you from Japan?' she asked.

'Most of us are, but I come from Thailand. I asked to come here for a year. An exchange,' she explained. 'My name is Phoon.'

'And mine's Anna. You all speak English so well. How is that?'

'Because we have many foreigners here. We feel we have an important mission. So many people come to this place and try to make some sense out of it. They think we have the answer and often they want to talk about it. Most people speak English whatever their nationality.'

'When the bomb dropped, Koji said the nuns helped the injured.'

'I wasn't here then, but yes, the nuns did do quite a lot. Some of them had trained as nurses. They went down to the town and helped the wounded. It was a privilege to be here at such a time. I wish I had been.'

Anna glanced at the fresh young face and judged Phoon could be no more than twenty-two or three.

'But what do you think about it all?' she asked the nun. 'How do you feel when so many people were killed? Aren't you surprised that your God could allow it to happen?'

'You say our God. Is he not yours also?'

'I'm not sure,' said Anna.

Phoon was silent for a moment before saying: 'It's a common question, isn't it? So many judge tragedy from a worldly angle. They look for wealth and security, yet it doesn't satisfy them and when things go wrong, they blame God. Yet it is often through suffering that people turn to him and find that he is a loving God and that he does fulfil their needs. Don't you agree?'

Anna noticed she was saying much the same thing as Hugh.

'I think there are plenty of people leading normal, happy lives who don't believe in God,' she continued. 'What surprises me is that the Japanese don't seem to blame us for dropping the bomb. I would expect them to.'

'I think perhaps what you say is true,' said Phoon, slowly. 'Perhaps they blame their Emperor who had promised them victory. I don't understand the political side of it, but I think there's something deeper to it than that. People personally involved in suffering, usually manage to cope with it. It's the others who do not fully comprehend it and are loud in their protests. I think that in suffering people can grow towards their spiritual potential but perhaps one has first to believe in eternity.'

'I had a twin brother,' said Anna, picking her words carefully. 'He died in a prisoner-of-war camp at the hands of the Japanese. He and his companions were brutally treated, starved, abused and tortured. I can't forget that. I haven't found any peace through his death.'

'And what about him? Did you ever find out how he felt about it?'

Anna thought of Hugh's letters.

'After the war,' she said, 'his friend who was in the camp with him came to see me in England. It surprised me because he had no hatred for the guards in that camp. In fact he had already forgiven them. He told me that my brother said before he died that he was glad that he'd had that experience. I find that hard to understand.'

'He had learnt to forgive,' said Phoon, nodding, 'and that in itself brings peace. It sounds to me as though you can't accept your brother's death and that makes you unhappy.'

They turned in at the gate of The Convent of Peace and walked under the cryptomeria trees.

'It must be very hard for you,' Phoon went on. 'I hope one day you'll find the peace your brother obviously found.'

'How can I find it, if I can't forgive?' asked Anna.

'By getting to know our Lord. He can give it to you,' said Phoon, serenely. 'It might take time, but it's worth finding.'

They had reached the house. 'I'll see you at the evening meal,' said Phoon. 'Perhaps you'd like to come to vespers afterwards. Most of our guests do.'

Anna thanked her. 'I'm glad we talked on the hill,' she said.

She was the only guest in the convent that night and at dinner she sat with the nuns. They were solicitious and politely interested in her, and she was happy to answer their questions, but none touched on the things she had spoken of with Phoon.

After the meal she made her way to the rest room. The French windows stood open, overlooking the bay and she stepped outside. It was not yet dark and the sky was that rich velvet blue that comes to Japan at twilight. Her thoughts dwelt on Jack and she wondered what he would make of this. He was, she felt, a part of it. A life could not be taken in isolation but was part of the whole of creation. As Yasuko had come to terms with Suzu's death and Koji with his family's, she wanted so much to accept Jack's. Perhaps love was the answer; God's love overriding the inadequacy of logic and meeting a deep need in the hearts of man. Was this Jack's secret?

She thought she would, after all, go to vespers. The nuns were making their way to the chapel now and she followed them and knelt down and tried to pray. She was quite out of practice and gave up trying to put her thoughts into words. Instead she let her mind drift, absorbing the profound quiet of the place, and presently a deep peace stole over her.

Afterwards in her bedroom, she opened her windows wide so that the mountain air filled the room. Her last waking thoughts were of Yoshi. If it had not been for him she might never have come. She was not depressed by what she had seen. There was hope. Out of destruction a seed was beginning to grow. There was no knowing whether it would flower, but it might already have entered her heart.

Chapter Eighteen

After visiting his mother in Osaka, Yoshi took Tama and the children to Kyoto for a few days holiday. Much as he enjoyed the company of his family he found these days away from work tried his patience, more so as he'd had problems with the old lady. He'd wasted a lot of time trying to persuade her to move to Tokyo where they had plenty of room to accommodate her, but she remained adamant. She had lived all her married life in the Kansai and had no wish to move at this late stage. At least, he consoled himself, her health was in the hands of a good friend of his, and he was confident that she was receiving the best possible treatment.

Tama helped him in this discussion, calming the old lady where he had ruffled her feelings in trying to override her wishes. In the end it meant staying on an extra day in Osaka, thereby curtailing their time in Kyoto.

As a result they'd had an exhausting day, fitting in more sightseeing than he'd originally intended. They had visited the famous Heian Shrine, the Silver Pavilion as well as the Kutsura Palace, and they'd had to miss the tea ceremony which Tama always enjoyed. Cheiko had become very fractious, complaining that she'd had enough of shrines and wanted to get back to the hotel. She was rewarded with sharp words from her elder brother which reduced her to tears. Yoshi had to admit that the day had not been a success.

The children were now in bed and having finished their evening meal, he and Tama were sitting on the balcony of their room overlooking the street. Rain threatened and already people were putting up their umbrellas as they tripped along the pavements in their wooden *getas*. Wind stirred the branches of a huge camphor tree, its massive roots exposed above the ground. Open-fronted stores were doing a brisk business as last minutes purchases were made for the evening meal. Not far away, they could hear the sound of a pichinko hall. Gambling on the pinball machines was all the rage these days with young people, and Yoshi was thankful that their children had not yet reached the age when they would have to face this problem.

'I should really go back tomorrow,' he said to Tama. 'I have this book I must make a start on. The publishers want it by the end of next year and there's a lot of research to be done before I can even start writing.'

'Now we're here, surely one more day will make little difference? You need the break, Yoshi.'

'I can't work under pressure. I must get some thoughts down and then I shall feel easier in my mind.'

Usually amenable, this time he found her remarkably stubborn.

'Yoshi, please, just this once. If you go tomorrow it will mean that we'll have to forego our trip down the rapids. The children are looking forward to that and we can't do it without you.'

It was true. He thought she might be willing to

give up the idea, but she seemed set on it and he certainly wouldn't want them to go on the boat without him. It could be dangerous, as the river was swift and the passage between the rocks narrow in parts. There had been accidents. He had promised them, and the children would be disappointed if the idea was abandoned. There was nothing for it but to go along with them.

'Very well,' he said, reluctantly. 'I will stay, but I must return to Tokyo early the next day. I shall have to work on the book some other time.'

She was visibly relieved. 'Now you're here it would be a pity to leave before we've done all that we planned to. It might be a long time before we come again.'

'You don't need to come home with me, Tama. You can stay on and bring the children back later.'

'It's not the same without you. There's so much for them to see here. We need this time together, Yoshi, to enjoy it properly and teach them what to look for on these expeditions.'

'That's something you can do equally well without me.'

Tama was not to be put off so easily.

'They enjoy learning from you. The boys are quite a handful, you know. They respond to you and you are far better equipped than I to answer their questions.'

Yoshi sipped his tea and reflected that perhaps he had been neglecting the family. Unlike some of his colleagues, he had always felt it important to be involved with the children's upbringing. He couldn't leave it all to Tama, especially now the boys were older. They received a good education at school, but there were some things that must be taught in the home and discipline was important. He suspected that sometimes Tama found it quite hard to keep them in order, though this was the first time she had voiced her anxieties.

He tried to calm her fears.

'I know I've left a lot to you but at the moment I don't see how I can do otherwise. I'll bear in mind what you've told me though. The children are developing well, Tama. They have enquiring minds and a natural appreciation of beauty. So long as we encourage that, they'll turn out all right.'

Outside on the street they could hear the tofu seller's flute as he pushed his cart along the street. People came out of their houses to buy the nourishing bean curd which he ladled into containers for them. Yoshi and Tama watched for a while in silence.

Presently Tama regarded him, her eyes sad. 'Yoshi, are you so busy these days that you haven't the time to teach our children or isn't it important to you any longer? You used to say that time spent in this way was never wasted.'

She waited patiently for his answer. Although her voice was even, it carried a hint of determination that irritated him.

'Of course it's important and perhaps I am neglecting these things. But you must understand that just at the moment I am extremely busy. Believe me, I don't want to tackle this book but I can't afford to pass over any opportunity to publicise the dangers that another war would bring. It's a responsibility I can't overlook.'

Was he being entirely honest with Tama, he asked himself. He should at least try to encourage her in her efforts to bring up the children.

'You're right though,' he went on, 'As soon as I can, I shall make more time for the family.'

'So you'll stay for the three days as you intended?'

This was not what he had meant to imply. 'No. I shall go back the day after tomorrow.'

Tama had said her piece. She accepted his decision, but he knew that she was upset. She had put her case well and whereas another time he might have been persuaded, the inclination to get back to the hospital was so strong that he would not consider staying on. He felt badly about disappointing her and ill-at-ease with himself. Perhaps he was overworked. He found it ever harder to concentrate these days and this was a sign of stress.

To make it up to her, he said, 'You're very patient, Tama. I'm a very fortunate man.' He held out his hand to her. 'I'm tired. Let's go to bed.'

Tama was looking very desirable that evening and as she gently caressed him, soothing away his weariness and all the tension, he turned to her with an urgency he had not felt for many months.

On his return to the hospital two days later, Yoshi went straight to the children's ward and checked on his patients. The following days were taken up with meetings and visits to other hospitals. He welcomed the busy schedule as it took his mind off Anna. He hadn't seen her for over two weeks, but now she had left the children's ward their paths rarely crossed. He found that this did little to decrease his desire to see her. Angrily he thrust his thoughts away but they refused to be banished and throughout the day returned to bother him.

It crossed his mind that she had left. It was always on the cards that she might have to go home. He couldn't rest until he'd found out, and thinking up some weak excuse, he visited the women's ward at a time when he would expect her to be there.

The staff nurse on duty was a complete stranger to him.

'When will Nurse Bradford be on duty?' he asked.

'I think she's away, but Sister will be back shortly. Can I give her a message?'

'No.' Yoshi had difficulty in hiding his impatience. He had expected to glean some information however slight.

The nurse shook her head. 'I'm sorry but I've only just come to work on this ward.'

He had to see Mother Agnes about the book. Some of his research would be done in this hospital, and he wanted her to know there would be times when he would be working on it in his office.

'That's all right, Yoshi,' she said.'You must work wherever it's most convenient for you. Any facilities we have here are at your disposal.'

He spent some time discussing the form it would take. He found her keenly interested in the subject.

As he was about to leave he said, 'I haven't seen Anna about recently. Is she still here?'

'She's on leave at the moment. I have an idea she went to Hiroshima.'

'I know she was thinking of going. Have you any idea when she'll be back?'

'Early next week. They'd have the dates on the ward.'

He shrugged. 'It can wait. Actually I was wondering if she'd be coming back to the children's ward? She was exceptionally good with them.'

Mother Agnes studied him so intently, he began to feel uncomfortable.

'Not for a while,' she said at last. 'We need her where she is and I think she needs a break from the children.'

'You mean after Suzu?'

'That's one of the reasons. The children's ward is fully staffed at the moment with excellent nurses. Don't you agree, Yoshi?'

He left the room with the feeling there was more to it than Mother Agnes cared to tell him. It could even be that Anna herself had asked to be transferred from the children's ward.

A few days later Yoshi was working in his office, surrounded by reference books and trying to get his thoughts onto paper. Exasperated by his lack of concentration, he pushed back his chair and went over to the window. He was standing deep in thought when there was a knock on the door.

'Come in,' he called absent-mindedly.

He was aware of the door opening, but a moment passed before he turned to see who it was. His reaction was immediate. A mask came over his face in an effort to hide the intense pleasure he felt at seeing Anna.

'You've been away?' he enquired, his voice indifferent.

'Yes. To Hiroshima.'

Unreasonably, he was annoyed that she had not informed him of her movements. 'You didn't tell me you were going.'

'No.'

'You went alone?'

He knew from the look of surprise on her face, that his questions were intrusive but he couldn't help himself.

'Yes,' she said. 'Why?'

'You said you wanted to go with someone who could explain it to you.'

'I had hoped it could have been you, but as that wasn't possible, I went alone.'

'Where did you stay?'

'At a convent in the hills.' There was a suspicion of laughter in her voice and the hint of a smile in her eyes, as though she found his questions amusing. It annoyed him.

'How did you find such a place?'

'A taxi driver took me there.'

It was beyond his comprehension. Here was a foreigner, a woman at that, who went off to Hiroshima because she wanted to find out something about that complex subject. Not only did she travel on her own, but she appeared to have had no difficulty in finding suitable accommodation, having put herself at the mercy of a taxi driver who, no doubt, cheated her of her money. A Japanese woman could never have done this, and such independence, such self-containment astonished him.

'I think you should have sought advice before you embarked on such a plan. Had you asked me, I could have given you some idea of what to see and recommended an hotel. Then you wouldn't have wasted any time.'

'But I didn't,' protested Anna. 'I had a very pleasant stay there.'

'You weren't shocked by what you saw then?' asked Yoshi.

'Yes, of course I was, but the books you lent me had prepared me to some extent. I came to ask if I could keep them a little longer.'

'Of course. I have more when you've finished

those. You went to the Peace Memorial Museum then?'

'Yes. I spent a long time there. I found it very moving and not as upsetting as I expected.'

His eyebrows rose. 'Why was that?'

'I'm not sure myself. It would take me a long time to try and explain how I felt, but I'm very glad I went.'

He looked at his watch. He had an appointment in ten minutes, but he didn't want to let her go. Once she left the room there was no knowing when he'd see her again.

'Unfortunately, I have an appointment,' he told her. 'But I would be interested to hear more about your trip. Perhaps we could discuss it some other time?'

'I'd like to,' she said, and obviously meant it.

Her pleasure at his suggestion was gratifying. Saturday might be a good day. Most of his colleagues would be at home then and it was unlikely that they would be interrupted. He had ear-marked Saturday to make a start on the book and he could ill afford the time. Still, he consoled himself, he would make up for it the following week.

'Perhaps something could be arranged for Saturday,' he suggested. 'I have to come into the hospital in the morning. If you're free in the afternoon, we might go for a drive into the country?'

He arranged to pick her up near the hospital. When she had left he settled down to work. He felt much more relaxed and could now give his full attention to his notes. He didn't pause to wonder why he had made this suggestion to her against all his earlier intentions, nor did he consider where it might lead. Enough for now that he would be seeing her again very shortly.

* * *

On Saturday afternoon the weather suddenly changed. A haze obscured the sun so that it became a shapeless blaze of light. There was a threat of rain in the air.

Anna was waiting at the appointed place, dressed in a light suit, when Yoshi pulled up and leaned across to open the door for her. He smiled at her as she slipped in beside him.

'Hello,' she said brightly.

He returned her greeting, somewhat more gravely.

There was little traffic and they were soon clear of Tokyo.

'Tell me about your impressions of Hiroshima,' he said as they entered a long straight stretch of country road.

If she were to tell him everything it would take the whole afternoon, she thought. So she selected the things which she thought of special interest to him.

'I was impressed by the layout of the Peace Memorial,' she said. 'I didn't find it at all morbid. It was a bright place and it gave a clear picture of what happened that day. I almost felt that I'd been there myself. It wasn't the history of the place though that interested me so much as the people I met there.'

'You found people who spoke English?'

'I found a taxi driver who spoke very good English. He took me everywhere and acted as my guide. Do you know, Yoshi, he lost his family when the bomb fell and yet he was incredibly cheerful.'

'It was a long time ago,' Yoshi said soberly. 'He has to get on with life.'

'That's what he said. But I would have expected some blame for what happened. That's the amazing thing here. There seems to be almost no resentment towards your late enemies.'

'What's the point? Recriminations are useless.'

'It makes it hard to understand how such a people could be so brutal in war.'

'War brings out the worst as well as the best. It's the same the world over. What else did this taxi driver show you?'

She went on to tell him about Koji and how she found the convent but presently it seemed to her that he was no longer listening. It was as if his attention had wandered elsewhere. She didn't resent it. She was content to be with him, and there were other things to talk about.

'I agree with Koji,' Yoshi said at length, to show he had been listening all along. 'It seems you spent a lot of time in the convent, when he wanted to show you the city.'

'It wasn't a sightseeing tour, Yoshi. More of a personal pilgrimage. I don't expect you to understand.'

'There are people who go there, probably the vast majority,' he said, 'who look for the horror of it and they'll find plenty to satisfy them. But there are others like you who look for deeper fulfilment, and for them it has a special meaning. I'm glad you found what you were looking for.'

He turned up a road that led into the hills and parked the car on a grassy verge.

'Shall we walk a little?' he suggested. 'There's a good view up here.'

They set off along a rough track until they came to a stream where water gushed down the hillside. Rocks had been placed at intervals to serve as stepping stones.

'There's a lesson to be learnt from rocks and stones,' said Yoshi, picking up a mottled stone and running his hand over it. 'Each one tells a story. In Kyoto there's a famous garden which is made entirely of smoothly raked sand and a few rocks. Nothing else.'

'Why not flowers as well?'

'We dislike gardens that look as though they've been tamed by man,' said Yoshi. 'Flowers are best seen in their natural state as they grow in the wild. A Buddhist believes that nature can't be improved upon. He'll try to walk through a forest without disturbing a blade of grass and on entering water he'll take care not to cause a ripple. What would a western mind make of that, Anna?'

'Perhaps we could understand it,' said Anna, 'but we wouldn't dwell on it for long. I think perhaps a poet would have a greater understanding. Shelly was a great lover of nature.'

'I've read much of his work.'

'In Japanese?'

'In English.'

He had crossed the stream and now held out his hand to help her. The flesh-to-flesh contact had the same devastating effect on her as before. How often had she relived physical contact with him and longed for it to be repeated? This time it was more intense than ever. She was certain that he too must feel it. He did not let go of her hand, and they went on together up the hill. She was afraid that at any moment the path might narrow and he would release her. When eventually he did, she felt as though she had been deprived of some vital force on which she depended for survival.

As they went along, he paused now and again to

point out a damp patch where a variety of moss and lichens grew, or to listen to the myriad noises that insects make on a calm day such as this. Each moment vividly imprinted itself on her senses, and deliberately she stored them away to be recalled to mind when they were no longer together.

They passed a quarry where labourers were loading slabs of stone onto a truck and presently came to a grassy plateau around a small mountain pond. The sky was a delicate mother of pearl, bathing the village below them in a soft light. There was not a breath of wind, and in the silence a frog jumped into the pond, making a splash.

Then she felt that he was no longer looking at the view but at her. She met his gaze and saw the tenderness in his eyes. For years afterwards, when she looked back and recalled these moments, she would think that it was always like this with Yoshi. Only his eyes spoke to her and no language was needed.

'How much longer do you have, Anna? I think that you'll soon be leaving. When will it be?'

'I don't know. I had a letter from my mother the other day. She said my father has been in hospital again undergoing treatment. They're hopeful he might improve but I suppose at any time they could send for me and then I must go.'

'I sometimes wonder what keeps you here at all?'

'I stay because the right time has not yet come for me to leave.' It was perhaps a very Japanese answer to the question, and he accepted it.

'You will tell me when you know, won't you?' He spoke urgently, his eyes searching her face.

'I wouldn't want to leave without saying goodbye to you.'

'I'd like to spend so much more time with you, Anna, but it isn't easy for me to arrange.'

'I know. You have many demands on your time.'

'That isn't the reason. I've explained before that in my position I have to be discreet. Anything which could be construed as an alliance particularly – please forgive me – with a foreign woman, would be frowned upon by my colleagues and I wouldn't want word of it to reach my family.'

'I understand that.' She looked at him steadily. 'Yoshi, I'm happy with what time you can spare. I like to be with you, but I do understand your committments.'

'Then I have something to ask you.'

He turned away and stood in silence looking down to the valley before continuing. 'I don't know how to put this. Please forgive me if what I am about to suggest is offensive to you and alien to your way of life. You know, of course, that I have the highest opinion of you and would not for a moment speak of it if I felt it might upset you.'

'Please go on,' she said, having no notion of what was to follow.

'If I found a place for you in Tokyo outside the hospital, a small house or flat for which I would be responsible, would you be willing to move into it?'

'You mean,' asked Anna, pausing uncertainly, 'that you want me to become your mistress?'

He was taken aback by her directness. His eyes were wary.

'Yes, though I wouldn't have put it so bluntly.'

'What about your wife?'

'Such things aren't uncommon in Japan. It

wouldn't affect her position at the centre of the family. Besides, there's no reason why she should know. It would be a purely temporary arrangement which might suit both of us.'

'But if she did know, she'd be hurt, wouldn't she?' pressed Anna.

'Yes. That would follow because she loves me, but she wouldn't question me on the subject, even if she suspected it.'

'And you, Yoshi? How would you feel?'

'Men have a certain amount of freedom. A public scandal is to be avoided at all costs because it would harm my family and my career but provided we are careful, it's permissible.'

'And me? What about my reputation?'

He looked at her, perplexed.

'I understand your anxiety, Anna, but there's no reason why anyone should know. I'm fond of you. Isn't that enough? I've tried to hide it, but it has become an obsession and I can't keep it from you any longer. I believe you feel the same about me?'

'I do, Yoshi. I've felt that way for some time. Unfortunately. I can't do as you suggest.'

'Why not?'

'Because I don't want to give up my work at the hospital and for that, I have to live there.'

'It's not necessary. We could find somewhere quite close. A lot of nurses live at home and come in each day. No questions would be asked.'

'I wouldn't be happy in such a situation.'

'You're offended then?'

She smiled at him. 'Not at all. How could I be when I feel the same way about you, though I must admit that you've taken me by surprise.'

'I'll give you time to think about it. It seems that we haven't many days left.'

'My answer will always be the same.'

She wondered herself why she felt so sure about this. Her desire for him was intense, but as her decision over Nigel was right, so now it was with Yoshi, and for reasons which she could not begin to formulate. There was Tama, the woman she had never met. She could not embark on a relationship which would cause her pain even though Yoshi had told her it might be expected of him. And then there was Jack. She felt that in some way it would be condoning all that he had suffered. Yes, Jack's memory would always stand between herself and Yoshi.

She could explain none of this to him. He wouldn't understand, let alone accept her reasons, though he expected her to understand his. In the end perhaps it was the difference in their cultures. He was making her an offer that a Japanese woman might have been honoured and pleased to accept. But he was asking her to fall in with his plans to suit his convenience. This she couldn't do.

The subject was dropped by tacit accord. As they came down the hill, the scene had changed. It no longer held that gentle peace she had felt so strongly on the way up. She paused to look at it once more. The sun was sinking low in the sky casting a glow over the landscape, but she was oblivious of its beauty. It had become distorted, as had the mood between them. For her, nothing would ever be the same again. They could no longer speak frankly to one another because the words would be misinterpreted.

There was nothing she could do to bridge the wall

of restraint between them. Whenever she looked at Yoshi, his eyes smouldered back at her, dark with restrained anger. She understood how he felt. He had put himself in a vulnerable position and she had rejected him. This was an intolerable blow to his pride. She longed to get back into a warm companionship with him again, but could think of no way of conveying her thoughts to him without making matters worse.

Crossing the stream, he went ahead and left her to find her own way over. She wanted to take his hand in an effort to reach him again but she didn't have the courage for fear of rebuff.

Reaching the car, he got in and opened the door for her. Starting up the engine he drove off in silence till they'd almost reached the hospital, then he turned into a side street and switched off the engine.

'I'm sorry I took you by surprise,' he said stiffly. 'I didn't consider it an unreasonable suggestion and I hoped that you wouldn't either. After you've thought about it and if you decide to make the most of the time we have left together, I'll be waiting to hear from you. Otherwise, I'm afraid that any effort to meet unobserved is too difficult.'

'I understand, Yoshi. I'm glad you've told me of your feelings. I'm very moved by them, and although I'd like to accept your proposal, I'm sorry, I can't.'

And then, because she thought it might restore some of his hurt pride, she added, 'You see, I wouldn't be willing to share you.'

She got out and, aware that he was watching her, walked to the end of the road and round the corner. The distance to the hospital was short and she walked quickly, hurt that after all he'd told her, he was unwilling to risk being seen with her by any of his colleagues. He had told her what she had longed to hear, then spoiled it with his proviso: either she must accept his proposal or terminate their friendship. The choice was hers.

Chapter Nineteen

Anna was in no doubt that Yoshi was going through a very uncomfortable time. He had allowed himself to be compromised and rejected by a woman, which was unheard of for a man in his position. Even worse, she was a foreigner. It was not only a personal affront, but disturbing to his deepest values.

It must be extremely painful for him. Although she'd told him that she loved him and had been as gentle as she could in explaining the reasons why she couldn't go along with his suggestion, she guessed he would interpret the stark reality of her refusal as a rebuttal and an insult.

For her part, she accepted that his family and his profession were paramount to him. She drew some comfort from his declaration of his feelings for her, yet she was hurt that he had made no effort to end their relationship amicably.

She thought of going to him, of at least trying to salvage something of their friendship, even though he had left little room for such manoeuvre. She could hardly remonstrate with him. He had said if she changed her mind he would be waiting, but since that subject was closed, she did nothing. Yet Yoshi continued to fill her thoughts and she longed for his affectionate understanding. She couldn't bear this cold avoidance of her.

Winter was here. She had no inclination to explore further afield than Tokyo. Wrapping up warmly in those crisp clear days, she walked briskly in the park, where frost touched the bare branches of the trees and a wintry sun shone through a grey sky. Children, bundled into quilted padded coats, skated on frozen ponds where a few months ago they had sailed their boats.

It was a time for indoor activities, and she had recently been to the Kabuki theatre with her Japanese teacher. The girl tried to explain the meanings behind the strange costumes and exaggerated movements, but it was utterly incomprehensible to Anna. She also continued with her Japanese lessons. She did these things as a matter of urgency as she felt her stay here was drawing to a close but she had little interest in them.

One morning she had occasion to go to the children's ward. She was in the office talking to Sister when Yoshi walked in. His presence filled the place. Her whole attention was immediately centred on him. He seemed surprised to see her. His mouth opened but no words came out.

'Hello, Doctor,' Anna said formally.

Still he didn't speak.

'Did you want to see me?' Sister asked, looking puzzled.

'Er . . . no. It will wait.'

With that he spun round and strode out like a man with a purpose.

Her need for him was as great as ever. She had only to go to him but the situation hadn't changed. His ultimatum made it impossible for her.

About this time she heard from Hugh in reply to a long letter she had written him after her visit to

Hiroshima. He had touched on something which Anna found disturbing as it was the first time that he had written in criticism of her.

I hope you'll forgive me if I comment on this but it seems from what you write that you're still clinging to your anger over Jack, perhaps through a sense of loyalty, when you should be making an effort to let go. Koji hit on the truth when he said that negative thoughts spoil happy memories. I'm sorry if I've hurt you, but I think it needs to be said.

The letter left her feeling uncomfortable. He was suggesting that the answer lay within herself and that she should be actively doing something about it. It could be the reason why she was finding decisions so difficult to make these days.

A recent letter from home warned her that when she returned, she would find a difference in her father. He had recently had another spell in hospital. She knew she daren't delay much longer if she was to see him, but she had some obligation to the hospital. She had more or less promised that she would stay a year and Mother Agnes would need time to find a replacement. Qualified staff weren't easy to come by.

She was helped by Mother Agnes who asked her to come to her office. Now the Sister was coming back on duty, would Anna be prepared to transfer to Surgical?'

'I don't think I should,' said Anna. 'My father is no better and I feel I ought to go home if I'm to see him again. It would be pointless to move for such a short time.'

'I'm sorry to hear this,' said Mother Agnes, 'but you warned me and I won't try to persuade you to stay if you've made up your mind. When are you planning to leave?'

'I'd like to be home for Christmas. That gives me another month.'

'Then I'll make the necessary arrangements. We're going to miss you, Anna. Perhaps one day you might consider coming back to us? If you do, I'm sure we could come to some agreement about the fare.'

Anna shook her head. 'I don't think so. Once I get home I shall look for a job so that I can be near my parents.'

Having made up her mind, she rang Jean and arranged to meet her in town.

'It seems a bit sudden,' remarked Jean. 'Anything to do with the Japanese doctor?'

Anna smiled to herself. 'Not in the least,' she said offhandedly. 'I want to see my father before it's too late, that's all.'

'You're probably wise,' said Jean. 'Does Nigel know?'

'Not yet. I'll ring him before I go. I hope he'll meet someone else soon, someone who'll make him happy. He deserves that.'

'Hmm. I rather think he still hopes that one day you might change your mind.'

'Then perhaps if you have a chance, you'd better tell him that it's unlikely. I don't want him pining fruitlessly for me.'

'If I have the opportunity I'll drop the word.'

'Thanks, Jean. When you come home on leave, you will come and see us, won't you? It's an easy journey from London and I don't want to lose touch.'

Anna had been thinking about Yasuko, Suzu's aunt, and one evening she went to visit her. It was a crisp starry night and a thin crescent moon shone through scattered clouds as she picked her way down the familiar street. There were only a few people about and they walked quickly, anxious to seek protection from the icy wind in the warmth of their houses.

It was the hour of the evening meal. Housewives were cooking on open *hibachis* and the smell, mingling with the more unpleasant street odours, wafted towards her. Last time she had come this way it had been O-ban and the place had been packed with revellers, gathering for the festival. Tonight all was quiet, except for the brisk wind scattering bits of rubbish about the street.

When she came to the house, she knocked. The door was opened by Yasuko herself. She drew Anna eagerly into the warm room. The family welcomed her with smiles and bows and invited her to share their meal.

Anna had brought gifts with her, a warm shawl for Yasuko, some tobacco for her husband and toys for the children, and she distributed these as they squatted round the *hibachi*. The children were trying to entice a kitten onto their laps.

'It's a stray,' Yasuko explained. 'It followed the children home and I've allowed them to keep her.

'Today she's nervous,' the eldest child said. 'She won't play.'

Anna stretched out her hand but the kitten backed away, hissing.

'Something's frightened her,' said Yasuko. 'Animals can always tell. She must have felt a tremor.'

Anna glanced up at the shelf just above the place where Suzu used to lie. She saw that the small light burned brightly, and the photos of Suzu and her mother were still there. Yasuko followed her glance and smiled in empathy.

'You're still at the hospital?' she asked.

'Yes but I'm returning to England quite soon. I've come to say goodbye.'

'We'll all be sorry,' said Yasuko. 'We shall never forget you.'

'Neither shall I,' said Anna, suddenly close to tears.

'Perhaps one day you'll come back?'

Anna grimaced. 'I don't think so.'

They had finished the meal and as she laid down her chopsticks, Anna felt the ground trembling beneath her. The vibrations increased until the doors and shutters banged and rattled. Alarmed, she looked at Yasuko, and the next moment the whole house shook, upsetting the *hibachi* and spilling red hot charcoal over the wooden floor. Yasuko leapt to her feet and shouted to her husband to fetch water. She grabbed a rug and flung it over the embers, as Anna searched for something to remove them with. By the time Yasuko's husband appeared with a bucket and threw the water over the rug, small tongues of flame were licking the fringes and taking hold, spreading rapidly across the floor of the flimsy wooden building.

Yasuko screamed and grabbed the children, while her husband picked up a few belongings and, flinging the door open, went into the street. The little girl slipped from Yasuko's grasp and ran back for the kitten. It struggled frantically in its terror, until she was forced to let it go.

Yasuko, bundling the children ahead of her, was on her way out. Anna made to follow, then paused and hurried back to whisk the two photographs from the shelf. Flames literally flicking her heels, she made a dash for the door.

Theirs was not the only house on fire. *Hibachis* up and down the alleyways were well alight and many were knocked over, spilling the red hot embers. Smoldering on wooden floors, and fanned by gusts of wind through open doors, the flames spread rapidly. Outside, other people were gathering, calling out frantically for missing members of their families. Panic broke out, impeding people's progress. In their confusion, some ran towards the heat.

Anna could hear the crackle of fire and looking down the street, she could see the flames fanned by a sudden gust of wind, coming rapidly closer. Taking the children by the hand, she and Yasuko pushed through the crowd.

They passed a family who were hampered by an old woman who could scarcely hobble. Her daughter was carrying a baby on her back and her husband held onto the other two children. He urged his wife to hurry, but she would not leave her mother.

"Go on!' Anna shouted to Yasuko. 'I'll help these people. Go ahead. Don't wait for me.'

'Come,' cried Yasuko, taking her arm. 'Come quickly,' but Anna shook herself free and ran back. Finding the old woman, she took hold of her and ordered the young couple to go ahead with the children.

In the distance she could hear the fire engines. The heat was intense as the flames engulfed the tinder dry buildings and spread rapidly through the houses. Most of the able bodied were well ahead now and only the stragglers remained, Anna amongst them. Smoke filled her throat, choking her as bits of debris fell about her. Terror immobilised the old lady and she was unco-operative as Anna urged her forward. It was then that a piece of boarding fell from a burning roof and crashed against her, a small part catching in her sleeve. She felt a searing pain up her left arm and tried to brush it off, but she daren't stop. At their slow pace, the fire would soon overtake them. Fighting waves of pain from her arm, Anna picked up the thin body in her arms and carried it to the safety of the road. Someone – a man – relieved her of her burden, and she sank unconscious to the ground.

She awoke to find herself in a hospital bed with Mother Agnes beside her. The pain in her arm was excruciating and, looking down, she saw it had been bandaged from shoulder to wrist. She tried to grasp what Mother Agnes was saying but drowsiness overwhelmed her. Her eyes closed and presently she drifted again into oblivion.

The earthquake was given extensive coverage in the national newspapers. It was the worst in years, and they compared it with the great earthquake disaster in 1923 when vast areas of wooden houses were burned to the ground, and hundreds lost their lives. This time the fire had been contained, but over thirty had lost their lives and many more were injured, amongst them the old, and children who had strayed away from their families. Others had been overcome by smoke or trapped by falling buildings or had lost their sense of direction as the wind fed the flames, cutting off familiar paths of escape.

The fire services and ambulances had been hampered in their task by the narrow streets and the density of the shacks. The whole squalid area had been razed to the ground, leaving an enormous social problem. There were still many people to be accounted for and the living would have to be re-housed as a matter of urgency. In planning a rebuilding scheme, safety and modern facilities would be given high priority and the popular answer, according to the press, favoured the construction of highrise flats with special strengthening to withstand earthquakes.

Anna lay in bed, sedated to relieve the pain, and slept for the next two days. Mother Agnes came to see her twice, and on the morning of the third day, when she opened her eyes, Yoshi was bending over her.

Very gently he removed the bandages and carefully examined the nasty wound running down the length of her arm. He applied an antiseptic ointment before expertly fixing a new dressing. The pain was so great that she couldn't help crying out. He looked at her with concern.

'I'm sorry,' he said. 'I know it hurts terribly, but it will heal. I'm afraid you might be left with a scar though.'

'That doesn't matter,' she said weakly. 'What's a scar compared to what those people suffered.'

'You showed great courage, Anna. We're all grateful to you.'

She smiled at him. 'It was worth it, to have you look after me.'

'You've no idea how much I've wanted to spend my time doing just that.'

They were alone and could speak freely.

'But you had to have an excuse?' she said.

He looked away. 'I'm sorry. I was being unreasonable. I hadn't thought how my plans would affect you. Can you forgive me, Anna?'

'I was upset at the time. I'm all right now.' She took his hand and squeezed it. 'Yoshi, do you know if Yasuko and her family escaped? We got separated in the crowd.'

'They're safe. They're being looked after with other families until they can be rehoused.'

'I managed to save Suzu's photographs. If I give them to you could you see that Yasuko gets them?'

'Of course, but when you're better, you could take them to her yourself.'

She shook her head. 'No. I won't have time. I'm going home soon.'

'Not yet. You're not well enough.'

She didn't have the energy to argue.

Thereafter, Yoshi came to see her every day, taking personal responsibility for her injury, and she experienced first-hand the compassion and gentleness with which he treated his patients. But for her there was something more. Slowly recovering, she luxuriated in his care and attention.

She was worried about her father but Yoshi had told her firmly she was not fit to travel yet. She wrote a note home explaining about the accident which meant a postponement of her return for a little while longer. It crossed with a letter from her mother, saying that her father seemed to be rallying and was looking forward to her homecoming.

This would give her a little more time. Her arm was still extremely swollen and painful. She felt very weak and suffered from bouts of nausea. At the moment she was unable to cope, but she made up her mind that, as soon as she could get a flight, she would somehow get home. She showed the letter to Mother Agnes.

'How soon can I leave?' she asked.

'You're not fit to travel on your own yet, Anna. Reckon on at least another two weeks. That arm has to be looked after or it could lead to trouble. You need to build up your strength before you leave here. When you get home you must be fit, otherwise you'll be a burden to your family at a time when they need your help.'

Frustrating as it was, she had to go along with it. 'I'll write and tell them I'll be home in a fortnight,' she said.

Mother Agnes was firm. 'I think you should wait and see how it goes. I want you to have a few days to convalesce. In fact it's an order,' she added. 'Have you friends in Japan?'

'I suppose so. I'll have to think about it.'

Where could she go, she wondered? She thought of Jean but with the new baby, it wouldn't be fair on her. Nigel was out of the question. As she sat reading, the idea suddenly came to her. She'd go to the Japanese Alps. Helen had once told her how beautiful they were. She had saved money since she had been working, and there was more than enough for her flight home and a holiday as well.

Mother Agnes approved of the idea and made the booking for her.

On a bright Saturday morning, her second in hospital, there was a knock on the door and in walked Nigel, bearing a large bunch of flowers. He came over and kissed her on the lips.

'Nigel! How did you know I was here?'

'Read about it in the paper. Jean rang me too.' He grinned like a naughty schoolboy. 'I had to see you, Anna.'

'You came down specially?'

'Yes, of course. How did it happen?'

'I got stuck in a earthquake,' she told him, laughing.

'There was more to it than that. I read about some foreign nurse who saved an old lady's life.'

'They exaggerate. If I hadn't helped her someone else would have done.'

'So what happens now?' asked Nigel, pulling up a chair beside her.

'I'll be going home soon. I've been away long enough. I want to see Dad.'

'You'll come back to Japan?'

'No. I think I'll get a job near Mum and keep an eye on them for a while.'

'Anna, is it any good asking you to forget the past? I want you so much.'

'No. I have to go home.'

'You don't have to stay there forever,' he protested.

'No, I don't. But I can't think about it now. I want to go as soon as they allow me to travel.'

'Who's they?'

'Mother Agnes and the doctor.'

'I've been thinking, Anna. If you don't want to live in Japan, I'll give up this job and find something at home.'

She stared at him. 'Oh Nigel,' she said softly. 'Do you love me that much?'

'You know I do.'

'I'm sorry.' She touched his cheek. 'I am fond of you, but I can't make any decisions at the moment.'

'He shrugged. I've waited so long. A little longer will make no difference.'

'Nigel, listen – I want you to forget about me. I've messed your life up enough. There's another girl somewhere who would make you far happier than I ever could. I want you to look for her.'

'Then you don't love me at all?'

She only knew that she loved Yoshi and she could see no future in that. She tried not to be too brutal.

'I'm not in love with you. Let's leave it at that.'

He stood up, his face impassive.

'Very well. When are you leaving?'

'Probably next week.'

She didn't want to tell him of her idea of going to the Alps. She wanted to make that journey on her own.

Anna travelled by train and was surprised to find how tired she was after the journey. Mother Agnes had been right in advising patience and persuading her to wait a little longer before returning home.

The choice of location for her convalescence was a happy one. The majestic beauty of snow clad mountains had always invigorated her and she rarely felt lonely when she was near them. There were few visitors in the hotel, as the ski-ing season had only just begun. Consequently, she had the place almost to herself.

She spent most of her time out of doors and soon she was well enough to ski again. At first she stayed on the beginners' slopes then gradually, as she grew stronger, she took the lift to higher places, discovering with satisfaction that once her confidence returned, she had forgotten none of her early skill.

She was reminded of those holidays with Jack long ago in Switzerland. At times when ski-ing, she had a strange feeling that he was right behind her. She half expected him to overtake her as they sped towards some distant winning post, as he used to do with a shout of laughter, in those long-gone carefree days.

It was while she was here that she had another dream. She awoke in the depths of the night, suddenly aware of something that had never occured to her before: her anger over Jack's death, and insistence on clinging to his memory, had preventing them both from moving on.

She got out of bed and crossed to the window. A brilliant moon shone over the snowy slopes and further peaks rose away in the distance. She had felt Jack's presence somewhere out there; Suzu's too, now free of the restrictions of her sick body. Jack was no longer part of her life any more than Suzu was part of Yasuko's. She felt it was important to make a deliberate act of renunciation.

She opened the window wide and let the cool mountain air caress her.

'Good-bye Jack,' she whispered. 'It's taken a long time, but now I'm ready to let you go.'

A burden had been lifted from her and with it her anger evaporated. Over the months it had imperceptibly merged into the past. Perhaps it was simply the passage of time, but she thought it probably had more to do with the people she had met here. They had helped her to accept Jack's death and now she found she could call to mind memories without the pain. She had taken Hugh's words to heart. In future, if ever she was tempted to think that way again, she would be able to put the thoughts firmly behind her.

Each day her strength was returning. Breathing the fresh mountain air, she absorbed the beauty surrounding her as she skied in great curves over virgin snow. It was years since she'd felt this thrill of excitement simply to be alive.

At the end of the week she felt restored, ready for

whatever lay ahead. On the last evening she packed her bags ready for her return to Tokyo the following day, and settled down in the hotel lounge to read a book by the blazing log fire. She lifted her head, thinking she heard Yoshi calling her name. It could only be a trick of her imagination. He was so often in her thoughts.

'Anna.'

She looked up and he was there, close enough to touch. She stood up, her book falling to the floor. It seemed quite natural he should be there. He looked tired and his face was solemn.

'I'm afraid I've brought bad news,' he said. 'Your father died early this morning.'

He led her to a corner of the room which was unoccupied and held her hands while she struggled to hold back the tears that threatened.

'How did you hear?' she asked.

'Mother Agnes showed me the telegram. I said I wanted to come and tell you myself.'

'Yoshi, what about your work?'

The first tear escaped and trickled down the side of her nose.

'This was more important.' He brought out a hankerchief and himself gently wiped the tear away.

'I missed him,' she whispered. 'I should have gone home.'

'You weren't fit to travel.'

Presently they went upstairs to her room where there were no curious eyes to witness her grief. He held her close until she was calmer. Even in her sorrow she was aware that he had disregarded any attention he might attract to be with her.

He took her to the window, to look out towards the mountains. Now her father, too, was somewhere out there with Jack. The thought comforted her and presently her grief subsided.

'I haven't booked a room,' he said.

'You don't need one, Yoshi. The bed is big enough for two.'

Then he kissed her, again and again, with a passion and longing that aroused an intense response in her. Slowly and with great gentleness, he undressed her and carried her to the bed. She lay there naked, watching him take off his clothes. Then he came to her and kissed and caressed her, until her grief gave way to her urgent need of him. It was the consummation of months of longing. That night he made love to her again and again with passion and tenderness and she knew a deep fulfilment, surpassing anything she had imagined, a joy which would remain with her all her life, a natural conclusion to her healing.

She woke as the sun rose over the mountains, shafts of light brightening the room. She turned to Yoshi and saw that he was already awake. He leaned over and kissed her.

'You're so beautiful, Anna. I can't live without you.'

'You can, Yoshi. I have to go home.'

'You will come back, won't you? I can't let you go. Not now.'

She traced the contours of his face with her fingers, and searched his eyes. She believed him.

'Anna, I will agree to anything you want. If necessary, a divorce. I have tried too long to persuade myself that I can and must do without you, but I was living a lie. I need you too much.'

She ached with longing to respond to him, but somehow she had to make him understand. She moved away and sat up, pulling the cover to hide her nakedness. Her hair hung loose about her shoulders.

'Yoshi, listen. I want more than anything to say yes, but I can't. You know and I know in our hearts that we wouldn't be happy. Neither of us would want to hurt Tama. You love her and I could never take her place. I wouldn't want to.Then there's your career. Please understand, I don't have a choice. I have to be with Mother now. I'm going home.'

This time Yoshi didn't try to persuade her. His eyes held no anger, only sadness.

'I'll take you back to Tokyo after breakfast,' he said.

On her last day in Japan, Anna rang Jean to say she would be leaving.

'I'm so sorry to hear about your father,' said Jean. 'I was hoping to see you again before you left, but we'll meet in England. I won't forget the message you gave me to pass on to Nigel, though I'm afraid he'll take it badly.'

'He'll get used to the idea once I'm gone,' said Anna, briskly. 'Please give my best wishes to Stan and hugs to the children. I shall always be grateful for your kindness at a very difficult time, Jean. You've been a real friend.'

She put down the receiver and went to say her goodbyes to her colleages at the hospital, last of all to Mother Agnes.

'I'm grateful that you took me on,' she said, embracing her. 'I shall never forget you and all that I've learnt here. I feel I'm leaving something of myself in this hospital.'

'Goodbye, my dear.' Mother Agnes said, and her eyes were moist. 'God bless you.'

* * *

For Yoshi, she had no words. She knew they would never meet again and she must accept that, like Jack, Yoshi too had to be relinquished.

At the airport, visibly distressed, he said, 'Perhaps one day I shall come to your country.'

'I hope so.'

'You'll write? I want to know what you'll be doing.'

'I don't think so, Yoshi. It's best we say goodbye now.'

For a moment it seemed that he would insist, then he said, 'You're right, Anna. That doesn't mean though that I shall forget you.'

'I know. It's the same for me.'

There was no kiss, no embrace. Just a clinical, necessary separation.

He came as far as the check-out. He was once more his professional self, though she knew he was struggling to suppress any display of emotion. Only his eyes spoke to her as she looked at him for the last time before going through the barrier.

Chapter Twenty

Hugh rose early. Anna's plane was due in at seven a.m. and he had promised her mother he would be at the airport to meet her.

He too had received a letter from Anna, telling him of her decision to come home. It had been written before her father's death and was in quite a different vein from her previous letters. He was relieved that she had not taken exception to his remarks as he had felt it important to make them. It was clear to him that Anna was still preoccupied with Jack's death and unless she was to be forever chained to the past, she had to cut the ties with her brother, painful though it might be.

He thought she had come a long way during her stay in Japan. She had had the courage to break off her engagement and find a good job. If it hadn't been for her father's death, he wondered if perhaps she might have stayed there, at least for a while. He thought back to when she had told him how uneasy she was at the thought of living in Japan. He just hoped she had been able to work through this.

How would she be feeling about coming home? He had only seen her that once just before she left, but she had made a deep impression on him. He remembered the frank way she had spoken of her fears and how she had listened so intently as he had described the prison camp. He need not have worried. Far from any public demonstration of her grief, she had behaved with restraint and dignity and he admired her all the more for it. Through their letters, he had come to know her much better. He valued her confidence in sharing her thoughts with him. She might need support for a while now, and for Jack's sake he intended to do what he could to help her.

He spotted her as she came through Customs, her trolley laden with luggage and packages, looking about her with an air of confidence. She had changed, he could see that. Her face was radiant but there was more to it than her outward appearance. It was the strong face of a woman who could survive on her own. It's beauty lay in its sensitivity. He hurried forward to meet her and took the trolley from her.

'How kind of you to meet me, Hugh.' She greeted him with a smile.

'Your mother told me you were arriving on this flight and asked if I would come. Welcome home. Did you have a good flight?'

'It was all right. I slept quite a bit and apart from refuelling stops, it didn't seem overlong.'

He led her towards the car park and transferred her luggage into the boot of his old Ford. She allowed him to negotiate the traffic out of the airport before she spoke.

'I'm so sad I missed Dad,' she said then. 'How is Mother coping?'

'Of course she's upset but looking forward to seeing you. Over the last few weeks she's become very tired. She didn't want your father to go into hospital and insisted on caring for him at home. About two weeks ago, he seemed to rally and was greatly looking forward to seeing you again. But it wasn't to be. He died peacefully in his sleep.'

'I wanted to come sooner,' she lamented, blinking back tears. 'I'd have been back in time but I had an accident. Did Mother tell you? They wouldn't let me make the journey till I was better and, quite honestly, I don't think I could have coped. I'd have been nothing but a nuisance and Mother might have landed up nursing me as well. I wish I could have been with them at the end though.'

'You mother mentioned the accident. It was bad luck. I've got to know your parents quite well,' Hugh went on in his easy way. 'Your father and I used to have long conversations together. He always felt it was right for you to go to Japan, you know. He had an idea you'd find what you were looking for there. It seems to me that perhaps you did, Anna?' He glanced sideways at her.

Tears still pricked her eyes, but nothing could bring lasting sadness because there were no regrets. In a way, her father had released her from any remaining feelings of guilt.

'I think so,' she said. 'Thank you for your letters, Hugh. They arrived when I was feeling a bit lost. Some good advice in them, too.'

He laughed. 'I hope you've forgiven me for that?'

'It was what I needed. I think I've got over Jack now. I learnt a lot in Japan, you know. The Buddhists believe that nothing is permanent and we mustn't try and hold onto things that we're deeply attached to. That includes relationships. I think we do sometimes, because we're afraid of change.'

'That's probably right,' agreed Hugh.

'The Japanese put a lot of faith in the spirit world.

How do you feel about that?'

'I can go along with it,' he said. 'Providing we don't meddle with it.'

'I like to feel that Jack's at peace now.'

'No more dreams then?'

'Yes, there was one. Not long before I left I was in the Japanese Alps for a few days, recuperating. I felt very close to Jack at the time and one night I did dream about him again.'

'Tell me about it.'

'It was different. Or perhaps it was that this time I understood what it meant.'

'Go on.'

'Well, Jack was sitting with you in camp whittling away at a piece of wood with that penknife I gave him. Remember?'

Hugh nodded. 'Strange how a small object like that should keep cropping up.'

'I was afraid someone might take it away, but when a guard did appear Jack didn't seem worried. He and the guard walked together across the compound and when they reached the gates, they slowly opened and the guard stood aside, allowing Jack to pass through.'

'Into the jungle?'

'No. Into a lovely garden. I knew I couldn't follow him there and I didn't want to.'

'And the guard?'

'He just closed the gates.' She frowned. 'Was Jack friendly with any of the guards?'

Hugh shook his head. 'No, but he wasn't afraid of them. He felt they were just as much prisoners in that place as the men they guarded. So now you're happy about him, Anna?'

'Happy? No, never. Content – yes.'

He was silent as he negotiated a roundabout. Then he glanced at her.

'And what about Nigel?' he asked presently. 'Where does he fit into all this? As I remember, your dilema about whether or not to go to Japan had just as much to do with him as with the Japanese themselves.'

'That's true.'

'And it didn't work out?'

Somewhere, he felt, there was a missing link. He couldn't pry too deeply. He could only assume that they had come to an agreement satisfactory to them both.

'Not at the time.'

Did he detect a a note of uncertainty in her voice. Unfinished business? He hoped not. All that should be behind her now, leaving her free to make a fresh start. He waited for her to elaborate but she was silent, gazing out of the window at the countryside flashing past.

'It's nice to be back, Hugh. I'd forgotten how beautiful England is even in winter.'

'Tell me about your accident.'

'I was with Suzu's family at the time and there was an earthquake. People were cooking their midday meal and the hot charcoal was scattered all over the place starting fires. We had left the house and were in the street when a bit of burning timber fell against me. It could have been much worse, but it made me feel groggy for days.'

'Sounds nasty. Were many people trapped?'

'A lot. The fire engines couldn't reach the houses because the streets were too narrow.'

He didn't let on that Mrs Bradford had already read him a letter she had received from Mother

Agnes commending Anna on her bravery. Sooner or later Anna would see that letter for herself.

'So what are you going to do now, Anna?'

'Try and settle down at home, I suppose. Find myself a job.'

'Your mother will be glad to have you back,' he said. 'At least for a while.'

'I owe her that.'

'Do you think you might go back to Japan one day?'

'No. When I'm sure Mother's OK I might go off somewhere, but I don't know where yet. I'll have to see. One step at a time.' She flashed him a smile.

'I'm glad you're intending to stay here for a while. Maybe we can meet up in Oxford one day.'

'I'd like that, Hugh.'

The girl sitting beside him was not the same as the one who went away, he decided. He was suddenly glad to have her back. Many had been the nights when he had mentioned her in his prayers, and he was certain she had needed that but he guessed there were other experiences of which she had not spoken. There was this Japanese doctor for instance, of whom she thought so highly. Perhaps it was he more than anyone who had influenced her. Whatever had happened in Japan there were some things he suspected that would forever remain her secret.

'Did Nigel mind you coming home?' asked her mother.

It was their first evening together. Hugh had dropped her and left with the promise that he would be in touch soon. They had finished their meal and were having a cup of tea by the fire.

'Yes. He came to see me in hospital. He tried to persuade me to stay.'

Her mother's expression became concerned.

'Is it really all over, dear? He's such a nice fellow. We both thought so highly of him. Your father always said that had Nigel been posted anywhere other than Japan, it would have worked out all right for you both.'

'I don't think so, Mum. In the end it was nothing to do with Japan.'

'Had your father lived,' her mother said, 'would you have come home when you did or would you have given it a bit longer?'

'I wanted to come home. I had decided to leave anyway. Then I had this accident. If it hadn't been for that, I'd have been home in time to see Dad.'

'He hoped you'd make it. He was looking forward to seeing you.' Her mother brought out her handkerchief and wiped her eyes. 'It seems so strange without him.'

'Perhaps I should have left Japan much sooner, then I could have helped you with Dad. It was selfish of me, but I felt I had to stay on until I had sorted myself out. First of all with Nigel, then taking on the hospital job. I had to give them a reasonable time. And another thing – it was the only place where I could come to terms with Jack's death. That must be hard for you to understand, but one day I'll try to explain.'

'Your father and I sometimes thought that it was Jack that came between you and Nigel. Jack wouldn't have wanted that.'

'I know. Perhaps it did have something to do with it, but that was my fault.'

'And Nigel?'

'He thought so too. He never wanted to talk about Jack and that hurt. It was so important to me, and I felt that Nigel never tried to understand.'

'Perhaps it was a form of jealousy. You seemed to be attaching more importance to Jack than to Nigel. A marriage could never work under those circumstances.'

'Mum, I don't want to discuss it any more. It's over now and I'm back home and intend to stay. We'll have a holiday somewhere and then I'll think about getting a job.'

Mrs Bradford smiled at her daughter. 'All right, my dear. I just want you to know that you must do what you think best. If that means leaving home and making your life somewhere else, that's what you must do.'

They went to Scotland. In those two weeks Anna felt closer to her mother than ever before. They talked about her father and Jack. They had spent a family holiday in the Highlands years ago and they revisited old haunts, walking in the hills and lingering a while wherever the mood took them.

By the time they got back home, Anna had come to a decision. She spoke to Hugh about it when they had lunch together in Oxford.

'Any plans yet?' he asked her.

I'm applying for a job at the Radcliffe. I feel I owe it to Mum to be around for a while. It will give me time to sort myself out.'

Hugh smiled at her across the table. 'I'm glad to hear it,' he said. 'I was half afraid you might be going back to Japan.'

'No,' said Anna. 'There was never any question of that.'

Hugh was silent for a moment. He seemed ill at ease.

'What is it, Hugh?'

'I was just hoping that one day there might be a chance for me?'

She looked at him with affection. He had taken her by surprise.

'You'll always be a dear friend, Hugh, a very special one, but I don't think you need me. You're sufficient in yourself.'

'Please, Anna. Don't take it lightly. I know you need time but I'm prepared to wait.'

'It might be a long wait, Hugh. A very long wait. I'm afraid I can't make any more decisions. Not yet.' Then she gave him a dazzling smile. 'But I do need you around to talk to. Will that do to go on with?'

'It'll have to, I suppose,' he said ruefully.

It was good to have the friendship of a man like Hugh. She felt happier than she had for months. She had been right to leave Japan. It was as though she had crossed an important bridge and reached the safety of the other side. The people she had met along the way would always hold a special place in her heart. Now she looked forward to a new beginning, to a past with a future.

THE END